Blast from the Past

Cathy lives in Bath with her husband and three cats. In her spare time, she is happiest digging, planting or reading in the garden or on a walk with friends in the local countryside – usually ending in a pub. For more about Cathy, find her on twitter: @CathyHopkins1 or Facebook: CathyHopkins or on her website www.cathyhopkins.com.

Also by Cathy Hopkins

The Kicking the Bucket List
Dancing Over the Hill

Blast from the Past

Cathy Hopkins

HarperCollins*Publishers*

HarperCollins*Publishers*
The News Building,
1 London Bridge Street,
London SE1 9GF

A Paperback Original 2019

3

www.harpercollins.co.uk

Copyright © Cathy Hopkins 2019

Cathy Hopkins asserts the moral right to
be identified as the author of this work

A catalogue record for this book
is available from the British Library

ISBN: 978-0-00-828657-6

Typeset in Birka by
Palimpsest Book Production Ltd, Falkirk, Stirlingshire

Printed and bound in Great Britain by
CPI Group (UK) Ltd, Croydon CR0 4YY

Know, therefore, that from the greater silence I shall return . . . Forget not that I shall come back to you . . . A little while, a moment of rest upon the wind, and another woman shall bear me.

Kahlil Gibran

1

It all began with a birthday gift from my friend, Marcia. Most people would think of giving a scarf, a pair of earrings, books or some scented bath oil but, oh no, not Marcia, not this time. She'd wanted to be different and present me something out of the ordinary.

'Today's our last day and you remember what we promised each other,' she said as we sat, ready for breakfast, in rattan chairs on the terrace of our brightly coloured heritage hotel on the shore of Lake Pichola in Udaipur, India.

'I do,' said Pete, Marcia's husband. 'Presents! Time to reveal what we've all been planning.' He reached down and produced three envelopes from his rucksack. He fanned his face with them then handed one to Marcia, one to me, and kept the last for himself. 'These are from me. Happy fiftieths. May we have many more decades together.'

'Especially in locations like this,' I said as I gazed out over the water which was shimmering in the early morning sun. Udaipur was my favourite part of the holiday so far, a fairy tale of a city with a scenic and romantic setting, marble palaces, courtyards, gardens, temples, ancient narrow streets and, of course, stunning views from our hotel of the famous lake. And to top it all, presents. I knew that whatever Pete and Marcia had got me would be thoughtful and generous – from Marcia in particular; she loved to spoil friends and always picked something that was just right.

'So go on, open them,' said Pete.

'I will,' said Marcia, 'but first . . .' She handed me a tube of lotion and pointed at my nose which was red from the sun.

I laughed. 'You never change.' She'd been telling me what to do since I'd met her on my first day at secondary school. Along with all the other wide-eyed new girls, I'd entered the school gates, looking around for someone, anyone, I knew, but there was no one I could see from my junior school. I'd followed the crowd into assembly, got in line, and there in front of me was Marcia, her wild, black hair tamed into a long plait. She'd turned around, looked me up and down, assessing me, then she'd pulled her jumper up and rolled the waistband of her skirt, making it inches shorter than the knee-length uniform rule. She'd indicated that I should do the same which I did without question. 'Welcome to seven years of hell. I reckon we should stick together.' I'd laughed, impressed, and stuck close to her, and here she was, almost forty years later, still looking out for me and telling me what to do. I applied the coconut-scented cream, though it was really too late, my face blared Englishwoman abroad. Marcia, being dark skinned, never suffered the same problem, nor did Pete; in fact, his tan had developed evenly into a deep nut brown.

A handsome young waiter in a white starched uniform

appeared and placed tall glasses of mango lassi on the table in front of us. Pete whipped out his iPhone and showed it to him. 'Please would you take a photo? Three of us?'

The waiter nodded so Pete handed it to him then indicated that Marcia and I should pull our chairs close while he went to stand behind us.

'Everybody smile,' said the waiter and we grinned into the camera. 'One more. Good.'

After he'd gone, Pete examined the results then showed them to us.

I grimaced as I stared at the photos. 'I look like an ageing elf. Your fault, Marcia.'

'Rubbish,' said Marcia. 'You're the epitome of style, as always.'

The photos showed a slim woman with short platinum-blonde hair between two vibrant-looking hippie types. Pete, with a goatee beard and navy scarf, tied bandana-style around his head, looked like an old rock star, Marcia, with her waves of long black hair, was in a red kaftan and amber beads, his rock-chick companion. I was wearing a long black linen dress, 1930s Prada sunglasses, a single, long rope of silver that matched my earrings, and had painted my lips bright red. It was a style Marcia had come up with when my brown hair had begun to grow grey in my mid-forties: 'Think Annie Lennox 1980 – spike it up at the front a bit,' she'd told me, 'add a slash of bright lipstick, then go for plain colours with your clothes and you'll be seen as cool and chic, not middle-aged. With your fine bone structure, you could take it.' I'd taken her advice, had my hair cut, and stuck to black, navy or white clothing ever since.

We'd planned the trip to India for months, the holiday

of a lifetime to celebrate our birthdays. We had agreed no gifts until the end of the journey, then we'd all surprise each other with something. So far on our travels, we'd had a chill-out week on white sands by the sea in Kerala, and drifted peacefully on rice boats through palm-tree-lined canals in Alleppey (the Venice of the East). We'd done the Golden Triangle: Delhi, insanely busy with traffic, where we'd had a near-death experience in a tuk-tuk; Agra where we saw the Taj Mahal before the crowds arrived, its iridescent white marble glowing rose pink in the dawn light; Jaipur, where camels, elephants, pigs, cats, dogs and chickens could be seen strolling along the streets, narrowly missed by mopeds sometimes carrying five or six people. Everywhere we'd been was photo-worthy: women in jewel-coloured saris on bicycles; big-eyed children waving or begging from the side of the road; honey-stoned temples with intricate carvings on pillars and arches; market stalls overflowing with fabrics, pashminas, jewellery, fruits and spices; lorries painted bright yellow, red and green, strewn with garlands of flowers and tinsel. I loved India and, although I'd been before on short trips buying jewellery and trinkets for my shop back in the UK, the vibrancy and beauty never ceased to impress and inspire me.

Four days ago, we'd arrived through the three-arched gate into Udaipur in Rajasthan, the last leg of the journey. We'd been on a budget for most of the trip, but had agreed to splash out for our last few days and stay in the Shiv Niwas Palace, a heritage hotel on the shore of the lake. Our time there was made even more special when, on hearing that we'd all just turned fifty, the hotel manager, Rakesh, an elderly man with an impressive white moustache and big smile, had insisted on upgrading us to the royal suites. 'My biggest pleasure,' he'd said when he showed us the rooms that were out-of-this-world fabulous. 'Hotel used to be royal guesthouse, long time ago. Suites empty today, now full with you my new friends. Everyone happy. Good to be happy on big birthdays.'

We couldn't believe our luck. The rooms were vast with high ceilings, and decorated in the glorious colours that India does so well. Mine was sugar pink and apple green, Pete and Marcia's pale grey with royal blue stained-glass windows and, hanging from the ceiling, an enormous chandelier in the same vivid shade. Both suites had arched doorways leading to balconies where we could sit and marvel at the magnificent City Palace to our right, the lake in front of us, and the purple and ochre mountains in the distance.

Pete indicated the envelopes again. 'Go on then, open them,' he said. Marcia and I did as we were told and found vouchers inside for Ayurvedic massages.

'Just what I wanted,' said Marcia.

'Perfect,' I agreed. 'Some pampering to end the trip. Thank you.' I pulled out two parcels that I had hidden under the table earlier. 'And these are from me.' I'd thought long and hard about what to get for Marcia and Pete. We were all at an age where we had most things we wanted, and at first I had been at a loss as to what I could possibly add to their lives. In Jaipur, I'd had an idea. I'd been out one afternoon buying merchandise for my shop and had passed a stall bursting with fabrics of every colour. I'd bought metres of gunmetal silk for Pete and scarlet for Marcia, then found a tailor in Udaipur with a sign outside his shop advertising that he could make anything in twenty-four hours. I'd asked him to make the material into long kimono-style dressing gowns and he'd been true to his claim: the gowns had been delivered to my suite yesterday evening and the stitching was immaculate.

Marcia and Pete ripped the wrapping paper to reveal the robes. Both immediately put them on. 'Wow,' said Pete, as he gave us a twirl, then looked at Marcia. 'You look amazing. Bea, these are fabulous. What a great idea.'

'Yes, thank you. I love it,' said Marcia as she stroked the soft fabric. 'I hope you're having one made for yourself too. In fact, you ought to think about manufacturing these and selling them.'

'My thoughts exactly,' I said. 'But Stuart gave me a stern talking-to before we left about not spending until business has picked up back home.' Stuart was my accountant and a good friend and I knew he was concerned about the drop in profits in the last year.

'The killjoy,' said Marcia.

'Looking out for me as always,' I replied. 'And he's probably right. I need to get things back on an even keel before I think about expanding into importing silk dressing gowns.'

Marcia sat down. 'OK. My turn.' Like Pete had done a few minutes earlier, she produced three envelopes, handing one to Pete and one to me and keeping the last for herself.

'Oo, what's this?' I said as I ripped mine open. Inside, there was a voucher not unlike the one for Ayurvedic massage, but this said, 'An hour with Saranya Ji.' I looked to Marcia for explanation.

Her face was glowing with excitement. 'She's one of the top psychics in India.'

Oh *no*, was my immediate reaction. I don't do clairvoy-ants, astrologers or palm readers: they're not my thing at all. I think fortune-tellers prey on the vulnerable and tell people what they want to hear, but this was a present from Marcia and the last thing I wanted to do was to hurt her feelings. 'Fabulous,' I lied.

Marcia laughed. 'You hate it. I know this isn't your bag usually but she has a fantastic reputation; all the reviews say that she is *amazing* in what she reveals.'

'No, no, I don't hate it at all. It will be fun,' I said. It was typical of Marcia to have done something like this. She had stacks of books on spirit guides and the meaning of dreams at home, was always a sucker for a card or palm reading, looking for someone who could draw back the veil to the unknown. Not me, and she knew that. I was the more rational of the two of us, my feet firmly planted on the ground, whereas Marcia had her head in the stars. Pete went along with her interests if only to keep the peace but, privately, the only spirits he was into were those of the alcoholic variety.

Marcia laughed again. 'You don't have to put on an act for me, Bea. But come on, keep an open mind. If nothing else, it will be a chance to get a look inside the Taj Lake Palace Hotel, because that's where she's staying and doing the sessions. She's on a tour and I was lucky to get us all in.' She pointed out over the water to the middle of the lake where there was a two-tiered white marble hotel with pillars and arches around the sides. It looked like an enor-mous wedding cake. 'It was originally built around 1743 as the royal summer palace, and it covers the whole island, which is why it appears to be floating. It looks straight out of Disney, doesn't it?'

'It does,' I agreed. 'And it will be great to take a look inside.'

Pete kissed his wife's cheek. 'Well I love it. What an original gift. Let's find out what our futures hold.'

'Can't wait,' I lied again. *Probably some charlatan who will tell me I am about to meet a tall, dark, handsome stranger,* I thought. As if that's ever going to happen. I'd given up on men many moons ago, but I'd go along with it for Marcia's sake. As she'd said, it was also a chance to look inside the world-famous hotel. 'I've read that it was used as a location in the TV series, *The Jewel and The Crown* – and in the Bond film, *Octopussy.* I reckon martinis will be in order when we get there.'

'Excellent idea,' said Pete. 'Make mine shaken, not stirred.'

2

The Ayurvedic treatments were to be at a health centre just outside the Udaipur City Palace, so we decided to make the most of our last day and explore the glorious-looking building on our way there.

'There's not a square inch that hasn't been painted or covered in mosaic,' said Marcia as we wandered through a maze of corridors and into vast, tall rooms interlinked with scalloped arches and carved pillars. We marvelled at the depictions of life-size elephants on one wall, a camel on another, Lord Krishna in shades of yellow glass, gods and goddesses in reds and blues. We passed through a gold door surrounded with a series of deep green arches that seemed to ripple out towards us, then we moved into and through a room covered in lines of silver, and scarlet tiles that had been set in dramatic zigzags across the walls.

'Wow, opulent,' I said as I looked at the lightning bolts of colour. Everywhere was a feast for the eyes: a gold and orange room; another that was pale turquoise with rust-coloured shutters; a ceiling covered with scarlet flowers on an emerald green background; a golden elephant against a royal blue wall; stained-glass windows with panes that shone like jewels with the light behind.

There were tourists in every room, all with their iPhones out. I was tempted to join them then decided not to. 'I'll take snapshots with my mind instead,' I said as I put my mobile away. 'And I can always revisit it on the Internet.'

'We'll probably want to do that when we get home,' said Marcia. 'I read that it's snowing back in the UK.'

'And of course it will be Christmas mania over there,' I said. *And not a time that I look forward to any more*, I thought.

'This part is famous,' said Pete as we entered a pretty courtyard with a huge green and blue mosaic peacock, then moved into the adjacent room where the walls were made from small squares of blue, orange, green and yellow glass.

'Colour combinations that are a million miles away from the pebble and taupe shades we live with back home,' I said.

Marcia nodded, 'Apple green and red, lime green and turquoise and everywhere gold, gold, gold. I love it. Pete, I think I feel some redecorating coming on.'

Pete rolled his eyes. 'Again?'

'The palace was built 450 years ago by Maharana Udai Singh II,' we heard a tour guide tell his party. 'It was added on to by subsequent generations, which is why it is now a series of palaces, eleven in all, measuring two hundred and forty-four metres long and thirty metres high. In days gone by, silk or muslin curtains, soaked in rose or jasmine water, would have been hung across the arched doorways and windows so that in the heat of the sun, the scent would waft through the palace.'

'So romantic,' I said to Marcia. Not for the first time on the trip, I felt a pang of regret that I wasn't there with a special someone to share it with. Not that Pete or Marcia made me feel as if I was tagging along, not for a moment; but, all the same, sometimes I felt wistful that there wasn't a hand to hold, or someone I could stop, look and treasure a moment with.

*

The health centre was a dark wood raised bungalow with a veranda at the front. It smelt strongly of herbs and sandalwood joss sticks, and in the background was the sound of chanting, Om, om, ommmmmmm.

We were greeted by a young Indian woman in a red sari, who took our names, then led us along a corridor and into treatment rooms. Moments later, I was undressed, on a couch, and had been anointed with what felt like a bucket of pungent-smelling oil. Soon, I was being pummelled and stroked by the two female therapists, one on either side of me.

They started to slap me lightly then poured on more oil and got to work. 'Rosemary, good for muscles,' said one of the masseuses.

As the massage continued, due to the copious oil that had been poured all over me, I found myself sliding forward and back along the leather couch at an alarming speed. I dug my fingers under the sides of the bed and held on in order to stop shooting out through the open window opposite, like a cannonball out of a cannon, into the courtyard at the back.

'You loosen up, lady,' said one of the masseuses. 'You very tense.'

Story of my life lately, I thought as I tried to let go and surrender to the rhythm.

'Let go, let go,' urged the other masseuse. I loosened my grip on the couch and tried to relax. Forward and back, up and down, they stroked and I slithered. It had been years since I'd had a massage and I felt I'd lost the ability to switch off. Life, work and commitments always seemed to take precedence. Running my shop was a full-time business, often spilling over into my evenings and weekends, so aspirations to have regular treatments or a facial seemed to get shoved to the bottom of the list. Even this holiday with Pete and Marcia had been combined with purchasing a small amount of merchandise to have sent back home. While my friends had been dozing on the beach in Kerala, I'd been combing the market stalls nearby, looking for appropriate acquisitions while trying to ignore Stuart's voice in my head advising me not to get into debt before I left. As the masseuse bade me turn over, I wondered what to expect this afternoon. A psychic? What would she see? Anything? I wasn't sure I wanted to be told about my future. It might be bad news. Life had been uncertain on so many levels before I'd left to come away. Business was slow and my love life at an all-time low. Could things change? Or would it be more of the same – work, work, work; getting older; more Friday nights alone in front of Netflix, trying to convince myself I was OK. I didn't need anyone. I was strong, independent. I *was* OK, and keeping busy provided a way to block out the fact that I was fifty, single, and all my previous relationships hadn't worked out for one reason or another. If I hadn't got it right so far, there was little chance I was going to succeed in the future, so I'd given up looking. I'd worked hard to create a life where it appeared that I had it all and I didn't need anyone. I had a lovely house, though I barely spent any time there, great friends, though mainly couples, but really nothing to complain about. My work was my life; that was an achievement, though lately I'd realized that I rarely got the chance just to kick back and enjoy life. The truth was, behind the mask of the independent, successful businesswoman, I was lonely at times. No wonder I was tense.

'OK, waking up now lady,' said the masseuse, just as I was finally beginning to doze off. 'Drink much water. Get dressed when ready.'

3

We set off for the Taj Lake Palace Hotel in the early afternoon, feeling soothed and scented after our treatments. I'd resigned myself to going along to keep Marcia happy, to smile and listen to whatever rubbish the fortune-teller had to say and not to let my cynicism be too apparent.

'A car's coming to take us down to the bay,' said Pete, as we made our way down to the hotel lobby. Two minutes later, a maroon and beige vintage Bentley rolled up. It was straight out of the days of the Raj. 'Is that for us?' I asked.

Marcia nodded. 'We're going in style. I thought it might sweeten the experience for you.'

'Blackmail,' I said, 'I like it.'

Marcia laughed. 'I wanted to make sure you came.'

The car took us a short distance to a car park by the lakeshore, where we got out to see a tall Indian man, in a white turban and Eastern-style gold uniform, holding a large fringed red parasol. He was waiting to escort us into a white tent. 'Your boat is ready,' he said as he led us through and down to the water. Minutes later, we took our places in a small speedboat, which was open on the sides and canopied on the top, the seats inside scattered with colourful cushions.

'I really do feel like I'm in a Bond film now,' I said as the boat whooshed through the water to the hotel. Looking back at the shore gave us the best view of the City Palace so far: with its domed turrets, terraces and balconies, it was a truly magnificent piece of architecture.

Our boat arrived at a small jetty, where another Indian man, this one in a red turban and navy uniform, stepped forward to help us up onto the marble landing area at the front of the hotel. A red carpet led to the reception area, which we could see behind a glass wall. From an open balcony on the floor above came a shower of rose petals. I looked up to see the faces of two smiling Indian women. 'Welcome,' they said, as they scattered more petals down on us.

We stepped through an open door where three smiling ladies in emerald green saris were waiting. They came forward and placed garlands of golden flowers around our necks. One of them introduced herself as Adita. She reached down to a brass tray on a small table behind her, then dotted red powder on our foreheads. The other ladies handed each of us an iced pink drink in tall glasses. 'Passion fruit,' said one of them, 'you will like.'

As I looked around me, I could see that the décor of the hotel was a mix of old and new, with marble floors, white arches and pillars and tall gold Indian statues placed in alcoves along a corridor in front of us.

'You here for Saranya Ji?' asked Adita.

'We are,' Pete replied, and he handed her our vouchers.

'Please you follow,' she told us, and led us into a white

courtyard with a pool in the centre of the hotel where she indicated we should take a seat in one of the alcoves. The atmosphere was very tranquil, the only sound from a bubbling lotus fountain in the middle of a pool of water.

'You two go first,' I said when Adita had left us alone.

'OK,' said Marcia, 'I can't wait to see her.'

On the dot of one, Adita returned and took Marcia away.

'You nervous?' asked Pete when they'd gone.

'Not at all. What is there to be nervous about?'

'She might see into the depths of your soul and all your dark secrets . . .'

'Stop trying to wind me up.'

Pete laughed. He always liked to tease, and had been doing so since I'd met him almost thirty years ago, when Marcia had brought him back from Glastonbury. They'd met there, then worked together manning a food stall. Pete was 100 per cent hedonist, with a particular love of good food and, with his clever business head, he had turned that passion into money. He'd started out doing food at the Glastonbury festival, which he and Marcia still went to every year, then moved on to running a café up north, then a small shop when he moved to London. Now he ran Harvest Moon, a food emporium in the city. It was a glorious place to visit and sold everything organic: bread, pastries from all over the world, fruit, vegetables, cereals, grains, every type of health food and supplement, cheeses, herbs and spices. There were also a couple of juice and healthy snack counters where local office workers could pop in for a takeaway lunch and get something tasty, fresh and good for them. Marcia worked there with him, running the office and keeping the admin side of things in order.

'But I do wonder what Saranya Ji's going to come up with,' Pete said. 'I know it's more Marcia's thing than yours but it could be interesting. I think there are some genuine psychics in the world, people who have a true gift.'

'But what if they see something awful, do they tell you? Like your plane is going to crash on the way home, you will lose all your money, and all your family are going to die in an attack by a plague of locusts.'

Pete laughed. 'Pessimist. I think they'd probably say something vague, like you're in for a challenging time.'

'I already know that I am,' I said.

'Are you worried about what you're going back to?'

I nodded. 'I am but I'm determined not to think about it while we're here. It's been wonderful to have a break from all my concerns back home. I'll deal with it when I get back. Heather's been texting but I purposely haven't read her or Stuart's messages.'

'Good for you. Heather's a good manager so I'm sure will cope if anything's come up. And you know Marcia and I will do whatever we can to help.'

'I do, but let's not talk about it now. If I start worrying here, there's not anything I can do, it's not going to make any difference, and it would only spoil our last day.'

'Exactly,' said Pete. 'Very wise.'

We chatted away about our plans for Christmas and the time flashed by until Marcia came back with Adita, who beckoned to Pete to go with her.

'So, how was it?' I asked.

'Not saying. I don't want to influence you. How about we tell each other what she said when we're all done,' she said, and with that, she went over to a sun-lounger, picked up a magazine from a nearby table and stretched out on the bed.

'OK, but good or bad do you reckon?' I asked.

Marcia put her hand up to her mouth and zipped. 'My lips are sealed.'

'Spoilsport,' I said. I could see she wasn't going to be budged, so I got out my book of puzzles to do while I waited. I loved puzzles and crosswords; they were great for passing time at airports, on planes and trains, or anywhere I had an hour to kill. I'd even been known to have a jigsaw on my dining table on a rainy weekend, something that Marcia found hilarious.

An hour later, Pete was back. He looked slightly dazed and, for the first time, I felt a twinge of apprehension. 'OK?' I asked.

'Fantastic,' he said as he went to sit by Marcia. 'She's definitely got something.'

Hmm, I'll be the judge of that, and I mustn't give anything away, I thought, as Adita beckoned that I should follow her. I got up and she led me back to the reception area, along a corridor to the left and into one of the hotel rooms. I knew from gullible friends that sometimes fortune-tellers fished for clues. Well, I wasn't going to give her any.

'Saranya Ji will come in short time,' said Adita, as she indicated that I should take a seat, then she left me alone to wait.

I looked around the small suite, with its closed shutter doors that I presumed led to a bedroom. The room was tastefully decorated in traditional style with cream walls, a red velvet sofa and chaise longue with gold cushions, a navy blue Persian rug on the floor and an antique-looking painting on the one wall showing a maharaja riding an elephant. *This must have cost a packet*, I thought. *Gypsy Rose Ji must be doing well out of the psychic business.*

Moments later, the door opened, and I stood as a small Indian lady in a white sari came in. She exuded warmth and came over and greeted me like a long-lost friend.

'My dear Bea, I am *so* pleased to see you,' she said as she clasped my hands in hers and I noticed the soft scent of roses and sandalwood. I couldn't help being charmed by her manner and found myself smiling back at her. 'Please, sit, sit. Would you like tea? They have mint here, made with fresh mint, no teabags. It's very refreshing.' She spoke with a perfect English accent and I found myself wanting to know more about her. I resolved to google her as soon as I got back to my hotel.

'Yes, that sounds wonderful.'

She picked up the phone and ordered tea then turned back. 'So my dear, how can I help?'

'Help? Oh no. I don't need help, no, my friend Marcia, the lady you saw earlier, she bought a session with you for me as a birthday gift.'

Saranya Ji regarded me in a manner I found a little uncomfortable. It wasn't that she looked at me unkindly, more that she stared right into me and I felt exposed in some way. I felt myself blush. After a few moments, she nodded and smiled. 'OK, a gift. So what would like to know?'

'I . . . I thought you were going to tell my fortune.'

'Ah. Fortune. I don't exactly tell fortunes. Is that what you want? Someone to tell you your future?'

She's fishing, I thought. 'No. Not that.'

'Good,' she said. 'The past has gone, the future is yet to be written; only the present is real.'

'True,' I said as there was a knock at the door and a waiter brought in a silver tray with tea.

After he'd gone, Saranya Ji poured and handed me a cup, then we sat in silence for a while which I found awkward. I didn't know where to look, so I stared at the carpet. *I am not going to give anything away*, I told myself.

Finally Saranya Ji began to speak. 'I feel sadness in you, Bea, and resistance. I feel scepticism, but this will change.'

Doubt it, I thought, *and as for appearing sad or resistant, that could apply to most of the population. Who hasn't got to the age of fifty without a few knocks?*

'Why are you here?' she asked.

'We're on holiday—'

'No, I mean here today, with me.'

'My friend Marcia, the gift, I couldn't refuse. I . . . there's nothing I want to know specifically.'

Saranya Ji sighed and then nodded to herself, as if accepting that I wasn't going to blurt out my whole life. 'OK. Give me your hands,' she instructed. I held my hands out and she took them in hers, turned them palm upwards and studied them. She closed her eyes as if tuning in to me, then opened her eyes and let go of my hands.

'You have known pain with love in this lifetime, no?' she asked.

'I . . . I . . .' I blustered. 'I've had good relationships and some not so good, probably like everyone my age.' I was about to tell her more, then remembered that I'd resolved not to give anything away.

'I mean the joy of love and contentment that comes from

meeting your equal and soulmate,' said Saranya Ji. She looked at me with such compassion that I felt my eyes well with tears. It was as if she knew, she understood how empty my life felt, but that couldn't be. I'd known her five minutes and some people I'd spent a lifetime with had no idea about what went on in my head and my heart. I had a good public mask of being cheerful, positive, not needing anyone. Only friends like Marcia, Pete, Heather and Stuart knew what went on behind the act. I blinked the tears away. Ridiculous. What was wrong with me? And what was happening here? Maybe Marcia had been filling her in on my past, or Pete? *I'll kill them when I get out of here*, I thought. Marcia saw my present lack of love life as her private mission, and was forever trying to pair me off with inappropriate single men.

'You have travelled far through time to be here,' said Saranya Ji.

'True,' I said again. 'It was a long flight from England and we go back tomorrow.'

'No. Not in India, I mean in this body you call Bea. What I want to talk to you about is your life as Bea.'

'OK.'

'What you must understand, Bea, is that in life, first comes destiny, next comes free will. Understand? How you react to what happens to you.'

I nodded. 'I understand.'

'Our soul has many lessons to learn on this journey. You have had many lives, many incarnations, gathering knowledge and experience to bring you here today in this lifetime as Bea. So far this time, you have not found lasting love, but it is there as your destiny, you could know the joy of finding your true companion.'

Me and a thousand others, I thought, and wondered how many people she'd fed the same lines.

She reached across, took my hands in hers again and closed her eyes. Her touch was soft and warm and it felt soothing. She opened her eyes again and continued, 'There is a reason for this and that is because you have it imprinted in your unconscious mind that lasting love is not for those such as you; for you it brings pain, that people you love, they leave you, and you are destined to be alone. In your attempt to go beyond this and not to get hurt further, you have repeated a pattern. You recreate the familiar in your relationships so you can think, yes, it is true, love hurts, no point. I am better off alone. I don't need anyone.'

Whoa, I thought, *steady on*. It was true, I did believe that love brought pain and that people leave, because so far that had been my experience, but imprinted on my unconscious mind so that I was creating it? I did not like what I was hearing. I glanced at the door and wondered whether to end the session there and then, but another part of me was fascinated as to what else she had to say. I stayed where I was. *Let's hear what baloney she comes out with next*, I told myself. *I can have a laugh about it later with Pete and Marcia.*

'I see a man, your soulmate. You have been together many times in many lives. It is a great love, powerful, and each time brought you a joy that you have not come close to in this life. He was and is your true love and you brought out the best of each other's nature. This was good. You encouraged each other to be open to learn, you challenged each other. Ah . . .' she paused then continued with confidence. 'Here it is. In your last life, you were Grace Harris. You worked as a dressmaker in London, England. You were to be married but . . . something happened to end that love.'

Saranya Ji was quiet for a few moments, and her head tilted as though she was listening to someone in the room, to her right, someone I couldn't see. She nodded. 'Ah, this could be where the pattern of belief that you carry now began. You were to be married but it was the war, Second World War. He had to go and fight but, oh . . . his life was interrupted. He didn't return. You were heartbroken. This loss caused you great pain because you believed you would have a whole life together in the future. This belief that love hurts went deep, deep into you, and you have carried this with you, the idea that a smooth love affair happens to other people but you lose those whom you truly love. This has made you cautious to give your heart and so you prefer to choose men who are wrong for you so, if they leave, it doesn't matter so much and if you do begin to care, you push them away so they cannot get too close and wound you.'

I almost laughed out loud. Grace Harris? A soldier killed in action? What a load of tosh. She'd probably seen an old war movie recently and was repeating the storyline back to me.

'What I want to tell you is that, as you are back in this lifetime, so is he. Like you, he has travelled far through many dimensions to be here. In this life, you must find him if you are to be truly happy. This is important, Bea. You are meant to be together. You *must* find him, recognize and let him in, if you are ever to know the joy of love.'

The atmosphere in the room felt charged and I felt a shiver go up my spine, but I was not going to be taken in. 'Was he by any chance tall, dark and handsome?'

Saranya Ji looked directly at me. 'You are cynical, Bea. Don't be, it doesn't suit you. It is a wall to protect yourself and is not your true nature. You have an open and loving spirit. You must learn to let go of your distrust if you are to progress. Yes, you may scoff at what you hear – many do when they hear a truth, and doubt me, but I simply tell what I see. It is always your choice to make of it what you will, but this man from your past who was . . .' She listened to her right again, 'He was known as Billy Jackson, he is your destiny. You can believe me and try and find him and who he is now in this life, or dismiss what I say and drift from one meaningless love affair to another, never finding the true contentment and companionship that your soul could know. Or you can immerse yourself in your work as you have done, so busy that no one knows that you are hiding. People see success but you are alone and . . .' She stopped and looked at me with tenderness, 'I don't think so happy with this, yes?'

You're beginning to freak me out, I thought as I looked away.

'Have you any questions?' Saranya Ji asked.

'There are millions of men on the planet, in different countries, how would I know him?'

'Recognition, there will be familiarity. A sense of, ah there you are. Have you ever met anyone and thought, *where do I know you from?* Yet you have never met them in this life.'

'I suppose I have felt it with some friends.'

'Yes, but it will be much more so with this man. A sense of, oh I know you. That is what you must look out for, but with your soulmate it will be stronger than with friends; it will feel exciting to find each other and maybe a little scary for you because it will confront your fear of loss and being hurt, so be careful not to push him away. Trust what you feel, as deep down there will be an awakening of that knowledge that yes, we belong together.'

I still didn't believe what she was saying. It was too unlikely, romantic fodder for the easy-to-fool, and I wasn't going to be taken in. 'OK, Saranya Ji, but what if we miss each other? He's on one continent, I'm on another.'

'Trust. Don't doubt that he will come into your life or has already come into it, that part is taken care of; but, as I said, it is your free will as to whether you accept him or reject him for fear of pain. You choose.'

'If you say he was Billy Jackson last time, can't you tell me his name this time? It would save a lot of time.'

She shook her head. 'I cannot, because then you would look for a name not for his spirit. You must recognize him, look into his eyes and connect with that soul you have known many times. If I give you a name, it would influence your search.' She regarded me again with her birdlike eyes. 'You are still sceptical, yes?'

'I'm sorry but I am, Saranya Ji. I'm afraid I don't believe in past lives or even soulmates, although it's a lovely, idealistic notion.' I didn't add that I thought that what she had said was ridiculous, preposterous.

Saranya Ji looked at me with a kind but weary expression. 'My dear Bea, open your heart and try not to be ruled always by your head. Change is coming to your life. Allow for possibilities that are . . .' she raised an eyebrow and smiled, 'ridiculous and preposterous. See where they take you. Life may surprise you yet.'

4

'So, what did she say?' asked Pete as soon as I got back to the courtyard and went to sit with them at a table where they were drinking ice-cold beers from tall glasses.

'Anything about what's coming?' asked Marcia.

I shook my head. 'She said something about change but didn't elaborate. I guess that could apply to anyone, though. Life is all about change, isn't it?'

'Did she say you'd meet the love of your life?' asked Marcia.

I laughed and shook my head. 'Not exactly, no.'

'So what did she say?' asked Marcia.

'I'm still processing it,' I said. 'It was . . . weird.' Despite my cynicism, I felt shaken by my session with Saranya Ji. She had not been what I expected at all and I wasn't sure what to make of it. 'You tell me what she said to you first.'

'She talked about my soul's purpose and journey,' said Marcia. 'She talked about how God is within all of us and the importance of recognizing that.'

'Yes, she said that to me too,' said Pete. 'And that we are not all born equal but eventually will reach a point where we are all equal.'

'And how's that supposed to happen?' I asked.

'Through knowledge and learning, through cultivating charity, hope, faith and love,' said Pete. 'And in my case, the importance of balance.'

'Good. You need that,' said Marcia. 'All or nothing, that's you.'

I smiled. It was true. Pete never did things by halves. One week, it was red wine and fine food, other weeks green tea and brown rice.

'And she spoke about making time to meditate,' said Marcia. 'Time to stop and tune into the peace inside.'

'No prophecies?' I asked.

'Not exactly. She spoke about my father, though, said he is with me in spirit and he was fine and that he said to tell me that I worry too much.'

Pete laughed. 'He was always telling you that.'

'And you believed her?' I asked.

'I did.'

'But I'm sure a thousand fathers would pass that message on to their daughters.'

Marcia shrugged. 'I found it comforting,' she said, and I realized that I should shut up with my doubts. I knew that Marcia had loved her father dearly and was still grieving, five years after his death. If what Saranya Ji had said had lifted some of that pain in some way, I didn't want to pour cold water on it.

'I'm sorry, Marcia, I didn't mean to be cynical. You know what I'm like. I guess we know so little about what happens after death. Why shouldn't your father speak through a medium?'

'Indeed,' said Marcia. She smiled. Like Pete, she was

easy-going, not one to pick an argument, nor was I, although privately I thought the chances of her father's spirit turning up to speak through a small Indian woman in Rajastan was about as likely as one of us winning the lottery.

'It's true,' said Pete. 'We know nothing about life after death, or if a spirit lives on.'

'Oh yes we do,' said Marcia, 'there are loads of books about reincarnation and accounts of people who have had experiences. So, what else did Saranya Ji say to you?'

I laughed. 'She spoke to me about a past life.'

'Really? Did you ask her about them?' asked Marcia.

'No, of course not. Why would I? Didn't she talk about past lives to you? I would have thought she would tell you two that you are soulmates and have been together life after life.'

'We already know that,' said Marcia, 'but no, Saranya Ji didn't mention anything like that. Why did she to you?'

'Because she said she sensed sadness in me and that I hadn't found true love. Did either of you say something to her?'

'Not me,' said Marcia.

'Nor me,' said Pete.

'Did she talk about you meeting the love of your life?' Marcia asked.

'Not exactly meeting him. She said I'd already met him.'

'Already? Great. So, someone you already know?' asked Marcia.

'Yes and no. I'm not sure I do know him.'

'Stop being evasive,' Marcia persisted. 'What did she say *exactly*?'

'She said I'd met him already—'

'Yes, you said, you've already met him. Michael. I bet it was Michael O'Connor. I always thought you two were meant for each other.'

'No. Not in this life.'

'What? So . . . ah, right, in a past life?' Marcia persisted.

'Yes, she said I'd met him before, in a previous life, when I was called Grace Harris; in many previous lives, in fact. She said we'd been together time after time.'

'A soulmate,' said Pete.

'Yes.'

'Lovely, how romantic,' said Marcia.

'And she said that as I am back now in this life, so is he, and that I must find him.' I filled them in on the rest of what Saranya Ji had said, because I knew that Marcia wouldn't let it go until I'd told her everything.

'Wow,' said Marcia when I'd finished. 'That's quite a story.'

'Exactly, a story, a big load of tosh, though it would be just my luck that my soulmate *is* dead . . . but I don't believe any of it for a second. OK, I'll acknowledge that Saranya Ji has some sort of spooky antenna for tuning into people, and she did pick up on a few aspects about my life that are true, but a past life as a Grace Harris? I don't think so.'

'I wouldn't dismiss it,' said Marcia. 'I've met a few people I believe I've known before. Pete, and you. I bet we've known each other before.'

'You were probably her mother,' said Pete. 'You're always bossing her around.'

'Yes, that's a very likely possibility,' said Marcia.

I put my fingers in my ears. 'Not listening. You really are bonkers sometimes, away with the fairies.'

Marcia laughed. 'That's no way to talk to your mother.'

I sighed. 'Honestly, I've never heard such nonsense.'

'I'd take on board what she told you if I were you.'

'Marcia, you know I love you dearly, and I am quite prepared to believe that Saranya Ji passed on a message from your father, but what she told me, I think not. I bet she gives loads of people the same spiel. I reckon she clocked that I was single because I don't wear a wedding ring then she made it all up from there. I can't be the only woman of my age who hasn't known lasting joy, as she put it, in my relationships.'

'But what if she didn't make it up? She said nothing to either of us about past lives,' said Pete. 'What she told me was very much about the present and about life's purpose and lessons to be learnt.'

'For me too,' said Marcia. 'But more importantly, what are you going to do about it?'

'Do?'

'About Billy and whoever he is this time round. What are you going to do to find him.'

'Find him? Nothing. Oh come on, I appreciate the gift, I really do, it's been a great experience,' I indicated the hotel. 'Coming here has been fabulous – the boat ride and the car, I loved it, and meeting Saranya Ji, it's been . . . er, different, if a little weird. But past lives? People called Grace and Billy. I'm sorry but I don't believe a word she said, not for a minute. She guessed I'd known some sadness. Who hasn't? Then she made the rest up and that's her gift – tuning into people then spinning a yarn. Obvious really.'

'Not necessarily,' said Marcia. 'You *have* to give it a chance and try and find him. She talked to me about destiny, it being what is fated to happen, and that free will determines how you react to that fate.'

'She also talked about the importance of keeping an open mind,' said Pete.

'She said that to me too,' I said. 'So OK, a soulmate? In what country? In what period of my life? She said I may have already met him. We could have passed each other on the street and—'

'You were probably looking at emails on your iPhone,' said Pete.

'Exactly. Missed him, darn it.'

'It's never too late,' said Marcia. 'If it's meant to be, it's meant to be.' She glanced at Pete for support but he just shrugged. He wouldn't take sides. He never did.

Adita appeared by our sides. 'Your boat is ready to take you back,' she told us.

I stood up. 'Great,' I said, and prayed that Marcia would drop all talk of past lives and spirits, 'now let's go and enjoy our last evening.'

5

The following day was an early start. A short flight to Mumbai then a two-hour delay before our flight back to London. When we'd found seats in a row in the airport lounge, I got out my laptop with a mind to google Saranya Ji and see if there was a reviews page. Although the rational part of me had intended to put the whole session to one side, another part of me kept going back to what she'd said, not just about the past lives but about my life and experience of love being painful. I couldn't deny that had resonated. I put in the name Saranya Ji only to find there were hundreds of them on the Net. Clearly it was a popular name. I scrolled down. There were pages and pages of women with that name.

'Anyone got any paper?' Marcia asked.

'Sure. What for?' I asked.

'I need to make a list.'

I always travelled with a notepad, so found it in my bag and tore out a sheet for her. 'A list of what?'

'Past lovers.'

'Oh *no*, Marcia. I know exactly what you're thinking.'

'I couldn't get what Saranya Ji told you out of my mind

and, as I was going to sleep last night, I thought that first we should look for someone named Billy Jackson. We could check records, you know, births, deaths, marriages, see where and when anyone of his name lived. It might give us some clues. We could look for Grace too. You never know what we might find and where it might lead us.'

'Good idea Marcia,' said Pete. 'So much history is on the Internet now, census records and so on. It shouldn't be too difficult.'

I groaned. '*Please*, don't encourage her.'

'I'd like to do it,' said Pete. 'You know I love stuff like that. A challenge.' It was true: he was a closet computer geek and was never happier than when researching history or suchlike on the web. 'I traced my father's family back to the seventeen hundreds on one of the ancestry sites.' He got out his laptop. 'In fact, I could start looking now while we're waiting.'

'Oh please don't. When you were looking you were tracing back a family tree, *your* family tree, not tracking down someone that a clairvoyant told you that you might have been in a past life.'

'What have we to lose by looking up the names that Saranya Ji gave you? It will be so easy to do. I have subscriptions to all the main sites and know my way around. I could put in the names and see what comes up.'

'Please, *please* don't do it on my behalf. Don't waste your time.'

'Someone has to do it and we know you won't. Pete is a whiz at it all now,' said Marcia. 'The woman, what was her name? The surname?'

'Harris. Grace Harris. A name Saranya Ji *made* up. I was

thinking about it as I fell asleep too. She could have plucked any names out of the air. You probably will find them if you look on your ancestry sites; there will be loads of people who lived with those names, just like there are hundreds of Saranya Jis on the Net.'

'Ah,' said Marcia, 'so you are interested. You looked her up.'

'Only to see if there were any reviews saying she was a charlatan. You *will* find a Grace Harris and a Billy Jackson, thousands of them probably, and not only in the UK but all over the place – Australia, America. It won't mean anything.'

'Didn't she say where they lived?' asked Marcia.

'She said London and that it was in the Second World War.'

'See, that narrows it down already.'

'Seriously? What's the point? So you find two people who had those names, they could be the names of people she met the day before she saw us, and now today she's telling some other sucker that they were Bea Brooks or Marcia and Peter Rodgers in a previous life. Grace and Billy could be the names of people she met anywhere on her tour. And if, by some miracle, you find that they did exist in the past, in London, there would be nothing to prove I was a Grace Harris in a previous existence.'

'We're going to look into it,' said Marcia. 'Let's see what we can find.'

I looked over at Pete who was still looking at his laptop. 'Can't you stop her?' I asked.

'I think you already know the answer to that . . . And what harm will it do?'

'Exactly,' said Marcia. 'Keep an open mind, Bea. So, second part of the plan, we look at your past lovers, where they are now and if, by any chance, there's someone you over-looked. It can happen. Twin souls or soulmates sometimes have stuff to work out on their own before they get together as a couple. So. Men. How many?'

'I'm not answering that,' I said.

'Well, I probably know most of them,' said Marcia.

Pete peered over his laptop. He had a mischievous look in his eyes. 'And so do I.'

No you don't, I thought. Although I'd known both of them through the ups and downs of most of my relation-ships, I'd had a few secret liaisons they knew nothing about.

'But maybe there have been others that we don't know about,' Marcia continued as if picking up on my thoughts. 'Was there anyone you felt that feeling of familiarity with that Saranya Ji spoke of? Think, Bea. Someone you let go and always regretted that it didn't work out?'

'All of them. All of them were my soulmates. I regretted that it didn't work out with all of them. Happy?'

'No, don't forget I lived through most of it with you, which is why I care so much.'

'Er . . . there was that bloke Michael,' Pete said. 'The musician. You were pretty keen on him as far as I remember.'

I ignored him.

'Yes, he was the first one who came to my mind,' said Marcia.

'Then you've both forgotten what happened with him. Anyway, what qualifies as a lover? I had a crush on my art teacher, Mr Doyle, at school – loads of us did, remember Marcia?'

Marcia wrote down the name. 'Course, he was gorgeous; half the school was in love with him. OK. We can make a first-division list and a second. Crushes can go on the second because they might be people that you recognized but didn't get to act out the feeling with.'

I rolled my eyes. 'OK, then you can add Idris Elba, George Clooney and Colin Farrell to that list. I think I've always known I belonged with one of them. Be great if one of them turned out to be my soulmate.'

'Start at the beginning, Bea. First love ever,' said Marcia.

'Jack.'

'Jack? I don't remember him. How old were you when you met him?' She seemed peeved that there was some part of my life that she didn't know about.

'Five.'

'And Jack?'

'He was a puppy when we got him, so he was probably about six weeks old.'

Marcia sighed. 'Oh *that* Jack, course I remember him. He was a dear old thing. I suppose it's vaguely possible your soulmate might have returned as a dog.'

I laughed again. 'You really are mad as a hatter, Marcia. But I did love Jack. I truly did. He was my best friend and constant companion. I was heartbroken when he died.'

'I remember. We buried him in your parents' back garden.'

'And I was heartbroken again when old Boris died, and Caspar.'

'Ah, we all loved those dogs,' said Pete. 'There's nothing as sad as losing a beloved pet.'

'I'll look into whether animals reincarnate as animals or if ever they cross over to being a human,' said Marcia.

'What planet are you on, Marcia? I'm not even entertaining this, not for a second.' I gave Pete an exasperated look. He grinned back at me and went back to his screen. 'I'm not sure if I even believe in reincarnation, animals or human. There's no real proof is there?'

'Oh yes there is,' said Marcia. 'I've read loads of accounts of people who have recall of past lives; people who have recollection of places that they've never been to in their current life and they remember specific details of the people that they used to be, who they used to know and where they lived. You should look it up. There's loads on the Net.'

'Think rationally for a moment, Marcia, that is if you're capable of doing that. These places that people remember – but have never been to – are probably from movies they've seen, or the Internet, or travel programmes. We're exposed to so much these days, these reincarnation-believers probably trot out something that they saw online but don't remember having taken in. Our brains are stuffed full of information.'

'You can believe what you want, Bea, and I *can* be rational, but I want to remain open-minded too. There are many things we don't understand with our limited brains.'

'True. And it's not that I'm not open-minded, I'm just saying many things have a rational explanation. OK, let's say we do reincarnate, there has to be good reasons why people don't remember who they were. Imagine you were some great artist or writer, someone famous now, in this century, but at the time you died in poverty. Imagine you were one of the Brontë sisters or Oscar Wilde or Vincent van Gogh? You come back in this life, then remember creating your past works, but no one will believe you. You see your books selling by the millions. You hear that your paintings go for billions. You watch as your books are made into TV adaptations or movies. How painful would that be? So, think about it, Marcia: if we do reincarnate, the fact that we don't remember past lives is probably a self-protection mechanism to stop us all going mad or getting angry or bitter and dwelling on how it's different this time round.'

Pete looked up from his laptop. 'Good point, Bea.' He sighed. 'Not having much luck on here. I need more time.'

'Good,' I said. 'It can't possibly go anywhere, so why waste your time? Like, what if Saranya Ji had told me that I used to be Jane Austen? And I believed her and went to her publishers saying, oi, you owe me years and years of royalties. I'd be locked up. No. I reckon focus on the present, this life, and make the best of it. Isn't that what all the great teachers say anyway? Be here now and all that good stuff. If souls evolve, then surely this present life has to be the best one yet. Would you really want to go back and relive past struggles and lessons? Never mind a past life, think about this one. I wouldn't want to go back to some parts of it, like I wouldn't want to relive parts of my teenage years again or some of my relationships. Surely it's best to move on.'

Marcia looked thoughtful. 'OK, I understand that, but we can still learn from the past, can't we? Especially if we're repeating a mistake or a pattern like Saranya Ji said you were.'

'No. I think it's best to leave the past in the past and that if I am to learn anything then it's that I have to move on, move forward, create a new pattern.'

I could see that I'd thrown Marcia with my argument

and she was considering what I'd said. 'Hmm. Maybe that's true, but what if you can't move forward because you're stuck in a pattern of thinking so sabotaging your relationships? I think this is exciting and I still think we should look into finding Billy Jackson. Who's next on your list of past lovers? And don't give me any more pets.'

I knew I'd have to humour her. When Marcia got the bit between her teeth, there was no letting go. 'OK. First love, er . . . that would have been Andrew Murphy.'

'And where was this? In case I need to track him down.'

'Manchester. I was ten. He was in my class in junior school, just before I met you.'

'Hold on,' said Pete, and he cocked his ear to listen to an announcement. 'Come on, looks like our flight is on time after all. We'd better go to the departure gate.'

Saved by the bell, I thought as we gathered our hand luggage and made our way to our plane.

*

Soon we were winging our way above the clouds back to London and Mumbai was receding in a haze of dust beneath us. Luckily Marcia and Pete's seats were across from me on the aisle so Marcia couldn't question me further. I did a few puzzles for a while then my eyelids grew heavy and, as I began to doze, my thoughts turned back to my early years.

Andrew Murphy. I hadn't thought about him in years, decades.

He'd lived round the corner from us in Manchester, in a Victorian house on the main road near the Golden Lion pub. I liked it because it had a wooden porch at the front and looked more interesting than the 1930s semi-detached house that I lived in with my parents and two brothers. Andrew and I were in our last year at the same primary school and the first time I really noticed him was in RE. Before that, apart from my brothers, boys hadn't been on my radar, I only saw them as annoying creatures who were too boisterous and smelt of stale biscuits.

Mother Christina had been talking to the class about God being omnipresent.

Andrew stuck his hand up. 'In that case, why do we only pray in church? If he's omnipresent, isn't it OK to pray anywhere, even in the loo?'

I'd turned to look more closely at who had asked what I thought was a brilliant question, and saw a good-looking lad with an open friendly face and shock of brown hair that wouldn't be combed down.

He got detention for being disrespectful and I was sent with him for laughing.

'So God is omnipresent apart from bathrooms and toilets,' he said later as we wrote out lines from the catechism.

'Good,' I said, 'I don't like to think of God watching while I do a wee.'

That set us off sniggering again and got us another telling-off. I didn't mind. I had a new friend. A boy. And with him came a relief that I wouldn't get called to be a nun. As Catholics, we'd been told about special people who got the vocation and were called to the life of a nun or priest. It sounded wonderful, like an early *X Factor*, when a hand would point from on high and a voice would say,

'You, you are one of the chosen.' My friend Denise and I talked about it a lot. Would we be amongst the special ones, singled out for a life close to God? It was made to sound like a great honour, but I had my doubts and so did Denise, because we had recently discovered that boys might have something more to offer us than being a bride of Christ and living a life of chastity. In the end, neither of us got the call from above and the notion of it was soon forgotten as our hormones took over and anxieties about how to be a good kisser took precedence instead.

Andrew got detention again soon after his question about omnipresence. It was coming up to Easter and, this time, we were in Father Pronti's class.

'So Mike Jameson, and what are you going to give up for Lent?' the priest had asked one of the boys in the class.

'Sweets and chocolates,' Mike replied.

'Very good, my son. And you Joseph O'Leary?'

'Watching TV, Father.'

'Excellent. And you, Beatrice Brooks? I can see that you're bursting to give us your answer.'

I was. I'd thought long and hard about this one. Nothing as mundane as sweets for me, oh no, I wanted to give up something impressive, and to show Andrew that, like him, I didn't go along with the rest of them. I waited until the room had gone completely quiet so that my answer would have maximum impact. 'Please, Father,' I said as the class strained to hear. 'I'm going to give up lies and stealing.'

The place exploded in laughter, including Father Pronti. I went scarlet. Why were they all laughing? It wasn't funny. Not that I made a habit of lying and stealing, but I'd been taught that at times like Christmas and birthdays, it was the thought that counted. Wouldn't that apply to Lent as well? Surely my ideas for abstention were more along the lines that God was after than giving up Mars Bars or Maltesers, but maybe I'd got it wrong, and cutting out your Cadbury's was the twentieth-century version of sacrificing a first-born or slaughtering a lamb. Across the room, Andrew gave me the thumbs-up. I knew he'd get it.

When Father Pronti got round to him, I could tell by his face that he'd thought about his answer too. 'And you, Andrew Murphy, what will you be giving up for Lent this year? Chocolate or,' he gave me a conspiratorial wink, 'or is it to be lies and stealing like young Beatrice? What's it going to be?'

'Catholicism,' said Andrew. That wiped the smile off Father Pronti's face, but it sealed the friendship between Andrew and me. After that, we walked home together from school or met up after his paper round and would climb up on top of the coal shed at the side of his house and eat salty chips with vinegar from the paper. I loved it up there. We could watch and comment on people going by on the pavement, wave at others sailing past on the buses. At night, I fantasized about what it might be like to kiss him, an actual boy, as opposed to an imaginary one or the back of my hand.

One afternoon, he arrived at my house looking tense.

'What's the matter, Andrew?' I asked.

'Is there anyone else in?' he asked.

'No. Everyone's out.'

'Good, because I want to kiss you,' he said, and stepped forward and pressed his mouth on mine. My first kiss at last. I wasn't sure what to do so moved my lips a little and he did the same then he stepped back. 'What do you think?'

'Er . . . nice, soft.'

'Let's try it with tongues, it's called French kissing.'

I was happy to oblige. I couldn't wait to tell Denise and everyone at school but Andrew must have picked up on my thoughts. 'Can we keep this between us for now? I want to get really good at it and I want you to tell me what feels good and what doesn't.'

'Sure.' I was flattered that he cared so much about how it was for me. I'd heard nightmare stories from other girls about boys who were sloppy, wet kissers, and who hadn't asked for any feedback about their technique. We spent the rest of the week kissing whenever we could. We tried soft, harder, with tongues, ear nibbling. It was great fun and we had to admit to each other that we were getting pretty good at it. Kissing felt great.

One night, after I'd gone up to bed, I heard a noise at my bedroom window. I went to the curtains and drew them back to see Andrew outside in our garden. He was throwing stones up to get my attention. It felt daring and dangerous because I knew my mum and dad were down below in the sitting room watching telly.

'Bea,' he called up. 'I have to ask you something important.'

'OK.' He was going to ask me out on a proper date, I just knew it. It was coming up to Valentine's Day and I hoped I'd get a card that year; like the kisses, it would be a first. And if he wanted to go out with me, surely we could go public? In my head, I was already telling my friends the story at school the next day. I'd be one of the in-crowd, a girl with 'experience'. A boy had come to my window at night, asked me out. My love life had begun.

I closed the curtains, put on my dressing gown and sneaked down the stairs. I could hear the TV was still on in the sitting room, so I crept past, into the kitchen, out of the back door and into the garden where Andrew was waiting.

'What is it?' I asked.

'I think I'm ready for the real thing,' he said.

Oh god, I thought, *sex, he wants to go further and practise that as well as kissing*. I wasn't sure I was ready. 'Real thing? I . . . Are you sure?'

Andrew nodded. 'Denise.'

'*Denise?*'

'Yeah. She looks like she's experienced which is why I wanted to get some practice in kissing before I approached her, but I think I'm ready now. Do you think she'd go out with me?'

It was a stab to the heart. As the implication hit me, I felt my hopes crumble and my dreams wither. He had been using me to *practise*. There would be no Valentine card, no date, no showing off to my friends. I wasn't a girl that a boy wanted for real. I was no more than a confidante, a mate, someone to practise on until ready to approach the real object of desire. God, it hurt, and it knocked my confidence to the floor. I felt such a fool but I knew not to give myself away. 'Ah . . . I . . . yeah, maybe, probably.'

'Can you find out if she likes me? If she does, I thought I'd take her to the Saturday matinée at the cinema.'

'I'll see what I can find out,' I said. I had to get away, get back inside, to my bedroom, to nurse my wounded heart and shattered ego. 'Got to go, my parents are still up.' I retreated back inside and ran upstairs. I was devastated but not surprised. Denise was a 'girlie girl', an early developer. She had breasts and glossy hair that fell in soft, brown waves to her shoulders and she smelt of strawberries. Boys were always looking at her. I was still flat-chested, despite my and Denise's regular arm-pumping exercises and chants of 'I must, I must improve my bust' and my hair, cut too short by my mother, was more hacked than styled.

Denise was thrilled about Andrew wanting to go out with her, her first boyfriend, and I, still coming to terms about having been passed over, didn't let on that I was gutted. They dated for a few weeks but she wasn't over-impressed by the romance of chips in the paper eaten on top of his shed, so she soon dumped him for an older boy who had a moped and took her to a posh café in town for coffee. Andrew came back to me to mourn his loss, but I wasn't interested in being a go-between for him and whoever took his fancy.

We went to secondary school soon after where I met Marcia, grew my hair, learnt about style and moved on. I vaguely remember seeing Andrew about locally, a gangly youth with spots, smoking in the car park of the Golden Lion. But I'd liked people who thought outside the box ever since, men with a different view on life. He had been the first I'd encountered who'd challenged the status quo.

Saranya Ji had said that I had an unconscious belief that love meant pain, a pattern I kept repeating. Was that when it had all started? When Andrew had overlooked me for my curvier friend and I'd been delegated to the part of the less attractive mate, the sidekick to confide in and cheer the main players, but not one to be desired or be centre stage myself? I'd learnt early, for fear of looking like a loser, to put on a happy face when others got the Valentine's cards and not to let my heartbreak at rejection be known. It didn't matter, I told myself. I didn't care. Love was something that happened to other people. I was cool with that. But I did care, and I wasn't so cool with it, not deep inside. *What became of Andrew? Had he maintained his rebellious attitude to life?* I wondered, as the flight hit some turbulence and I opened my eyes to see that the 'Fasten your seatbelts' sign had come on.

6

'And don't let us see you here again in a hurry,' said the prison warden as he handed me my keys, wallet and belt.

Always the same banter, every time I left. I smiled in acknowledgement of the familiar line as I walked towards the door that had been unlocked in readiness for my exit. Once outside, I breathed in the fresh, clean air and headed for the bus stop. It always felt the same when I got out of the bleak and oppressive atmosphere in a secure unit, the wonderful sense of freedom, the open sky above, heading home.

It would be Christmas in a couple of days, another New Year looming a week later. Time to take stock. I was never usually a man for making resolutions, but this time I would; a resolve concerning someone I couldn't get out of my head or heart. I'd been thinking about her and the possibility of us for many months – longer, if I was honest. Beatrice Brooks, Bea. Just the thought of her made me smile but how, where and when to approach her and tell her how I feel?

7

The journey home in the taxi from the airport was like driving through a winter wonderland, buildings and streets were white with snow, the pavements lined with festive lights. We sat in the back, shivering at the change in temperature from India, even though we'd pulled out winter coats and scarves the moment we'd collected our luggage at Heathrow.

As we drew up at Marcia and Pete's three-storey, Victorian house in one of the back roads in Hampstead, I glimpsed their eldest daughter, Freya, peering out of a downstairs window. She was twenty-seven, a beautiful, long-limbed girl with her mother's dark looks, she lived in her own flat in Camden but had moved back to the family home for the duration of the Indian trip. I reckoned she'd be relieved to give her siblings, Ben and Ruby, back into her parents' care. Not that either of them needed much care: Ben was in his last year at Nottingham University and Ruby in her first; both were now home for the holidays. Freya disappeared, then reappeared moments later at the front door and came tumbling out with Ruby, a younger version of herself with the same stunning looks. In the background, I could see Ben, so like his father, too cool to rush forward, but Marcia was already out of the car, gathering her girls into her arms before moving up the steps to embrace Ben who, despite himself, looked pleased to see her.

I waved to them all from the back of the car and wondered how many parties they'd held with their uni mates in their parents' absence, and what Marcia and Pete were getting back to.

'Call tomorrow when you've had a chance to settle,' said Pete as he hauled their last case from the boot of the car. 'We need to talk plans for Christmas lunch, it's only two days away.'

'I will,' I promised. 'Tell me what to bring and I can shop tomorrow.' It had already been arranged that I'd spend the day with them and the rest of the waifs and strays they always gathered. They wouldn't hear otherwise, although I'd have been perfectly happy to curl up in my pyjamas and watch *It's A Wonderful Life* for the fiftieth time and *Love Actually* for the hundredth.

'No need. I'll get it all from Harvest Moon,' said Pete. 'Just bring yourself.'

*

The taxi continued up the hill and into Highgate. It had long been one of my favourite parts of London, one of the few places in the city that had maintained a village atmosphere. It was picturesque in all seasons, with the Georgian houses surrounding Pond Square, but particularly so now with the snow-covered trees that were twinkling with

Christmas lights. We drove through the square, along the High Street, down the hill and at last I was home, a one-bed-room terraced house where I'd lived for the past ten years.

As I put my key in the door and stepped into the small porch, I was struck by how quiet it was in contrast to where I'd been for the last two weeks. The whole world and everyone in it had appeared to be out on the streets in India, a life where people spent so much of their time outside, as opposed to the closed doors and curtains sealing everyone inside in their homes in the winter in England.

The house was lovely and warm, a lamp on in the kitchen and a note propped up by the kettle. It was from Stuart. *Welcome back to the snowy UK*, it said. *Milk, bread and a few provisions in the fridge. I've put on the heating. Get out your thermals!* What a sweetheart he was. I'd given him a key because, after he'd heard about a recent spate of burglaries in the area, he'd been insistent about calling in from time to time while I was away to make sure everything was OK.

I had met Stuart almost a decade ago in the autumn, just after I'd moved into my house in Highgate. I had been out on the Heath with my dog Boris, and he had dug his heels in at the bin area by the gates and was refusing to move.

'That's how I feel some days,' said a voice behind me, and I'd turned to see a tall, dark-haired man in a long herringbone overcoat with a red scarf wrapped around his neck. He was smiling at me while trying to control a golden Retriever puppy. He looked interesting, not conventionally good-looking, but there was something attractive about his features and I immediately felt drawn to him.

'He will not budge,' I said as I pulled on Boris's lead. 'I think I might have to carry him home.'

Stuart laughed. 'Good luck with that.'

'I know. I'd need a wheelbarrow.' Boris was a big dog, a black German shepherd.

'How old?'

'He's twelve now. Actually, he's my parents' dog – or rather *was* my parents' dog – but they moved to Spain and weren't sure he'd adapt well to the hot climate at his age. They couldn't bear to put him in a rescue centre and nor could I, hence here we are.'

Stuart pulled a dog treat out of the pocket of his coat, knelt down and held it out to Boris, who miraculously recovered his mobility and trotted over to him.

'Looks like you've got trouble too,' I said as I noticed his puppy, who was on his hind legs, chewing on the end of Stuart's scarf as he leant over to fuss Boris.

'This is Monty,' he said. 'I got him for my daughter, she's always wanted a dog, but look who's ended up looking after him.' I checked his left hand for a wedding ring. *Of course*, I thought when I saw that he was wearing one: *all the good ones are taken*. 'He eats everything – socks, scarves, dirt, leaves, you name it,' Stuart continued. 'I've already been to the vets' twice with him and I've only had him three weeks.'

I laughed. 'I'm sure he'll learn.'

Boris decided he might walk after all, so we strolled along together sharing dog-training tips. Conversation came easily and I felt as if I'd known him for ever, an old friend I happened to have come across on the Heath. As he talked about his family and his wife, I'd quickly pushed away the initial attraction I'd felt for him. I never got involved with married men, never had, never would – not that he gave me any encouragement anyway. But I knew I wanted him in my life. When he'd said he was an accountant, I'd told him I was looking for one, and so the deal was sealed and, as I re-read his note by the kettle, I felt thankful that here he was ten years on, a friend I valued greatly.

I checked the heating was going to stay on then went from room to room switching on more lamps to give a sense of life in the place. On the ground floor, there was a large kitchen-diner, with glass folding doors at the back which opened onto a tiny courtyard garden. The sitting room and cloakroom were on the first floor, then up to a bedroom and bathroom on the second floor, from where there was access to a roof terrace, which was a heavenly place to retreat to in the summer.

Having checked that all was in order, I went back downstairs to the kitchen, opened the fridge and poured myself a glass of Chablis. I picked up the large pile of post that had been left on the island in the kitchen, took it up to the sitting room and sank into one of the sofas there. I could see that they were mainly Christmas cards, a few bills and one official-looking letter. I felt a knot of anxiety in my stomach. I had an idea of what it might say. I'd look at it later, not today. Why ruin a good holiday on the first night I was back?

It felt strange to be on my own after having had constant company and, despite my attempt to warm it up, the house felt empty of colour and life. *Now don't get maudlin*, I told myself, and said my mantra. *I'm OK. I have a good life.* I'd worked hard to create it and, although the house was small, it was a space that was a pleasure to come back to. The rooms had been painted in the neutral shades of Farrow and Ball: Cornforth White, Skimming Stone, Elephant's Breath. Pale linen and silk curtains hung at tall windows on the upper floors. Large, overstuffed, dove-grey sofas were in the sitting room, with cushions a few shades darker. Tasteful artefacts from my travels to India, Morocco and Turkey were placed on shelves and surfaces, not too many to look cluttered; big art and travel books were stacked on the coffee table. The atmosphere was elegant and serene. That was what people said. That was what I worked so hard to present to the world. Hah. What a joke. If only they knew. It was all so perfect but sometimes it felt sanitized, a show house, and I longed for the clutter and chaos of Pete and Marcia's home, always full of people and mess, their children and friends. I felt a sudden urge to have the whole house repainted in lime green and turquoise with a gold loo and red ceiling, then go and . . . and buy a dog, two dogs; but knew I wouldn't. I'd drink too much wine, sleep fitfully, then get up tomorrow and carry on, because that's what I did best, I carried on. Saranya Ji's words replayed in my mind: 'You believe that people you love leave you, and you are destined to be alone.' Bah. I'd got used to being on my own; it had made me what I am, independent and strong, well . . . most of the time. I had good friends. What more did I need? As I sat, sipping my wine, I thought back to a time when even Marcia had disappeared.

*

I had been eighteen when my parents left home. Not only did they move out, they left the country. Dad had tried to emigrate and get a job abroad before – Hong Kong, Singapore, Canada, Kenya. He had considered them all over the years but, this time, it was definite. He longed to get away from rainy, grey Manchester, and when a post as a senior lecturer at a university came up on sunnier shores, it was a dream come true for him. Apart from my elder brother, Matthew, and me, my family were off to New Zealand and taking everything I took for granted with them – regular meals, Sunday lunches, family Christmases, my mother's words of concern and care on days of exams, interviews or illness, bills paid, warmth and company when I returned at night. With them went a sense of belonging, security, a home.

Not that I cared at the time. I couldn't wait for them to go, particularly my father, who in my late adolescence had become increasingly critical and sarcastic. No, their departure meant independence. I had a place at Manchester Art College. A world of possibility would be opening up in front of me, and there would be no one to hold me responsible. At last, the freedom to live the kind of lifestyle I'd longed for, all my teenage years.

Of course, we made lots of jokes about them going at the time, like ha-ha, Matthew and I were so dreadful that not only did Mum and Dad leave home, they went as far as possible. But I wasn't laughing when it came to the day for them to go. Watching them load everything up one day in July, get a taxi to Piccadilly Station, get on a train and disappear: not my happiest memory. Mum was crying as they boarded and my younger brother, Mark, kept asking, 'Why aren't Matthew and Bea coming with us?' I burst into tears, which set Mark off too, even though he was sixteen at the time. Mum was too busy trying to get everything on the train to notice that I was freaking out inside. I was determined not to make a scene. I didn't. I turned away and put on a cheerful mask. Dad kept saying, 'You can still change your mind. There's a place at the university over there if you want it.' But no way was I leaving Manchester, Marcia, my place at art college – no way.

I felt weird all the same.

When the train started up, took off along the track then disappeared, I thought, *Right, that's it, now you haven't got any family*, like they'd died or something.

There was still Matthew but he rarely showed his feelings. He didn't that day. He just shrugged and set off to meet his girlfriend, Juliet, so I went home alone.

The house felt eerily quiet when I got back.

Mum had left us food in the fridge so I made some cheese on toast and went to sit on the bench in the garden where I told myself it would be OK, I'd manage. I would.

Later that night, I went to the downstairs loo. Mum must have been in there before she left because I could still smell her perfume, Chanel No 5, powdery and light. I realized that the scent would fade then disappear just as she just had. But what really got me was that in all the packing and last-minute panic, preparing for their new life abroad, Mum hadn't bought any loo paper for the downstairs cloakroom and there wasn't any. It was then that I realized I really *was* on my own: no one was going to take care of me any more, fill the cupboards, buy the necessaries. My mum was gone.

I sat on the loo and sobbed my heart out.

The next day felt strange too, getting up; no familiar

smell of toast and coffee from the kitchen, Radio Four playing as Mum got everyone sorted for the day.

The feelings didn't last long. Yes, I was sad that they'd gone, but I also knew that I was liberated. No one to answer to, ask if I'd been to Mass, done my homework, tidied my room, got in late. No one to tell me I wore too much make-up, my skirts were too short, tops too revealing. No one to question my friends, my taste in music, how long I'd been on the phone. And, best of all, Marcia would be moving in.

The family house was a four-storey, Edwardian build, with five bedrooms and a basement. The plan was to let the empty rooms to lodgers – students mainly. Marcia was one of them and we both had places at art college. It was summer in the city. Life was great.

The two attic rooms up top were taken by Matthew and Juliet, who had decorated them with the kind of flock wallpaper you used to see in Indian restaurants. They'd chosen red and it looked cosy and exotic up there. There were three more rooms on the first floor, where Marcia and I lived along with a pale-looking sociology student with curly dark hair called Mark. Red-haired Ed, a physics student, was in what had been the front sitting room on the ground floor. Meanwhile the back sitting room became a communal place for us all, and we'd fashioned a make-do bedroom in the basement for Ron, who promoted local bands and had nowhere else to go. Despite having the physique of Desperate Dan, he seemed happy enough down there in the small space, and had pinned swathes of gold silk on the ceiling and walls, which hid the pipes and plumbing and billowed out, giving it the look of a harem.

I loved going from attic to cellar, seeing how each character had made their space their own. As soon as Mum and Dad had gone and the tenants had moved in, the house had taken on a new atmosphere; a poster of Grace Jones appeared in the hall, another of Madonna in the sitting room. We ate what we liked when we liked, stayed up late, got up late. The house became a social centre for many friends who, like us, had little money to frequent bars or clubs and so loved to come and hang out. Phil Collins playing 'One More Night' was on a loop tape in the sitting room, and the house was always full of students or musicians, rolling joints, drinking tea, getting stoned and putting the world to rights.

It was perfect, and I had Marcia to share it all with.

*

Marcia rolled the most elegant joints I'd ever smoked. Not those fat, loose ones with tobacco and hashish spilling out of the end that got covered in spit because no one could get their mouth around them. Hers were long and slim, like panatella cigars.

On the low table in front of her in her room, she'd laid out her supplies: Rizla papers, king-size; silver cigarette case containing menthol, not regular tobacco; silver pill box with mother-of-pearl inlay containing her stash, and several immaculately cut pieces of white card for making roaches.

She reached for her Zippo lighter and lit up.

I smiled. 'It's like attending a Japanese tea ceremony, having a smoke with you.'

'I like to do things properly,' she said as she inhaled deeply. 'Er . . . thing is, Bea, I've got some news.'

She was always coming back with news for me, as I did for her. We were Marcia and Bea, Bea and Marcia. We did everything together, had done since we'd met that first day in secondary school. We shared all our discoveries: men, music, fashion, feminism, books, heroes or heroines to be admired or discounted as we pleased. We made all our decisions together; the most recent to decorate her room in the Zen style she'd got into. We'd painted her room white, took away the base of her bed and put the mattress on the floor, a bamboo blind at the window, a single poster in black and white depicting yin and yang in a circle on the wall, a small Buddha in the corner and books on Mahayana Buddhism piled up by her bed. I went for a more bohemian look. I liked the Pre-Raphaelites and we chose posters of Ophelia by Millais, Beatrice by Rossetti, Hylas and the Nymphs by Waterhouse for my walls. We bought vases and a chenille bedcover from an antique emporium in town, used embroidered silk shawls as throws on the sofa. Marcia said it had the look of a Victorian brothel. I was happy with that. I was the romantic back then; Marcia, ever the seeker, had just got into yoga and meditation, interests she tried to pass onto me but without much luck: I could never sit still for long enough. After years of friendship through school, it was great to be actually living together, and it was really thanks to her that I didn't miss my family more in those early weeks after their departure. She more than made up for them.

'It's about Pete,' she said as she handed me the joint. 'He wants to take a year out to go travelling before university.'

I took a drag. 'Oh Marcia, I am sorry,' I said. She'd just met him at Glastonbury back in June where he'd been manning a food stall, and I knew she liked him a lot because he'd been staying at the house every weekend for the last month.

'No,' she said, 'it's me that's sorry.'

'Of course you are. Where does he want to go?'

'All over. Cuba, Goa, Thai Land.'

'Sounds wonderful. You must be gutted.'

She looked away. 'No, you don't understand. I'm going with him.'

'*With* him?' My heart sank and my head swam as the marijuana took effect. 'But you can't. Your place at college—'

'I've already spoken to them. It's OK. I can start next year instead. Look, I am sorry, really I am, but it's too good an opportunity to miss.' What was she saying? She'd been making plans and not telling me? We told each other everything, *everything*: periods, moods, how far we'd gone with boyfriends and how they rated as lovers; everything. My heart sank further. This was the first time I'd ever been excluded. 'And you'll be OK here, you've got Matthew and Juliet. You'll meet people.'

I laughed. My brother and his girlfriend had even put in a mini-kitchen up on the top floor so they could be self-contained, away from the rest of us.

'When?' I asked.

'In a week or so.'

'Or so?'

'On the twenty-eighth of August.'

I felt sick. She couldn't be going. We had everything worked out. The house. Parties. Barbecues. College. We'd bought secondhand bikes to travel in together. We were going to bunk off in the afternoon to see movies. Go shopping. Bake our own bread. It was all planned.

'Come with us if you like,' she added, though with little conviction.

'I can't. You know I can't. Mum and Dad left both Matthew and me in charge here. I can't abandon him. Anyway, I couldn't come and be a tagalong with you and Pete – that would never feel right.'

'They shouldn't have left you with all this,' said Marcia, ever my champion. 'What about your Aunt Carol or Uncle Mike? Can't they take over?'

'Not that simple. I mean, yes, they're meant to check in on us every now and again, but they have their own families. Anyway, it was my choice to stay. Dad did keep asking if I wanted to go with them. I insisted on staying.' I didn't add that it had mainly been because I thought that, as long as I had Marcia for company, I didn't think I'd need anyone else.

'Yeah right, some option, the middle of nowhere, a million miles away,' said Marcia.

'You'll be going that far. Millions of miles.'

'Different. We'll be travelling.' She could see she had no argument and blaming my parents didn't wash. She was abandoning me and she knew it.

'We'll have to find a new lodger to take your room.'

'I guess.' She couldn't look at me.

I couldn't help it. My eyes filled with tears. 'Is it definitely definite?'

Marcia nodded. She still couldn't look me straight in the eye. We'd had our own plans to travel in the holidays:

Europe, maybe India. But why should she hang around waiting for me just because I had responsibilities? She had a boyfriend, was in love. I couldn't blame her for wanting to go.

'Maybe you'll meet someone when I'm gone,' she said.

'Yeah right,' I said. By that time, I'd had a few boyfriends: Bruno who was my brother's exchange student and here for a summer. Before him there had been Kevin, but I'd lost touch with him when his family moved away; a few dates in between, but no one special like Pete was to Marcia.

'You're too fussy,' said Marcia.

'I just don't see the point of compromise, that's all.'

Marcia smiled. 'Some day your prince will come. In the meantime, get a bit of practice in.'

'Maybe.' But I knew I wouldn't, not unless it felt special, and the idea of 'practice' was not one that appealed, not since the Andrew Murphy disaster, a time I'd told no one about. Despite him, though, I still was a romantic at heart, hoping that one day I'd run into a man who looked as if he'd stepped out of a Pre-Raphaelite painting by Burne-Jones or Rossetti – a King Cophetua down the deli, or Hylas buying hummus at the corner shop.

She left two weeks later. I sat in her empty room after she'd gone and thought: family gone, best friend gone. I'd never felt so alone in my life. *It's sink or swim time*, I told myself, and decided I'd swim. I'd be strong, become the type of person who didn't need anyone; not in a cold-hearted way, but in an independent, self-sufficient way. I'd become cool. I'd be more Zen and detached than Marcia could ever be. If I didn't need anyone, I couldn't be let down.

Marcia did come back a year later, but she didn't return

to the house or go to college. She and Pete had got married on a beach in Goa, so it wasn't Marcia and Bea any more, it was Marcia and Pete. Her parents helped them buy a small house near Chorlton Green, and he started his vegetarian café serving Eastern-style food with Marcia by his side as manager. Though I grew to love Pete, and Marcia was still my dearest friend, it was never the same again. The lesson had gone deep: people move on, make their own plans, and I could never depend on anyone. *You're born alone, you die alone and sometimes you have to live alone too*, I'd thought, even though by that time I had a boyfriend, Sam, who had declared undying love for me. I kept him at arm's length. I wanted to make a life where I needed no one, and was perfectly happy with my own company.

*

A noise outside brought me back from my trip down memory lane. I ran to the window to see what had happened. A blonde lady at the wheel of a Mercedes sports car was attempting to park in a space much too small for it, and had reversed into the Volkswagen Golf behind: my Volkswagen Golf. *And we're back to reality*, I thought as I raced to the front door. My neighbour, Jon, had also heard the commotion and was outside on his pathway laughing. *Probably pissed*, I thought.

'Sorry, sorry,' he called when he saw me. 'Hey, you're home. Have a good time in India?'

'That's my car she's bashing into,' I said. I could barely believe it. I'd been back five minutes and he was already causing problems. There was always something with Jon, usually involving one of his many conquests, parking in my space or parking without a permit, or generally causing problems. We'd had many altercations over it. Parking was sparse on our road and each resident had a limited number of permits to give out when there were visitors. With his many callers, Jon abused the system. He had so many women arriving at all times of the day and night that I'd joked to Marcia once that he was maybe a male escort for women who liked older men. Not that Jon was that old: he was in his mid-fifties, his brown crew-cut hair had only a little grey around the temples, and he had twinkly eyes that looked full of mischief. He worked hard at staying fit and lean, too. I often saw him out jogging or off to play tennis when I was leaving for work. *And another one bites the dust*, I thought, as the latest leggy girl got out of the car and tossed Jon the keys. 'Be a darling,' she said. 'Parking never was my strong suit.'

Jon headed for the car as I sighed and turned to go back inside. It was freezing out there, I was tired, and I could examine any damage better in the daylight the next morning.

'So sorry Bea,' called Jon. 'I'll make it up to you. Welcome home. Happy Christmas.'

Without turning back, I waved. 'And Happy Christmas to you too.'

I couldn't be bothered to get into an argument at that moment. The silver-tongued charm that won his women over had ceased to work on me months ago when, as well as the parking, he repeatedly left his rubbish in front of my house. He hadn't got the hang of separating plastics from cardboard from glass, and I'd had to do it for him on more than one occasion for fear of inciting the wrath of the bin-men. God, he made me cross!

Once back inside the warmth of my house, I found my laptop and googled Saranya Ji again to see if anyone had left a review of her readings. Once again, the pages came up showing links to people with that name, but not my Saranya Ji. I googled psychics in India and found that there were hundreds, some with thousands of reviews, many who claimed to do past life readings but, again, no sign of the woman we'd seen in Udaipur. Marcia must have found her somewhere, but I was hesitant to email or text to ask her where. It would indicate interest, and that would be adding fire to Marcia's flame, something I did not want to do. *Best I forget all about it*, I told myself, *it's a pile of nonsense anyway*.

I went upstairs and flicked the TV on; I could unpack later. The screen filled with a commercial showing the perfect Christmas, a big happy family around a festive table, everyone laughing and smiling as newcomers arrived and were welcomed at the door. I changed channels to see that a rerun of *The Holiday* had just started. I'd seen it before. Two women, Kate Winslet in the UK and Cameron Diaz in the USA, do a house swap and find the loves of their lives. Now there's a thought. Maybe next year I should do just that: take off to a house in the middle of nowhere and hide under a blanket until Christmas – and all its reminders that I was on my own – had passed. And maybe, just maybe, some handsome hunk in an Aran sweater, looking like Jude Law, would turn up and rescue me then . . . with my luck, would probably run off with one of my friends.

8

Should I text, phone, turn up with a bunch of flowers? Send a card? Send something amusing? What should I say? And what if my feelings for Bea aren't reciprocal? I'm not her type, after all? I don't know. Not really. Am I mad to imagine she would want a man like me? That's just a chance I'll have to take. Faint heart never won fair lady, and all that. Nor is this the time for self-doubt. Does she even suspect I harbour such deep feelings for her? I think she must know but then . . . why would she? But is it the right time? I have complications that I need to clear. Best wait a while? Yes. Clear the decks. The timing must be right.

9

'Love the tree and it smells wonderful in here, of pine forests,' I said when I arrived at Pete and Marcia's on Christmas Day to see a Norwegian spruce, as tall as the ceiling, in the hall. It had been decorated in red and gold and piles of presents were heaped around the base, to which I added the bag-full I had brought with me.

'Ben and Ruby did the decorations yesterday,' said Pete as he ushered me through into the kitchen diner, which was already full of family and friends.

'Looks fab and I can smell cinnamon and nutmeg too. Mulled wine?'

Pete nodded. 'Just made. I'll get you a glass. It's all been a bit of a rush this year, though Marcia did some preparations before we went away.'

'She ought to run the country,' I said. Despite some of Marcia's far-fetched ideas and predilection to be irrational at times, she was the most organized person I knew when it came to her family and work. She'd always had a gift for admin, project managing, and generally running things, though Pete often remarked it was actually just that she liked bossing people around. This season, she'd bought her Christmas cards back in October, had all the presents wrapped in November before we went away, and I'd seen her in the airport lounge in India ordering the fresh food online to be delivered on Christmas Eve. I hadn't even bothered decorating my house because I'd missed the run-up, nor had I bothered buying any special food: there was only me at home and I didn't plan on doing any entertaining this year.

'Any news?' asked Pete.

'I have a letter waiting for me at home but have put off looking at it until after Boxing Day.'

'It's not like you to procrastinate.'

'I know, but everywhere is shut over Christmas, everyone's on holiday, so what's the point in getting all worked up when no one's in their office? So I'm having a bit more time off – proper time – and when everyone's back at work, I'll get in gear.' Actually, part of the reason I'd been delaying the moment was that I wanted to be sure Stuart would be around to advise and, of course, he'd be busy with his wife and family over the festive period. He'd already seen me through some tough times with my business and finances, and I valued his calm approach and steadying influence.

'I think that's very sensible,' said Pete as he handed me a steaming mug of mulled wine. 'Good decision. Now get a drink and let's put all thoughts of work, worry and changes out of our minds. Let's eat, drink and be merry, for tomorrow we may diet.'

All the family were wearing their traditional jumpers: Pete's with a pudding that lit up on the front; Marcia's had a Santa on it, and Ruby was in a red sweater with a snowman grinning from her chest. She offered me a canapé of gravadlax and dill on rye from a tray, and I spent the next half-hour catching up with everyone who was there – Pete's parents, down from Scotland; Marcia's mum from Manchester who was busy preparing vegetables; Pete's uncle Tom in charge of drinks; Marcia's sister Yaz laying the table with Freya. Ben was sprawled on a sofa in the sitting room watching TV with his cousins; Pete's younger brother Ted and his wife and twin girls waved from across the room where they were playing a game which involved one person wearing inflatable antlers' horns while the others tossed rings onto them. Neighbours Jess and Ian Ward were settled with their glasses in the conservatory off the kitchen. No single men this time, I noted with relief. One year, they'd invited Nigel, a neighbour and bachelor, in the hope that we'd hit it off. We didn't, though he got the idea that we did. There was a reason that he was single, and that was that he was the most boring man I'd ever met with a particular passion for lawnmowers, something I knew all about by the end of the afternoon.

'And where's your jumper?' asked Marcia. They'd bought me a blue one with a penguin on it last year, which I had dutifully worn at the time then taken to a charity shop in January.

'Ah . . . shrank in the wash, so sorry,' I said. I was dressed in my usual black, a small nod to Christmas being the tiny silver holly-shaped earrings I'd had made and also sold in my shop.

'You were never a good liar,' said Pete. 'Here, have these.' He handed me a headband of antlers' horns instead. Nobody got away with looking cool at their house on

Christmas Day. I'd spent many Christmases there over the years and, though I'd offered to host at mine, there was no point really: we'd never all fit in. It was tradition now. Marcia and Pete's every 25 December, apart from one winter when I was living with my last long-term partner, Richard Benson. He'd come along to their house for Christmas Day for the first two years we'd been together, but wasn't happy either time. He was threatened by the ease and familiarity I felt when I was with my two oldest friends, especially Pete, who he felt he had to compete with. After weeks of complaint, on the third year, I'd given in and agreed to have Christmas at home, just the two of us.

It had been OK but hadn't felt right. I missed the pandemonium that had become part of my life. After we'd split up five years ago, I'd made a new condition to my relationships, and that was 'love me, love my friends.' Trouble was, there hadn't been anyone since to try the condition out on. I wondered where Richard was spending his Christmas this year. In fact, I'd been thinking a lot about all my past partners since India, reviewing who they were, who I was at the time, and asking myself if there was one who had got away. I hadn't been thinking of them because I believed that I'd known any of them in a past life, but what Saranya Ji had said had got me thinking about the choices I'd made to get where I was today, and if there was anything I could learn from the past in order to go forward.

*

Richard Benson. I'd met him over ten years ago when he'd come into the shop in Hampstead, on one of the rare days when I was behind the counter and not up in my office on the floor above.

I'd heard the door open and looked up to see a tall, well-dressed man in his fifties coming in.

'I'm looking for a gift for my niece,' he'd said in a public school voice as he perused the counters and cabinets displaying jewellery. 'It's her twenty-first and I don't want to go the usual Tiffany route, I'd like to give her something more personal.'

Hmm, a thoughtful man, I noted. 'Any ideas so far?' I asked.

'Her name is Rose, maybe a chain with an "R" on it?' he suggested as he pointed at a display of alphabet letter charms in gold and silver.

'Oh no, they're popular with the teenagers but maybe not for a twenty-first. Rose you say? How about something like this?'

I drew a quick sketch showing a bracelet with slim linked leaves with one charm on it, that being a single rosebud. 'Far more subtle and unusual than an R,' I told him. 'Be lovely in silver. What do you think?'

He smiled. 'Delightful. How clever of you just to draw it like that. It's just the thing. Could you do it in time? The birthday's in a few weeks.'

'I'm sure we could,' I said. I had a few contacts in the area who could make up a design for me.

He had returned to the shop to pick up the bracelet, then again a month later to tell me that the gift had been a great success and to ask if I'd like to go for dinner. I said yes.

Richard and I dated for a year before he moved in with

me and I was impressed by his taste and initial generosity. With his army background, immaculate clothes and thin frame, he wasn't my usual type, but I was ready for someone different. Richard was quite posh and I liked that about him – his impeccable manners, the way he spoke, the way he dressed in suits and shirts from Jermyn Street in Piccadilly, and wore handmade shoes. He always smelt wonderful, too, of Czech and Speake No.88 cologne. The typical English gentleman. He showed me another side of life. We ate in acclaimed restaurants in Mayfair, he got tickets to Glyndebourne, best seats at the theatre, taught me a lot about fine wines; we had weekends in France with his sister and a fabulous safari holiday to the Masai Mara in Kenya. It was a lifestyle I could get used to, I thought, and I did at first. I wasn't used to being looked after so well and told friends that it was nice to have a father figure. Another plus had been that he didn't come with any baggage or children. Richard's first wife had died in her early twenties, a fact he'd grieved over and moved on from. 'Life is for the living,' he used to say. He didn't drink to excess, didn't take drugs, wasn't moody and said what he meant. It was exhilarating after some of the men I'd known or thought I could change or stayed with because they appeared to need me. I wasn't after a grand love affair. At that time, I wanted stability: a man I liked, loved even, but not too much because that way, there was less chance of getting hurt. He'd rented out his flat in Kensington and moved in with me in what was supposed to be a temporary measure. We even talked about marriage, though neither of us wanted to rush into it. We discussed buying a place in the country. We planned a future.

The first years were good but an adjustment. Richard had his way of doing things, I had mine. Slowly, over the years, it became more his way of doing things, and I felt I'd begun to lose myself in wanting to live up to his high standards, rigid routines and expectations. Even sex was like a military operation: you put this bit here, then that there, twiddle a bit, oo, ah, then done and into the shower. Hardly passionate, and it soon faded to less and less frequent. I did wonder sometimes if Richard's first wife had died from boredom.

The final straw was when he became controlling over money and too possessive of my time. I wanted a relationship but never to be joined at the hip. Richard resented me being away too long if I was abroad on shopping trips, and even suggested that I give up my work and let him support both of us. When I refused to do that, his already thin lips became pinched as he insisted that I use my money to pay off as much of my mortgage as I could every month. He would pay for everything else. I agreed to it because I could see that he was the kind of man who needed to see himself as the breadwinner, but that was the beginning of all the trouble. Richard earned plenty of money as a barrister but, as the months went by, I realized he was rather tight. He'd question if I *really* needed an item if I'd splashed out on a pair of shoes or expensive make-up. I felt I had to defend any extra purchases, so I took to hiding things in the back of the wardrobe then, when I wore something new, would say I'd had it for years. Lying like that never felt right. He made a budget for our household expenditure and went through it with a fine-tooth comb at the end of the month. He told me to fire Stuart because he could do my accounts for me instead. I refused and, when I confided in Stuart about the suggestion, he asked if I was truly happy with Richard. It was probably then that I began to really question if I was. Richard sulked if I wanted to go away with a friend and argued that I should be using the extra money to pay off the mortgage. He even tried to control what I ate, frowning if I chose to have a dessert, banning chocolate from the house.

I began to feel hemmed in, that I was losing my independence and my space. Richard didn't want to do Christmas at Pete and Marcia's. He wouldn't wear the antlers' horn headband they gave him; he couldn't let go of maintaining the proper image. He never accepted any of my friends, and soon I was reluctant to have them round for fear of him criticizing them later. Although I thought Marcia had some whacky ideas, I didn't like hearing Richard call her and Pete a couple of old hippies. He just didn't get them, and was jealous of anyone who took my attention away from him. He even thought something was going on with Stuart, and watched him like a hawk if he ever dropped by the house. As if. I realized that what Richard really wanted was a stay-at-home wife who was there to cook his meals, keep his (my) house tidy and sweet-scented, plan his social diary, be there for him and him alone. I got bored with the predictability of our life – a G and T at seven, supper at seven thirty, a concert midweek, a theatre outing on Fridays, a proper roast lunch and walk on Sundays. The stability I had craved was suffocating me, and I began to feel like rebelling, not that I ever did. I toed the line and, with it, shrank inside from my true self.

When Richard sipped at his one, and only one, glass of

fine wine with supper, I started to feel as if I'd like to polish off the whole bottle, then dance on the table. Anything to evoke a reaction. He disapproved of smokers, which made me want to go out and buy a pack of Marlboro and smoke the lot. He insisted on regular exercise and a long walk on Sundays, which made me want to slob about in my pj's, watching trash TV, instead of one of his high-minded documentaries. I wanted to eat crisps and marshmallows instead of his only allowed TV snack, which was a bowl of olives from a deli in Kensington. And I was pretty sure his mother disapproved of me. She never thought I was good enough for her golden boy, though helping myself to the potpourri – thinking it was a bowl of crisps – when we first met, didn't help improve her view of me. In the last year we were together, the cracks had begun to show in our relationship, and I was slipping down and through them. When Richard started telling me what to wear and advised me to cut up my credit card, I'd decided that was enough. I wanted my life back.

Was he the one I'd let go? Definitely not. He was a decent man, kind when he wanted to be, but we were done. Saranya Ji had said a true soulmate might bring challenges, but I'd breathed a sigh of relief when Richard had moved out and I never looked back.

*

After lunch, Ben, Freya and Ruby disappeared up to their rooms; others settled on sofas to snooze, others helped with the washing up.

'Pete's been online,' said Marcia, as we cleared plates from the table and stacked them in the dishwasher.

'What for?' I asked, as if I didn't already know.

'Billy and Grace.'

'Ah. I thought he said it was going to be impossible to find them.'

'True. It's not easy but there's so much information online now, we have made some headway.'

'And how many people with those names have you found?'

'Loads. You were right, Bea, both are common names, but I did find a whole family with the surname Harris who lived in Ireland then Manchester then in Cambridge. Pete's going to get on to it in the New Year. When he has time, he's going to do some more research for us. Is there anything else you can remember from what Saranya Ji told you that might be helpful?'

'I told you everything.'

'OK. Any places you've ever felt a feeling of déjà vu when you've visited them?'

'Can't say I have.'

'Maybe you should try and contact Saranya Ji, see if she had anything else to add?'

'She was on tour in India, wasn't she? She's probably gone from Udaipur by now. How did you find her, Marcia? Was it online or did someone recommend her? Has she got a website?'

'Not that I know of. It really was coincidence, as if meant to be. Someone at work told me about her ages ago and then, when we got to India, I saw a leaflet in one of the hotels advertising her tour in India.'

'So how did you get in touch?'

'I called the number on the leaflet and a man told me where she was going to and when and, amazingly enough, she was in Udaipur the very same dates that we were. Why? Do you want to contact her?'

'No. I just wanted to know more about her, to see if there were any reviews about her.'

'I don't think I kept the leaflet but I'll look. In the meantime, think back, Bea: is there anything else that you remember from your session; anything you didn't tell us?'

'I don't think so. Second World War and . . . actually, I do remember something. She said Grace worked as a dressmaker in London.'

'Bea, that makes all the difference. I seem to remember that the census records show occupations. It could narrow the search down significantly.'

I sighed. 'OK, but say you did find one of them, or both of them, as I keep saying, so what? All it proves is that two people of that name existed, end of story.'

'You don't know that. You'd have made a crap detective, Bea. You look at clues, one leads to another. Anyway, I'm not giving up. So. London. Excellent. Second World War and Saranya Ji said that he went to war and didn't return. If they were to be married, chances are they were quite young.'

'Not necessarily. They may have met later in life.'

It was no use. Marcia was away. 'The dates of the Second World War were 1939 to 1945. If I allow for them being engaged as young sweethearts, they could have been eighteen, nineteen or early twenties, and often young men of that age went away to war.'

'Apparently some lads of only sixteen went to fight.'

'Doubt if they'd have been engaged to be married at that age, though. And what was the maximum age for soldiers?'

'I seem to remember it was forty, but older if called for Home Guard duty. I know because Richard was always watching documentaries about the war.'

'But Saranya Ji said he went away to war, right? So he wouldn't have been in the Home Guard.'

I nodded. 'I think she said that. I didn't make notes because it's a load of *baloney*, Marcia.'

Marcia ignored me. 'Hmm, but you're right, Grace could have been in her thirties or forties.'

'Unless he liked older women. He might have had a mother complex. She might have been ancient.'

'I'll get Pete to find out. I'll ask him to look up the exact age men were no longer eligible to go to war so that we're certain. He'll probably already know but, by my reckoning, it gives us about twenty-five years as a time frame to look at. Men between sixteen and forty, women the same. If Grace was born around 1919, she'd have been around twenty when the war began. We can begin with that, and the fact that we're looking in London also narrows the field. Other facts, her name and that she was a dressmaker will also help. I'm sure Pete will find her.' Her face looked flushed with excitement. 'Don't you see, Bea, we're making progress.'

I laughed. 'Not *we're* making progress: you're on your own with this. I'm really not interested.'

'Spoilsport. Where's your sense of romance?'

'As you know, that died a long time ago. Look, you go ahead, but don't ask me to get involved.'

'Too late,' said Marcia, 'you already are. Now, have you thought any more about your list of past lovers, though of course, we may be barking up the wrong tree looking back in time. It may well be that you are yet to meet this special man, so keep your options open, be on the lookout. In the meantime, though, how's the list? Have you started it? So far, we have Andrew Murphy, and the recent ones like Richard and before him, Michael O'Connor, Joe Wilding and Graham, of course, plus the odd one I can remember from our earlier days. Pete might be able to track them down, no problem, but it would help if you put them in some kind of order according to dates.'

'Are you suggesting that I look them all up?'

'Yes.'

I rolled my eyes.

Luckily Pete came to the rescue. 'Fill your glasses everyone,' he called from the sitting room, '*The Snowman* is about to commence.'

'Oh come on, Marcia, we can't miss this. Tradition and all that, and they're playing your song.' I pulled her towards the sitting room where people were already gathering and we could hear the familiar strains of 'We're Walking in the Air'.

*

I got home around midnight to find that there was a package and card on the steps up to my front door. I took them inside and opened them.

'Happy Christmas and sorry about the car, looks OK but if you see any damage, let me know. In the meantime, I got you a new one. Jon. XX'

I opened the parcel to find a box containing a toy Volkswagen Golf. *Hah. Funny. Well, you know where you can stick that*, I thought as I put the car in the waste-paper bin.

10

Boxing Day was traditionally time to catch up with my family. Sadly it took place in cyberspace because, after living in New Zealand and returning to the UK for a decade, my parents now lived in Spain. My elder brother Matthew and his family were in South Africa, my younger brother Mark up north in Manchester.

It was still too early to call them, so I made tea and toast and sat down in my pj's – grey silk ones that I'd bought after Richard had left and I could run up my credit cards again – at the dining table to go through the pile of cards still waiting to be opened. There were about sixty from family, colleagues, friends, an embossed card from Richard with a message saying, let's get together in the New Year. It was hand-delivered so he must have popped it through my letterbox when I was in the shower this morning. *Why?* I thought. *And had he been hoping to see me when he brought the card?* Our time together hadn't ended well; it was the only time I'd really witnessed his controlled persona break down when he'd begged me to give us another chance. I felt bad that I'd hurt him because he was a nice man, but he was just not for me. I think he had loved me in his own way – or at least the me I'd tried to be for him – but I wasn't that person. Something had been missing and I hadn't been prepared to compromise.

I texted Stuart to see if I could see him as soon as he was free, then I sifted through the cards. My phone pinged that I had a text. *Will be back in London tonight, need to see you urgently, coffee tomorrow? Heather XX*

Heather was one of my closest friends. We'd shared a flat together when I first came to London and we'd worked together almost as long as I'd had the shop. She also took care of business in my absence and I trusted her completely. I texted back, *C U here at 10? BX*. Urgent, she'd said in her text. Maybe she already had wind of what the letter said.

I sent messages to my parents and my brothers that I would be calling them later, then busied myself tidying and catching up on domestic jobs. Stuart texted back that he could see me on the 28th. *Phew, it would be good to talk things through with him*, I thought, as I finally sat back at the table with my laptop and phone to call Mum and Dad in Spain where they now lived in happy retirement. I had been a couple of times to join them for Christmas. Other years they had come back here but, as they'd got older, I had sensed a reluctance to travel, hence our cyber catch-up. I texted them: *Are you there?* No reply.

Next I tried my elder brother, Matthew, in South Africa. He was home, and soon, thanks to FaceTime, I had the whole family filling my screen: his wife, Juliet, son Tim and his wife Marie, and their four-year-old daughter, Phoebe. All were glowing with health with tanned faces and sun-kissed hair. They lived in Constantia in Cape Town, near to Juliet's parents, and it was summer over there, sunlight streaming in through an open door behind them. They lived in a colonial-style bungalow with dark wooden floors, whitewashed walls, a veranda at the front and a garden full of bougainvillea at the back.

'We've prepared a song, Bea,' said Matthew and, on his nod, the whole family burst into a few rounds of 'Ding Dong Merrily On High'. I laughed as they went at it with great gusto.

'Now you sing,' said Phoebe when they'd finished.

'Oh er . . .' I settled for a few verses of 'We Wish you a Merry Christmas', which they joined in with on the last lines.

'Weird having our Christmas visit in cyberspace, isn't it?' said Matthew.

'I guess – still, it's magic to be able to see you and your gorgeous house.'

'I've been drawing,' said Phoebe. She disappeared for a few moments then came back and held up her artwork. It showed two stick people holding hands.

'And who are they?' I asked.

'S'me and Jessie,' said Phoebe.

'Lovely,' I said, 'and is Jessie a friend?'

Phoebe nodded. 'My sister.'

In the background, I noticed Tim and Marie exchange glances and smile. 'Come on you,' said Marie. 'Time for bed.'

'But Jessie's not tired yet,' said Phoebe.

'OK,' said Marie. 'Well she can come and sit on the end of your bed while you go to sleep.' She looked back out of the screen. 'Merry Christmas, Bea, lovely to see you.'

'You too,' I said. 'And have a great New Year.'

Tim, Marie and Phoebe waved from the screen and left me with Matthew and Juliet.

'OK, so who's Jessie? Have they adopted a child and you haven't told me?' I asked.

'Oh no. Jessie's not real,' said Matthew.

'Ah, so she's a doll or something?'

Juliet shook her head. 'She's her imaginary friend. Phoebe's hilarious. She's always talking to her or about her and says she's her sister.'

'Probably because she's an only child,' said Matthew, 'so until another comes along, she's created her own fantasy sibling.'

'We've had to accept her as part of the family,' said Juliet.

'Hey Bea, remember you had an imaginary friend when you were little?' Matthew asked.

'Me? No. I don't remember that.'

'God, I do. You used to threaten me with him if I'd annoyed you.'

'Him?'

'Yes. I can't remember his name, but if I'd ever done something you didn't like, you'd say your friend was bigger than me and would get me.'

'I have no recollection at all,' I said.

'Why would you? You were about Phoebe's age.'

'And often children grow out of these imaginary friends and don't remember them at all,' said Juliet. 'No doubt Phoebe will in time, especially if Tim and Marie have another child.'

'That's right. I don't think you mentioned your friend

after a certain age, maybe after Mark came along,' Matthew continued, 'but . . . I remember! You used to say that you were going to marry him. I remember that. You were forever making wedding plans and collecting old bits of material and making them into dresses.'

'You're making this up.'

'I'm not. Ask Mum and Dad, I bet they'll remember. Oh, and by the way, Michael O'Connor got in touch with me on Facebook. He asked for your address and mobile number. I hope you didn't mind me passing on your details. I seem to remember you being broken-hearted over him at some point.'

'It's fine, it was a long time ago. I got over it.'

'Who was he?' asked Juliet.

'Friend of Matthew's,' I said. 'They played in a band together.'

'The Glow Sticks. We were terrible, least I was,' said Matthew. 'I think Michael still plays though. We keep in touch on Facebook and he often posts photos of him, guitar in hand.'

'Beer in the other?' I added. 'Last I heard he was running a beach bar in Thailand.'

'Think he still is, though I think he runs more than the bar out there now,' said Matthew. 'He's become quite the entrepreneur. It looks like a nice location from the photos he posts. I think he's heading your way for a family wedding or some event.'

'Oh, I remember him. He broke your heart?' asked Juliet.

'He was commitment-phobic, never one to be tied down. I thought he was the great love of my life, the One. He thought I was the one, too, but sadly the one of many.'

'Ah.'

'But we were young. He might have changed.'

'Hey, maybe the old spark will be there,' said Juliet.

'Doubt it, and don't you two start as well. It's bad enough with Pete and Marcia forever trying to pair me off. I've grown up since Michael; he wouldn't be my type any more.'

'So what type is that?' asked Juliet.

'Someone who has a job and a house, for starters. His resistance to commitment applied to material things as well as women.'

'He has his own house now,' said Matthew.

'Stop it, not interested.'

They laughed. 'If it's meant to be, it will be,' said Juliet.

'You always were hopelessly romantic, Juliet.'

'Come and see us soon, Bea,' said Juliet. 'We miss you.'

'I will. I promise.' I missed Matthew as well as my parents, but I had to get used to it, just as I'd had to get used to Marcia moving on so many moons ago. Matthew had been with Juliet since university and moved to South Africa straight after they both got their degrees. He loved it, and soon got a job working as an engineer. The climate suited him, and he and his family had a wonderful life over there. I got out to see them when I could, but Cape Town was a long way from London and air fares were costly.

'I will, and you know you're welcome back here any time.'

Matthew pulled a face. He'd never liked the cold weather.

We caught up on recent news, said our goodbyes and, when they'd gone, I texted Mum and Dad again.

A message came back, ready and waiting, I pressed FaceTime again and then there they were – or rather, there were the tops of their heads.

'Mum, I can't see you. Adjust your screen, that's it. Oh, and now I can't hear you. Is your sound button muted?'

I could see them faffing about and I felt a rush of affection. At last Dad pressed the right button. 'Can you hear me? CAN YOU HEAR ME?'

'I can Dad, no need to shout.'

It was good to see their smiling, familiar faces, and I felt a stab of nostalgia for Christmases we'd spent together, singing carols out of tune, swapping presents, playing charades. They both looked well, Dad white-haired and suntanned, Mum ash-blonde and glowing. The Mediterranean climate suited them. As with Matthew, I filled them in on my Indian trip and, in turn, they told me about their past weeks. They lived in a community for Brits abroad and it was reassuring to know that they were never lonely.

'Any chance you might get over?'

'I'll try, Mum, but having been away for two weeks, I have to make sure everything's OK with the shop.'

'When you can, love,' said Dad.

'Have you spoken to either of your brothers?' asked Mum.

'To Matthew just now. They all look disgustingly well and Phoebe's absolutely gorgeous, very creative and oh . . . do you remember me having an imaginary friend when I was little?'

'Imaginary friend?' Dad asked.

'Oh yes, I do, course I do,' said Mum. 'Billy.'

'Billy?'

'You couldn't have been more than five. You were such a funny little thing. Why? What's made you think of him after all this time?'

'Phoebe. She has an imaginary friend and Matthew reminded me that I'd had one too, though I don't remember. Are you sure I called him Billy?'

'Absolutely sure,' Mum replied. 'You grew out of it soon enough but there was a time when you talked about him non-stop. You even insisted we had to set a place for him at the dinner table.'

'How embarrassing.'

'If Matthew was making you cross, you'd tell him that your friend was bigger than he was and would get him.'

I laughed. 'Yes, he told me the same. Sounds like I created a sort of monster to get my own way. Good to hear I was so imaginative.'

'He didn't sound like a monster. You loved him, were planning your wedding.'

Dad nodded. 'That's right. Billy. I remember now.'

'Are you sure?' Billy was the name that Saranya Ji had given me. It was a coincidence, had to be. Loads of kids had imaginary friends, Billy was a common name. It didn't mean anything.

'Oh yes, you were going to marry him,' Mum continued. 'You were forever working on your dress, making it from odd scraps of material, dressing up in veils and flowers. In fact, you said you were going to make dresses when you grew up.'

A dressmaker, Grace was a dressmaker. A shiver ran through me. *No, get a grip, Bea*, I told myself. *I've started imagining coincidences when there probably aren't any.*

'And then you made real friends once you started school and never mentioned him again – least I don't think so,' said Dad.

'I honestly have no recall at all.'

'Why would you?' said Mum. 'It was a long time ago and you were little, but suddenly he was forgotten; though I do remember finding you in floods of tears one day and asking why you were crying. You told me that it was because of Billy; he was a soldier and had to go away to the war. I remember that day distinctly. You were inconsolable, but then life took over, school started, you got older and he was never mentioned again.'

Dad checked his watch. 'Have to go, I have a golf game in half an hour.'

'Me too. Bridge calling,' said Mum. 'Call again soon, in the New Year.'

'I will.'

We said our goodbyes and they were gone. The move to Spain had been a good one and kept both of them occupied and active. I was grateful for that, even if it was usually them who cut the FaceTime calls short. They were always off to some event or activity.

OK, that was weird, I thought as I closed my laptop. What they'd said had shocked me and I wished I could remember more but I couldn't. Billy, a soldier off to war, and I'd been planning to marry him? A girl making a wedding dress from scraps of material. A dressmaker? That was spooky. My mind went into overdrive. It was almost word for word what Saranya Ji had told me. Where had this invention of my imaginary friend come from? A past life? No. I'd known someone called Billy and remembered him when I was young? No. Could what Saranya Ji said have some truth in it? *No. It's coincidence*, I told myself again, *get a grip*. I was reading too much into it all. And, if it wasn't coincidence, then Saranya Ji was one of these people who could tune into a person's memories, a mind-reader. Yes, that could explain it, of course; she'd merely picked up on some lost memory of mine from my childhood and played it back to me, embellishing it with nonsense about a soulmate from a past life. Billy. Clever of her, quite a skill; only he wasn't from a past life, he was from my early life, no more than an imaginary friend, someone created to play with when my older brother was busy with his friends. I'd probably seen a TV programme about a handsome soldier and his fiancée and it had captured my imagination. Or heard one of my aunts talking about some distant relative who had gone to war and another who worked as a dressmaker. That would be it. Children were forever making up stories and pretending to be other people. Billy and Grace were nothing more than the results of a child's vivid imagination.

I felt happy that I'd found a rational explanation, and I'd almost convinced myself, but not quite: what Mum and Matthew had told me had niggled. *Why do so many children have imaginary friends?* I asked myself. I got out my laptop and googled 'imaginary friends in childhood'.

There were pages of sites, and I felt reassured as I read that inventing an imaginary friend was 'a healthy part of childhood that helps develop vocal skills'. 'Gives children a chance to tell someone else what to do', was another comment. That made sense. With an elder brother always telling me what to do, I'd probably imagined this Billy as someone I could boss around. 'Invented when lonely or bored'; 'Evidence of a child tapping into its imagination', other sites suggested. I felt a sense of relief as I read the explanations but then – oh no

– as I continued scrolling, there were sites linking imaginary friends to past life memories.

'Children recall people or events from past lives, often up to the age of five, after which they are usually overlooked.'

'Soulmates they didn't want to forget are remembered as imaginary friends.'

'Evidence of children remembering past lives or previous incarnations.'

'Children can sometimes recall memories from a past life.'

What? Noooo, I thought, *I will not entertain this idea. It is ridiculous*. With that thought came the memory of the last thing that Saranya Ji had said to me, 'Allow for possibilities that are ridiculous and preposterous. See where they take you.'

'OK, I will, Saranya Ji,' I said out loud. 'I'll show you I can be open if only to prove to myself and Marcia and Pete that there is some kind of rational explanation. Here I go. See. Open-minded, that's me.'

I spent the next hour googling case histories of children who had remembered past lives. It appeared to be a phenomenon all around the world, with many famous examples. I tried not to balk when I saw the stories labelled 'extraordinary', 'astonishing', or 'amazing', or read that some children had a birthmark or scar that related to the story they told of a wound they had received in their believed past life. One young boy had three birthmarks that matched injuries of his elder brother who had died twelve years previously. The boy appeared to know details of this brother's medical history, even though he had never been told them, and he kept insisting he was the elder brother returned. *Such tosh*, I thought as I continued reading. *There has to be some rational explanation.*

A young boy kept having nightmares about an aeroplane crash and fire. He claimed he had been a World War II fighter pilot, who had been shot down. He knew details of the aircraft, and that he remembered flying off a ship called the *Natoma*. Other very specific details kept emerging which led eventually to his parents linking their son to the pilot James Huston, who had flown off the ship and had been killed in action. The biggest sceptic in the case was apparently the boy's father but, after researching what his son recalled in detail, he came round to believing that there was indeed a link between his son and the dead pilot.

I bet the boy heard the story somewhere or saw a DVD, I thought. There had to be an explanation.

Next I read about a famous case, when a young woman, Jenny Cockell, was convinced she'd lived before as Mary, an Irishwoman who had died leaving young children. For years, she was painfully conscious of having left her children without a mother. She finally went to Ireland, where she was able to point out the house where Mary had lived, locations in the village and give details of Mary's children's lives. One of Mary's remaining sons, an old man when Jenny met him, came to accept Jenny as his deceased mother.

On and on they went, case after case, and when I looked at the clock, two hours had gone past. There was even a quote from the Dalai Lama, 'There are incidents where people, in childhood, recollect and recognize past life experiences and environments. Furthermore a considerable number of scientists are taking a keen interest in this field.'

In another article, a scientist noted that 'one area that deserves more study is when young children report details of a previous life which, upon checking, turn out to be accurate and which they could not have known any other way other than reincarnation.' The article said the memories could begin as early as three years old and fade between five and seven years.

I didn't know what to believe. My initial reaction had been they were all kids with overactive imaginations, but it appeared the evidence was there in some cases to say otherwise. I liked to think of myself as an open-minded but sensible person, but what I'd read had confounded me. *Could there be anything in it?* I wondered. Or maybe these children had a gift for tapping into a collective memory, including the memories of people who were deceased? Yes, that could be it. Carl Jung spoke about a collective unconscious tapped into by beings of the same species. Maybe it worked like iCloud; some sensitive souls could tune into that and remember other people's lives in the process. Why not? Whatever the explanation, I wasn't so sure of my position any more. Saranya Ji's words played and replayed in my mind: 'Allow for ideas that are ridiculous and preposterous.' The case histories that I'd found were certainly that; it was hard to know what to think any more. *No one really knows anything for sure*, I thought.

I gazed out of the window at the bare branches on the tree outside and it struck me that there was so much evidence of rebirth in nature. In winter, there was no sign of the buds or leaves that would appear in spring, the colour that would follow, as pale green foliage became bright in summer then a last burst of glory in the autumn only to disappear without a trace as branches became bare once more. So much of nature is cyclical. Maybe it was all there in its ever-changing glory, trying to tell us something. Birth, life, death; birth, life, death.

Oh no, I thought as I closed my laptop, *I'm turning into Marcia. I'll be talking to fairies next.*

11

Two items of post plopped through the letterbox the next morning. One looked official, the other looked like a late Christmas card with a foreign stamp. I ripped the card open and looked for the signature. Michael O'Connor. Hah. Just seeing his signature made me smile; it was still the same, a forward-slanting scrawl. It had been years since I'd heard from him, decades since I'd seen him. His card was cheap-looking with glitter on the front, and inside he'd enclosed a handwritten note.

Dearest Bea,
How the hell are you? I got your address
from your brother. He said you're doing
well, quite the entrepreneur these days.
I always knew you'd shine. I've often
wondered what happened to you and this
is the thing, I'm going to be in London
in February, fancy a catch-up? Here's my
number, 076633322. I've got yours from
Matthew so I'll text when I'm in town

or maybe before to let you know when I'm arriving. Keep some space for me, Love Michael. X

Michael O'Connor. Interesting that he should pop up at this point in my life. Synchronicity, Marcia would say. Just looking me up on a trip to England, I would reply. Whatever, I couldn't deny the frisson I felt inside at the thought of seeing him.

I'd met him in the queue in Pete's café in Manchester when I was at art college and I was on a lunch break from my classes. We both chose the lentil soup.

'Doesn't get more romantic than this,' Michael had said when we found ourselves also sharing a table. 'When we're old and our grandchildren ask how we met, we can say, it was over a pan of chickpeas.'

I laughed, flattered. Michael was a stunningly good-looking man, a mane of dark hair swept back from a face with a chiselled jaw line, a trimmed beard, truly beautiful sapphire blue eyes and a wide smiling mouth. 'Our grandchildren?'

He nodded. 'Lucy, Ben and Sky.'

'And our children's names?'

'Moonbean and Star.'

I shook my head. 'Hmm, not sure. I might like to call them something more traditional. Arthur and Alice.'

He put down his spoon and put his head in his hands. 'Oh god, we haven't even spent a night together yet and already we're arguing. Moonbeam and Star. Has to be.'

We haven't even spent a night together yet? There was a pre-supposition, one that I might have balked at normally but now I felt a rush of anticipation at the words. 'That's some chat-up line you've got going there – a tad presumptuous, I think. Do you use it on all the girls?'

Michael feigned offence. 'Only the ones who have the lentil soup.'

We spent the rest of the lunch arguing over names for our children like we'd been together for ever. On his way out, he handed me a leaflet. 'We're playing on Friday night at the Pig and Whistle in Deansgate. Please come.'

'I might.'

He smiled. 'Playing hard to get, eh?'

'I don't even know you.'

'Michael O'Connor, so now you do – know me, that is.'

'And I'm Bea Brooks.'

'Short for Beatrice? As in Rossetti's wife?'

'Probably. My parents love the Pre-Raphaelites, as do I.'

'Brooks? You don't by any chance have a brother called Matthew, do you?'

'I do.'

Michael put his hand over his heart. 'Fated. He plays in our band sometimes.'

'Oh! So you're in The Glow Sticks?'

'I am. See, if we hadn't met here, we were bound to have met somewhere. It's fate. Meant to be, like Moonbeam and Star. See you Friday, Bea Brooks.'

And off he went. I did go to the gig, of course I did. He was drop-dead gorgeous and had flirted with me: how could I resist? Matthew warned me against him as soon as he heard, saying that Michael was the sort who would never settle, but it was too late. I was smitten from day one and, miraculously to me, the feeling appeared to be mutual.

I fell hopelessly in love. We dated, we spent nights talking about everything from the silly to the sublime, we moved in together or, rather, Michael moved in with me. I was still living at my parents' house but no one objected to having an Adonis padding around the corridors in his boxer shorts, least of all me. I knew from the beginning that he was a restless soul, a Peter Pan, and I put that down to the artist's temperament. And I didn't care that he attracted women like a magnet or that he liked to flirt; he came home to me.

Until . . . a group was going to India to stay in an ashram. I could go with them, he said, but I hadn't finished college. 'I'll be back in a few months,' Michael promised. It was like Marcia leaving all over again and I hardened myself with the mantra that people I loved, left. I didn't need anyone, I told myself, but I felt his absence like a missing limb. But he did return, full of newfound wisdom about the importance of detachment from worldly possessions and the idea that attachment to people causes pain; the world was illusion, a dream. *No problem*, I thought. It was pretty close to what I'd come to believe, anyway. Plus I'd learned about Eastern philosophy from Marcia. I joined him in meditating, read the Buddhist and Hindu scriptures, put posters of Lord Krishna up on the wall, had statues of the Buddha on shelves, but it wasn't enough. Something had changed. Michael's aspired detachment from the world appeared to include me, and the East was calling him back. A few months later, he took off again. 'What we have is special, you know that,' he said before he left. 'If it's meant to be, our paths will cross again.'

It hurt. *I* hurt. It was true what the Buddha taught:

attachment did cause pain. I withdrew and nursed my broken heart. I got a postcard from Delhi, then Goa, then nothing. A year later, Matthew told me that he'd heard on the grapevine that Michael had married an Australian girl called Celia. *So much for detachment*, I thought. He taught me a big lesson in love, which was that when a man said he didn't want to settle, he meant, not with you, anyway. I went wild for a short time. I needed to know I was attractive, and could get a lover if I wanted. I proved that I could, but sex without love felt empty, the phase didn't last long, and I can barely remember the names of the men I slept with.

*

I put Michael's Christmas card to one side. Would I call him? See him? Could I risk what feelings he might evoke? My relationship with him had been a long time ago. What could he possibly want now? To relive old times? Was he still married to Celia? Was he still as beautiful as he had been when young, or bald as a coot and dried up from the sun? My curiosity was aroused. Maybe I would see him if he got in touch. I could ask him what became of Moonbeam and Star; had he had them with some other woman? *Ouch.* A wave of regret rose in me. Michael might have been a long time ago but the wounds he'd inflicted had gone deep.

My phone pinged with a text from Marcia. *Send list of past lovers, locations and any other details before work starts up in the New Year and takes us all over. Pete has some spare time and can get on the case of looking for your exes plus continuing to look for Billy and Grace. MX*

She was not going to let it go, and I knew I'd get no

peace until I wrote a list for her, so I opened a new page on my laptop and began to write.

1) Aged 10 years: Andrew Murphy. St Mark's, Manchester. Preferred my friend Denise.

2) 15 years: Mark Crosby. Manchester. Had a schoolgirl crush on him, along with most of the girls in our year – you included, Marcia, remember? Not worth pursuing as I don't think I ever even spoke to him.

3) 15. Kevin Grisham. Manchester. My first proper boyfriend and we swore to love each other for ever. His family moved away when he was sixteen – I seem to remember it was to Devon. I was heartbroken for months and we wrote for a while then it faded. Don't know where he is now.

My trip down memory lane was disturbed by the doorbell. Heather. 'Hey, you look great Bea, fab tan,' she said as she came inside, gave me a hug, then took off her red coat and fuchsia pink scarf. 'God, it's freezing out there.'

'You look good too,' I said. She always did; she was a fireball of energy, which was reflected in her colourful style, shoulder-length glossy red hair, green eyes and pink and navy polka-dot vintage dress that nipped in at the waist then flared over her hips, teamed with a pale green short cardi.

She pinched her stomach and groaned. 'No I don't, I've eaten and drunk far too much over Christmas and must start on some sort of detox soon or my liver's going to explode.' Heather was always on some sort of diet; not that she needed to be but, like most women I knew, she wasn't happy with her shape which was naturally curvy. 'You're lucky, you never put on weight. I look like a stuffed pig.'

'Rubbish. Stop it. New Year's resolution for you this year is to stop being so self-critical.'

She made a face. 'Why change the habit of a lifetime? Anyway, enough of me and my crap, it's boring. Today's the day of reckoning, right?'

'It is,' I said, as I indicated the letters that were lying on the dining table. 'One was waiting for me when I got back from India and another came today. I've been putting off opening them until you got here or I could see Stuart for his input. A trouble shared is a trouble halved, and all that.'

'Coffee and catch-up first or shall we get the letters over with?'

I put the kettle on. 'Coffee, definitely, but tell me your news – you said it was urgent.'

'Ah yes, OK.' She took a deep breath. 'Actually, it's probably what's in one of the letters. Greg Jefferson came in to see me before Christmas, while you were away. He seemed very agitated.' Greg was an old friend and he owned the building where I had my shop in Hampstead. 'I did text you, then was going to call you, but I thought, why ruin your holiday?'

'Oh. That bad, eh? So what did he want?'

'He's selling up.'

I sighed. 'I had a feeling. I'd heard a rumour before I went away and hoped it was just that. One of the other shopkeepers said they'd seen an estate agent casing the place after we'd shut up shop one evening. I hoped that he might just be getting it valued.'

'He's putting the whole building on the market. We have three months to vacate.'

'*Three* months? But why? Why now?'

'Divorce. He's splitting up from his wife.'

'Ah. I'd heard rumours about that, too.'

'He has a new lover, younger lover, so he's consolidating all his assets and getting out to go and live in France.'

'Wow,' I said, 'I was not expecting that. He didn't say anything to me last time I saw him, at least not about the shop. I knew his marriage was going through a rocky patch.'

'I think he feels bad, that's why he was so agitated. He knows he'll be letting you down. Also we've been good tenants. He said it might not sell in the three months he's given us to quit so maybe there's no hurry, but he wanted to let us know at the earliest. Maybe whoever buys it would let us stay?'

'Maybe, but you know Greg gave me mates' rates. He's kept the rents low for years. If someone new buys it, they'll put the rent up in line with all the other shops in the area.'

'I know, that's why there are so many empty shops round there. Not good news. Maybe something else nearby?'

'Oh Heather, you know we're just about breaking even as it is. I can't afford a higher rent and I can't borrow any more money to put into the business. I'm already remortgaged up to the hilt. We'll never find another place with the terms he gave us.'

'I know, not around there anyway. Prices have rocketed in the last few years; so many small businesses and independents have had to close and move on. I am sorry, Bea.'

'Me too, but I won't let this mean that you're out of a job.'

'Hey, don't worry about me.'

Heather pointed at the letters waiting on the table in

front of us. 'I guess he's put it all in there. He said there'd be an official letter. Let's see exactly what we're facing.'

I ripped the first envelope open and read, 'Yep, it's from Greg.' I quickly scanned what he'd written – 'sorry, no choice, feels bad, blah-de-blah.'

I passed her the letter.

'So what are we going to do?' she asked when she'd read it.

'Rethink the plan.'

'Join a nunnery?'

'Could do. I need to change something, though. The signs have been there for a few months now – longer, even. Fewer people passing through come into the shop, and those that do want a bargain. I can't compete with eBay, Amazon, Wowcher and all the other lower-cost sites that offer more for less.'

'Tell me about it. I've had a number of customers lately who come in, look, then announce that they could get similar stuff cheaper elsewhere. But come on, we've ridden a few storms before, it's not over yet.'

'Of course not. We will just have to reorganize things. We might have to let the part-time staff go, though,' I said. 'God, I hate having to do that. No one wants that kind of news first thing in the New Year.'

'I know.'

'And we've still got the website, though sales through that have been slow over the past year too.'

'You OK, Bea?'

'Sure. I just didn't expect it to be so final, or so soon.'

'Me neither. Will you look for other premises?'

'Possibly not. I'll have to think about it. Talk over options with Stuart. In the meantime, it might be best to sell off stock.' I grimaced. 'And I just ordered some things to be sent from India too. Stupid of me really, but it was hard to resist when I was out there.'

'Don't worry, it always goes in the end if we price it right. We had a decent December while you were away but we both know January will be our lowest month. People have spent up, everyone's cutting back.'

'New Year sale then, that might shift some stock.' I picked up the envelope that had arrived this morning and ripped it open. 'One more letter. Maybe it's someone telling us we've won the lottery.' I read the contents and groaned.

'What? Good or bad?'

'Bad. Worse.' I waved the letter in the air. 'Interest rates are rising. My mortgage is going up.'

'*No!*' said Heather. She knew that in order to keep things going at the shop, I'd remortgaged my house. It had seemed like a safe bet at the time. There had been a golden phase about seven years ago. I'd had an article in *Vogue*, another in a local paper, and for a while I'd been flavour of the month, with all sorts of people wanting my personalized jewellery. However, the last few years had been like swimming upstream. I worked seven days a week, kept the shop open on a Sunday when the weekend crowds descended on Hampstead, but still I was barely breaking even. I'd ignored the signs for as long as I could. It was time to take action.

'OK, I have a plan,' said Heather.

'Good. Because my brain seems to have frozen.'

'Lunch. I'm taking you out. We can talk it all out over a glass of Prosecco.'

12

'OK. Job number one, meet with Stuart and go through the accounts tomorrow. In the meantime, we could do some number crunching,' I said when Heather and I had settled at a table at the back of a café on Highgate High Street.

'What's that famous quote from *Gone with the Wind*?'

'"Frankly, my dear, I don't give a damn."'

'No, not that one.'

'"You should be kissed by someone who knows how." That was always a personal favourite of mine.'

Heather groaned. 'No, not that either.'

I laughed. '"As God is my witness, I'll never be hungry again,"' I said in my best Texan accent.

'Things aren't that bad, Bea. No, the one I meant was, "After all, tomorrow is another day."'

'Ah, yes, exactly.'

'Let's do a Scarlett O'Hara. I think we should sleep on the news; you meet with Stuart then we reconvene when we've had a chance to give it some thought. In the meantime, tell me about your holiday.'

'God, India seems a million years ago now. Talk about back to reality with a bang.'

'Forget about that for now. Photos. I want to see photos.'

'Are you sure? I took hundreds.'

'I am sure.'

I got out my iPad and we spent a pleasant time revisiting scenes from my time abroad; it did cheer me up to look back and see all the great locations I'd been to. 'I bought some earrings and ankle bracelets for the shop when I was in Jaipur,' I said as I showed photos of the Amber Fort. 'And it was probably foolish of me to have shelled out on going away at all, especially at a time like this.'

'Don't talk rot,' said Heather. 'You deserved a break. You haven't had proper time off in years, and it's not every day you turn fifty. So . . . best moment of the trip?'

'The City Palace in Udaipur, out-of-this-world wonderful,' I said as I found her the shots I'd taken from the speedboat on the lake on our way over to the Taj Lake Palace Hotel.

'Wow, it looks so glamorous,' she said as she scrolled through.

'It was. India is a country of such extremes: amazing wealth on one hand and awful poverty on the other.'

'Worst moment?'

I laughed. 'Throwing up in Jaipur. I got what they called the Jaipur jitters, a sister of the Delhi belly. Took a while to adjust to the spicy food. And also . . .'

'What?'

'Not exactly worst moment, but something did happen that was weird; in fact it spooked me out a little.'

'Sounds intriguing.'

I filled her in on my session with Saranya Ji. She listened

without interrupting, which was unusual for Heather, though she did look highly amused and burst out laughing when I'd finished. 'Sounds crazy.'

'I know. It was typical of Marcia to get me something like that and at first I thought it was a load of nonsense.'

'At first? Oh no, Bea, you don't for a minute believe any of it?'

'I can't deny that it's got me thinking. Marcia's completely on my case now and she's got Pete looking at ancestry records.'

'Ancestry records? What's she hoping to find?'

'A record of Billy Jackson and Grace Harris. I keep telling her, even if she finds them, it doesn't prove anything.'

'No, only that people with that name existed. Doesn't mean that you *were* Grace in a past life. Sounds like a lot of baloney made up by this Saranya Ji person to me.'

'I thought the same but then . . .' I told her about the imaginary friend I'd had when I was little and the research I'd done last night.

She burst out laughing again. 'OK. Now I've heard it all. Bea, I think it's stress or jet lag or eating too many spicy samosas have addled your brain. I mean, come on, this isn't like you. Past lives? A soulmate in another body in another time? One that's in a grave somewhere?'

'Saranya Ji said that just as I am back as me, he is back in a new body.'

Heather put her forehead on the table, groaned then sat up again. 'Oh, and did I tell you I had an alien visit when you were gone? Yeah. Spaceship hovering over the garden, then they beamed me up.' She sighed. 'Do you have any idea how ridiculous you sound, Bea?'

'Yes. No. So you don't think there's anything in it at all?'

'Of course not. I think people believe in reincarnation because they can't handle their own mortality. I think, you live, you die, so make the most of it now. All that past life stuff feeds an idea that somewhere, sometime, it was all better than it is now. Grass is greener sort of thing, an escape. And if there is any truth in it, which I don't think there is, then if you evolve from life to life, then surely this has to be the best one yet, so why look back?'

'Those were exactly my first thoughts.'

'And as for soulmates, pff: it's pot luck, forget fate or destiny. You meet people, sometimes you're lucky, sometimes you're not, but generally I think you create your own destiny through the choices you make.'

'Saranya Ji said destiny is fated, the only choice we have is in how we react to it.'

Heather studied me closely. 'She really got to you, didn't she?'

'I . . . no, oh, I don't know, Heather. Maybe it is all an escape from what I'm facing. I keep telling myself to get a grip.'

She reached out and put her hand over mine. 'We'll get through this, Bea; there's a lot of sorting out to do but . . .' She stopped and laughed, 'I don't think looking for a soul-mate from a past life is going to help in any way, unless he's reincarnated as a multimillionaire.'

When she put it like that, I realized that it did all sound insane and I laughed too. 'You're probably right. Too much sun and spicy food addled my brain.'

'It's not that I'm close-minded, but you have to admit the past life bit does sound way out. Still, OK, just for a moment, let's go with it. Saranya Ji said that there will be a recognition if you meet your soulmate, in which case, why do you have to do all the running, trying to find him or get Pete or Marcia to find him? It has to work both ways. He should want to find you as much as you him. Let him come to you, find you. You are a strong, independent woman, used to making things happen so, for once in your life, let go. If there's any truth at all in what your psychic lady said, then it will happen when it's meant to, as she said: first comes your destiny, then it's your choice how to react to it. So let it be, let him come to you, then decide if you like the look of him and if there's any kind of cosmic recognition.'

'I hadn't thought about it that way. I like that. Yes, if it's meant to be, if we're meant to be and if there's any truth in it, yes, let him find me.'

At that moment, my neighbour Jon came into the café and spotted us in the corner. He came straight over. 'I thought that was you,' he said, which caused Heather and me to burst into laughter. 'What's so funny?' he asked.

'We were just talking about recognizing people and you came over, that's all,' said Heather.

'Ah. Synchronicity,' said Jon, and gave me a meaningful look.

'Thank you for your note, Jon, and the car,' I said.

'You're welcome. It's my New Year's resolution, not to annoy Bea so much,' he said.

'I doubt that's going to happen.'

Jon grinned. 'Anyway, just popped in for a take-out latte. Happy New Year to you both. Do you have plans for the thirty-first, Bea?'

'I . . . Oh yes, there's a thing at—' I started.

'Jacob's, yes, I'm going too. Should be good, he always throws a fabulous party,' said Heather. 'Anyway, Happy New Year to you too, Jon.'

He got that he was being dismissed and didn't hang about.

'That man fancies you,' said Heather when he'd gone.

'That man fancies half of London, the female half, so you can drop it right now. And who's Jacob? Is he having a party?'

'No. You were stumbling and you've told me what a pain Jon was. I made Jacob up to get rid of him.'

'Get you with the fast thinking. I knew there was a reason I hired you to be a manager.' Heather had a great talent for getting out of awkward situations, something I'd witnessed with awe over the many years I'd known her.

'Though you do know that if this were fiction or a movie, Jon would be The One. It's always the one the heroine dislikes the most.'

'Yeah, then she realizes that he's really a prince or Mr Darcy, like that's ever going to happen with Jon,' I said as I watched him buy his latte – no, two lattes – then go out to greet a blonde lady with a dog who was waiting outside.

'He is attractive though, come on, you have to admit it: twinkly eyes, good head of hair. I would have thought he was your type.'

'Zip it, Heather, believe me, that's never going to happen. Now, where were we?'

'Oh, usual stuff. Past lives, reincarnation and imaginary friends.'

I laughed. It was good to spend time with Heather and get a more realistic perspective on how ridiculous it all was.

'I'm not averse to the idea of soulmates,' Heather said, 'but I think we have a few of them for different aspects of our lives and personalities. We're all multi-faceted, so to expect one person to satisfy all sides of us is a big ask. For example, I have one person for hanging out and going to the movies with, talking about books to, etc., you know – "cultural me"; another friend for "organic healthy me" to go hiking with, do yoga with, keep fit and get out in open spaces with; another mate for being "naughty me" with – drinking too many cocktails, having the occasional fag with; another for girlie stuff, shopping and spa days. Before I married Anita, I had one soulmate for sex, passion and great chemistry, but we had nothing to talk about, so I had another for romance and talking but the sex was crap, and I also had a third one for companionship and talking about politics and world news. I'm sure most people do the same. Lovers can all be different, like you can be down and dirty and try new things with one yet, with another, it wouldn't feel right. To get all those aspects in one person would be like winning the lottery, so different folks for different times. Friends or soulmates don't all have to be one sex, either. I'm sure I have soulmates who are men as well as women.'

'Makes sense. But what about Anita?' I asked. 'Why did you marry her if you have different people for different sides of you?'

'She fits a few of the categories, but I don't expect her to satisfy every part of me. Like she would go ballistic if she knew that I had the occasional fag, so I keep my naughty soulmate, Jill, for when I fancy one. And of course, there's a different kind of soulmate to be had in a pet.'

'True. No one does unconditional love better than a dog.'

Heather hadn't finished. 'And I think if there was such a thing as a past life, then we'd remember them and there's a reason that we don't. Like all that, *why are we here?* stuff. *What's it all about?* Those deep questions come on you at funerals when you're standing there watching someone take off into the unknown and then are usually forgotten by the time you get to the wake in the pub. And why is that? Because it would drive you mad otherwise. Because we humans have pea brains, that's why. Not in the sense that we're stupid, but our intelligence is limited; even the most brainy of us don't have answers to the big questions. It's an arrogance to imagine that we could comprehend it all so, I say, just get on and experience day-to-day stuff, that's what is real.'

'Wow, Heather, you're really quite wise under that mop of red hair, aren't you?'

'Not at all, just practical. I also think the idea of rein-carnation is an easy way out, a way for people to explain their troubles and understand why some have it all, while some have so little. Like . . . ah, it was because they were wicked in a past life and are suffering for it now. Seriously? That's bollocks, if you ask me, and cruel to put it on someone as if they're responsible for their own bad luck, whether in terms of their health or their situation. Truth is, shit happens to the best of people and, ultimately, we know nothing – not about where we came from, what we're doing here, or where we're going.'

'Sounds pretty scary when you put it like that.'

'It does, and reincarnation gives you a trouble-free answer – you've lived before, if you're good this time, you'll come back and all will be well. I don't think it can be that simple.

I could go along with our souls having some kind of genetic memory from generations before, though. We're all made up of our parents, grandparents and great-grandparents, going back for centuries, so we're bound to have all sorts of stuff imprinted in our DNA. But reincarnation ? Nah.'

'OK, forget about past lives for a moment. What about karma? As you sow, so shall you reap? I think there's something in that.'

'Maybe, but only to a degree. Sometimes it's true – what goes around, comes around – but, as I said before, shit happens to the best of people, and other people who are real shits seem to have it all: wealth, health, good looks. What about all the souls who have died in atrocities or are suffering now in refugee camps? You can't tell me it's karma. That would be too cruel. I don't know. Who knows how any of it works? I gave up trying to figure it all out years ago. Love the ones you're with, be kind and help out when you can, and don't try to overthink it: that's my philosophy. But, going back to what you were saying earlier, have you ever felt that sense of the familiar that the psychic lady talked about?'

'Not a knock-out blast of oh, I know you.'

'Me neither. I'm probably too preoccupied most of the time but there are people I've been drawn to and others I've disliked on meeting. Know what I mean?'

'I do. I have had a sense of the familiar with some of my girlfriends so maybe you're right, maybe some of my soul-mates are female and not just one. I felt it with Marcia, and you, like you're family, comfortable, you both get me and I know I can say anything.'

'In that case, maybe this Billy soul has come back as a

woman – have you considered that? He may be in a female body, in which case you're going to have to become a lesbian like me.'

'Tempting,' I said as I watched Jon chatting with his new friend outside. 'I think generally women tend to be more straightforward.'

*

Jon Howard. He was one of the secret liaisons Marcia and Pete didn't know about; no one knew about, in fact, not even Heather. Ours was an encounter I preferred to draw a veil over and certainly one I would never repeat. He was good company until you got to know him and learnt he was a first-league womanizer. The phrase 'notches on the bedpost' came to mind when I thought of him and I was embarrassed by the fact that I'd been one of them.

He'd turned up on my doorstep about three years ago.

'Just moved in next door,' he said, brandishing a bottle of champagne. Cristal, I noticed as he handed it over. I was impressed. A man of taste. 'Thought I'd come over and introduce myself and ask a favour,' he continued as he shifted on his feet and, for a moment, looked vulnerable. *Why not?* I thought. An attractive older man at my door. It didn't happen often.

'I'm desperate for a good meal,' he said when he left a few hours later. 'I've no cooker until my kitchen's done.'

I laughed. 'Is that a hint?'

He grinned back at me. 'I could help. I'm a good cook.'

'No, no, come. I'd be glad to.'

And so he'd come back the next night, and the next. He

asked for advice on local tradesmen, admired the house, admired me, my choice of furnishings, asked me to keep a spare set of house keys for him in case he lost his. I felt useful, respected and desired. I listened to the story about the end of his marriage, noting he was a single man about to embark on the divorce process, just a few years older than me, a rarity. He was making a new start, worked as an architect specialising in institutions like hospitals, schools or prisons, moved from St Albans. He was lonely. Didn't know anyone in town. Said he felt a connection with me straight away. How was it possible I was on my own? And we had got on at first. The sex wasn't bad either, though it only happened once. I thought it was all too good to be true. It was. After he'd made his conquest, suddenly he wasn't as available, didn't appear to be so lonely after all. He even took the moral high ground when I called him out on the number of women who seemed to be passing through.

'I made no promises,' he said. True. He hadn't. Bastard. Marcia would love it if I told her about him, and he'd be moved up her list of contenders straight away.

13

'Coffee?' asked Stuart as I took a seat in his office. It was a cosy, wood-panelled room above an estate agents' on the High Street in Highgate and was a great place to retreat to on a cold, frosty day. With the bookshelves full of art, music and history books, old rugs and prints on the wall and a vintage guitar on a stand in the corner, it was more like a man's den than a place of work. Stuart didn't look like your average accountant either, with salt-and-pepper hair that always looked in need of a cut, an aquiline nose and heavy-lidded brown eyes. He was dressed in jeans and had his customary long red scarf wound around his neck, giving him an appearance that was more bohemian than executive. 'I've just made some.'

I sniffed the air. 'I know, I can smell it. I'd love a cup – and hello to you, Monty,' I said as he got up from under the desk and padded over for a fuss. He always accompanied Stuart to work and his presence made my visits all the more enjoyable. 'And thanks so much for looking in on the house while I was away and the provisions in my fridge when I got back. You really are a pal.'

'No trouble, there's nothing more boring than not being able to make a cup of tea when you get home from a long trip,' said Stuart.

'It was very thoughtful of you and thanks also for seeing me today. I know a lot of people don't work at all between Christmas and New Year, so it's much appreciated.'

'I'm happy to, I was in the office anyway. Everywhere is quiet, so it's a good time to get things in order before the coming onslaught on the second of January and . . .' he grimaced, 'well, I could see the urgency when I got your text outlining your current situation. I've had a look through and—'

'I know, not good,' I said.

'No, not good. This is serious, Bea.' He looked at me sternly. 'You're paying out extortionate amounts on two properties that you can't afford, your shop and your house. Your outgoings far outweigh what is incoming. It's not looking good at all.'

I felt like a naughty schoolgirl who had been called in to see the headmaster. I often felt that way with Stuart. 'I know, that's why I came to you.'

He shook his head. 'Well, clearly something's got to go, you can't go on like this. Going bankrupt could be an option to look into.'

'Not one I want to take.'

'Second option—'

'Sell my house.'

'It's the largest debt, get rid of that, then we can rethink. Pay off that remortgage which I seem to remember I told you not to get in the first place, but you went ahead anyway.'

I always felt comforted when Stuart said things like 'we

can rethink', as if we were a team. Stuart had always had my back and been 100 per cent supportive over the years. He always made me feel less alone, even if he was a tad critical of how I dealt with things sometimes. 'It kept me going at the shop for a few years.'

'It was a hell of a risk borrowing that much money, and the monthly repayments are enough to give anyone sleepless nights.' Stuart glanced down at the figures on the paper in front of him. 'Too many dry periods and you haven't been in profit for well over a year. Sounds like the shop is going to take its own course if the building is up for sale, but even if your landlord there gets a buyer imminently, which I doubt, it could still take months to complete.'

'I was wondering whether to look for alternative premises when the time comes.'

'I'd think about that very carefully. It would have to be the right place with—'

'Lots of passing trade.'

'Exactly and, as we both know, you pay through the nose for locations like that. For now this is my advice: one, put your house on the market; two, get rid of what stock you can in the shop; three, do *not* borrow any more money.'

I laughed. 'You sound so strict, Stuart.'

He smiled. 'Someone has to tell it like it is, and it's what you pay me for.'

'Right, of course. I'll do what you say.'

'And you have a tax bill to pay at the end of January. I hope you've made some provision for that. It's not massive because profits were low but, all the same, it's another debt,' Stuart sighed. 'What do you want to do, Bea? What does your gut tell you?'

'Buy a camper van and go travelling.'

Stuart laughed. 'Good plan, I might come with you.' I knew it was impossible for him but sometimes I got the feeling he'd like to kick back and do something different to accounting.

'If I can sell my house,' I said, 'that will solve a lot. I'll have some equity left after I've paid debts, tax included.'

'Where will you live? House prices in London are still on the up, at least they are on desirable properties.'

'Marcia and Pete have offered me a room at theirs until I decide where I want to go and what I want to do next.'

'Good. Tread water for a while. You'll be a cash buyer and in a much stronger position than trying to downsize in a rush and maybe get gazumped. Do you know where you want to relocate to?'

'Nope. I love Highgate. I love where I live, the village atmosphere; nowhere better in all seasons.'

'What about India? How was that?'

'Glorious. Are you going to tell me off for spending on such an exotic trip?'

'Absolutely not. You deserved a break. I'd love to do something like that. Maybe one day. And it was a big birthday, so why the hell not?'

I nodded. 'Turning fifty gets you thinking about what's really important.' I looked out of the window at the blue sky above. 'It feels unreal to be indoors talking over money matters. We should be out on the Heath, breathing in the air.'

'Monty would like that but . . . stop trying to change the subject. Where will you live after staying with Marcia and Pete? Property prices are high here. You owe more than half of the equity in your house to the bank. That doesn't leave you with a lot.'

'I know.' I'd been determined to go in and be businesslike, no emotion, no tears but, suddenly, I felt myself crumbling. It all seemed to be happening so fast, everything I'd worked so hard for disappearing before my eyes. *Change the subject, quickly*, I told myself, before I started full-on blubbing. 'How's Janet? And your kids? Your Christmas?'

'My wife and kids are fine though, as you know, hardly kids any more.' Stuart sat back in his chair and looked at me kindly. 'I know it's tough for you, Bea, believe me, you're not the only one in this situation. Times are changing. You've been resisting it for a long time, but it's time to give in and face the music. You have some hard decisions ahead of you, but you started from nothing; you could rebuild again but without the risks.'

'I could.'

'If that's what you wanted to do. Question is, do you want to?'

'Honestly, I don't know any more. For the last year, I thought if I put the blinkers on and just tried to plough through, everything might be all right. I couldn't have done more. However, when I was away in India, I realized that my whole life now is all work, no play – and what for? I barely get to enjoy the lifestyle I've worked so hard to create.'

Stuart nodded. 'That sounds familiar. Janet is always saying the same thing about me. I guess we both need to find some balance in our lives.'

'I . . .' I was about to confess to the fact that I worked to blot out how empty my life was at the moment. For the last years, I hadn't wanted balance, I'd wanted distraction, projects, to fill the hours with things to do so that I didn't have to face the fact that I went back to a silent house and the prospect of more years alone, but I bit it back. Stuart didn't need me having a breakdown in his office, and what could he say anyway? It was my problem. I was going to have to sort it.

'It's not so bad, Bea, but you have to be strong and make the changes; know when the time is right to consolidate what you have, and put your energy where it can work. It's like someone who has been pushing the car from the inside, wearing themselves out – they have to recognize when something isn't working, get out and push from behind.'

'Understood.'

'And you, are you OK? I appreciate this must be difficult for you.'

'I'll be fine.'

'Anytime you need to talk things over. We'll take a walk on the Heath and grab a coffee or something, and please don't do anything – and I mean anything – without consulting me first.'

'I won't.'

'You mustn't worry. You'll get through this. It's like in a marriage, rough patches, smooth patches. . .' he hesitated then looked at me intently as if weighing up whether to say more.

I looked away. I always found it hard to look Stuart straight in the eye because it awoke too many feelings in me that I knew could never be reciprocated. 'Up and down and round and round we go. The rollercoaster that is life.'

'And love.'

'Love?'

Stuart shrugged. 'I meant life. . .' This time, it was Stuart who looked away. 'Right. So . . . we have a plan?'

'We do. First thing in the New Year, house on the market, sell off stock. Got it.'

'You know I'm always here for you, don't you?'

'I do. And thanks.'

*

As I left the warmth of Stuart's office and headed back out into the cold December day, my mobile pinged that I had a text. I glanced at the message. It was from Marcia. *Pop in if you have time, am home. Have news for you about Grace and Billy.* I put the phone away. Looking for past life lovers was the least of my concerns. OK, I'd had a moment of wondering about it on hearing about the imaginary friend from my childhood, but I wasn't going to waste time pursuing it, especially now that I had more pressing things to do in the here and now. My next job was to visit the team of designers I used when I needed a particular piece of jewellery made up. I owed it to them to fill them in on what was happening. Most of them displayed their own designs in the shop as well as doing my commissions. They weren't going to be happy.

14

Why Bea? And why now? If I am honest, the connection was always there, a sense of familiarity, but it wasn't the right time for either of us. She makes me smile. I like her company, her face, her eyes; more than that, the spirit that lives inside of her. I can see us together and hope that she will too. In the meantime, a few issues still to deal with, cutting a few ties to places and people, then I will be ready. In the meantime, there's a dog by the door, and he's waiting for a walk.

15

'End of an era,' I said to Marcia as I took a seat at her dining table early in the evening.

She went to the fridge, got out a bottle of wine and poured two glasses. She hadn't asked if I wanted one, didn't need to. 'Endings can be beginnings. End of a chapter, beginning of a new one.'

'End of my first fifty years, beginning of the next fifty. I didn't really think about it when I was away, but it's hit me since we've been back. Fifty, half a century old.'

'None of us looks it and we probably don't act it either,' said Marcia. 'Fifty is the new forty and all that.'

'Thanks to hair dye, for me anyway. You still don't have a grey hair, and believe me, I've been checking. I remember when I was younger, fifty seemed so old, and so many that age seemed to look it: the same hairstyle, comfy cardis, slacks with elasticated waistbands.'

'Well, we're not going there.'

'But with everything that's happening, it really does seem like the end of one part of my life.'

'Does it have to be an end? Do you want a change? No one knows the jewellery business like you do.'

'Maybe. I don't know. I certainly never imagined I'd be where I am – unsure where I'm going to live or what I'm going to do next.'

'Where did you think you'd be?'

'More financially secure, maybe married with kids, though it's too late for that now.' I thought of Graham and the time a family had seemed possible; I thought of Michael, of Moonbeam and Star, children I'd never had, and felt another stab of regret.

'It's never too late for anything,' said Marcia. 'You could still marry and adopt if you really wanted to go that route. Is that what you want?'

'That's just it. I don't know.'

'Maybe the universe is trying to tell you something. If it was just your mortgage repayments or just the shop, it could be seen as a blip, but for both to come at you at the same time, I wonder if it's a sign telling you that it's time for a life change.'

'Do you really think that? That the universe gives us signs?'

'Sometimes, yes.'

'I don't. I think that what's happening to me is more to do with world economics. Things change, so many people in different areas of business have to adapt or go under. It can't be that the universe is giving us all a sign.'

'Sometimes it can; sometimes there are world shifts that affect everyone, a global sign that things must change. Sometimes the signs are more personal, but does what's happening to you mean your business has to come to an end? You've spent too long building up contacts and researching the market to let it all go. Can't you reinvent things? Adapt to the changes and evolve?'

'Like a cockroach? I don't know, Marcia, I probably could, but the thing is, I'm not sure I want to go on as I was – all work and no play.'

'Pete and I have been saying that to you for years.'

'Trouble is, if I did find myself with time on my hands and not so many commitments, I'm not sure what I'd do.'

'Then surrender to that. There are many times in life when things seem to come to an abrupt end so, instead of fighting it, embrace it and see what unfolds next.'

'How?'

'Take some time out, go with the flow. As one of the hexagrams in the I Ching says, no harm in waiting. I think times of inactivity are as important as the active phases. Rather than rushing headlong into something else, take a few weeks or even months off and reassess everything.'

'Stuart said something similar; he said to tread water for a while until things become clearer. Sounds scary – and don't say, "Feel the fear and do it anyway".'

Marcia laughed. 'I was just about to. You know you can stay here as long as you like if you get a quick sale on your house, which I think you will. We'll love having you here. And if you need to borrow money, just say.'

'Thanks for the offer, but that was number three on Stuart's list for me: no borrowing more money.'

'Yes, but we're different. We could lend you some and we wouldn't charge interest and we wouldn't put a deadline on any loan.'

'I'm lucky to have friends like you but I won't. I like the

idea of clearing the slate. I'll take it a step at a time. The next few months are going to be about clearing and selling what I can, then I will do as you say and re-evaluate the situation and, maybe, as you suggest, take some time out. Perhaps by then it might be clearer what's next.'

'Exactly, you don't have to decide anything immediately. Just deal with what's in front of you. You've seen Stuart, what else have you been up to?'

'Meeting with people on the back-up team, all the individual jewellers I have called in to make up designs.'

'How did they take it?'

'Resigned to it. I think a couple of them knew it was coming. I've encouraged them all to up their social-media presence – Instagram, Twitter, Facebook – and update their websites. It's the way things are going.'

'And your website?'

'I'll work on mine too and put any stock that doesn't sell in the shops on there. I can put some on eBay too, though you get nothing for it on there, everyone wants a bargain.'

'And have you got any further with your list of past lovers for me?' she asked.

'Argh. I thought you'd forgotten about that.'

'Why would I do that? So how's it coming on?'

'Er . . . I got up to number three.'

'Good. I shall expect it first thing in the New Year,' said Marcia.

'Bossy is your middle name.'

'It's because I care. In the meantime, I've got some news for you, developments on the Billy and Grace front. Look at this.' She got her laptop and brought it over to the table.

She opened a page and went to her emails where she found one from Pete. It showed a link, which she clicked on. 'Pete's been busy.'

I put on my glasses and peered at the page that opened in front of me. 'What is it?' All I could see was a page listing names.

'It's a list of men with Billy's surname who died in action,' said Marcia. 'Pete found them last night. I've emailed what we found to you so it will be there on your computer.'

I peered at the screen. 'William Jackson. There are loads of them. Where did Pete find this?'

'On one of the war memorial sites, I think. He found a few men with that name – different ages, different addresses.'

'How would we know any of them were the Billy that Saranya Ji talked of?'

'I don't know, but it's a start. Pete said he's happy to keep looking up information for you, but if you ever want to have a look yourself, most of the sites offer a free trial.'

I shook my head. 'I've too much else going on at the moment, but do thank him.'

*

When I got home, I went to my laptop and opened the email that Marcia had sent. Despite myself, I was intrigued. I clicked on the link that took me to the site showing the war records. It looked easy enough to use. A page came up asking me to put in a name and the period I wanted to see. I put in the name Jackson, then I clicked on Second World War. Five pages came up but, before I could go any further, I was asked to subscribe, so I closed the site and went to get a glass of wine. When the going gets tough, the tough turn to vino had been one of my and Heather's mottos when we lived together.

I went back to the laptop and found an ancestry site. Once again, I put in the name Jackson, added the date 1940, and clicked on military. On this site, lots of Jacksons who had fought in the war came up. 'Hah, see Pete, I can do research too,' I said out loud.

I scrolled down the list: Kenneth, Gordon, Peter, David. I clicked on the second page. Horace, Richard, ah . . . a William! I clicked on the name and the details showed he had lived in Glasgow.

I continued my search and found more Jacksons. It was then I noticed that there were two hundred pages. *What am I doing?* I asked myself as I shut down the site.

Five minutes later, I went back to the laptop and continued clicking through. It didn't take too long to scroll through a page then another and another. Mark, Frank, Albert, more Williams. On page twenty-five, I found another William Jackson. I clicked for more details. Place of birth, Lancashire, resident of London. Died 25 May 1940. Could he be the one? I clicked on and on, scrolling through until I'd found five William Jacksons, all of whom had lived in London, with the dates of their deaths. Some were with the Royal Artillery regiment, one with the 30th Motor Brigade. Surely I could find a death certificate if I kept looking?

A loud knock on the door disturbed my research. I got up to answer and found Jon on the doorstep. 'Oh!' He was completely naked apart from two recycling boxes, a small black compost one held over his groin, another slightly bigger one, used for plastics, covering his backside. I burst out laughing. 'Well here's a sight you don't see every day. What the—'

He pushed past me. 'Let me in, *please*. I'm freezing my balls off out here.'

I shut the door behind him. 'So? What happened? Someone's husband returned and you had to make a fast exit?'

'No, *no*. How could you think that?'

I rolled my eyes.

'I got locked out. I need my key. You do still have it, don't you?'

'Ah, leaving your key here: has this all been a ploy to present yourself on my doorstep?'

'Ploy? God, no, Bea, not at all.'

I looked down at the strategically placed bin boxes. 'Oh, so doing your recycling at last, were you? Couldn't decide whether to put yourself in with the compost or the plastics.'

Jon sighed. 'I'd just come down from having a shower in my dressing gown and thought I heard someone at the door. I opened it, Chief ran out before I could stop him—'

'Chief? Who's Chief?'

'My dog . . .'

'You have a dog?' This was news to me.

'Long story. I'll tell you one day when I'm not *naked*.'

'So he ran out the door?'

'Yes. I leant out to grab him, only just caught him, and shoved him back inside, and then the door slammed shut, catching my gown in the door and leaving me starkers outside.'

I started laughing again.

'Not funny, Bea. It's below zero out there.'

'And there was me thinking you'd come over to do the dance of the seven bin boxes.'

'All I could find,' said Jon, but he laughed too. 'I know, not my sexiest outfit. I am truly sorry, so could you let me have my key . . . unless you'd like me to stay, that is? You know we have a connection, you must have felt it the first time we met—'

'Nice try but no thanks.' I turned around and rummaged in a bowl where I kept assorted keys.

'I appreciate how things may look to you,' Jon persisted. 'I just think when I moved here, it wasn't the right time for us, but—'

'Ah, here it is, and you'd better get back, your dog will be waiting.' I was about to give the key to him, but both his hands were occupied with the crucially placed bin boxes. He gave me a look as if to say – and now what? I leant over to put the key in his mouth and he obediently parted his lips. I ushered him towards the door, opened it and indicated he should leave. 'Heartless woman,' he muttered as he stepped out, just as a group of people passed by on the pavement below. They took one look at him and hooted with laughter as he hotfooted it back over to his house.

'Got shut out, got shut out,' he mumbled out of the corner of his mouth as he raced up his front steps. I couldn't resist waiting to see what he did. He turned away, gingerly lowered the box covering his backside, took the key from his mouth and opened his door. He backed into his doorway, shut the door and the spectators walked on. A few moments later, a text pinged through. *You could have lent me a dressing gown at least.*

I texted back. *Sorry, didn't think. Not every day a naked man turns up on my doorstep. Besides, why spoil all the fun by giving you clothes?*

He texted back. *I get a feeling you enjoyed that, Cruella.*

I texted back a smiling emoji.

I went back to the sites I'd been looking at. I closed the military links, cleared what I had put in and typed in 'Grace Harris, birthplace London'. The site asked for a year of birth. *Hmm*, I thought, *let me think. As Marcia said, if Billy died in the Second World War, he might have just been in his twenties or a little older so that narrows the margin a bit. Grace would probably have been born around the same time.*

As when I looked for Billy, there were pages and pages of women with the name Grace Harris. Two thousand in all. *Can I be bothered?* I asked myself. *Surely this is madness?* But something had gripped me – not the fact that I believed for a moment that Grace and Billy had anything to do with me, it was more like doing a particularly challenging puzzle. I wanted to see if I could find two people with the names I had been given who lived reasonably near to each other. If I could, the chances of them having known each other was likely. As I continued my search, some pages connected to different links, some showing the censuses taken, which revealed addresses and occupations. *Now I know why people get hooked on this*, I thought as I continued scrolling through. *It's addictive stuff.*

I spent time looking at pages and pages that blurred as I moved through them; some I printed out then cross-referenced links and names. The bottle of wine went down until I realized it was empty.

OK, I've drunk too much wine, I thought as I looked at my watch and saw that it was 3 a.m. I was exhausted. I gathered up my pages, stacked them in a pile and went up to bed, where I fell into a troubled sleep, dreaming of Dunkirk and dressmakers.

16

O n New Year's Eve, I went through to the sitting room and switched on the TV. Three hours to go before midnight. I flicked through channels then looked in the *Radio Times*. 'I'll be seeing midnight in with you, Jools, my old pal,' I said to the TV then switched it off. I felt restless. I could read. I could visit a friend. I could go to one of the several parties I'd been invited to, but I wasn't in the mood. Marcia, Pete and family had gone up to Scotland to stay with Pete's parents, as they did every year, and had invited me to go with them, but I'd declined the offer. It was their family time and I had things to be getting on with in London. So it was 31 December, I was fifty, single, an old maid practically; it didn't bear thinking about. I knew the feeling would pass come 2 January. Christmas and Easter breaks were designed to make people on their own aware that they were alone, lonely even, but once the holidays were over, it would be straight into action, with people to see, places to go, so much to sort out. I just had to get through this evening.

Don't get maudlin, said an inner voice that sounded

distinctly like Marcia's. *If it bothers you, do something about it.* Saranya Ji's words also came back to me, 'You can believe me and try and find your true love and who he is now, or dismiss what I say and drift from one meaningless love affair to another, never finding the true contentment and companionship that your soul could know. Or you can immerse yourself in your work as you have done, so busy that no one knows that you are hiding. People see success but you are alone and . . . I don't think so happy with this, yes?'

Blargh, and you can get out of my head too, Saranya Ji, I thought as I glanced at my laptop on the coffee table. I hadn't told Marcia and Pete that last bit of what Saranya Ji had said, though I was pretty sure that they sensed I wasn't 'so happy'. Anyway, people weren't going to look at me for much longer and see success; they were going to see a closing-down sale and my house on the market. I had to find a way to present the changes to the world in a positive light, as though it was all intended, another step on my business plan, and not like I had failed in work and in life. Saranya Ji had said that things were going to change, though she hadn't specified how. Maybe the collapse of my business wasn't what she had meant; maybe she had imagined that the change would be internal, because I did feel that I was changing inside as well as outside, and that striving for success at work and having the perfect house didn't hold the appeal it once had. If I was honest with myself, having someone to share it all with was more important, though I hadn't let myself go down that route of thinking for a long time. I felt a sudden yearning for my family. I did miss them at times like this. I got up, hauled my photo albums off the bookshelf and took them over to the sofa, where I began to look through, just to see their faces. Mum. Dad. Matthew. Mark. I flicked back to pages showing times with them in my twenties, my thirties, my teenage years. *Marcia would love this*, I thought as I spotted various past boyfriends smiling out of faded photographs. Andrew, Kevin. Bruno . . . *Why not?* I thought as I found a pad of paper and pen and began to write. If nothing else, it would keep Marcia happy.

The romantic life of Bea Brooks.

1) Aged 10 years: Andrew Murphy. St Mark's, Manchester. Preferred my friend Denise.

2) ~~15 years: Mark Crosby. Manchester. Had a schoolgirl crush on him along with most of the girls in our year. Not really a contender.~~

3) 15. Kevin Grisham. Manchester. My first proper boyfriend and we swore to love each other for ever. His family moved away, I was heartbroken for months, and we wrote for a while then it faded. Don't know where he is now, though. Devon seems to ring a bell.

4) ~~17 years: Jim Winstanley. Manchester. Lousy kisser and he often tasted of the cheese and onion crisps he liked so much. Lasted one date. Do not pursue.~~

I crossed him off the list. He wasn't even worth mentioning.

5) 17 1/2. Bruno Romano. My brother Matthew's exchange friend from Italy.

It was love at first sight. With his dark Mediterranean looks and beautiful clothes, Bruno had been a cut above the other boys around in Manchester back then, and he was a great kisser. He was heady stuff for a teenager used to the local lilywhite boys with lank hair, pre-shaving chins covered in peach fuzz, no sense of style and whose kisses were timid and soft. Bruno knew how to kiss and did so with passion. Matthew did not like me spending time with him. 'He's *my* exchange student, not yours,' he said. My parents saw the way I lit up when Bruno was around and were keen to keep us apart too, but that only added to the excitement. It was a forbidden love, and we spent the summer creeping into each other's room after lights out, stealing kisses and making declarations of love when no one was around – usually in the linen cupboard because that was the only place where anyone could get any privacy. We promised to meet up in the Christmas holidays, which was postponed to Easter. Then I got a letter saying that he'd met a girl, so he had to curtail our letters and, anyway, long-distance love affairs rarely worked. He was sorry and hoped we might meet again some day. It didn't stop me dreaming of him and I doodled his handsome face in the margins of all my school notebooks throughout the rest of sixth form. Sadly my trip to Italy never happened, but there was a connection with him, most definitely.

6) 18 years: Sam Gorman. Manchester Art College.

Ah, Sam. He was intense, eccentric and romantic, and easily the most talented student at college. He really liked me, but dope was his first love, and it got boring when his eyes glazed over and he spouted rubbish about the universe or fell asleep listening to music. I'd heard he'd moved to London, but that was years ago. I am still in touch with his sister Kate on Facebook. Could he be The One? Maybe, maybe not, but he was the first man I had sex with. We did hit it off when he wasn't stoned. Be interesting to find out what became of him.

7) ~~18 1/2 years: John Burke. Manchester at Umist. Dated him for a few months then discovered he had several other girlfriends. Never felt myself with him, like a square peg in a round hole.~~

Nah. Sorry John, you're not going to make the final list.

8) 19 years: Jed Nash, at art college. Checked him out from afar for one term; like Sam, he was very talented. I hung out with him another term. Things were just beginning to hot up with us when he moved to do his post-grad in London. Potential?

9) ~~20 years: Rick Jones. Manchester University. Cheapskate who expected me to pay for everything which was unfair because we were both students. Felt the world owed him and women were there to serve him. Arrogant tosser. Do not pursue.~~

10) 20 years: Michael O'Connor. Friend of my brother's. Knew him in Manchester, lives currently Thailand. Was with him for a year and a half. Fun, interesting. I thought he was The One, he thought I was one of many. Met him when I was too young?

11) ~~22 years: Ian Kennedy. Dated him for a term. Fitness fanatic, weeks of hiking, walking, rowing, plus he was hung up on an ex and it wasn't my idea of fun to act as his private counsellor as he mourned her departure. Know for a fact that he is now married and living in Cheltenham. Do not pursue, another one I never felt I could be myself with.~~

12) ~~25 years: Joe Wilding. London. Lived with him for five years, which of course, you know, Marcia. I thought I could change him. Couldn't. Definitely not the one. Not going back there.~~

13) 30 years. Graham White. Well, you know all about him too, Marcia.

14) ~~40 years: Richard Benson. Noooo. Not going back there either.~~

15) ~~46 years: Jon. One-night stand.~~

Deleted Jon from the list. I don't want Marcia to know about him.

Wow, I thought, as I counted fifteen but I'd crossed out eight. That left seven. Was that normal? Too many? Slut-worthy? Or not enough? And had I crossed out someone who might have been The One and I'd missed the connection at the time? OK, there had been a few in between – inconsequential lovers or disastrous blind dates set up by well-meaning friends; a few equally crap dates from my brief attempts at Internet dating – but, for the last few years, I had been single and celibate.

Looking back over the list, I couldn't see any discernible pattern. Saranya Ji got it wrong when she said that I had it imprinted in my mind that love was painful. It wasn't that, it was more that I believed that falling or being in love was a waste of time. There was no one I really felt had got away, or who I mourned having broken up with. Graham White, maybe, but he's another story and, OK, maybe Michael as well, but I had been young and we had never got the chance to play out the potential of our love affair, at least not to my mind.

I glanced back at the photo album lying open on the sofa. It was open on the page showing Andrew waving from the top of the coal shed. *Why not call Andrew's parents now?* I asked myself as I glanced at my watch. It wasn't too late. I could find out what became of him. I got up to rummage through a drawer where all my old address books were and soon found the one I wanted. There it was. Andrew's old address. I doubted that he would still be there but his parents might be. I quickly dialled the number before I had a chance to change my mind.

'Hello?'

'Er, yes, is that Mrs Murphy?'

'It is. Who is this?'

'My name is Bea Brooks, you probably don't remember me. I used to be a friend of Andrew's, many years ago.'

'Yes, dear, and how can I help?'

'Well . . . I was wondering if you could give me a contact number. I'd like to get in touch.'

'Oh no, I don't think that's going to be possible. He doesn't live in this world any more.'

'Oh, I am so sorry. When did he die?'

'Die? Oh no, he's not dead, though he might as well be. So you don't know?'

'Know what?'

'He became a Trappist monk in his thirties. That's the order where they take a vow of silence. He doesn't even speak to us.'

'No way.'

'Oh yes. What did you say your name was?'

'Bea Brooks. We were in junior school together.'

'I'm afraid I don't remember you, dear. I'm sorry I can't help.' She hung up and I burst out laughing. Marcia would too when she heard. *So if Andrew is, or was, The One, I'd have to go and talk to him in sign language*, I thought. *Or take a load of cue cards that said: are you my soulmate? Do you believe in past lives?*

I crossed Andrew's name off the list. 'And now we're down to six,' I said.

*

I transferred my list on to my laptop so I could put it into an email to send to Marcia when she was back. Job done. *Now what?* I glanced over at my laptop again. It seemed to be calling me in that way Häagen-Dazs can from the freezer.

'Oh OK,' I said out loud, and leant over and put it on my lap. This time I googled census records and I clicked into the site that appeared. I read that records had been taken every ten years since 1801, excluding 1941. I put in my dad's details and there he was, in a few seconds, as was the address he'd been living at when the census had been compiled. I did the same for Mum, putting in her maiden name. She too appeared immediately. *Now . . . shall I? Shan't I? Shall I, shan't I? I shall.*

I looked for the dates of the censuses taken in the 1900s.

1901. Probably too early.

1911. Maybe also too early?

1921. Records were destroyed in World War Two.

1939. I'd start there. If Grace was born around 1920, she would have been about fourteen or fifteen when that census was taken in 1939. If I have no luck there, I will go back earlier.

I filled in the details I knew. Name, place, 1900s. A list came up immediately. I clicked on the London, England option. I continued clicking through until I found one that said London, 1939. Maybe I could find out where Grace had lived. But Saranya Ji hadn't specified which part of London. I clicked randomly on one of the Graces, just to see what sort of information was revealed. *Interesting*, I thought as I saw that the census recorded not only who was in the house at the time it was taken, but also their occupations. It was going to be a long task, but it was either that or watching some round-up programme of the past year on the TV. I stuck with the census records, fetched my printer and printed out parts that seemed relevant. I placed them on the coffee table and the floor and was soon absorbed in puzzle heaven.

After another half-hour of clicking through, I found a census record showing a Grace Harris and her relation to the head of the house – daughter. It showed that her mother was Alice Harris, father Edward Harris; that Grace Harris had been aged nineteen at the time the census had been taken, and there was also an older sister, Lily Harris. I went back and traced the mother through various census pages. I found a page where it stated occupation: dressmaker. *Dressmaker*, I thought. Saranya Ji had said that Grace was a dressmaker. If this was the right Grace, she had clearly gone into the same profession as her mother. I glanced back at the page. Registration district Fortis Green. I knew that area well. It was between Muswell Hill and East Finchley; there were some lovely old properties around there. Next I searched through sites that had records for death certificates. I found a Grace Harris, born 1920, died in 1943. Could that be her? That would explain why her name wasn't on the later census, or perhaps she had moved out of the family home.

I then repeated the process for Billy, with the addition of some of the material I had found a couple of nights earlier. Soon I had more papers all over the floor with parts highlighted, others screwed up into a ball to be discarded.

Could they be the ones? I asked myself. I needed a second opinion and resolved to send my findings to Pete and see if he could confirm what I had found or if I had been off on a wild-goose chase. In the meantime, I wondered – could Grace and Billy have met in a local pub? On the Heath? In a church after a Sunday service? I clicked on images from Fortis Green from the 1930s and 1940s and pages of black-and-white photos came up, some showing monochrome streets, others showing people in parks, in front of shops, posing, smiling at the cameras. Who were these people? All with a story to tell, a life behind a photo that captured a moment in time. Was one of them named Grace Harris, waiting for news of a soldier fighting in the war?

*

A few seconds after midnight, my mobile pinged with messages. One from Marcia and Pete wishing me *A Happy New Year, New Start, New Everything*; another from Heather saying *Onwards and don't look back*. I wondered if she was referring to the past life story as well as life in general. Another was from Stuart saying, *The best is yet to come.*

If only, I thought, as I looked at a couple of others from friends texting their messages of hope for the next chapter. I sent my own good wishes back and, when I put my phone back on the table, I spotted the piece of paper with Billy and Grace's addresses. I reopened my laptop and looked for Google Maps.

The address I had for where Grace had lived was in Northern Road in Fortis Green. I had driven through it a thousand times on my way up to Muswell Hill. *Had I ever felt a sense of recognition there?* I asked myself. I couldn't say that I had. I liked the tree-lined streets around there – the houses all had what the estate agents would call character – and, in fact, I had even looked at a property near there when I was looking to buy many years ago. I checked for the house number for Grace. No. 176. *Might take a drive past one day*, I thought.

It was 12.15 a.m. I felt a rush of curiosity. I could go and have a look now. Start the New Year by being daring. I'd go now. I put my coat on and opened the front door to a blast of cold air.

'Happy New Year,' called a voice to my left. Jon. 'Off to your party? You're a bit late.'

'I . . . no . . .' How could I explain? I was off to drive past the house of someone I might have been in a past life. He'd think I was bonkers. 'I . . . er, have you been to one?'

Jon shook his head. 'I took a late-night walk. Fully dressed this time, you may have noted, er . . . sorry about the other night.' He opened his car door and out jumped a border collie. 'This is Chief.'

'He's gorgeous,' I said as I went down the steps and over to stroke him. 'The one who ran out the other night leaving you starkers? How come you have a dog now?'

'He's always been my dog but it got a bit complicated in the . . . you know—'

'Divorce?' I asked as I fussed the dog, who was wagging his tail like I was his oldest, best friend.

Jon nodded. 'Fran, my ex, she's away for Christmas with her new . . .'

'Ah.'

'Yes. So I said I'd look after Chief while she basks on

some island in the Caribbean. It's been great having him back. He was always more mine than hers.'

'I get the impression you'd like to keep him?'

'God, yes. I'll be working on it when she gets back. I'm not sure Fran's new chap is much of a dog lover.'

'Well, if you ever need someone to walk him . . .' I said. 'I used to have a dog. I still miss him.'

'Deal,' said Jon, then hesitated, 'though it might be a while before he's here permanently. I may have a few things to attend to in the New Year but once all that's settled, I'm hoping Chief can live here with me. So you? Where are you off to?'

I decided to tell the truth, see how he reacted. 'I thought I'd drive past a house where I might have lived in a past life, to see if I remember it.'

Jon looked puzzled then nodded and laughed. 'Ah. Sorry. Of course, I get it. None of my business.' He began to walk towards his front door. 'You take care, Bea, and once again, Happy New Year.'

'And to you too, Happy New Year,' I called after him.

He put his key in and turned back. 'Hope to see more of you in it.'

'Sure, sure,' I replied. *And pigs might fly*, I thought.

Peculiar old life, I thought as I let myself back into my house. He hadn't believed me for a second when I'd told him where I was going. I took my coat off. The moment for exploring the address had passed. It made more sense to do it in the daylight, and if and when Pete confirmed that I had the right place. I'd do it another time when I was more sure of where I was going.

17

'So trousers down, up on the couch, lie on your side and take a deep breath,' said the young Indian nurse as she put on white latex gloves and lubricated her fingers ready to examine my prostate.

'We haven't even had dinner and a date,' I said in a weak attempt at a joke. She didn't laugh. I guessed she'd heard similar from embarrassed patients all the time. A year ago, someone close to me died of prostate cancer. He made me promise to have regular check-ups and I wanted to honour that. 'Prostate cancer is treatable if it's caught in time,' he said. Sadly it was too late for him by the time they diagnosed it, and it had spread. They tried everything – hormone treatment, chemotherapy, various clinical trails – and he cursed that he hadn't taken heed when invited by his local surgery to have regular checks, or seen someone when he'd started needing to get up to use the loo four times a night. 'Like most blokes, I thought it won't happen to me. I'm going to live for ever,' he said. His passing was a shock. First of my inner circle to leave the party. I missed him sorely and his death was part of the reason I'd been taking stock of life and making some changes. He had a lot to say before he went, urging friends and family not to waste time with people they didn't want to be with or doing things they really didn't want to do. 'Life is not a rehearsal,' he said. 'You only get one crack at it.'

*

So much for a great start to the New Year, I thought after the nurse had taken blood for the PSA test and I'd left the surgery and headed for my car. What would I do if I had bad news? Maybe this wasn't the time to try and convince Bea Brooks that I was the one for her; maybe I'd wait to get the results or else it might be a case of 'hey Bea, I want to be in your life, to love, cherish and the rest of it. And oh . . . just one thing, might be that none of the equipment will work if I have to have surgery or radiotherapy or whatever, er, sorry about that, bad timing eh?' I was looking forward to a chapter or chapters with Bea, had it all planned out – how I was going to woo and win her, but now I felt it might be best to leave it a while, see what the outcome of the tests were. It might not be the end of the world, I might even get the all-clear, but I've done my research. Even if you do have to have treatment, some chaps are lucky and sail through it, and some recover all the necessary in time.

There's that saying that life is what happens to you when you are busy making other plans. How true. I had it all worked out for this year. Bea Brooks. A new start for both of us. But this might be a hiccup on the way. Waiting for results is always the worst part and the imagination can have a field day – mine, anyway. Like Tom Sawyer sobbing as he watched his own funeral, some dark part of my mind was envisaging mine – who'd be there, what hymns and readings to have. *Get a grip man*, I told myself. *Everything may well be fine*.

In the meantime, my furry friend was waiting for me in the passenger seat of my car. A long walk with him should blow away a few anxieties.

18

On Friday afternoon, I gave Heather a lift to our local pharmacy to pick up a stash of cold and flu remedies to keep at the shop as everyone that came in was coughing or sneezing. As we headed across the car park, I noticed a familiar figure in front of us coming out of the surgery. I nudged Heather. 'Oh no, I think that's Joe Wilding.'

Heather looked over to see a dark-haired man of medium height in front of us. 'Oh no. How long is it since you've seen him?'

'Must be twenty years, yes, we lived together for five so—'

'Do you want to avoid him?'

'Yes. I . . .'

Too late, Joe had seen us. His face registered surprise and I sensed a reluctance to engage, but there was no avoiding the situation. 'Bea, I . . .'

I was shocked to see how he'd aged, but then he was probably thinking the same about me. 'Joe, I thought that was you. How are you?'

He shifted about on his feet and laughed. 'Older, not much wiser. You?'

'I'm fine.'

Heather waved a hand. 'Hi Joe.'

Joe looked over. 'Oh, hi Heather. All right?'

She nodded.

Joe looked over at the line of cars behind us. 'Er . . . better dash, sorry.' He glanced at his watch then back at me. 'Bea, lovely to see you, I'll get in touch, I . . . I've been meaning to get in touch for a while.'

'Sure,' I said. He probably didn't mean it. It had been a clean break when we parted and I'd hardly seen him since, although I was aware that he still lived in the area.

Heather and I watched him walk away.

'That was weird,' she said, once Joe was out of hearing distance.

'I know. And why would he get in touch?'

'Is he on your list of men to look up?'

I shook my head. 'No. I heard on the grapevine that he'd got married and had kids.'

'Probably divorced by now, knowing him,' said Heather. 'You never know, it's been a long time, and he was good company when he wasn't drunk.'

'That became more and more infrequent.'

'Don't worry,' said Heather, 'if he hasn't conquered his demons, you have me to watch out for you.'

'No, not going back there. It wasn't a particularly happy period of my life and not one I want to return to.'

Joe Wilding. I had been aged twenty-five when I arrived in London. Pete and Marcia had moved down the year before, got a ground-floor flat in Crouch End, and Marcia had sent for me. 'You'll love it here, pack your bags, you have to come,' she'd said. 'It's where everything is happening.'

I'd stayed in Manchester after college, not sure of my place or what I wanted to do, so when the call came from Marcia, I dutifully did as I was told. She and Pete delighted in spending their weekends driving me around – north, south, east, west London – so I could get to know the areas and decide where I wanted to live. I was wide-eyed with anticipation as I explored the streets lined with brightly lit shops, bustled my way through the crowds in the West End, learnt to manoeuvre through the busy traffic. I remembered vividly the first time I drove with Pete and Marcia along Hampstead High Street. It was dusk, the tall houses and artisan shops lit from within and casting a warm glow out onto the streets. As we turned right at the traffic lights and up the hill, I thought, *This is where I want to be.* The area, popular with artists, writers and actors, was well known for its bohemian atmosphere and when I came across the vast expanse of parkland nearby that was Hampstead Heath, I felt it couldn't get any better.

'You have chosen one of the most expensive parts of London,' said Marcia, who encouraged me to look further north in Finsbury Park, Muswell Hill, or close to them in Crouch End, but I was determined to live in Hampstead. When I saw an ad in the local paper for someone to share a garden apartment in a big old house on one of the back roads, I was over the moon. I was interviewed by two women, Katie and Heather, who were also in their twenties and, like me, were eager to get out there, find lovers, find our careers, be part of the buzz. I passed their test, moved in, and couldn't have been happier. The world seemed full of possibilities as a single woman in a big city. NW3 was the home of the famous and the fashionable, and I aspired to be one of them. I trod the cobbled back streets, met friends in the olde-worlde pubs, was in awe to discover the many famous people who had stayed or lived there in different centuries: Gerald du Maurier, actor and father of Daphne, authors H. G. Wells and Robert Louis Stevenson, actor Peter O'Toole, musicians Boy George and Sting, and the film director Ridley Scott, to name only a few. I'd often spot comedians Peter Cook and Dudley Moore on the pavement outside a restaurant, always laughing; they clearly relished each other's company. I loved to walk down Church Row with its tall red-bricked houses, then through the gates and into St John's Church at the end, where there was an overgrown graveyard in which the artist John Constable was buried. I discovered the open-air ponds on the Heath where we swam amongst the reeds, birds and dragonflies in summer. One afternoon, I came across the Vale of Health, a village of individual cottages and hidden gardens built in the 1800s. I was captivated by their names – Rose Cottage, Woodbine Cottage, Vale Lodge. I saw a plaque on the wall of one house that said that the novelist, D. H. Lawrence, had spent time there; nearby was a house that the Romantic poets, Shelley, Byron and Keats had frequented; in another the Indian poet Rabindranath Tagore had lived. I found Keats's House, the home of the poet, had tea in the café at Kenwood House, a white stately home built in the 1700s, which stood in the middle of the Heath and displayed paintings by Gainsborough, Reynolds, Vermeer, Rembrandt. Hampstead High Street was alive with cafés, independent and quirky shops, butchers', bakers', florists', and art galleries.

On days off, Heather, Katie and I would take off for Portobello Road in Notting Hill or go to Camden Lock and spend any spare money we had on vintage clothing and bits of jewellery, beads and crystals from the stalls there. I loved all of it. I felt I had found my place and, with Heather and Katie, my tribe. For my first years, I had four jobs to keep up living expenses. I worked as a receptionist in a health spa in St John's Wood three days a week, as a photographer's assistant two days a week for a lovely man, Robin Mayhew, who had a studio in Camden Town. I did bar work in a pub near Highgate five nights a week, and on Saturdays I helped Pete and Marcia out in their shop. On Sundays, I'd go out with my camera, taking pictures of my new world and the people in it. I'd fall into bed each night exhausted but content. I was where I wanted to be because, in my last couple of years in Manchester after college, I'd felt as though I was drifting. I'd done an extra year at college to give myself a teaching qualification but, at the end, I hadn't applied for any jobs because I wasn't sure that was what I wanted to do.

A year after my move to London, I'd met Joe at Robin Mayhew's sixtieth birthday party. Joe was in the kitchen, manning the bar and concocting his famous cocktails for the guests – he always made a mean mojito.

'And for the lady in the red?' he asked when he saw me, then began to sing the song so badly that I had to laugh.

'Just white wine,' I said.

We spent the rest of the evening chatting, getting very drunk, and although I thought he was flash and bit of a name-dropper, it was hard not to be seduced by his charm and eagerness to please. I learnt that he worked as an art director in advertising, loved his job, and lived in Camden Town; I went back there with him that night and awoke the next morning with a humming hangover. It was a super-trendy maisonette with white walls, black leather sofas, glass and chrome furniture, and Andy Warhol prints on the wall.

We soon fell into an easy routine, weekends together walking his spaniel, Bertie, on the Heath. On my nights off, one of us would cook or we'd go out for dinner in Notting Hill Gate or Covent Garden or to a movie. We were officially a couple, Bea and Joe, Joe and Bea and, six months later, I moved in with him. I gave up my bar work so we could have more evenings together, and Joe encouraged me to think about my career, which I did, starting by doing a course in jewellery design. He was my greatest supporter and we were never happier than when scouring Camden Lock looking for vintage jewellery that could be adapted into modern designs – to the point that I took on one of the stalls there on a Saturday, so I could be on site to scoop up any finds as soon as they appeared. I soon had boxes and boxes of brooches, rings, old necklaces, all ready to be reworked. Joe created my first BB logo, had cards made up for me, advertising that I would make bespoke items and, before long, one of his friends gave me a space in his shop in Notting Hill Gate to display my own creations.

Sex with Joe was wild, and the creativity and need for approval that he manifested in every area of his life, he also applied to our lovemaking. He prided himself on keeping it interesting from the very first time, which I seem to remember was up against a wall. We did it over sofas, on the kitchen table, in a lift, in the loo on a train, and even half in the wardrobe on one occasion; I still have a vivid memory of being face down in a sock draw. Oh yes, we did it in all the most romantic locations. One night, he'd been reading that porn stars used toothpaste to keep an erection for longer, and he dutifully rubbed some on to his penis. Sadly, he hadn't taken into account that he'd used menthol, and hopped around the place in agony, finally plunging his burning minty-flavored willie into a sink of cold water. I couldn't stop laughing. We did laugh a lot in the first years we were together, and I'd never been fitter in my attempts to keep up with the gymnastics that were our sex life. With Joe, it was always as though he had to prove himself to someone, and when I met his parents, I realized why. His mother was warm and adored her son, his father distant, critical, and never praised Joe, though it was clear how desperately he craved his father's approval. I understood then where the insecurity that was behind Joe's successful mask had come from. He was really just a boy wanting to make his dad proud of him. Sadly that never happened, but it made me love and care for him all the more. *I would make up for the lack from his father*, I'd thought. *I'd cherish and change him.*

We talked about getting married; so many of our friends were tying the knot and we had wonderful weekends at their weddings in country hotels, some in the UK, one in France, another in Italy. Our early years were happy ones; Joe was full of life, energy and fun, and so generous, always buying gifts or clothes or perfume. He appeared to adore me, and it was heady stuff after Michael's rejection and departure. I loved having a home, keeping it nice, cooking for him, having someone to share my life with.

At first, Joe's drinking didn't bother me – everyone drank

too much; hangovers were par for the course – but then, over time, I began to notice that he quaffed wine down as if it was water and, by the time a friend or colleague had finished their first glass, he'd already polished off four. After a certain number of drinks, he changed: his voice got louder, his eyes slightly out of focus, and he became argumentative; he liked to rile people and see if they'd take the bait. He never remembered in the morning and would be back to the sweet and vibrant man I'd moved in with. However, when the drinking escalated and cocaine was added to the mix, I grew more concerned. We had heated rows. I tried to get him to slow down, though I learnt fast not to argue when he'd been drinking or was high. Stress, Joe said; his job was stressful, I didn't understand the pressure he was under.

I tried to. I thought I could be his rock, his shelter in the storm; I could change him, calm him down. I learnt to avoid certain situations, certain people but, as time went on, I didn't like who I was becoming – always on edge, on the lookout at functions to see if Joe had had that drink too many, the one that turned him nasty; always checking to see if he was still being civil. He accused me of being a nag. Our lives were no longer fun. When he lost his job after having had a go at a client in a meeting after a long boozy lunch, he fell apart. He needed me more than ever, so I stayed, supported him, even paid all the bills in the end. He was full of resolutions and good intentions to reform, but I still found bottles tucked away at the back of cupboards or in boxes hidden in our cloakroom. I was no longer sure he was faithful. I'd become Miss Prim in his eyes, his conscience. Joe balked at the words addict or alcoholic, called me names – uptight, prissy, superior. I wasn't; I just didn't like living with someone with a drink problem and all that went with it. He wanted a fun girl to share his binges.

The nights he didn't come home grew more and more frequent. In between, Joe was full of resolutions and good intentions. He would get on a detox program, life would return to normal and we'd get on again for a while. Then something would happen and, again, he'd fall. My friends grew concerned for me. It was clear Joe was an addict but I kept hoping that he'd change. Marcia suggested Al-Anon for me and I attended meetings for the best part of a year. Heather bought me a copy of *Women Who Love Too Much* and I began to question what my part in it all was. Was I enabling him? What was I getting out of it? Why did I stay? After a series of blow-up rows over the summer, I decided I'd had enough. I didn't like who I was any more and I'd lost respect for Joe. I also realized that the reason I'd stayed too long was because I needed to be needed; I had an important role as the one who was there to care for him on the morning afters when he repented and regretted his behaviour of the night before. As long as I had him to worry about, I didn't need to think about myself and my shortcomings or needs.

One night Joe didn't come home, and when he did eventually return the next day, I finally faced the fact that I'd lost him. He hadn't left me physically as Michael had done, but I'd lost him to his addiction. There was no more denying it, and I left to move back in with Heather.

*

I felt sad about bumping into Joe. It was a reminder of a turbulent time in my life, but also a time when I was just starting out, so full of ambition and energy. *Would we have made it if I'd stayed, ridden the rollercoaster with him?* I wondered, as Heather and I picked up our purchases. *Might he have changed? And the sweet, vulnerable Joe have won through?*

'No, he wasn't the one, *isn't* the one,' said Heather, picking up on my thoughts. 'You've been there, done that, got the T-shirt.'

'Noted,' I said.

19

The following weeks went by in a haze of activity as Heather and I went into top gear. I got three estate agents over, got quotes, and put my house on the market. They all said it would be an easy sale and at first I thought, they all say that, even when a house is a hovel but, sure enough, once I'd chosen my agent, potential buyers seemed to be inquiring about it, even before it went live on the Internet.

When Marcia, Pete and family returned from Scotland, they all had stinking colds. They took to their beds and, from there, Pete emailed to say that he had looked into my research about Grace and Billy. I hadn't had a moment to look at his email properly though – there was far too much going on to get distracted.

Heather and I spent long days in the shop. When I'd first taken it on, I'd wanted it to have the look of an art gallery, and we'd achieved that with the stripped and varnished floors, white walls and plenty of light streaming in from the south-facing window that looked out on the main road.

I'd chosen the art-deco style for the furnishings, so all the light fittings and furniture were from that era, and my BB logo had been done in art-deco style in black and silver outside. In the window display, I'd not wanted to go the traditional route with the jewellery shown on a series of neck dummies, I'd wanted something more original. Heather and I had gone searching in the antique markets in Notting Hill Gate and found a fabulous, reclining, life-size figure from the 1920s. It had cost a bomb but I bought it instantly and had it sprayed black. We called her Daphne and she now lay in the window wearing an assortment of necklaces and bracelets. To her side was a small table displaying a range of earrings.

'What will you do with Daphne when we finally leave the shop?' Heather asked as we took down the last of the silver Christmas decorations and put up sale signs.

'She'll come with me. Maybe she's my true soulmate: she's consistent, stable and never answers back.'

'Sounds like the perfect match,' agreed Heather.

*

In the evenings, we went through all our stock in the back room, pricing things down, displaying the better items in counters and cabinets at the front, ready for the day and opening hours. We advertised on Instagram and Facebook, then tweeted times and bargains of the day. Our efforts paid off and the shop drew a steady flow of people most days in the first two weeks of January. The hardest part was letting the suppliers of the filler items that we sold in the shop – mainly greetings cards handmade by local artists

– know that I wouldn't be using them or restocking their work for a while, if ever.

*

On the way home one evening, I took a trip to my lock-up to drop off some boxes that were cluttering up the shop. I also wanted to look out some bits of old jewellery that I'd collected over the years. I kept the lock-up – a large double garage in a car park in Highgate – to store bits of furniture and items that didn't fit in my current home, but that I didn't want to get rid of. When I got there, I went inside, switched on the light and almost gave up there and then. I'd forgotten there was so much stuff crammed in. Stuart had helped me shift some of it after Richard and I had broken up, and I can still see him struggling with curtains, pictures, mirrors, endless boxes, and making me laugh as he feigned backache, knee-ache and even toothache. He'd been a tremendous help, and I remembered one particular afternoon especially, because there was something in the air – maybe because I'd just reclaimed my freedom, or was on the rebound but, at one point, I slipped on a bit of bubble wrap and fell into him. He reached out to help me stand up and, for a brief second in his arms, I felt a tug of chemistry, drawing me to him. We both pulled back and busied ourselves immediately, and it never happened again, but that same intensity has hung in the air on occasion when we're in close proximity, heads bent over papers or accounts. I've always had to remind myself that he is married and whatever I felt that afternoon was just wishful thinking on my part.

I began to shift things until I came to the boxes that might possibly hold what I wanted. I opened the nearest and sifted through books, paper, more bags of beads and old jewellery that I'd picked up over time. An old album with a red velvet cover was at the bottom and, as I pulled it out, a few loose photographs fell out. I made a make-do chair on a box heavy with books and opened the album. It had been years since I'd looked at it and there he was, smiling out at me from the pages: Graham White, a typical photo with him in his gardening togs at the allotment, our dog Casper by his side.

It was painfully noticeable to me that no one talked about him any more, aware that it would be opening an old wound, one that none of them could heal because there was no going back there. But I wanted to consider the option. If there was a shred of truth in what Saranya Ji had said, had Graham been my Billy and I'd had my time with him?

*

Graham White. The years after Joe and I had split up had been bleak when it came to men. I'd moved back in with Heather and we'd watched our flatmate Katie get married then move to a rustic idyll in Wiltshire.

And so there were two of us.

Heather and I went all out to meet The One. Heather particularly; she was ready to settle. I was less enthusiastic about committing again but was happy to accompany Heather to places supposedly good for meeting new people. We did the wine bars, which I grew to hate – the noise, the crowded pubs, men just wanting a one-night stand. I did date a man called Keith for a short while, but he was the grumpiest man on the planet once you got to know him, a glass half-empty type of person. I'd counted his complaints on one outing to see friends in Bristol, and by the time we'd got to Paddington Station from north London, there had been eighteen – about bin men who hadn't made their collections, people who chucked chewing gum on the pavement, tourists who gathered at the bottom of escalators, the government, taxes, the weather, politics; all legitimate complaints, perhaps, but it was oh so wearying to listen to. I felt any joy I'd found in the day seep out of me like air out of a balloon, until I was as flat as he was and had a sudden urge to leap under the nearest train, or push him under one. We didn't last long, and I hadn't mentioned him for 'the list' because I knew there was no point. He most definitely wasn't The One. Plus the few times we had had sex, it had been awful, soulless; I wasn't that desperate. It was around the Keith time that Heather met Anita, love of her life, swing-dance partner and all-round fabster. I watched them fall in love, move in together then get married, and I was genuinely happy for her.

Then there was one. Me.

'There's someone out there for you,' both Heather and Marcia had told me. 'You'll find him.'

I wondered if I was too picky, if I was difficult, unattractive, demanding, too independent, too needy. In the end, I gave up looking, and filled my time with classes – yoga, Italian, art, film study. I'd be fine on my own. I dug up my mantra from my teens and my twenties. I didn't need anyone. I was fine, just fine.

I met Graham just after I'd turned thirty-three and had been unattached for four years. I'd signed up to do a life-drawing class in the evenings in the church hall in Highgate. I had arrived ten minutes early and found my way to the classroom at the back of the building, and there he was, at a desk in the corner, looking like Santa Claus's younger brother with his sandy-coloured hair and beard. 'Hi, find a place,' he said. 'I'm Graham White, the tutor for the evening, and you are?'

'Bea Brooks.'

'Ah, like that Hollywood movie star from the 1920s?'

'You're thinking of Louise Brooks.'

He smiled and ticked my name off his list. 'Probably. Must be the hairstyle as well as the name.'

I'd had my long hair cut into a short bob after Joe and I had split up, and taken to wearing tailored vintage riding jackets, usually sourced on Portobello Road, jeans and brogue shoes. Graham looked in his forties and appeared to also favour clothing from past decades, with his corduroy trousers and Harris jackets, picked up from the charity shops he loved to frequent.

Other students arrived, our life model appeared. She was a young, stick-thin girl with a shock of soft blonde hair. She stripped off, took her pose for the start of the evening and off we went, beginning with a series of quick charcoal sketches, then moving on to a longer study until the end of the class.

Graham was a good teacher, encouraging as well as critical, and my drawing improved enormously under his guidance. There wasn't an immediate attraction, although I liked him from the start. There was more a feeling of respect for his knowledge and his own considerable talent. He taught at an art college in the day, spent his Monday nights doing the evening class I attended, Saturdays he volunteered and taught art in a local prison. Our tutor/ student relationship grew into a friendship. We spent time in the pub after classes with other students, all of us eager to learn from him.

It was in the term after Easter that I began to have feelings for Graham and found myself looking forward to Monday nights, hanging about afterwards with some excuse or other, feeling that I'd miss our times together once the class broke up for the summer. I never imagined the feelings were mutual because there wasn't the slightest hint or glance from him to say that he felt the same way.

On a balmy summer's night, the last evening of the term, a group of us went to the pub as usual. When the others had gone, I took the plunge and asked if he'd like to accompany me to a Picasso exhibition at the Tate the following week. He leant over and kissed me lightly on the forehead and said, 'Love to. I made it a rule never to see a student alone out of class, but now that the term's finished . . .' I reached over and took his hand. It was soft and warm. We interlocked fingers and it felt intimate and sensual. Graham smiled back at me. 'I'm so glad you feel the same way. I've been wanting to ask you out since the classes began.'

We spent the whole summer getting to know each other. As neither of us had much money, Graham suggested that, instead of a holiday away somewhere, we should be tourists in London and treat the city as though we were visitors. We took the tourist bus around the sights, got the boat from Westminster to Greenwich, walked up Pall Mall to

Buckingham Palace, saw the latest plays and exhibitions, walked the green areas – St James's Park, Regent's Park, Hyde Park, Richmond Park. We researched the restaurant reviews and deals and dined out in those that claimed to offer best value for money. It was a great few months and, when the summer was over, he asked me to live with him. I agreed without hesitation, moved into Graham's terraced house in Crouch End, and so began the most stable period of my life.

He was the total opposite of Joe, who had been flash with his brand names and designer clothes. Graham was as comfy as an old jumper and, like me, loved to find a bargain in a junk shop or stall in Notting Hill. Our happiest times were spent looking for finds in the various antique and junk shops around the capital, Camden Passage in Islington being our favourite, and we would head home after a morning outing with old books, chipped or cracked Lalique and mismatched art-deco crockery. He was so easy to live with, conscious and considerate, a man who grew his own vegetables on an allotment nearby, a caring man, kind to animals and to our two black cats, Bing and Bong and collie dog called Casper. I liked Graham's friends and they adopted me as one of their own. They were a bright bunch: some were academics, who were clever and informed and taught me a lot about local politics and causes; others were artists like Graham. They made me think, read books I hadn't considered, expanded my horizons, and I liked that. I felt I was moving in the right direction again after a period of swimming against the tide.

It was then that my stall at Camden Lock began to really take off, and I began to rent the space for the whole weekend plus one day in the week. Some jewellery I had made, some I sourced at trade price. Weekends at the market were buzzing with people, many tourists, eager to buy a trinket to take home with them. I found I had a good eye for purchasing what would sell and the stall grew to be a huge success. Heather, who was eager to find flexible work so she could be home with the daughter that she and Anita had adopted, came in with me. As I made money, I started travelling, and Graham was happy to accompany me. We went to Turkey, India, Bali, Morocco, and always returned with contacts and merchandise to sell.

We had a comfortable life – not rich, not poor, not passionate, not dull. I could see myself growing older with him; greyer, more wrinkled, always at each other's side.

After three years, one morning, he got down on one knee. 'And will you, Bea Brooks, take this old codger to be your lawfully wedded wotsit?'

'I will,' I said.

We planned the wedding for the following month, a small do in the local register office, sausage and mash later at the Old Bull and Bush near the Heath. I bought a dress from a boutique in Notting Hill that specialized in vintage clothes, a slip of ivory silk and lace, and I found the most divine and delicate hairband made of tiny seed pearls, miniature white fabric roses and leaves made of old white lace. It was perfect. I glanced down at the photo in my hand.

'Where are you now Graham?' I said out loud as tears spilled down my cheeks.

*

My trip down memory lane was halted when Heather suddenly appeared in the lock-up's entrance. 'I thought you'd be in here. I hope you're not getting maudlin on your own.' She picked the photograph out of my hand. 'Ah.'

'I was just wondering if Graham was The One.'

'Of course you were, we've all wondered that, but I think Saranya Ji would have said something about that, surely?'

We sat in silence for a while and looked through the album. No words were needed.

20

Late afternoon one Saturday, Stuart dropped in with Monty to see me at the shop. 'Just thought I'd see how it's all going,' he said as he looked around the shelves. He was wearing the long grey herringbone coat that he'd been wearing the first time I met him, and had his thick red scarf wound around his neck.

I put on my smiley face. 'Sales are great, better than great, though it feels a bit sad to think that this is the end of an era and I'm still not sure what I'm going to do next.'

'You'll think of something,' he said, 'and let me know if there's anything I can do to help.'

'Gift for the missus,' Heather piped up from behind the counter. 'We have bracelets, earrings – you name it. Earn yourself some Brownie points.'

Stuart smiled. 'Bit late for that, I think.'

Monty started pulling on his lead so Stuart headed for the door. 'Stay in touch and don't do anything rash.'

I laughed. 'Heather and I are on the next plane to Brazil. We'll send you a postcard.'

'I might even come with you,' he said, then let Monty

out of the door. A moment later, he came back. 'Don't suppose you can get away for a walk? We could talk over your future plans.'

'Or lack of them,' I said. 'But I—'

'Go,' said Heather. 'I can man the shop. Take a break.'

'Great,' said Stuart. 'I have a few things to do then I'll come back for you in about an hour?'

I watched him walk off down the street and thought he seemed subdued. Maybe it was him that needed to talk over his future.

'That man fancies you,' said Heather.

I laughed. 'You say that about everyone. You said that about Jon too.'

'Both of them fancy you. You just don't see it, Bea; you're blind to your fatal attraction. Loads of men fancy you.'

'Yeah right, not Stuart though. OK, yes, he's a friend, but also one hired to oversee my finances, which explains his concern, it's his job. Anyway, you know he's married.'

'Shame. So many of the good men are taken. But how do you feel?'

'About what?'

'You know very well about what, I mean who: Stuart.'

'Don't be ridiculous. Drop it, Heather. Ours is mainly a professional relationship and, even if it wasn't, I think he believes I've messed up, made some bad decisions of which he disapproves. If you had your way, I'd be sleeping with half the men in Hampstead.'

'Why stop there? Go for all of them. You have so much to offer – you're attractive, good company, I'd like to see you shacked up with someone.'

'I am fine. I have Daphne. I don't need anyone,' I replied.

'I've managed on my own and will continue to do so.' And to prove my point I sang the opening lines of Gloria Gaynor's 'I Will Survive'.

Heather grimaced. 'And you can't sing either. When you do meet The One, please don't try and serenade him, because that will be the end of it.'

'Thanks for the vote of confidence. And now I am going upstairs to go over a few figures. Can you manage down here?'

'Sure,' she said.

*

After I'd done most of the admin that needed doing, I finally got around to looking at personal emails and the one that had been waiting for me from Pete.

Darling Bea,

Spot on re Grace. I think there's no doubt you have found her. I looked at a couple of others with the same name in London around the time we're looking at, as you probably did, but none of them gave dressmaker as profession of the mother, so I think it's highly likely that the one in Fortis Green is our girl. Born 1920, died 1943.

Re. Billy. Now this is interesting but I believe I have your man. Sadly died in the defence of Calais in 1940. From what I can find, he was in the 30th Motor Brigade.

The address I found for him in the military records is Kentish Town.

Not far from Grace so it's likely they could have met up. Worth checking out further, anyway.

At the bottom of the email, Pete included an attachment that showed a death notice for a William Harris, killed in action, 25 May 1940.

I knew a little about the defence of Calais. It was a story from the Second World War that had always particularly touched me. The lives of the soldiers there enabled the mass evacuation, and Operation Dynamo at Dunkirk, which saved hundreds of thousands of men. For those left behind in Calais, though, there was no hope.

I googled 'defence of Calais 1940.' Photos showing men in uniform staring back. They looked so young. Some were group shots, men smiling, but one in particular struck me and that was of a group of men marching. They looked utterly worn out and depleted of any of the spirit shown in the pre-battle images that showed bright young men, full of life and vigour. So many would have been killed, as would Billy Jackson. Looking at them made me feel over-whelmingly sad. So many lives cut short. All of them with families, wives, fiancées and a life back home that they had to leave. Would Grace have known the truth about that period in history, as we do now? Would the defence of Calais have been reported in the papers as we now know it happened? Or would she have been waiting to hear, ignorant of the true facts? Hoping that Billy was amongst those soldiers due to be evacuated and brought home? And did one of those faces looking back at me from the photos belong to a man I knew in another time? A man I'd loved and lost?

I was about to google more images when I heard Heather calling. 'Oh my god, Bea! Get down here now. I mean *now*. The most gorgeous, *gorgeous* man is walking up the High

Street. He's coming this way. He's looking up and down the street.'

Heather always did this when she was bored, looked out the window for suitable men for me.

'Not interested. I bet he's young enough to be our grandson.'

'No *seriously*, he's about our age. George Clooney, eat your heart out. Come, come and look.'

'I am not going to gawp out the window at some stranger.'

'Bea, *Bea*, he's looking in the window. Come down NOW.'

'He probably wants to buy a gift for his beautiful young Swedish wife.'

'Who cares? Eye candy like this doesn't come this way that often. Come *on*. You have to see him. Oh . . . I think he's going to come in.'

I sighed, saved the file I was working on, and went down to the shop, if only to shut Heather up. A tall man with cropped grey hair had just come in; his face was turned away from us. He was wearing jeans, denim blue Converse sneakers, and a navy Aran sweater. I glanced over at Heather. She grinned at me and indicated the man with a flick of her head then made the heart sign with her fingers. I rolled my eyes.

'Can I help you with anything?' I asked as the man closed the door and turned to face us. Heather was right. He was drop-dead gorgeous with truly beautiful sapphire blue eyes.

'Michael!'

'Bea Brooks,' he said as he strode over and gave me a bear hug. 'How the hell are you?'

21

'I told you I'd come back,' he said once we'd settled at a table in the Coffee Cup along the High Street. It was my favourite café in the area, a cosy 1960s-style place with wood-panelled walls, floors and tables.

I laughed and glanced at my watch. 'Thirty years later.'

'I know. Where *has* all that time gone? So tell me everything. You look great. I like the short hair. How are you? What's happening? Where are you going? Goals, dreams, aspirations?'

I was still in shock, to be sitting opposite him, gazing into those oh-so-familiar eyes that were looking back at me with such intensity. I was back at twenty years old, high to be in his company, happy to see him again, conscious of the admiring looks he was getting from other women in the café. He'd aged well, a suntanned face with a neatly trimmed grey beard, laughter lines around his eyes, slightly broadened but still fit looking.

'I'm good, sort of at a turning point.'

'Crossroad in life?'

I nodded.

'Me too. Tell me all about it. Your shop? Looks good and you design jewellery?'

'I'm letting go of the shop and not sure what I'm going to do next. That's the turning point, that and I'm selling my house – moving on but not sure where to.'

'Great timing, then. Come to Thailand. Have a holiday.'

'I can't do that, or at least not just yet. I have to oversee things over here.'

'Have you ever been?'

I shook my head.

'Think about it then, in the summer maybe, though I think November to April are the best months. You'd like it there and, of course, I can show you round all the spots the tourists never see.'

'Tempting but what about you? You got married? Run a bar?'

'I manage a couple of bars now. I like the lifestyle over there and the climate but . . . I don't know, I may relocate, come back here. I'm undecided but I feel like I'm ready for a change. Er . . . what else can I tell you? I was married to Celia, still am, though we're not together, haven't been for ages. We're still good friends.'

'Why still married then?'

'Just haven't got round to doing the legal bit, but it's all happening now, in fact, because she's got herself another fellow and wants to remarry.' He laughed. 'So much to catch up on. Where do we start?'

'Children?' I was about to add, *Did you ever have Moonbeam and Star?*, but I bit it back.

His face clouded. 'A boy, Dylan.'

'Is he in Thailand with you?'

'He is now.'

'Now? You mean he wasn't?'

'He lived with his mother in Australia after we'd split up, but he visited regularly or I went to them.'

'So he's with you more permanently now?'

'Not exactly with me. He's been a complete and utter idiot. He got involved with a bad crowd on his last visit, into the drug scene; it's not wise to have anything remotely to do with drugs over there. Truth is, Bea, he's been in prison for a year.'

'I am sorry.'

'So am I. Thai jails are not like over here. Not an experience he'll want to repeat. He came out to see me for a break then got persuaded to be a mule, to carry drugs back to Australia. Not a large amount, his sentence would have been worse if it had been. It was stupid and naïve of him to think he could get away with it. The police picked him up at the airport.'

'I am sorry,' I repeated.

'This too will pass,' he said, as much to himself as to me. 'He'll get out and at least he has learnt his lesson.'

'I imagine it's been hard for you too, visiting him.'

'Awful. Not an experience you'd ever wish your child to have to endure. The prison visits are truly awful, knowing I can't fix it and just get him home. That and dealing with his mother. She went ballistic. Of course she blames me but, hand on heart, I had no idea what he was up to. I genuinely thought he had more sense. But what about you? Any children?'

'No. Didn't happen.'

Michael looked thoughtful. 'You pay a price. As much as they bring you joy, they bring you sorrow.'

I could see it made him sad to talk about Dylan so decided to change the subject. 'And you're over here for a wedding, I believe?'

'In March. Melanie, she's my niece. Did you ever meet my brother Rob?'

'You talked of him but I never met him.'

'He died just over a year ago, prostate cancer . . .'

'Oh, I'm sorry.'

'Me too, he was a good guy. As both my parents have gone now, Rob's wife, Jess, wanted someone in the family to give Melanie away. I came over early for that, and also a couple of things to attend to, boring stuff. I'll catch up with Jess and Melanie, family, old friends while I'm here, and of course you were top of the list. I've been meaning to get in touch for a long time, but then all the cyberspace stuff just isn't my thing, not my style. I thought I'd wait and catch up in person.'

'And here you are.'

He reached out and took my hand. 'And here I am, and it is *really* good to see you.'

We sat drinking coffee and soon fell back into the ease of conversation we had so long ago. I learnt that, after Celia, he'd had another long-term relationship that hadn't worked out, had taken up painting, and had his own studio over-looking a beach, played with a local band, had a rescue dog he adored called Buster. His life sounded idyllic.

'Are you still into meditation and Buddhism?' I asked. 'I remember that was really your thing when we were together.'

'I lean that way, am vegetarian, don't like to kill insects, but I could never do the monk bit.'

'The Buddhists believe in reincarnation, don't they?'

'They do believe the spirit lives on.'

'Do you believe in past lives?'

'Yes, in a way. I think we all go through many lives in this life and are different people, you know – child, student, lover, husband, father, worker and so on.'

'I meant lived before, as in a different body?'

Michael laughed. 'That's what I always liked about you, Bea. You were always different.'

'Was I?'

'Well, not having seen each other for ages, most people would chat about their families, what they've been doing, what they're having for supper, but you're straight in with a metaphysical question like that.'

'Not usually, really, I'm pretty normal most of the time. So . . . do you have any sense of having lived before?'

'No, no idea. I wouldn't rule it out but I have no memory of previous lives. I can hardly remember what I did yesterday. Why are you asking?'

I wondered whether to tell him about Saranya Ji but decided not to. We'd only just met up again, and I didn't want him thinking that my head was too full of mad fantasies. 'Oh, no reason, just with you being in Thailand and being so into the Eastern philosophies . . . I was curious to know if you still were, if you ever asked yourself if some of us here, now, have met before – in some other time or place – and if maybe we come back time after time.'

'It's a nice idea, romantic. Honest truth, I don't think about it much any more. I know I did when I was younger, but these days I try and live in the present. I suppose I view it all as a dance, a country dance: people come forward in your life, you dance a few steps with them, they step back and another person steps forward, you partner up and on it goes. Some people return in the dance later, others move on to another dance and you never see them again. Whether that takes place over one life or many, I have no idea.'

At that moment, I glanced out of the window and saw Stuart on the opposite side of the street, walking down the hill with Monty. My heart sank. I'd completely forgotten I'd said I'd go for a walk with him. I looked at my watch and realized that we'd been sitting there for over an hour. 'God, look at the time. I'd better get back to the shop to take over from Heather.'

'Me too. I'm going to drop in to see Melanie and her fiancé, then I've got a train to catch. I'm going to stay with Jess, in Oxford, talk wedding plans.'

'Oh.' I'd hoped that he would be staying in town and we could have met up later. The feeling of disappointment felt only too familiar.

'Don't worry. I'll be back.'

I made myself smile. 'You've come over all Terminator,' I said, then did an appalling impression of Arnold Schwarzenegger saying, 'I'll be back.'

Michael laughed, got up and paid the bill, and we walked up to the tube station, our arms linked. When we got there, he put his hands on my shoulders and held me at arm's distance and looked me directly in the eyes. I felt the old chemistry still there, blushed and looked away, uncertain how to react.

'I'll be in touch, Bea Brooks,' he said. 'I've got your number.'

'Will that be in another thirty years or sooner?'

'Sooner. Just got a few things to sort – I'll give you a call.'

I watched him go through the turnstile and disappear down into the station. As I walked back to the shop, I felt unsettled. Michael O'Connor. Would he have changed? What did he want? Anything? Nothing? And why was he going to stay with his sister-in-law when he could have stayed with me? I should have asked him. It had been so good to see him but I didn't dare let go to imagining that we were any more than two old friends meeting up. He'd hurt me once before and, by the attraction that I'd felt, could probably hurt me again. *Forget about him*, I told myself. Last thing I needed was a long-distance lover in Thailand. If he got in touch, fine, I could ask him why he'd come to see me, why I was, as he had said, top of his list. But in the meantime, best not to get my hopes up. Until then, I'd put him out of my mind.

'So?' asked Heather, the minute I walked back into the shop.

I sighed. 'So . . . I don't know. He said he'd be back at some point, but if he's at all like the Michael from the old days, that's not a promise to be relied on.'

'You're both older. Maybe he's realized what he missed with you.'

'I'm not even going there.'

'Stuart came in. Did you forget you said you'd go for a walk with him?'

'I did. What did you say to him?'

'That an old friend of yours had turned up and you'd probably gone to the Coffee Cup.'

'I think I'm in his bad books now. Do you think I should text him?'

'Of course, definitely, say you're sorry. Jon popped in too, after Stuart had gone. He had a look around, didn't buy anything. I got the feeling he was hoping to bump into you.'

'Doubt it. He was probably looking to stock up on gifts for his girlfriends.'

'Funny,' said Heather. 'It's like that programme *Blind Date*, where you have to choose from three contestants.'

'Not really. Stuart's never been on my radar in that way,' I lied. Even though Heather was one of my closest friends, I'd never confided in her or Marcie about the attraction I felt for Stuart. Nothing was ever going to come of it and I didn't want either of them getting on my case about him. There was no point. 'Jon is a womanizer so not for me, and Michael lives on the other side of the planet in Thailand.'

'You're too picky.'

I laughed.

'And Michael's not in Thailand now is he?' Heather pointed out.

'We'll see,' I said. 'I am not getting my hopes up there. Been there, done that, got the T-shirt.' Those were the words that came out of my mouth, but inside was another story. Some ever-hopeful part of me thinking, maybe time for a new T-shirt?

22

Heather and I continued working every day to prevent any shelves looking sad or empty. By evening, I was exhausted, but when I put my head on the pillow, sleep wouldn't come. My mind was on high alert, firing off ideas, filing things I'd done, listing things to do, people to contact, thinking about Grace Harris waiting for Billy to return to the war and how anxious she must have felt, debating whether to text Michael or not. It had been two weeks since he'd come to Hampstead. I had his number, he had mine, but he hadn't been in touch. Had I dreamt he'd been? Had I been too aloof? What was he doing in Oxford? And what was going on with Stuart? He'd gone quiet too. I'd texted my apology for not being there for our walk, but he hadn't replied which was unlike him, and when I'd dropped in to see him at his office on my lunch break yesterday, it had been closed up, which was most unusual.

At night, as I desperately sought sleep, I reminded myself that I must keep the house immaculate for potential viewings. There'd already been an offer, which I'd accepted. Should I have waited until a few more people had seen it?

I would have to check out storage units and costs for if/ when the house sold and I moved to Pete and Marcia's. I would have to make a list of people to inform if I did move.

And on and on it went.

I couldn't switch off and, as the days went on, the lack of rest began to take its toll. I needed to sleep.

'Hypnosis,' said Marcia.

'No thanks,' I said.

'Nytol One-A-Night,' said the lady in the chemist. It worked for three nights.

'Night Nurse liquid variety,' said Heather. Knocked me out for a couple of nights then it was back to staring at the ceiling.

'Easy Sleep pillow spray with lavender,' said Marcia. It had no effect but made the room smell lovely.

'Valerian,' said the lady in the health shop. No sleep and made me feel drugged the next day.

'Remove all electric appliances from the bedroom, phone, digital clock, laptop, TV and don't look online after eight p.m.,' Heather read to me from a magazine. Tried that. I was still wide awake most of the night.

'Wine, and lots of it,' said Pete. It did send me to sleep but then I was awake at 2.30 a.m. with a cracking head-ache.

'Mindfulness, meditation.' Marcia again. I tried it. It did make me feel calmer but when I slid down under the duvet, suddenly my mind was filled with all the things I had to do, places I had to go, and I was off again.

Back to the health shop. 'Put crystals next to the bed,' said the girl on the till. I came out with a selection of amethyst, ammonite, angelite, black tourmaline, clear quartz, hematite, jade, labradorite and rose quartz. Can't say they worked but they did look nice.

'White chestnut Bach flower remedy,' said Marcia. 'Helps stop unwanted thoughts.' Helped a little, but not enough to give me a night of deep sleep.

I googled websites that offered so many ideas and solutions. There was so much advice out there, from drinking banana-peel tea to smelling an onion. I tried no coffee after midday, warm milk and honey before bed, chanting, ensuring I had a daily walk in the fresh air, had hot baths with sandalwood and marjoram, tried breathing in, breathing out in a whoosh, counting sheep, but sleep still evaded me. My mind was active and on the go.

'The trouble is, I'm wired and starting to connect with my inner psycho,' I said to Marcia one day when she dropped into the shop. 'It's like I've drunk three shots of espresso just before going to bed. I haven't slept properly for weeks.'

'Ah, that might be it. Do you drink coffee?'

'Not any more. I've gone decaff but that hasn't helped either.'

'It's not surprising really,' said Marcia. 'There's a lot going on in your life. As we get older, we don't respond so well to changes in routine, and this is major.'

'Any more suggestions? I'll try anything.'

'Then why not give hypnosis a go? I reckon you have to get to the root of the problem then let that go,' said Marcia. 'And I know, that's hard to do, easy to say. I know a good guy in town, down near John Lewis. Simon Jenkins. Pete went years ago when he wanted to stop smoking and it worked, though it took a few sessions.'

She found the number and gave it to me, but I didn't feel very enthusiastic about the idea and I put the number away. However, after another few nights of tossing and turning, drinking passionflower and camomile tea at 2 a.m., I was desperate. I had nothing to lose and thought that if hypnosis didn't work, at least I could pop into John Lewis and invest in some new bed linen.

*

Simon's practice rooms were on the first floor of one of the imposing five-storey terraced houses overlooking the square behind Oxford Street.

A slight-looking man in spectacles, dressed in a red fleece and brown cords, came out to greet me once I'd been buzzed inside to a musty-smelling hall and had climbed up the carpeted stairs. He looked to be in his forties. 'Simon Jenkins,' he said as he gave me a strong handshake. 'Come on in.'

I followed him through into a room that was sparsely furnished. It had two chairs, one reclining, one upright, and a small table displaying leaflets and brochures. On the wall, there were several framed certificates, and a Japanese painting showing a blossom tree by a lake. There was also a window, but at a height where one would have to stand on tiptoe to see out.

Simon indicated that I should take the reclining chair and he sat opposite me.

'How are you feeling?' he asked.

'Bit nervous to tell the truth.'

'Is this your first time?'

I nodded.

'A lot of people are anxious in their first session – it's only natural when trying something new – but I think you'll find that the apprehension will soon go away. Most people's concern is that they're going to be out of control and that something may be suggested that they don't want to go along with. That can't happen. If you decide to go ahead with the hypnosis, your body will be relaxed but your mind will be alert. I couldn't suggest something that you disagreed with.'

'Like make me do the chicken dance on my way back to the tube?'

Simon smiled. 'Exactly. I can assure you that won't be happening. So. How can I help?'

I filled him in on my sleep problems and he nodded and took a few notes. 'I think I can help with that. Can you tell me if you're a visual person or someone who responds more to sound or touch? It will help me to know when making suggestions.'

'Oh . . . visual, I would say.'

'OK, so let me tell you a bit about what I do, then you can tell me if you want to go ahead. First of all, hypnosis is not sleep; it is a state of heightened relaxation when certain commands can be accepted by the subconscious. Your subconscious accepts programming from your conscious mind and that can be positive or negative. With me so far?'

'I think so.'

'Under hypnosis, the subconscious can accept suggestions that otherwise have been unaccepted. In order to do that, you must desire change, and also have confidence in me.'

'And what sort of things do you change?'

'I can programme in new beliefs, like how to become successful, to relax, stop smoking, lose weight, accelerate learning and healing. Hypnosis is a way to bypass the conscious mind and whatever patterns are already programmed there but are having a negative effect.'

'I see.' *It sounds similar to what Saranya Ji said in India*, I thought as he continued his explanation. She'd said the reason I had not found love was because I had it programmed into my mind that love was painful and so kept repeating the pattern. I wondered if Simon could help with that. I decided that – if he managed to help cure my insomnia – I might ask him.

'I can work on programming, that is adding a new belief, or reprogramming, that is taking something away like a fear or trait that isn't helpful.'

'In my case, not being able to sleep. When I lie down, I feel wired and can't unwind at all.'

'I understand and the more you don't sleep, the more it can become a vicious circle because your mind is saying, "I can't sleep" or, "I'm wired". That is the message your subconscious is receiving and so it makes it a reality. Thought is very powerful. What I'd work on is removing that belief and suggesting to your subconscious mind that you *can* sleep. Any questions so far?'

'I don't think so. Sounds good. I think I would like to go ahead if you have time today.' So far, I liked Simon. He had an easy way about him and his explanation made sense.

'I do. I always allow time for a bit of a chat beforehand and then the actual session.'

He told me to get comfortable and close my eyes. 'I want you to breathe deeply, into your diaphragm. Hold your breath there as long as possible, then let it out through parted lips. Good, you are beginning to feel calm. Again, breathe in . . .' As he continued talking, I felt myself beginning to relax. He had a very calming voice and it felt wonderful to stop for a short while and just be there listening, '. . . safe, you are calm, going deeper, five . . .' I was beginning to feel drowsy. 'And now you're going to, four, mentally relax one body part at a time, three . . . You feel a relaxing power in the toes of both feet, moving into arches, heels and up to ankles, completely relaxed now . . .'

For the rest of the session, I was vaguely aware of his voice, soothing, taking me deeper, I heard him count down from ten to one, then count down again. He repeated words about being able to sleep, to rest deeply, waking refreshed. His voice droned on and on . . .

'And three *two one, wide awake now* and *back* in the room.'

I opened my eyes to see Simon smiling opposite me. 'How are you feeling?'

'Fine. Good. I . . . Is that it? Did I fall asleep?'

'Not exactly,' said Simon.

'I felt as though I did, though I was vaguely aware of you talking. It's annoying that I can sleep here but not in my bed.' I checked my watch. It was an hour and a quarter since I'd arrived. 'Wow. I . . . So what now?'

'I'm going to get you a glass of water while you gather yourself, and then we'll have a further chat. After a first session, some people can feel slightly disorientated.' He left the room. I didn't feel odd in any way, in fact I felt great, like I'd just awoken from a good night's sleep. I was amazed that the time had passed in what felt like five minutes. While I waited, I had a look at the leaflets on the table in front of me. I read a little about Simon and then, on the back of his brochure, the list of issues he dealt with.

Hypnosis can help with:
- Confidence building
- Stopping smoking
- Stuttering
- Nail biting
- Fitness and health
- Weight loss
- Stress and anxiety problems
- Sexual problems
- Insomnia
- Motivation
- Phobias
- Relationship issues

Simon Jenkins is also trained in past life regression and tracing unresolved issues and deep-seated trauma.

Simon came back into the room and handed me a glass of water. 'I'd like you to do some homework,' he said as he sat down. 'It's to support the session today. Although you may not be aware of it, you have been telling your unconscious mind, I can't sleep or I'm not sleeping and, as I explained earlier, that became your reality. What I'd like you to do is simply to change that to "I can sleep" or "I sleep well and awake refreshed and alert". I want you to be aware if you find yourself going back to thinking, I can't sleep. Suggestions *must* be positive.'

'Like affirmations.' I knew all about them. Marcia was

into the power of positive thought and she was always giving me lines to say about feeling good and creating success.

Simon nodded. 'A mental mantra. Repeat what you want to say over and over as you go about your daily tasks; visualize it too. See yourself sleeping well and awakening fresh and alert and that will become your reality.'

'OK, I can give it a try.'

'Don't try, do. And lastly, if you have time, I'd like you to write down these affirmations; that way, you're doing everything you can to convince the subconscious mind that you have no trouble at all in sleeping. You're thinking positively, visualizing, and the repetition in the writing will help override the old beliefs.'

I held up the brochure. 'I see that you've also trained in past life regression.'

'I have. Why? Are you interested?'

'I . . . no, well, yes . . . I mean, do you really believe people can relive past lives, or that there's even such a thing?'

'Two questions. Yes, I do believe there is such a thing and that we have lived before. I believe that in the same way we discard one set of clothes and put on another, the soul or spirit discards the body we have worn at the time of death and enters a new one at the time of birth. These bodies that we wear are not our true selves, we are the being inside, the being that looks through the eyes, hears through the ears, feels through the skin. The body is merely the outer clothing of our true self and, in the same way that we change clothes daily, we change our outer body from life to life.'

'Wow. That's deep for a Monday evening.'

Simon laughed. 'To answer your other question, yes, I

believe some people can relive parts of their past lives, though not everyone. I have witnessed it many times.'

'How do you know that they're not just reliving something in their imagination or memory, a movie they saw on Netflix?'

'Because of the detail. People remember things they couldn't possibly have known from watching a film.'

'And why would anyone want to go back?'

'Because sometimes trauma is very deep. A pattern has been ingrained in the unconscious mind and it is negatively influencing events in this present life. Thought patterns like – I always suffer, or things always go wrong for me, and so on. These beliefs can come from a past life of having experienced such things but have been carried forward into the present life. Although it sounds as if past life regression is looking backwards, it is really to help a subject move on in their future.'

I thought about Saranya Ji's words again. 'So you're saying you could help remove a pattern that is negatively influencing this life?'

'If I can get to the root of the cause with my subject, yes. You sound very interested. Has something been troubling you?'

'I . . .' I glanced at my watch. My time with him was up. 'I'd like to make another appointment. I don't think I want to do past life regression, but would maybe be interested in removing what you call a negative pattern that I have in my subconscious.' I could hardly believe I was considering this, but I felt comfortable with Simon and if it worked, well and good, and if it didn't, at least I'd tried.

'We can certainly look at whatever has been troubling you.'

'Maybe we could talk about it next time?'

'Whenever you're ready and, in the meantime, we can continue to work on your insomnia – that is, if it is necessary.'

'Deal,' I said.

I left his treatment room feeling more rested than I had in weeks. When I got home, I googled Simon. It appeared he had done a degree in psychology, worked as a psychiatrist in a hospital for many years, then left to study hypnosis and had been working in that field for the last twelve years. He'd written three books about the subject, including one on past life regression. It also said that he gives talks around the world on the subject. I had a look at a couple of other sites listing hypnotherapists. Some sounded genuine, others sounded flaky.

So Simon's a bit of an expert in his field, I thought. *Maybe I could trust him to look back into my past? What have I got to lose?*

That night, I slept like a baby.

23

On Tuesday morning, I called for the results of my PSA test. 'All fine. Nothing to worry about,' said the doctor's receptionist.

Excellent, I thought as I clicked my phone shut. *So all systems go.*

Next on the list was to pack a few things and find some temporary accommodation, a place to hang my hat until I had decided where I wanted to be more permanently. A lot of that will depend on Bea, of course. Just a few more things to attend to, then I shall make my move.

24

When I got home from work on Wednesday evening, Stuart was sitting on my doorstep with Monty by his side. He got up to greet me as I got out of the car.

'Hello stranger,' I said.

'Been working late?' he asked as he approached and gave me a hug.

'I have. You been here long?'

'Few minutes. I was just texting you. I'm about to take Monty for his evening walk and wondered if you wanted to join us.'

'Sure. I could do with some fresh air. Give me two minutes to change my shoes.'

*

Stuart drove us down to Cherry Tree Park where we let Monty off the lead and strolled along behind him. I filled him in on the latest on the shop and house and he listened, nodding every now and then.

'I think you're going to be OK, Bea,' he said when I'd finished. 'But have you any idea what you want to do yet?'

I shook my head.

'You going to tell me who that chap was in the Coffee Cup?'

'I am so sorry about that Stuart and missing our walk, I really am. He turned up out of the blue and it kind of threw me, time-wise.'

Stuart shrugged. 'Old flame?'

'He was, a long time ago.'

'So what does he want now?'

'Nothing. He's just passing through so looked me up. He'll be returning to Thailand soon, I reckon.'

Stuart put his arm around me and gave me a squeeze. 'Thailand? Long way away.'

'Exactly.'

'And do you still have feelings for him?'

I knew I could confide in Stuart. He'd been there with a listening ear and kind words many times. 'Mainly hesitation. He was always a restless soul and I never knew where I stood with him.'

'I wouldn't want to see you get hurt.'

'Don't worry. I doubt if he'll even get in touch again. I'm not going to get involved.'

'Do you want a relationship?' he asked. He still had his arm around me and, although it felt good and natural, I suddenly thought, *What if someone saw us?* His wife? Or someone who knew both of them? Although it was innocent, it could be misconstrued. I pulled away slightly and Stuart removed his arm.

'Do I want a relationship? Possibly, but things change as you get older, don't they? You find you want different things.'

'Sure, and we should find the time to identify them.'

'What about you, Stuart? What do you want? I mean in life.'

'Me? I've always wanted to play music so I've started. A few old codgers like me have formed a band. OK, so we'll never be the greatest, but I love it.'

'Can I come and see you play?'

'Hah, if we ever play in public, I'll let you know.'

As we continued on our way, I thought how it always felt so easy with Stuart and how much I was enjoying just strolling along, two people and a dog, just normal. 'It would be nice to have the companionship,' I said, 'that's for sure, someone to do the everyday things with.'

'Companionship? That sounds a bit dull.'

'OK, more than that, but I've got used to being on my own too, set in my ways. I'm not sure I want to share my space with someone. I've got used to making my own decisions and not having to compromise, like I did with Richard the control freak. I like that aspect, but then there are times when yes, I feel alone. I guess I want it all. A lover who's there when I want him to be, then disappears when I want space, like that card that was going around a few years back – what's the definition of the perfect lover? An Adonis who makes love all evening then turns into a pizza.'

Stuart laughed. 'I'm sure you'd make it work if you were with the right person.'

'Yeah, like that's going to happen. No. I think I just have to accept that I'm going to be on my own.'

'Never too late . . .' said Stuart, and was about to say

something else when he took off after Monty, having seen that he was in pursuit of a squirrel.

Once we had Monty back on the lead, we headed for the far end of the park so we could walk through the streets back to the car. As we left the gate and found the alleyway up to Southern Road, I realized that we would be near where Grace Harris was supposed to have lived.

'Can we take a short detour?' I asked when we reached the main road. 'Just down here. I want to look at a property.'

'Sure. Why? Are you thinking of buying round here?'

'Oh no, nothing like that. Now OK, this is going to sound crazy . . .' I filled him in on what Saranya Ji had told me about Grace and Billy, then the research I'd done to find them, which had resulted in coming across the whole Harris family at the address nearby.

'Are you telling me you believed this woman?' Stuart asked.

'Oh god no, not that I was Grace, but Saranya Ji got their names and situations from somewhere and, having looked into it a little, I have to admit their story captured my imagination. They've become more real to me and I've enjoyed the challenge of working out where they might have lived, and so on.'

'A wartime romance, but it sounds like it ended so sadly if Billy didn't come back.'

'I know. That's what struck me. Forgotten people and yet they had their story, like so many.'

'And do you have an inkling who this soulmate might be? Your Michael chap?'

'*No*. Why? Do you believe in reincarnation?'

Stuart shrugged. 'Why not? My belief is that we know

so little about the big issues. I don't discount the idea of rebirth, nor do I believe. I'm somewhere in the middle and will happily admit, I just don't know.'

'Me too.'

'Though I have to say when my kids, Fi and Jack, were little, Janet and I always said that Fi was an old soul. From an early age, there was a wisdom in her eyes as she took everything in, whereas Jack, first time on the planet without a clue what was going on. He hasn't changed much.' He laughed. 'So why are we going to look at this house? Are you sure you're not more taken in than you're letting on and want to see if anything resonates?'

'No, no, of course not,' I lied as we reached Northern Road. I did want to see if it seemed familiar. 'I've driven this way a million times. I think if I was going to feel something, I would have done so by now. Curiosity, that's all, honest.'

'What number is it?' asked Stuart.

'176.'

We continued walking along the street. Number 176 was a semi-detached Edwardian house on the left with a small front garden.

'So there it is,' said Stuart as we gazed up at the first floor. He closed his eyes and began to sway. 'Oo, I think I'm getting something, yes, going back . . .' He started laughing.

'Oh stop it. Be serious. And, even if I was looking to see if it was familiar, which I'm not, I can't say I'm getting any sense of déjà vu, apart from it being a route I've taken many times.'

'I like the look of the property, though,' said Stuart. 'I

wonder how long this Grace lived here. Did you find out any more about her or the family?'

'Oh yes, a couple of nights ago I looked on the census taken in 1951. Grace wasn't listed on there. It was just her parents and her sister, in fact . . .'

'So maybe they still live here? What do you think?'

'I think her parents will be long gone.'

'Yes, but not the sister. Do your maths. You said that the sister Lily was only just older than Grace who was born in 1925. She might just be around still.'

'Spoken like a true accountant. I guess she might be, but she'd be very old.'

'So go and ask,' said Stuart as he opened the gate.

'No! You can't just go barging in there asking something like that . . . Come back. What would we say?'

Too late. He'd already rung the doorbell and I had to admit I was curious too. He rang the bell again but there was only silence from within. 'Nobody home,' he said. 'Never mind. You can always come back.'

'I don't think so.' I'd had a better idea. I could look on Zoopla or Rightmove. Zoopla tells a bit about the history of a house, when the last sale was, and so on. If there had been a sale in recent years, it was very likely that the property details would still be on line. I could see inside the rooms, the kitchen, the upstairs, the bedrooms, and so on.

*

After Stuart had dropped me off, I went straight online and looked for 176 Northern Road on Zoopla, under current house prices and values. It listed all the houses along the road, stating their worth plus any recent sales. When it came to 176, it said current value not known, which I knew meant there hadn't been a recent sale. *Even if there had been*, I thought, *and I'd found recent photos, the house had probably been updated and redecorated many times since the 1930s, or whenever it was that Grace lived there. Owners might have knocked walls down since, built on, changed windows, extended.*

'Ah well, it was worth a try,' I said as I closed down my laptop. 'I seem to have come to a dead end.' I laughed. 'Hah. Dead end. Funny.'

25

'How are you feeling today, Bea?' asked Simon, as I took my seat opposite him for my second appointment.

'Glad to get out of the rain outside,' I replied. 'And all good otherwise, whatever you did seems to have helped and I've been sleeping well.' I didn't tell him that I'd almost cancelled the session about ten times because part of me wondered how, in the space of a few weeks, I'd gone from sane business woman to the sort of person who was considering talking to a stranger about patterns in the subconscious mind. My Bea from last year wouldn't have entertained it for a second yet, here I was, the beginning of February, about to broach the subject with Simon.

'Excellent.'

'Plus some of the issues that were causing the lack of sleep are beginning to be resolved.'

'So do you want to have another session on relaxation? I sensed last time you were here that there was something else you wanted to talk about.'

'I do, did. Er . . . bit awkward. It was something you

said, about patterns that can repeat in someone's life due to a deep-seated belief that can have a negative impact on life.'

'You think you have such a belief?'

'Maybe, probably, yes.'

Simon laughed. 'Maybe, probably. So what is this belief?'

'It's to do with relationships. I'm currently single, have been for a while, and I wondered if somehow I might be sabotaging them myself by my thoughts . . . God, this sounds mad now that I'm actually saying it.'

'Not at all. Makes perfect sense to me. We create our lives from our thoughts, our choices. Opportunities can arise in life, but really how they play out is how we respond to them and that applies to relationships too.'

'I saw a psychic on a recent trip to India. She said something similar: that first comes destiny, and then our free will in how to respond to it. She said that I have it ingrained in my unconscious mind that love is painful and, because of that, I keep recreating that pattern.'

'And you believed her?'

'Not at first. My more rational side said it's all nonsense and that she probably told the same story to everyone she saw – or something similar, at least.'

'You were cynical?'

'I guess.'

'That's not a bad thing; in fact I think it's wise to question, but you mentioned your "more rational side". Does that mean that you have another side? Not so rational?'

'I suppose I do, and often they're at war with each other.'

Simon nodded. 'Indeed. Do you believe that love is painful?'

'Partly. The getting-left-behind part, not the falling-in-love stage.'

'Is that what has happened? That you've got left behind? Is that what you've come to believe always happens?'

'It's been my experience, so yes, I do, but I can't be the only person who has been left or abandoned. We can't all be making that happen by our thoughts.'

'Indeed. Sometimes bad things just happen, a part of life. Loved ones die, move on, meet someone else.'

'Thing is, what if I've met the right one then ruined it all by this subconscious attitude that I have?'

'Is that what you think has happened?'

'I'm not sure, but the idea of that has made me think, and my friend Marcia won't let it drop.'

'How's that made you feel?'

'Pressured to do something about it, to a certain degree, and the session with Saranya Ji, she was the psychic, was a birthday present. I'd hurt Marcia's feelings if I dismissed it all.'

'What else did this psychic say?'

'I . . . It sounds insane.'

'Believe me, I've heard it all in here. Whatever you tell me is in the strictest confidence, plus the more direct we are with each other, the more you will get out of the sessions. I am not here to persuade you into anything. I am here to guide and to help.'

'Saranya Ji said that in a previous life, I was . . .' I filled him in on the whole story, 'so if there's any truth in any of it and if I am to find this man now, how will I know him? I find myself looking at everyone from the cab driver to the postman and thinking: is it you? But he could be in

Australia or married and I might as well not waste my time. Really, I don't know what to think or do.'

Simon nodded and looked thoughtful. 'I can understand your dilemma – what to believe? But from what I've read and witnessed here with clients, it does appear that souls are reborn in clusters.'

'Clusters?'

'In families, groups of friends, bound together through time; maybe because of unfinished business, so the chances are that he isn't too far away or that you have already come across him. A daughter may be a mother in another life or a grandparent may return as a son.'

'Really? That sounds far-fetched to me, or wishful thinking.'

'Why not? We don't actually know a lot about where we've come from or how we got here, do we? But haven't you ever had that feeling when you've met someone: that they're familiar; like you've met them before but can't place them?'

'I did with my friend Marcia. I think she's hoping that the search for Billy and Grace might lead to me finding a soulmate.'

'I see. You do know that if you *do* find him, he might not be what you expect. A soulmate can be the one to teach you the hardest lessons; someone who challenges as well as cherishes you. It might not all be candles and roses, because a meeting of an equal soul may confront you, press all your buttons.'

'A few of my exes did that all right.' I thought of Richard and hoped that it wasn't going to turn out to be him.

'If you did go ahead with a regression and remembered

something from Grace and Billy's time, that might help you recognize him.'

'That's what I wondered. I mean, the Internet can come up with birth or death certificates and census records, but what do they really prove? Nothing. But if memories of another time are still inside me, as you said, as part of my soul's journey, if I remembered being Grace, then that would convince me more than any census record or piece of old documentation.'

'Possibly, but regression isn't for everyone, only if it's appropriate and comes up spontaneously in a session. It can't be forced. The unconscious mind tends to throw up what is most useful to us, and that might not be going back to another life.'

'Does anyone ever go back and then get stuck there?'

'No. There's no danger of that.'

'So what do you do?'

'A past life session is similar to what we did last time, but I would guide you to go back to certain key points in your life, to see if we can determine at what points the negative patterns began. With you, we'd try to identify where the belief about love that you carry has come from, and then reprogramme it to something more positive. But each session is different, just as each person who comes here is an individual. I can't guarantee anything but, if you're willing, we can see what happens.'

I took a deep breath. It felt daring to be trying something so new and different to anything I'd done before. I almost laughed as the theme tune to *Star Trek* played in my head along with the voiceover – about going boldly where no man had gone before. When we were fifteen, Marcia had a pair of knickers with the line embroidered on them. She got me a pair too, though – because I was still a virgin – mine said 'The Final Frontier', with an arrow pointing down.

'I think I'd like to try.'

'Well, we can see where this session takes us but, as I said, it will only happen if it's going to be useful and the time is right. Your unconscious mind and higher self will decide that and you can trust them.'

'Can you bring me back at any point if I don't like it?' Despite my curiosity, I felt a rush of anxiety. Did I really know what I was letting myself in for? No. And, despite having read up about Simon, I hardly knew him.

'Nothing can happen without your consent, and although I will be making suggestions, it will really be you who is in control,' said Simon. 'When you're ready, I want you to close your eyes. Let's start by getting you to relax. I'll make some further suggestions to reinforce that you continue to sleep well, then take it from there.'

I closed my eyes and he began to talk me through the breathing, then the countdown. At first I felt tense and was particularly aware of it as he talked me through letting go of different areas around my body. I willed each part to let go and, after a few minutes, I found myself relaxing a bit, my limbs beginning to feel heavy as I listened to his soothing voice.

'Good, good,' Simon continued. 'Keep focusing, safe and warm, two, relaxed and floating . . .'

I was vaguely aware of his voice droning on in the background as he instructed me to imagine that I was in a lift going down, down . . . Going down a set of stairs, further down, down . . . 'Now I want you to go back to a time when you felt very happy and safe, a time of comfort.'

I immediately recalled a time with my parents. We were on a beach with our dog, Jack. 'How old are you Bea?'

'About six.' I didn't feel as if I was hypnotized, just recapturing a memory from my past, albeit one I hadn't recalled for many years. It felt good.

'And where are you?'

'Southport Beach. The sea is miles out. It doesn't matter.'

'Good, good. Now, I want you to go back to another time. A time when you felt let down. A time when you felt loss.'

Another memory came to mind. I was older. Our cat, Samantha, had just died. Matthew and I were in the back garden, digging a hole in which to bury her.

'How old are you now, Bea?'

'Eight.'

'And where are you?'

'Outside, it's raining. We're sad. Our cat died.' My mind flashed forward as if scanning for other times when I felt abandoned or sad. I remembered the time my parents left England, then soon after when Marcia had gone, then Michael, Graham; the sense of loss weighing down on me as more memories loomed like dark, threatening shadows, ready to emerge from some deep, buried place inside.

'OK, now I want you to relax, let go and move away from those times,' Simon continued, and I was glad to leave that pit of recollections behind. 'You're safe and warm, going further down . . .' Again his voice droned on, and as I drifted I felt I was beginning to fall asleep. The room felt warm, I was oh so comfortable. My body felt so heavy, so . . . 'Further back, down, down . . .' I felt myself floating. I could see a mist in front of me.

'Bea, where are you?'

'Nowhere,' I wanted to say, 'on your couch, here in London.' I knew where I was but to say so felt like too much effort, like my whole being was made of wet sand.

'Deeper, down, feeling relaxed . . .' For a while, I wasn't aware of his voice, just of a lovely sensation of drifting, safe and warm, on soft clouds. 'Where are you now, Bea?'

'Not sure. It's misty. Very comfy.'

He gave further instructions and I felt myself letting go, letting go. 'Good, good. Now where are you?'

The mist began to clear and I had a sense of being somewhere, though not sure where. I struggled to see.

'Where are you, Bea? What do you see?'

'I don't know.'

'OK. I want you to look down at your feet. Tell me what you are wearing on your feet.'

I tried to look down but everywhere was misty, and I couldn't see through it. I wanted to imagine my feet, shoes. I wanted to see something from Grace's time. I felt uncomfortable and felt myself stir out of the pleasant reverie I'd been in. 'I'm sorry, Simon, I feel I ought to say something about Grace, because I've been told about her, but I don't feel or see anything. I don't want to lie to you.'

'And you mustn't. Don't try and force this. Lean back, keep focusing on your breath, Bea. Of course you mustn't lie. Only what's appropriate will come up. Relax. Let go. Trust. You don't have to do anything or make anything happen. If the memory of Grace is inside of you, it's there, if it's not, it's not. If it is to be useful to you to remember her, then you will. You don't have to do a thing. Like sleep, you can't make it happen, it just happens. You can't dictate your dreams or who you are going to dream about, so let go, let go, let go. You don't have to control this. Your unconscious mind is your friend; trust in it. It will lead you where you need to go, so just relax, let go.'

As I listened to his voice, I felt myself drifting off again. It felt good to be told that I didn't have to do anything. I felt relieved.

'Breathing in, breathing out . . . relaxed and feeling calm. Moving down down . . .' I was vaguely aware of him talking about another lift, another set of stairs, something about a door. I felt like laughing again. *I must be so far underground by now that I should have reached the centre of the earth*, I thought as I followed his instructions and fell back into the peaceful doze. 'Good, good, safe, warm, comfortable.'

His voice became distant, or maybe he'd stopped talking. It felt quiet, then suddenly it was like watching frames of a film inside my head – or were they pieces of a mosaic? That was it: a mosaic or a jigsaw puzzle. I could see images from my life, people I knew so well, all there from different times, but I was seeing them all at the same time. My life streaming back, moving but not moving. Odd but not scary. Yes, I was looking at a mosaic made up of pieces of my life. I felt overjoyed; there were all my pets going back in time: Boris, Casper, Jack, the cats Smokey and Samantha. Friends were there, too, they had their own colours; each person was on a different piece of the mosaic. Marcia's was autumnal, reds, browns and oranges; Heather was in vibrant greens; Pete was blue. Old friends: Jane, Greta, Carol, Rosie. I could see friends I'd known but had lost touch with over the years: Bernie, Fran, Jean, Annie. In one mosaic piece, I saw a scene from my life. I was in Harrods with Marcia, up on high stools, drinking hot chocolate. In another, at a wedding with Heather, talking to her friends. In a car with my brother Matthew, him driving so fast, my foot on an imaginary brake. Back, back. It was a moving mosaic, beautiful; vibrant, as if lit from within. There was Marcia at school in sixth form. Another segment shows us on the bus, on a back seat with a bag of Liquorice Allsorts. We're laughing until it hurt.

'Where are you, Bea?'

'Remembering friends. Time is moving back but also standing still. I can see everyone I know, all at once, like they're in a living mosaic.' At dinner with Richard, in bed with Jon, bicycling with Graham, singing with Michael: they were all there; all my past lovers in a jigsaw made from mosaic pieces. Was a piece missing? Where was it? Or was I imagining a gap? Oh, there's my brother, I'm studying in Central Library with him. And Sam, stoned again, headphones on, crashed out on the sofa. I wanted to laugh. Some of the mosaics were so perfect, a tiny embodiment of a moment. Bruno. Jim. Andrew. Everyone was there.

Again I was drifting, vaguely aware of Simon's voice in the room on a grey day in London. I could see fractured images. I'm in my bedroom with Marcia, doing a makeover. I see a bicycle in the hall. Matthew's. It was always in the way. So clear: red, black and silver. I hadn't thought of it for years. In a paddling pool at home. Dad leaving for work. Mum cooking. I could smell burnt toast. Lying in a cot. Nice. I am a mosaic baby, a piece of a whole mosaic picture that is constantly changing yet stays the same. 'Loss,' I hear Simon say. He's saying something about loss. I don't want to think about that and then I feel it, ripping through me; more than that, it hurts. I want to move away from the feeling. I become aware of another mosaic, to the left and separate from the one I was looking at. It's darker, greyer, and I am in one of the pieces of it. It's not such a big mosaic but I see a woman: is it me? I'm not sure. On a bed, giving birth. Can't be me. I have no children. I see her again in another part of the mosaic in a garden, a baby with dark hair toddling towards her. It's not me but I feel her as me.

'Where are you, Bea?' asked Simon.

'Not sure. Looking at mosaics.'

'How many are there?'

'Two, no . . .' I looked around and saw that I was in a spacious, light hall.

'Can you describe them?' Simon asked.

'There are many mosaics. It's an art gallery. I am in one room in an art gallery. I get the feeling that it is my room, though, because I can see through openings that there are other people in adjacent galleries looking at their mosaics. 'Many. Maybe fifteen maybe twenty.'

'What do they show?'

'I can't see the others clearly. Mine shows my life. People. Places. Colour.'

'You said two mosaics . . . what does the second one show?'

I looked at the darker mosaic again but felt myself getting anxious. I could see the woman: she had light brown, soft, wavy hair to her shoulders; she was in a garden, by a tree, bent over, she was weeping. *I know that garden. Where have I seen it before?* I felt my chest tighten; it was hard to breathe.

'Bea, Bea, relax, breathe, look back at the first mosaic. What do you see?'

I felt the tension ease almost immediately, but the mosaics were beginning to fade. I wanted to sleep and began to drift again, though was still aware of Simon's voice in the distance and I felt myself begin to emerge as if coming up through water. It felt good, there were circles of light, and I was swimming through them, so beautiful '. . . on the count of five, you will be awake. Four, coming up, coming up.' I got the sensation of being pulled up from the depths of water, pulled by my solar plexus; propelled up. 'Three, further, at peace with life, two, waking up now.' I was flying, up, up. 'Three, two, back into the room and one. *Wide awake.*'

I'd landed. Back in the room. I opened my eyes and smiled at Simon. 'Wow. That was amazing.'

26

'Sounds like you fell asleep and had a particularly vivid dream,' said Heather the next day in the shop after I'd told her about my session with Simon.

'That's what I thought, but I know I wasn't asleep. I was aware of being in the room and of Simon's voice.'

'Snoozing then. I'm not dissing it. I think the unconscious mind can throw up fantastic creative ideas during that in-between sleep and waking state. Loads of artists and writers say that they get inspiration from their dreams. It does sound like you went into a dreamlike state. So, the second mosaic felt different?'

'It did. Like the first one was everything to do with this life, all the people I know or have known and places and experiences, and the second one was something to do with me – but what, I don't know. I remember telling Simon that I felt as if I was trying too hard to remember Grace because I'd been told about her. He said if it was in there, it was in there, so I didn't need to force it. And the mosaic pieces because I've been thinking about puzzles. Maybe I saw the second mosaic and the woman in it because I'd been thinking about Grace; you know, like often if you've been watching something on TV, it gets into your dreams somehow.'

'Makes sense, and your subconscious came up with that amazing interpretation of it all. And you say everyone had a colour?'

'Yes, you were shades of green or rather vibrations of green. It was weird, not in a bad way – beautiful, in fact.'

'Well, I'm glad I am beautiful in your unconscious mind, that's a relief. And are you going to have another session?'

'I'm not sure.'

'OK, I've just had an idea. Let's say for a moment that there is anything in it, and that the first mosaic represented this life and the second mosaic your last life, OK?'

'I thought you didn't believe in past lives?'

'I don't, but I do believe in dreams and the power of the subconscious mind. I love the idea that it came up with the mosaic of your life and I think you got that idea, not just because of your love of puzzles and jigsaws but also from your trip to the City Palace in India, remember? You showed me loads of photos of the beautiful mosaics there.'

'Of course. I never thought of that.'

'It doesn't matter. As you said, what you've been doing on a certain day can get into your dreams, and India and all the impressions you took in there are bound to be stored in your mind somewhere, so it's not really surprising that your unconscious or subconscious used them. Anyway, here's an idea. If you could go back to that art gallery room in another hypnosis session, study the first mosaic again, take note and remember the colours of old boyfriends, then go to the second mosaic and see if there's any piece of that mosaic that matches with the first one, then bingo, you'll have found him. Like those games we used to play when we were kids: match the similarities or like *Where's Wally?* You have to spot the soulmate amongst all the pieces in the second mosaic, so it's not *Where's Wally?* It's Where's Billy?'

'That's brilliant, Heather. But what if I don't ever go back there?'

'Then your unconscious mind might serve up something else. As the hypnotherapist told you, it throws up whatever is most useful.'

'Sounds like a cat vomiting,' I said.

27

We were sitting in Marcia's Volkswagen Polo outside her house the day after my hypnosis session. On my knee, I had the paper with the address that I had for William Jackson. 'I still can't believe you went to see Grace's house without me,' she said as she started up the car.

I laughed. 'We were passing. I didn't mean to leave you out. Anyway, you've been out of action with that virus.'

'Not my fault.' Marcia stuck out her bottom lip like a five-year-old. 'So, which way?'

'Kentish Town. Down the hill and I'll direct you from there.'

'OK, and tell me everything on the way, how's it all going?' said Marcia, as she started up the car.

'I've accepted an offer on the house.'

'What? *Already?* That's amazing.'

'They offered the asking price so we've exchanged solicitors' details. They're a sweet couple, newlyweds, who came to see it before it even went on the market. Although there are a few other interested parties, none of them are proceedable buyers.'

'So will you take the house off the market?'

'The estate agent says to leave it on a while because even what appears to be the most safe and sound transaction can fall through at the last minute. People don't get mortgages or they see other places they prefer. He said we should generate interest and be ready with a back-up list in case things go awry.'

'Sensible man. So if the sale does go ahead, that will ease things up for you, won't it?'

'Financially it will, but we'll see how the rest of the week goes.'

'I'd say you've done the right thing, because I always thought this was dead time for selling houses, so to get an offer is good.'

'That's what I thought – that things only really picked up in the property market in spring – but apparently that's exactly why I've had a good response. A lot of people are waiting for the better weather before marketing their places, so there's not a lot on.'

'Have your neighbours been in for a nose? No doubt they want to know what's happening.'

'Curiously no, and all's quiet from Jon. I haven't seen him for a few weeks either.'

'He's probably away.'

'Yes, probably gone skiing with one of his many.'

'Well, at least you won't be bothered by him and his comings and goings any more when you move. And how's it going with the shop?'

'It's been good there too. I'm almost tempted to get more merchandise because we've been selling out so fast.'

'So everything will be OK then?'

'If the house sale goes through, then yes. I can repay outstanding loans and – for the first time in years – be debt free.'

'Are you tempted to look for another shop?'

'Curiously, I'm not. I want to consolidate, and then who knows? Maybe I will begin again in a different location, but I'm not going to rush into anything.'

'Good girl,' said Marcia as we reached the traffic lights near the tube station. 'Has there been much interest in anyone buying the building where the shop is?'

'A few people interested but no one definite; in fact, there are a few premises standing empty now. I don't think people can afford the rising rates and rents there, not just me. But for now, I can stay until it sells. Over the lights,' I said as I checked my phone and then the street names. 'Here, coming up, the street on the left, then we look for number thirty-three.'

Marcia turned the car into the side street and, as we drove along, I looked out for house numbers. There was a row of terraced houses, a medical centre, a school, a pub, a church on the left side and, on the right-hand side, a few houses: number three, five, seven, then a large block of flats.

'It's not here,' I said, as Marcia found a space, pulled in and parked. We got out and walked up and down the street. It wasn't a long one and was clear that there was no number 33.

'I reckon it's been knocked down,' said Marcia, as she indicated the tall block of flats. 'It could well have been over there because the houses that are on that side end at number seven.'

I felt disappointed. I wasn't sure what I'd thought we'd find but, whatever it was, wasn't there.

'Do you feel anything?' asked Marcia, as we looked up and down the street. 'Any sense of recognition?'

'Nope. Just a street in London like any other I've been down.'

Marcia began to walk towards the pub. 'Let's go and ask in there.'

'Ask what?'

'You'd have made a lousy detective,' said Marcia. 'You check out the area, ask around, look for clues.'

'Well I suppose at least we can get a drink,' I said, as we found the entrance then went inside. The pub was empty apart from a bald old man sitting at the bar. Marcia ordered two glasses of wine from a young girl with pink hair behind the counter.

'Don't suppose you know when that block of flats further down the road was built, do you?' Marcia asked the barmaid.

'Nah. I just work here Tuesdays.'

I smiled to myself and wondered what that actually had to do with anything and, maybe if she'd worked on Thursdays, she could have answered our question.

'I can tell you,' said the old man. 'There was a row of terraced houses on that side of the road, all bombed in 1941, and they put that eyesore of a block up in 1960. Used to be a lovely street this, families out, a real sense of community; all gone now.'

'Did you live in the terrace?' Marcia asked.

'Not me but I knew people.'

'I don't suppose you knew a Jackson family, number thirty-three?'

The man shook his head. 'Can't recall that name,' said the man. 'But if you say they lived locally, they might have a record of them in the church.'

As soon as we sat down with our drinks, Marcia got out a sheet of paper. I glanced down and saw that it was the list of past lovers that I'd emailed to her.

'I have a bit of an update for you,' she said. 'Pete's been on the case and found a couple on the list. So . . .'

We both bent our heads over the page as Marcia went through.

'Number one. Kevin Grisham. Pete's found him and got an address in Kent. From what he could discover, he was married, has three kids, but currently single.'

'Wow, it's amazing you found him.'

'Number two. Bruno Romano.'

My brother's exchange student. 'Matthew might know where he is,' I said. 'I'll email him, promise, I just haven't got round to it yet.'

'OK. Number three, Sam Gorman, the dope head.'

'I'm friends with his sister Kate on Facebook, so I'll contact her. I will, promise. It's not been top of my list lately.'

'Number four. Jed Nash from art college. Pete found a website of his work and an Instagram account.'

'Let's have a look then,' I said, and got out my phone. 'Although I don't hold out much hope for him as we never really got together. He was more someone I admired from afar.' I soon found his page on Instagram. There was a link to a website displaying his paintings – huge colourful canvases which showed well against the white walls of three interlinked rooms, which reminded me of the art gallery rooms I'd seen in my hypnosis session. There was only one photo of Jed, professionally taken, by the look of it. He looked great: slim, fit; he had lost most of his hair but looked very dapper.

'Try Facebook,' said Marcia, 'see, there's a link at the bottom of the website to his page.' I did as instructed and clicked on the link.

It was easy enough to scroll down and look at his photos; he clearly had them all on public not private. He looked nice, attractive . . .

'Ah . . .' said Marcia, and started laughing.

I peered more closely at the photo she was looking at. 'Ah. Yes. Oh . . .' The Facebook page showed a wedding, smiling faces gathered outside a country location. Jed and his partner, a nice-looking man with a goatee beard. 'So he's married and gay. I always suspected as much. Well, good for him, he looks happy. So . . . another one off the list, I guess, though I would like to connect up just to make contact.'

I decided to get in touch with him regardless. I'd always liked Jed; maybe we could be friends after all this time.

'Number five. Ah. Michael O'Connor. Has he been in touch since his visit?'

'Not a dickie bird.'

'Well he's staying on the list, isn't he?'

'I guess.'

'Joe Wilding. He wasn't on your list but surely he's a contender? Pete has his current address. He's still in North London. Married with two kids.'

'Really?' I had heard a rumour that he'd got hitched up but I'd always imagined Joe being the eternal bachelor.

'On or off the list?'

'Off. Whatever we had to play out is over.'

'Number six. Graham.'

I shrugged and Marcia didn't pursue it.

'And Richard Benson. Off the list?'

'Off. Definitely.'

'OK. So . . . there are fewer options now,' said Marcia as she turned over her page. 'We have Kevin, Bruno, Sam, Michael and Graham. I think we have to have Graham on the list, despite what happened, so that makes five.'

Six, don't leave Jon off, said some rebellious part of my mind that a more sensible side of me immediately tried to quash.

We finished our drinks, thanked the man for his help, then went back onto the street. Marcia headed straight for the church.

'But what do you hope to find out?' I said as I trooped after her. 'The idea was to see if I felt any sense of familiarity, which I don't.'

'We might find a record of the family in the church, if anyone knew them; meet some ancient old priest who baptized the family, married any of them, buried them. We could find their graves.'

'Billy might not have a grave in this country if he was killed in action.'

'Grace's then.'

'*No*, finding Billy's or Grace's grave, soulmates or not, is a bit too Goth and spooky for me, Marcia.'

'Well, I'm fascinated even if you're not,' said Marcia. 'I've been reading up a lot on reincarnation since we went to India. Some of it makes perfect sense – like one man just couldn't get into sex with his wife, even though he loved her. It turned out he had been a priest in a past life and had taken a vow of celibacy, so sex felt improper.'

I burst out laughing. 'Oh come on, Marcia, you don't really believe that? Sounds like an almighty good excuse for not being able to perform in the bedroom.'

Marcia looked miffed by my reaction. 'Might be true. There was another case of a woman who was told that her husband had been her brother in a past life; that was the end of *their* marriage, too.'

I cracked up again. 'God, I'm loving this. What fabulous, creative excuses to get out of a tricky situation and a great change from the "let's just be friends" line. You can say, it's not you, it's me, I was a nun in a previous life and just can't do sex; or, so sorry, but I can't get past the fact that you were my dad in a past life and sex just seems . . . wrong.'

In the end, Marcia laughed too. 'I guess when you put it like that, it does sound a bit mad. Maybe that's why we don't remember. It would cause way too many problems.'

She opened the small wrought-iron gate and walked through to the church door. She tried the handle. It opened. Inside was cool, calm and quiet. No one appeared to be about and Marcia and I spent a few minutes looking around at the various inscriptions on the walls.

'Hey, come and look at this,' said Marcia from the front.

I went to join her and saw that she was looking at a memorial for men who had died in the Second World War. At the top of the stone was a carving of a soldier, then beneath that were two long lists of names.

'So sad,' said Marcia as we scanned the names. 'There

are five here with the same surname. The war must have wiped out whole families and, oh . . . look, there he is!'

I looked at where she was pointing, on the list on the right-hand side, towards the bottom. William Jackson. 'I wonder if his parents saw this,' I said, 'and did they survive the bombing of their house?'

'And if Grace saw it? She might have stood right here where we are now,' said Marcia.

'I doubt it; these kinds of memorials were probably put up quite a long time after the war.'

We stood for a moment in silence. Marcia put her arm around me. 'Sad,' she said. 'But I reckon he must have come in here as a boy, attended Sunday services with his parents. You might have been planning to get married in here.'

'You mean Grace might have been and, if she was, there are much nicer churches in the area for a wedding.'

'Ah, so you are beginning to see it as a possibility?'

'No, not that I was Grace . . . but I don't doubt her or Billy's existence and I feel great sympathy for what they must have been through.'

'But what about your hypnosis experience and the woman in the second mosaic?'

'I think that was my brain putting it together. It's no proof, Marcia. It's not like I have her memories or came up with anything I didn't already know or had been told. As well as the fact that I've been to the street where Grace lived, Billy's street, this church, even the place that was probably their pub, and nothing resonates, not even slightly. What I am drawn to is their story.'

'And what Grace lost.'

'Yes, absolutely.'

Marcia looked at me closely. 'Love was painful for her.'

'It was.'

'Must resonate with you that, that feeling of loss.'

'It . . . and you can stop it right now,' I said. 'It's a story, from the past, captured my imagination a little, end of.'

'Sure,' said Marcia. 'If you say so.' She had a smug look on her face. Smacking her over her head in a church was probably not the best place. I'd wait until we were outside.

28

'In blue or red, sir?' the shop assistant asked when he saw me holding up shirts against myself in a mirror. 'Haven't a clue.'

Maybe it wasn't such a good idea to come shopping, but I thought that it was about time I updated my image, bought a few new clothes. I needed to make an effort. It was when I got to the men's underwear department that I started to feel my age. There were rows and rows of them in every colour and design. I'd always been a boxer man but I'm told that's old fashioned now, bit like my worn and weary body. My knees creak. My back goes if I exert myself too much. Will Bea find me attractive – sexy, even? Good sense of humour, that's what women like. Getting my kit off, that might give her a laugh. Not that I'm overweight or unfit . . . It's not just women who worry about their looks. A haircut? Some new aftershave? I feel like a teenager again, unsure what to wear, what to say, how to approach a girl I have a crush on.

Recent events have been a wake-up call, that's for sure. Life is short, as they say, nothing lasts forever, and it's time to make some changes to the script and the characters within it. Now I'm truly a single man again, it's time to say goodbye to many elements of my old life and really think about where I want to be and who with. Time to live life to the fullest, hopefully with Bea Brooks. Time to declare my feelings for her, but not just yet; I don't want her to find me with a suitcase full of old moth-eaten clothes and a bad haircut. But, in the meantime, I could let her know that someone's out here, thinking of her. I shall send her something. A gift? Flowers? Poetry? What? A grand gesture from a man presently in need of a makeover. I'll rack my slightly befuddled brain for something that Bea would like. Will I say who it's from? Not yet. I need to check out if I have competition, so I shall be her mystery man for a while yet.

29

Five minutes after I'd got home later that evening, the doorbell rang. I opened it to see a delivery man with a bunch of white flowers.

'Someone's thinking of you,' he said as he handed them over, then took off back down the steps. Twenty gardenias. The scent was stunning. I closed the door and looked for a card. *Thinking of you*, it said. No name. Who could they be from? I looked for the number of the florist's on the card and called them.

'Your company just delivered some flowers to me. There was no name,' I said.

The woman at the other end took my details. 'No. No name.'

'Please could you tell me who sent them?'

'I am sorry, but we are not allowed to pass on that kind of information without the buyer's consent.'

'Can't you make an exception?'

'Sorry, love. More than my job's worth, especially on a day like today.'

'Day like today?'

'Valentine's Day.'

'Of course.' I'd forgotten. It had been so long since I'd had a card or gift, the date no longer registered with me.

'Sounds like you have a mystery admirer.'

'It does, doesn't it?'

'Don't worry. He'll probably reveal himself at some point. You can be sure of that.'

After the call, I put the flowers in a vase and inhaled the heady scent. A mystery admirer? Michael? No. He'd never sent flowers before. Jon? He'd sent me white flowers as a thank-you just after he moved here and I'd cooked for him. Richard? He didn't often buy flowers but, when he did, he didn't spare any expense. Or maybe Marcia? It was the kind of thing she'd done in the past when I was going through a difficult time. Yes, probably her, but then again, she'd have said they were from her. She didn't do mystery. Heather's words from a conversation weeks ago came back to me. 'If you have a soulmate out there, then let him come to you,' she'd said. *Could these flowers be from him?* I wondered. If they were, then he'd left one clue, and that was that he was a man with good taste.

30

On Sunday morning, Marcia texted me to meet at Waterlow Park, by Swain's Lane gate, at eleven.

I texted back: *Great. Need some fresh air after being cooped up in the shop.*

It was one of my favourite spots to walk in all seasons, with lakes, bridges, a great variety of trees, and the added bonus of a charming café in the old house up near the main road.

Marcia was waiting for me at the entrance when I got there and, instead of heading off into the park, she started off down the lane towards Highgate Cemetery further down.

'Where are you going?'

Marcia pointed ahead. 'To see if we can find Grace's grave.'

I groaned. 'Why? What's that going to prove?'

'More evidence that she existed.'

'We know she existed.'

'I want to make it real for you, then maybe you'll take what Saranya Ji told you more seriously.'

'I don't think we have any doubt that she was a real person; what is in doubt is that I used to be her in a past life. Besides, wandering around a cemetery on my day off is not my idea of relaxation.'

'Ah, but have you ever been to these cemeteries?'

'No but—'

'They're amazing. Come on, trust me, you'll like them and, you never know, something might act as a trigger.'

I followed her down the lane like a reluctant toddler following her mother, kicking the ground as I went.

'There are two parts to Highgate Cemetery, East and West,' said Marcia. 'I think the East one on the left has more recent graves, so the West side is the one we want.'

'How do you know if she's buried here and, if she is, where she'll be?'

'This is the main cemetery for the area, so there's a good chance that this is where her grave is.' Marcia pointed to an eccentric-looking building further down the lane to our right. It appeared to be a mix of architectural styles, with Tudor windows, Victorian turrets and a Gothic-looking wrought-iron gate in the middle. 'There must be a records office in there. We'll go and ask.'

'I'm not going,' I said. 'What are you going to say if they ask how you knew Grace? The truth would sound bonkers.'

'You stay here then,' said Marcia, who went up to the office and knocked on the door. As I waited, I looked around in awe. The place was straight out of a Gothic movie, with many of the gravestones worn or broken, overgrown with ivy and moss. Some had Victorian statues marking them. Behind the entrance and across the courtyard behind the office was a colonnade that looked like the front of a horse's stable, only made of stone.

Marcia came out a moment later. She gave me the thumbs-up. 'The lady in there suggested that we talk to one of the guides. We have to pay to get in and go round with one of them. The next tour is on the hour.' She glanced at her watch. 'That's in ten minutes. You up for that?'

I shrugged.

'Good,' said Marcia, 'because I've already got us tickets.'

We noticed a bunch of tourists gathering by the gate and went to join them. We were soon joined by our guide, an elderly man with sandy-coloured hair who was wearing an old cardigan and cords. He introduced himself as Nigel, then indicated that we should follow him into the wood.

'The West Cemetery opened in 1839 as one of the seven new cemeteries,' Nigel told us as we walked down the moss-covered paths. 'They were known as the Magnificent Seven.' As we trooped along with the group, I stopped to read some of the inscriptions along the way:

To Edna, beloved wife.

For Marcus who fell asleep.

Forever in Our Hearts Agnes.

Or simply *John Richards RIP.*

'What do you think you'd like on your gravestone?' asked Marcia.

'Cheerful,' I said. 'I've never really thought about it. You?'

'Nothing. I want to be cremated and my ashes scattered down on our favourite beach in Dorset, or in our garden with a tree or flowering shrub planted to mark the spot.'

'I read somewhere that D. H. Lawrence's wife had his ashes made into a fireplace,' I said. 'And I had a client once who wanted his wife's ashes made into cufflinks – so she'd always be with him. There's a whole line of cremation memorial jewellery – lockets for the ashes, rings made out of them; some of it is really tasteful too.'

'Not sure I'd want to go round wearing my dead husband, though,' said Marcia, 'although my aunt Iris wanted her husband's ashes to be put in an egg-timer, she said that way he'd finally do some work.'

I laughed, which caused an elderly lady in the group to turn around and frown at me, but the place, the conversation, the sombre atmosphere gave me the giggles, which soon set Marcia off too.

'And of course there's the famous joke about the mother who wanted her ashes scattered in Brent Cross shopping centre,' said Marcia. 'She said that way my kids will definitely come and visit once a week.'

Another of the tourists, this time an elderly man, gave us a filthy look for sniggering like a pair of teenagers, so we immediately attempted to straighten our faces.

'And you can have your ashes shot up into space in a rocket. Some people even have them made into fireworks and go out with a bang,' whispered Marcia.

'I read somewhere that one of the most common last sentences that women say when they're dying is, "Where's my handbag?" It's going to happen to everyone but I guess no one's ready.'

'I read that the most famous last words are "Oh shit!"'

'Figures.'

'And of course,' Nigel went on, 'one of the most famous people buried here is Elizabeth Siddal.'

That caught my attention. I still had my poster of her

posing as Ophelia, painted by Millais, on my bedroom wall, and her tragic story and beauty had always captured my imagination. 'Would it be possible to see her grave?' I asked.

Nigel shook his head. 'Not today. If you come back on Friday, one of us is doing a special tour of that area.'

'You in, Marcia?'

She shook her head. 'I can't Friday. I'm in the shop. What about you?'

'Absolutely. I'll make time. I had no idea she was here but, now I know she is, I'm not going to pass up an opportunity to see her grave.'

'About one hundred and seventy thousand people are buried here in fifty-three thousand graves,' Nigel continued, 'which vary from the minute plot markers for foundlings and small children to the more ornate and ostentatious monuments we will see later.'

'Sobering, isn't it?' said Marcia as we continued on past headstone after headstone. 'We're all going to die but it's rarely talked about. If reincarnation is true, I wonder how many of the people under there,' she pointed to the ground, 'are out here now living new lives.'

'Whatever the truth, being here makes you realize you really do have to seize the day and live the life you have now to the fullest.'

'Which is why I think this search for Billy is important,' said Marcia. 'Of all the things that makes life the best, love has to be number one.'

As we continued on, I thought about the loves I had lost in different ways. Being in the cemetery, surrounded by death, was bringing up to the surface so many feelings I'd worked hard to bury. 'This place is getting to me,' I said. 'I think we need to do something more cheerful afterwards.'

Marcia put her arm around me and gave me a squeeze. She knew what I was thinking.

'The Victorians loved the symbolism of death,' said Nigel as he indicated a statue of an angel. 'For example, an upturned torch in an angel's hand was to show life extinguished; another popular symbol is the broken pillar showing a strength cut off.'

We turned a corner and I gasped. In front of us was a wide stone gateway flanked by massive obelisks that were worthy of the entrance to a temple in ancient Egypt. It was stunning and so unexpected to come across in the middle of a graveyard on a grey day in North London.

'And now we come to the most famous part of the cemetery,' said Nigel as we followed him through into a tunnel lined with tall chambers with classic columns surrounding them. 'Sometimes called the avenue of death; other times it is called Egyptian avenue. If you follow me through, you will see it leads to an area named the Circle of Lebanon.'

'I feel like Alice who's fallen through into some weird wonderland. I had no idea this existed.'

'Yes, but don't forget why we're here,' said Marcia. 'Keep looking at the headstones for the Harris family and, if we don't see one, we can ask Nigel.'

At the end of the tunnel, we were led up some steps to where there was an enormous cypress tree on top of a circular corridor, lined underneath with grand doorways leading into tombs behind them.

'I doubt if we're going to find Grace here,' I said. 'These

tombs look like they were for people who were seriously loaded.'

We followed Nigel on through the maze of lanes and saw that nature had been left to run wild. It was unlike any cemetery I had ever seen. Far from having ordered lines of stones, this place was overgrown with weeds, moss and ivy, giving it the eerie but enchanting atmosphere of an eighteenth-century film set. As we progressed, we saw headstones with kneeling angels, bowed Madonnas, statues of women in veils, urns partially covered with cloths carved from stone.

'You may look around now and we will reconvene in ten minutes,' said Nigel, so Marcia and I took off to study the inscriptions on the headstones. We searched and searched but there was no sign of Grace Harris.

'I'm going to ask Nigel,' said Marcia, and marched over to where he was resting on a bench. 'Excuse me, sir, but we're looking for the grave of a Grace Harris, died 1943, and maybe the rest of the Harris family. Do you by any chance know where that might be?'

Nigel nodded. 'I think I do. I know every grave in the place. I've been tending them for over fifty years.'

'Might you be able to tell us where it is and if we may see it?' Marcia persisted.

'On the way back I'll show you where to go,' he said.

Marcia thanked him and came back over to me.

'I'm not sure I want to find her grave,' I said.

'Oh come on, we can't give up now,' said Marcia, 'we're almost there.'

Our small party reconvened and, when the tour was over, Nigel led us back towards the entrance. As the tourists dispersed, we hung about until Nigel was free.

'Now then ladies,' he said. 'What was the name again?'

'Grace Harris, died 1943,' said Marcia.

'Give me a moment. I just want to check inside then I'll be right back.'

He returned moments later. 'I thought I recognized that name, I was doing some cleaning up that way only yesterday.' He beckoned us to follow him back down the lane.

I hurried to keep up with him. 'Don't you get lost sometimes?'

He smiled and shook his head. 'Doesn't take long to find your way around, especially when you've been working here as long as I have.'

'And to see the Lizzie Siddal grave, I have to come back on Friday?'

'That's right. If you come along for ten o'clock, a guide will be taking a group there.'

'Great, thank you.'

Nigel led us off the main path and into an area where the headstones were less ostentatious. After a few minutes, he stopped. 'I think this is the one you're looking for. I'll leave you alone for a while then, when you're done, come back to the entrance. I'll be waiting for you there.'

We thanked him and, when he'd gone, we went over to the grave. It was a small, simple grey slab overgrown with moss. After the grand and ostentatious ones we'd seen in the other parts of the cemetery, it looked bare and sad.

'She's buried with her parents,' said Marcia. 'Look.'

I leant over to read the inscription and could just about make out the words. *Alice Harris. Edward Harris*, then *Grace Harris, 1920–1943*.

'I found her listed on the site that records deaths. She was only twenty-three when she died,' I said.

It felt odd to be standing there looking down at the grave of this person Grace, who had begun to feel like someone I knew. *So there it is*, I thought. *A gravestone amongst so many others, with just a dash between two dates to represent a person and a life and experiences we'll never know about.* I wondered what she was like. I shivered. Months ago, before India, I had been so sure of who I was, so sure of my life. Now I felt like I didn't know anything.

'You OK, Bea?' Marcia asked.

I nodded. 'This is weird,' I said. I felt strangely emotional and shaky. 'I mean, we have no real proof that I used to be this person, but never in a million years did I think I'd be standing in a cemetery looking at the grave of someone I might have been in a previous life; or at least the body of someone I was in another life, but not her spirit, because that has continued on in me. If what Saranya Ji said is true, then that spirit is now in me, looking through these eyes down at my own grave. I know nothing about her. Was she a fun person? Was she gloomy? Confident, or shy and retiring? What was she like? Who stood here on the day of her funeral as we are standing today?'

'It does make you think, doesn't it?' said Marcia as she looked around. 'I wonder if the sister is here as well. Lily.'

'Wouldn't she be with the others if she had died?'

'Not necessarily,' said Marcia. 'She's not there in the family grave. She might have got married, in which case she'd have had a different surname.'

We looked around at the other gravestones nearby but couldn't see any with the inscription Lily.

I was beginning to feel cold. 'Let's go, Marcia, this place is making me feel spooked.'

'OK,' said Marcia, but as we made our way back to the entrance, she continued to look at the gravestones. 'Here's a Lily, surname Marks, no, couldn't be her, too young.' A moment later, she found another Lily, but she too was dismissed as being too old.

'Come on, Marcia, let's go. I need to get back to the world of the living,' I said, and pulled her away. 'I'll buy you a hot chocolate up in the village.'

'Sounds like a plan,' said Marcia. 'Lead the way.'

*

After Marcia had gone home, I called Heather. I needed her reassuring angle on life after the atmosphere at the cemetery.

'Doesn't mean anything,' she said after I'd told her about finding Grace. 'Don't let it bother you.' She laughed. 'It's not like she can come and haunt you.'

'No because, in a way, she already has.'

'Haunted by your own spirit.'

'Stop it. Oh, but one thing that was worth the visit was that I found out Elizabeth Siddal is buried there.'

'The one in Millais's painting of Ophelia? Where she's lying amongst the reeds?'

I nodded. 'Apparently she was ill after posing for that painting; it was after lying in a bath in cold water for hours.'

'Let's see what it says on the Net,' she said. 'Let me get my laptop. Give me a minute . . . Here it is. Lizzie Siddal, 1829–1862. Buried in Highgate in the West cemetery in the

Rossetti family grave. She died of an overdose of laudanum – no one knew whether it was intentional or an accident.'

'Apparently, on the day of her funeral, her husband, Dante Gabriel Rossetti, placed a book of his poems next to her face in her coffin. Seven years later, the coffin was reopened and the book taken out and published, a fact that some art historians believed haunted him for the rest of his life, and is the reason that he wasn't buried in the family grave. There is also a story that – when the coffin was opened – she was in pristine condition and her beautiful red hair had continued to grow.'

'I heard that story, but apparently it's been exaggerated, because everyone's hair continues to grow a little after death. There is another story that the man who ordered the exhumation made up the story about the hair to tantalize Rossetti.'

'Good story all the same,' I said. 'Want to come? It's on Friday at ten. We could skive off and not open the shop until lunchtime.'

'Wow, you have changed your tune. Months ago, you would never have suggested skiving off. You bet I'll come. Christina, Dante's sister, is also buried there. I loved her poems when I was going through my "tragic heroine" phase in my twenties.'

'Ah, those happy days,' I said as I clicked off my phone.

I arrived back home just as Jon was getting out of his car with Chief.

'Hey Bea,' he called as he put Chief on a lead, 'where have you been?'

'Cemetery in Highgate.'

'Oh. I am sorry. A funeral? Someone close?'

'Yes and no, and not a funeral. I was visiting the grave of the lady I used to be in my last life. She died over eighty years ago, before I was born . . . obviously. Quite spooky looking down on the grave of someone you used to be in a previous existence.'

It amused me to tell Jon the absolute truth and see what he made of it. He looked startled by my reply, then he creased up laughing. 'God, I love you Bea Brooks. OK, OK, I get it. None of my business again. Sorry. Won't ask again or . . . maybe I will, just to see what story you come up with next.'

'No, Jon, I am serious. I am telling you the truth. That is where I have been.'

Jon laughed again. 'Sure, sure. Last life. Love it. And I've just been made prime minister. Let's get together sometime and compare fantasies. Could be fun. My place or yours?'

'I'll have to consult my diary, but I think I'm busy for the next millennium.'

'I can wait.' He went off chuckling at what I'd said.

31

On Friday morning, Heather and I went back to Highgate Cemetery, paid an admission fee and soon we were off on a tour again. This time the guide was a middle-aged woman with short brown hair and a friendly face called Margaret. As we walked through the graves, she gave a talk similar to the one that Nigel had given earlier in the week. Like me, Heather had never been inside the cemetery, and was awe-struck by it, especially when we passed the Egyptian gate. 'This is like a film set,' she said.

'That's what I thought.'

Margaret overheard us. 'It is indeed; it was used as the location for a number of horror films: *The Picture of Dorian Gray*, *Taste the Blood of Dracula* and *Tales from the Crypt*, as well as *Fantastic Beasts and Where to Find Them*.'

'Why have I never been here before?' asked Heather as she looked around. 'I love it.'

We learnt from Margaret that Charles Dickens's parents were buried there, as were the artist Lucian Freud, actress Jean Simmons, singer George Michael and actor Bob Hoskins, to name but a few, but the one that we and the rest of the tour were really interested in was that of Elizabeth Siddal.

Margaret led us through the lanes. She stopped at a gravestone that consisted of a tall stone with the top shaped like a four-leaf clover. 'The grave of Elizabeth Siddal. Many of you will have heard the wild stories about her being dug up by her husband Dante . . .' She filled us in on the story about the hair and the poems.

'It seemed a fitting place for her to have ended up,' I whispered when Margaret had finished, as she indicated that we should follow her back to the entrance. 'It's romantic and poignant,' I added.

'Can you show me Grace's grave before we go?' asked Heather. 'We might as well take a look, seeing as we're so close.'

'I think we have to ask for permission.' I said and, in typical fashion, Heather went straight over to ask.

'Yes, you can see the grave, but I'd have to accompany you,' Margaret said, so we waited until the group had gone then she took us back to the area where Grace was buried. 'I will wait for you at the front. Take as long as you like, but let me know when you go as we don't want to have to come looking for you in the dark.'

As soon as she'd gone, we stepped forward for a closer look. 'Wuhoooo,' said Heather as she gazed down at the stone. 'Spooky hey?'

'It is a bit. I felt really weird when we were here the first time, though there's nothing really to see and, as you said, it doesn't prove anything.'

'Apart from the fact that she died as a young woman,' said Heather as she examined the inscription. 'I wonder what she was like; in fact, all these graves in here, who were they?'

To the left of Grace's headstone, I noticed a grave that had fresh flowers on it, white roses. Out of curiosity, I went to look at the inscription. The stone was very worn but I could just about make out the names.

'Whose is that?' asked Heather.

I read what I could make out, 'Amelia Jeffrey and underneath Howard Jeffrey and Lily Jeffrey. Oh, a Lily.'

'Who are they then?

'Not sure, but Lily might be Grace's elder sister. We noticed she wasn't in the family grave so Marcia suggested that she might have got married and changed her surname. She was looking for all the Lilys last time we were here, but she missed this one.' I looked at the ages. 'Lily Jeffrey 1918–2006. The birth date fits with her being Grace's elder sister.'

'Oh but look, Amelia,' said Heather, 'she died at . . . not even two years old. How sad. Must have been Lily's daughter.'

'Sounds like it.'

'But then who left the flowers? A living relative? Maybe Lily had another child or even a grandchild. Bea, do you realize what this might mean? If this is Grace's sister's grave, then whoever left those flowers, they knew Lily and maybe the family. Let's ask at the records office. Margaret seemed very nice. I'm sure she'd help.'

We made our way back to the entrance and found Margaret having a cup of tea. 'You off now?' she asked when she saw us.

'Yes,' said Heather. 'Er . . . we noticed that someone had

left some flowers on one of the graves that we had come to look at. I wondered if you knew who that was.'

'Which grave?'

'One next to the Harris family. Names are Howard, Lily and Amelia Jeffrey.'

Margaret shook her head. 'I don't but Robin might. He tends a lot of the graves and knows most of the people who come regularly. You'll find him if you follow the main lane.'

We set off back in the direction we'd come from and soon found an old man with white hair in gardening clothes who was cutting back shrubs. Heather filled him in and asked if he knew who had left the flowers.

'Ah yes, I know exactly where you mean, Jeffreys' grave. Lady came late afternoon yesterday. Comes every year around this time.'

'You don't happen to know who she was, do you?'

He shook his head. 'Older lady but I don't know her name. I only know the ones under the ground. Sorry I can't help more.'

We thanked him for his time then made our way to the exit.

'So what do you think?' asked Heather.

'It's not so unusual,' I said. 'People come and leave flowers all the time, but I do think the proximity of the graves and the names and dates lean towards the fact that Lily Jeffrey might have been Grace's sister and that she and her husband had a little girl.'

'You could look them up now that you have a possible surname,' said Heather. 'Maybe find death certificates and what the cause was.'

'Or Lily's marriage certificate; that would give her maiden name.'

Heather rubbed her hands together. 'Exciting, isn't it?'

'You're supposed to be my voice of reason,' I said. 'Don't you start getting into it all now.'

'I'm still not sure of the past life thing but, you have to admit, the rest of it is all intriguing.'

'And spooky,' I said. 'Gives me the shivers.'

32

I have a reception to organize. I'd booked a private room in a pub over the phone and wanted to check it out in person. I found the place easily enough, parked and got out. Although it was my first time there, without thinking I went to the right side to look for the entrance, only to find that there wasn't one there. I walked round to the back to explore further and found a man having a cigarette on the back steps.

'Good morning, sir. Can I help you?'

'Oh yes, thank you. I was looking for the way in and thought the door was on this side.'

The man smiled. 'Not any more. Here, follow me.' He led me back to the side of the pub. 'Your instincts were correct, though; the entrance used to be here.' He pointed at the brickwork. 'Look closely.'

I looked at the wall, unsure about what I was supposed to be seeing.

'New bricks,' said the man. 'The whole wall was rebuilt after the bombing in the Second World War. The road took a bad hit: whole of the terrace over the road went; this side of the road stayed mainly intact, but the right wall and entrance of the pub took a knocking. When it was rebuilt, the chaps who did it decided to block up where the old entrance had been and put the door on the other side.'

'So the door's round the other side?' I asked.

'It is,' said the man.

I walked round to the other side and went in and over to the bar, where a young barmaid with pink hair was standing behind the counter. 'I'm here about the gathering next month, just to run through a few last details.'

'I'll get John,' said the barmaid. 'He's just upstairs. Can I get you a drink while you wait?'

I ordered a beer and went to sit at a table in a corner while the barmaid went to find the events manager. As I waited, I noticed there was a selection of old black-and-white photos on the wall. I got up to take a closer look. They showed the pub and street before the bombing. A row of terrace houses on the right, the pub on the left side, looking pretty well the same on the outside as it did today, old red brick with some tiling. The only change that I could see was that the entrance back then had clearly been on the right-hand side. Funny I'd gone there automatically. I must have seen the old photos of the street on the pub's website when I was searching for the wedding location and forgotten that I'd seen them. Must be that. All the same, there was something familiar about the place. I had a sense of déjà vu, though couldn't for the life of me remember having been there before.

33

I was in Simon's office for my third hypnosis session. I was looking forward to it this time and all the apprehension I'd felt in the first two appointments had gone.

We chatted for a while then Simon said, 'Shall we get started and see where it takes you this time?'

I knew the drill so sat back in the reclining chair and closed my eyes. Simon began to talk me down, '. . . and the relaxing power moves up to knees, up to thighs, hips, every cell and atom, into fingers of both hands, relaxing, moves up to forearms, and upper arm, fingers hands forearms so relaxed, imagine a warmth . . .' I surrendered to his voice and the words and felt myself letting go and sinking back into the chair with no resistance. '. . . all tension is gone, going down down, three, deeper, down down, four, deeper deeper down down, down, five, deeper deeper down, six, deeper, down down, seven, down deeper deeper eight, deeper, deeper, down down, down. Nine. Now relaxed and at ease, imagining the most peaceful situation that you can, total peace. And ten. Now I want you to go back to the time when you first began to believe that love can be painful.'

I consciously thought of the times I had felt abandoned and sad and, in my head, I began to feel as if I was watching a film, images from my life on an inner screen: leaving Joe, him turned away on the sofa; Michael leaving for his travels; before that, Marcia heading off on her gap year; my parents leaving, standing at the train station, waving them off and returning to an empty house; later standing in Marcia's room, looking at the mattress, stripped of bed linen. Although the images made me feel deeply sad, I decided that this time I would face the shadows, not fear them or deny them. They were a part of me as much as the good times.

'Where are you, Bea?' asked Simon.

'Just thinking about people leaving, watching people go. My parents, friends . . .'

'I want you to go further back,' he said, and I listened and followed his voice as he took me further down steps, in a lift, more stairs, 'down, down.'

I felt so heavy, my eyelids heavy, everything heavy. '. . . to a time when you knew true love, your soulmate, long long ago . . .'

I continued watching the images from my life on the inner screen, when I suddenly felt a jolt in my solar plexus, a sensation of a shift, falling; then I could see a park, a man and young woman, holding hands. I felt drawn in, pulled towards them, as if I was in the picture but above, looking down. Then I got the feeling of sinking, and sensed that the man was holding my hand. I felt slightly seasick as I moved into the image. I was in the movie. I turned to look at the man. 'Oh!' I felt a jolt of recognition and sense of 'Oh there you are, of *course*, I know you. I would know you anywhere.' A rush of joy flooded through me, relief; there he was, so clear. 'I thought

I'd never see you again.' I felt tears come to my eyes and an overwhelming surge of happiness at being reunited with him. How could I have forgotten him? He was the love of my life.

'Who, Bea?' I heard Simon ask. 'Who are you talking to?'

'Man in the park.'

'Where is the park?'

I made myself concentrate and look around. 'Wood. Of course, I know where I am, it's Cherry Tree Wood.'

'Who's looking at the wood?'

'Me but not me. I know I have my eyes closed, but I can see and I can talk but I don't think he can hear me.'

'And are you all right where you are?'

'Oh yes, very happy but no, wait . . .'

I sensed that the man was distressed and that the woman was also becoming upset. I experienced a ripping sear of pain. He was talking to her, to me. I felt myself detach from them, and again it was as though I was looking down from above. I could feel my breath becoming ragged. I didn't want to leave. I sensed the man was going to go away and that I wouldn't see him again. I felt an unbearable sense of loss, an empty dark chasm that I was falling into. Or was this what Saranya Ji told me? Was I dreaming it? Whichever, I didn't like this feeling. I couldn't bear that he was going to go. I struggled to breathe. 'I don't know if I am making this up, seeing what I've been told,' I said.

'Don't worry,' said Simon. 'Don't concern yourself with where the images or feelings are coming from. If you can, stay with it.'

I focused back on the scene in the park but it was too painful. 'I saw him but I know I'm going to lose him again, forget him and it won't be real. I'll have lost him again.'

'Moving on now,' I heard Simon say. 'Moving on to a happier time.'

I scanned the film that I could see inwardly. I could still see the young woman in the park. This time, she was alone. 'Go to a happier time,' I heard Simon say again, and I felt I was jolted forward and I was in a garden. I knew it so well, it was full of sunlight, an apple tree to the left. I was with a small girl with blonde wavy hair; not a girl, a toddler, she was just learning to walk. I got a strong sense that she was my child.

'Bea, what's happening?' Simon asked.

'I'm with Minty.'

'Who's Minty?'

'My baby girl,' I replied as I moved through the frames of the film. 'But that can't be right. I don't have a baby girl.' The film seemed to go into reverse, as if on rewind. I watched the woman, inside the house now, washing up. She looked up as another woman, an older women, brought her a letter, a telegram. The other woman looked concerned. It was bad news; the younger woman was distraught, staggered and reached out to steady herself, then there was a sense of moving on, as if someone had pressed fast-forward on a TV. The younger woman was in a hospital by a bed, the little girl was in it, moving on again, the bed was empty, the woman seated, bent over, sobbing. The older woman was with her, her arm over her shoulder.

'I don't like it here,' I said. 'You lose those you love.'

'Can you find them again?' asked Simon.

I vaguely remembered the mosaics from the previous session and tried to will myself to see them again. 'Where's Wally?' I said.

'OK,' said Simon. 'Can you tell me what that means?'

'The mosaics, they're all in there.' I felt a wave of hope. 'I have to match the man from the park with my mosaic, then I'll know who he is now and won't have lost him.'

'OK,' said Simon, 'but just let go, don't try to force anything, let your unconscious mind reveal to you what it wants to. Just let go . . .'

But all I could see was a light mist inside: no mosaics, no art gallery room. I let myself go back into the comfy state of drifting. I felt so tired and then Simon was counting me back up, '. . . three two one and *wide awake*, feeling refreshed.'

*

'Do you think Grace had a child?' asked Heather when I met her after my session in the café on the fifth floor in John Lewis.

'It was definitely her baby,' I said, 'but I got the feeling that the baby died.'

Heather looked thoughtful. 'Hmm. Could be that your subconscious is interpreting events again. It could be that the baby represented an innocence lost.'

'Maybe, but she looked very real. She had a name too. Minty.'

'Sweet,' said Heather, 'but . . . if you ask me, I think that after our trip to the cemetery and finding Lily's grave as well as Grace's, and then discovering that Lily had a daughter who died at an early age, on top of what Saranya Ji told you about Billy going off to the war, it's been on your mind, literally. Also, if Grace had had a child, surely she'd have been in the grave with her. I think your subconscious concocted it all into a story to make sense of it all: that's the power of dreams. And I seem to remember reading somewhere about how death in dreams isn't necessarily a bad thing. It can represent the death of something – of a chapter in your life, and that birth usually means new beginnings, so maybe this baby indicates a new start for you.'

'Maybe.' I took a sip of the tea that Heather had bought me. 'Sounds like gobbledygook to me, certainly felt like that – a mishmash of events and thoughts and ideas. Whatever the explanation, I get a very strong feeling that it is time to move on. Whatever happened in that session, if I really did go back to a past life, or if I just fell into a deep in-between-sleep state and, as you say, reimagined the story that Saranya Ji had told me, it doesn't matter which, but I don't feel that dwelling on it all is helping. Grace, whoever she was, lived a long time ago. I, on the other hand, am alive now. This is my time. This is the real time and I need to focus in this century, this decade.'

'I agree,' said Heather. 'Will you talk to Marcia about any of this?'

I shook my head. 'Maybe . . . So far I've told her that the hypnosis helped with my sleeping and she seemed happy enough with that. You know what Marcia's like. If I told her what I'd experienced, she'd be off on one and telling me to do all sorts of whacky things. It's been so intense and I'd like some time to mull it over myself. It's different talking to you, you're more impartial.'

'So what's the plan?'

I laughed. 'Move on, stop hanging about in graveyards, get on with this life.'

'I'll drink to that.'

34

On our way home, I took the route through Muswell Hill. As we drove along the High Street, I spotted Joe Wilding with an attractive redhead who was holding hands with a young lad. Joe was pushing a pram. He said something and the woman laughed and kissed his cheek.

'Looks happily married,' I said as we continued on our way. 'And really well too. Maybe he's kicked the demon drink. I do hope so because he was a nice guy when he wasn't high on something.'

'Even sober, he was never the one for you.'

'I know that.' I turned down Fortis Green and headed for the lights. 'No regrets.'

'Isn't this near where you said Grace lived?' Heather asked.

'It is, just round the next corner.'

'Oo, let's have a look.'

'Why? There's nothing to see.'

'I know, but she's captured my imagination as well as yours and you know what a nosey cow I am so, seeing as we're passing, let's have a look.'

I turned left and slowed down as we got to the house that the census had given as Grace's address. 'There it is,' I said as I pointed to the right side of the road.

'Let's get out,' said Heather. 'I want a closer look.'

I parked the car, we got out, and stood on the opposite side of the road to where the house was.

'Nice little house,' said Heather as she looked up at the first floor. 'I wonder which was your bedroom.'

'Stop it, Heather,' I said. 'I told you, I'm letting it all go now, moving on.' As we stared up, a small white-haired woman who looked in her seventies came out of the gate and noticed us looking up at the windows. She came straight over. 'Can I help you?' she asked in a tone that said she didn't want to help us at all, more that she wanted to know what we were doing checking out where she lived.

'I . . . No, sorry,' I said. 'I . . . I . . . wah . . .'

'What she's trying to say,' said Heather, 'is that she's been researching a family tree and looking into census records and this address came up.'

The woman's face softened. 'How fascinating. I love all that stuff. I always watch *Who Do You Think You Are?* So what have you found?'

'Er . . . that the Harris family lived here and they had two daughters, Grace and Lily.'

'That's correct,' said the woman. 'Lily was my mother, Harris was her maiden name. So, are we distant cousins or something?'

'Oh, I—'

'Six degrees of separation,' Heather interrupted.

'What does that mean?' asked the woman.

'It's the idea that any person on the planet can be

connected to any other person on the planet through a chain of acquaintances that has no more than five intermediaries. The connections are amazing.'

'So you knew Grace Harris?' I asked.

'Sadly not. She would have been my aunt but she died before I was born.'

'What about her daughter Minty?' Heather asked.

The woman went white. 'Did you say her daughter? And you know her name?'

Heather nodded. 'Grace's daughter.'

I was taken aback. What was Heather saying? We didn't even know if Minty had been a real person, or just someone I dreamt up, but that was Heather, always rushing in. She'd always been the same, straight over to talk to people, not thinking through what she said.

I tried to pull Heather away back to the car. 'Sorry to have bothered you.'

The woman's expression changed to that of a very stern and scary headmistress. 'Hold on a minute. I think you'd better come in. I'd like to know exactly what you know about Minty.' She indicated that we should follow her back through her gate to the front door.

'Oh my God,' I whispered. 'What have you done?'

Once inside, the woman closed the door and led us through to a back room overlooking the garden. 'Right. Introductions. I am Eileen Jeffrey,' she said.

'And I am Bea,' I said, 'and this is Heather.'

Eileen studied us hard again. 'Now tell me *exactly* what you have found out in your research.'

I looked over at Heather. 'I . . .' As I looked out of the window, I noticed that there was an apple tree to the left, just as I'd seen in my hypnosis session. I took a deep breath. 'OK, this is going to sound completely bonk—'

'We've only just started looking,' Heather interrupted. 'We found out your family lived here and—'

'But what about Minty?' asked Eileen. 'What do you know of her? You said Grace's daughter?'

'I dreamt about her,' I said. It wasn't exactly a lie and I was still unsure whether she was a figment of my imagination or not. 'A very vivid dream.' I pointed out to the back garden. 'I'm sure it was out there, Grace with her little girl.' Inside I was panicking and wanted to get out of there as soon as possible. 'I . . . maybe because I'd been researching about Grace, my mind made Minty up.'

'No, she was real enough. Her name was Amelia,' said Eileen. 'Minty was her nickname. It's extraordinary that you dreamt that. How could you have known that?'

'So she did exist?' I asked.

'Oh yes, but why did you say *Grace's* daughter?' asked Eileen.

'I'm not sure. I felt it.'

Eileen sat down heavily on the chair opposite. '*Felt* it? Are you some kind of psychic?'

Heather burst out laughing.

'No,' I said. 'Not at all. To be honest, it's as much a mystery to me as to you. I guess Grace has kind of captured my imagination.'

'Nobody knew,' said Eileen. 'No one knew that Minty was Grace's daughter. I only found out when my mother was dying. I always thought she was my sister – or would have been had she lived.'

'Your sister?' I asked.

'Was?' Heather asked.

'She died when she was two years old.'

I gasped. So Minty had been real and my memory of Grace at the hospital bed must have been real. So much for Heather's idea of it being a clever way of my subconscious interpreting things.

I glanced over at Eileen. She looked emotional. 'Excuse me a moment,' she said and disappeared from the room.

'This is amazing, isn't it? God, Bea, it might all be true. Does this room seem familiar?'

'I don't think so, but probably because the overriding feeling I have at the moment is *pure panic*.' I took a deep breath and looked around. It was then that I noticed a collection of photos on the wall in the corner. I got up to look at them. There was the woman I'd seen in the park in my hypnosis session, Grace, no doubt about it, a slender figure with brown wavy hair. She was with the older woman I'd seen bring her the telegram. Eileen came back in. I pointed to the photographs. 'This is Grace and her mother?'

'It is,' she said. She pointed to another photo showing an elderly woman. 'And that was my mother, Lily.'

'Grace's older sister.'

'You seem to know an awful lot about my family,' said Eileen.

'I do and I don't. Only what I've found on the Internet.'

I was fascinated by the photo of Grace on the wall. It had obviously been taken in a photographer's studio. She had bright eyes and a friendly looking, open face. *Could that have been me in there, in that body?* I wondered. I felt faint and put my hand out to steady myself on a chair.

'Are you all right?' asked Eileen.

I sat down. 'Not really.' My mind was reeling. This was far beyond a bit of fun with a fortune-teller, a session with a hypnotist, speculation about a lost soulmate. Eileen had confirmed that Minty had existed and her real name was Amelia. Saranya Ji hadn't mentioned that Grace had had a daughter. No one had, not until now: that had come from inside me. The only way I could possibly have known about her was if, as Saranya Ji had told me, I had been Grace Harris. The implication hit me like a brick. Grace, Billy, past lives, soulmates; it could all be true, after all.

'My mother died thirteen years ago and Grace, well, she died when she was twenty-three, not long after Minty. My mother said she reckoned that she died of a broken heart so soon after—'

'Losing Billy too,' said Heather.

God, that woman never knows when to shut up, I thought. Eileen nodded. 'So you know about him as well?'

'Oh yes, he was killed in action, wasn't he?' said Heather.

'He was, in France. A tragic story. He never knew about his daughter.'

'But you said you thought that Minty was your sister? Why was that if she was Grace's daughter?'

Eileen hesitated for a moment. 'I can only assume that it was because it would have been a scandal. Grace was unmarried, you see. She and Billy were due to be married as soon as he returned but of course—'

'I don't suppose you have a photo of him, do you?' Heather asked. Eileen hesitated again but Heather continued, 'When we heard the story, we were captured by the romance of it, weren't we Bea?'

'I . . .' I seemed to have lost the ability to speak.

'Romance?' said Eileen. 'I don't think there was much of that, at least not from what I heard; just loss . . . For Grace to have lost the two people closest to her must have been unbearable, but then that's war for you. From what I know, my grandparents looked after Grace and Minty. My mother was newly married at the time and living here too, so I imagine that – in order to save Grace's reputation – they said that Minty was Lily's daughter. Who was to know? Of course I never knew Grace or Minty, but my mother always talked about Minty as if she was my sister; until she was dying, that is: then she told me the truth.'

She got up and went to a dresser where she searched in one of the drawers, then pulled out an ancient-looking leather photo album. 'I think this is the one,' she said as she placed it on the table in front of us, then flipped over a few pages. 'There,' she said as she pointed to a photo of a young man in army uniform. 'That was Billy, just before he went off to war. Handsome chap, wasn't he?'

I took a sharp intake of breath when I looked at the photo. *Ah, there you are again*, I thought as I saw the face of the man from the park staring back at me, a face as familiar as family. He had indeed been a handsome chap, dark haired with fine features. I felt tears come to my eyes and brushed them away. 'Such a sad story,' I whispered.

'And there's one of Grace and Minty,' said Eileen as she pointed at another photo. 'I was sad not to have known them. Lily said that Grace was such a joy before she lost Billy and Minty but sank into a depression afterwards.'

Heather and I looked at the photos and I could see that Heather was as moved as I was. Minty was a little cherub with curly blonde hair. I glanced out of the window and, in my mind's eye, I could still see the image from the hypnosis session: Grace in the garden, Minty toddling towards her.

'I'm sorry that I haven't better news,' said Eileen. 'Both Grace and my mother are buried up at Highgate Cemetery, as are my grandparents. Grace is in my grandparents' grave and Minty was buried with my mother and father. Amelia Jeffrey, it says on the gravestone. That was my mother's married name and, of course, my surname.'

I prayed that Heather didn't reveal that we'd been up in the cemetery or else Eileen would really be suspicious. Luckily she didn't.

We left half an hour later, and as we got into the car and drove away, Heather burst out laughing.

'What's so funny?' I asked.

'Think about it. Consciousness is the greatest mystery in the world, but it's pretty clear now that what your lady in India said was true; in which case, you were Grace, and that elderly woman back there, Eileen Jeffrey, was your niece.'

I groaned. 'That's too weird to even think about. In the meantime, I think I need a stiff drink.'

'Me too,' said Heather, 'and we need a new plan.'

'Which is?'

'Obvious, idiot. Billy. We *have* to find out who he is now. No question about it, after this latest development. Grace was real, Minty was real, Billy was real. You knew Minty's nickname, and even Pete with all his sleuth skills on the ancestry sites couldn't have found that out. The whole story was buried in your subconscious somewhere.'

'It was amazing looking at those photos. They were

exactly the people I saw in my regression session. I have Grace's memories.'

'So you believe it all now?' asked Heather.

'I do. Absolutely. No doubt.'

'Me too. So, you're here again and, as Saranya Ji said, so is he. You *have* to look for him, discover where he is now, and who.'

'The latest model.'

'New version Billy.'

'My new edition soulmate.'

'Talk about blast from the past!'

We both laughed. Today had changed everything and I felt fired up to continue the search for who Billy was now.

35

When I got home, I made a quick note of who was on my contenders' list.

Kevin
Bruno
Sam
Michael
Jon

Get out of my head Jon Howard, I thought as I crossed his name off the list, then I texted my brother Matthew to ask about Bruno. He texted straight back. 'Look on my Facebook page, Bruno's on there, but we haven't actually been in touch for years. You thinking of looking him up? Think he got married.'

I went straight to Facebook, found Matthew's page, and scrolled down to his friends. I soon found Bruno. His profile picture showed a dark, handsome man, but he looked younger than the fifty-something man I knew he was. *Can't be current*, I thought as I clicked on his page. It showed his address as Milan but no more than that. He'd obviously put his privacy settings to friends only. I took a deep breath and clicked on Add Friend. There. Done. *Will he accept me as a friend and will he even remember me?* I asked myself.

While I was on Facebook, I typed in Kevin Grisham, my first proper boyfriend, who had moved away with his family, to see if he had a page. So many with that name came up: a couple in Devon, one in Manchester. Pete had given me an address for Kent but I couldn't find a Kevin Grisham in that area. Next I tried Sam Gorman, who I'd been with at art college. OK, so he had been a dope head back then but if Joe Wilding could clean up, then maybe Sam had too? There was a Sam Gorman listed in Dublin, others in London, Newcastle, New York, but none that I recognized as the Sam I'd known.

On a whim, I typed 'Jon Howard' into search. Again no luck, perhaps my Casanova neighbour didn't use Instagram? *More likely to find him on a dating site*, I thought. Which one? Guardian Soulmates? I went to their site but didn't get very far because it asked me to register and I didn't want to do that. No matter, why was I even looking for Jon? I knew where he was and wasn't interested in him anyway . . . So. Back to Kevin Grisham in Kent. I found the contact details that Pete had given me. *No time like the present*, I thought as I picked up the phone and dialled.

The phone rang then a recorded message played. I panicked and put the phone down. What would I say? Bea Brooks here. Long time, no see. Am looking up past boyfriends because . . . Because what? I wasn't like Heather who could come up with a story at the drop of a hat. I should think through what I wanted to say and be prepared. I'd call again later.

Thirty seconds later, the phone rang.

'Hi, did you just ring here?' said a man's voice.

'I . . . I did.'

'Sorry, I was in the shower and didn't get to the phone in time. Who's calling?' He sounded nice, friendly.

'I was calling for Kevin Grisham.'

'Who wants him?'

'Er, it's . . . Bea Brooks, I used to know—'

'Bea? Bea from Manchester? I don't believe it.'

'Yes. Me, er . . . long time, no see.'

'Certainly is. Must be years. Wow. I don't know what to say. This is . . . this is synchronicity.'

'It is?'

'Yes. I was just thinking about you recently and had a mind to look you up.'

'You were?'

'You're in London, right? A friend of a friend from Manchester said you'd moved there.' He laughed. 'Must be the time of life, you know, reviewing the situation, looking back over past times. Wow. I think I need to sit down. Talk about a blast from the past. How did you find me?'

'I have a friend who's a computer geek. He tracked you down.'

'Well I never. I'm flattered. So, to what do I owe this honour?'

I racked my brain for the sort of excuse Heather would come up with. 'I . . . er . . . a project I'm working on. I'm thinking about writing a book about the Manchester area when we were there, so I am getting in touch with people I knew from that time to see what they remember.'

'Fiction or non-fiction?'

'Oh er . . . fiction, but of course the facts and the setting must be right.'

'I'd be glad to help. And am I right in thinking you've just had a big birthday? I seem to remember your birthday was a few weeks before mine.'

'I have. You have a good memory.'

'Mine was the month after yours, so I always remember. Hey, we have to meet up.'

'Yes, that would be interesting after all this time.'

'When? Damn it, I've just been up to London recently. I could come up there, see where you live . . .' He sounded eager, too eager.

'Or I could come to you. I'm just in the process of moving, you see.' *That way, I can get away if necessary*, I thought.

'OK. Come here. Sure. Great. Let's do it. How you fixed for this weekend?'

'*This* weekend?' It all seemed to be happening a bit fast, but I knew I had nothing urgent on and it had been me who had contacted him, so why were alarm bells ringing and why was I feeling hesitant? What did I have to lose? 'I . . . OK, why not?'

'Will you drive or get the train?'

'Train probably.'

'Great. Saturday then? Get the train to Westgate-on-Sea. I'll pick you up from the station and rustle up some lunch. Be fantastic to see you again.'

'Just remember I am thirty-five years older.'

'Me too, Bea, but it will be great to catch up, relive some old times. Here's my mobile, you can text me the details of your arrival time when you know and then I'll have your number in case of delays.' He gave me his number then I heard him laugh. 'Unbelievable that you should get in touch when I'd been thinking about you.'

'I know.'

'Oh. Right. OK. See you Saturday,' he said and hung up.

What just happened there? I asked myself. I have a date. I don't remember him being so in charge when I knew him, but he had only been fifteen years old then. I sat down. Kevin Grisham. Relive old times. Hah. Fumbling our way around each other's bodies when he'd sneaked up into my room when Mum and Dad were out. Long snogging sessions. He'd been a good kisser, but that had been as far as it went. We were both virgins and, though he'd pushed to go further, we hadn't. I hadn't been ready.

I went to train enquiries online and found out the train times. There was one from London Victoria that would get me in about twelve. *Perfect*, I thought. *So who's next? Sam Gorman.*

I looked up his sister Kate's Facebook page and sent her a private message.

Hi Kate, long time no see. How's life? And your kids? Do hope all is good with you. I'm writing to ask if you could let me know where Sam is now. I've been thinking about old friends . . . I crossed that out. *I've been taking a trip down memory lane.* I crossed that out too. What would Heather write? I asked myself. *There's going to be a college reunion next month and the woman who's organizing it asked if I was in touch with anyone from back then. Of course I thought of Sam. He might not want to go but I thought I'd let him know anyway, so if you could put me in touch, that would be appreciated. Love and best wishes, Bea Brooks.*

I put my contact details at the end, then clicked for the message to be sent.

Lastly, I texted Heather and Marcia to let them know where I was up to. 'So that's it. Homework done.'

Messages done, I went back to Kate's Facebook page and clicked on her photos to see if there were any with Sam in. I scrolled through to see plenty of her with her husband and family, but none with her brother, which was strange because they'd been close when I'd known them. I closed the page and let my thoughts drift back to the time we were together.

Sam Gorman.

He was a handsome devil: tall, fine featured, with longish brown hair, a Shelley or Byron manifested in the canteen at the art college that we both went to.

'I believe we are meant to be in each other's lives, Bea Brooks,' he'd said one night when we were curled up in a bed at his parents' manor house in Cheshire. He came from a wealthy family, though you wouldn't know it from the way he dressed in faded velvet jackets, flamboyant scarves and paint-splattered jeans.

'But we are in each other's lives,' I said.

'No, I mean in the future. Shall we make a pact? One of those, if we're not married by the time we're fifty, we look each other up.'

'Fifty? That's a long way off. Who knows if we'll even be here then?'

'True, but how about it? If we're both single at fifty, we get back together and dance over the hill into a fabulous and decadent old age together.'

I laughed. 'Sure. Why not? But why not before? Like thirty or forty?'

'Fifty is a good age. We'll be half a century old. We'll both have lots of experience under our belt. I'll be a very successful artist with my own studio, a multimillionaire who has gallery openings in New York, Milan, Paris and Hong Kong, and a string of mistresses and illegitimate children.'

'And me?'

'You will be a grandmother with four ex-husbands in different parts of the world and coach-loads of beautiful grandchildren with big eyes. You'll live in a remote spot in Arizona with horses and chickens and wear colourful clothes, swear a lot and dance naked at full moons.'

'OK. And why would I want to get back with you?'

'Because of the connection we have. You do feel it, don't you? We have something special.' He moved on top of me and stared into my eyes.

I pushed him off. His long, meaningful looks made me feel uncomfortable sometimes. 'OK. Deal. If we're single at fifty, we get back together.'

He sat up, leant over to the bedside cabinet, rummaged in a drawer and found a safety pin. 'Prick your thumb. These things must be done like a sacred ritual. We have to seal the deal in blood.'

I groaned. 'We do? Really?'

'Yes.' He pricked his thumb, yelped, then handed me the pin.

I took a deep breath, pricked my thumb and put it against his.

'Excellent. It is done. Blood lovers. We are bound together.'

'Either that or we end up in A and E with blood poisoning.'

'Where's your sense of romance? Destiny? If it's fated, we will go into old age together.'

I wasn't so sure. I liked Sam a lot, but wasn't sure if I wanted to spend the rest of my life, or second part of my life, with him. I loved his paintings, admired his considerable talent – his life drawing especially; his figures had weight and the right proportions, whereas mine always looked as if they were floating. And I enjoyed his company when he wasn't stoned. He read poetry to me at night, was the first man to bring me flowers and gifts.

What he didn't tell me that night was that it was already over between us. He had dropped out of college and was planning a trip to Paris 'to experience life as a true artist.'

He was gone a week later and, for a few months, I got postcards depicting famous works of art from London, Paris, Morocco, then nothing. I wasn't too heartbroken. I hadn't been ready for his intensity. I was only eighteen and, like Sam, wanted to experience life, love and all it had to offer.

36

The following day, I made a start on moving some of my things over to Marcia and Pete's house. As soon as I'd unloaded the boot, they sat me down in the kitchen and made me bring them up to date about everything; all about the hypnosis session, meeting Eileen and seeing the photographs, though I sensed that Marcia was peeved that I'd gone with Heather and not her. 'Heather's absolutely right,' said Marcia. 'You *have* to find him now.'

'I agree. No more need to persuade me,' I said. 'I'm in.'

'And I'll help in any way I can.'

'Yes, but we don't know if Bea has still to meet her soulmate,' Marcia pointed out. 'Saranya Ji never said if she'd met him already, or was to meet him in her future, only that she had to find him.'

'Good point,' said Pete.

'And of course,' I said, 'addressing the elephant in the room, what if he was Graham? And I've had my time with him already?'

'What do you think, Bea?' asked Marcia.

I let out a deep breath. 'No doubt I loved him and he loved me.'

'I'm sure Saranya Ji would have said if Graham was the one.'

'I looked for her on line,' I said. 'There are thousands of women with that name, but I couldn't find our Saranya Ji anywhere. I can keep trying, as maybe she could add something to what she told me already.'

'So where are you up to with your list?' asked Marcia.

'I contacted Kevin Grisham and we're meeting on Saturday.'

'Excellent. I remember him but . . . I know you liked him but there was something – how can I describe it? – a bit limp about him. My gut tells me it's not him.'

'Who knows? He sounded friendly on the phone, if a bit eager.'

'That was it,' said Marcia. 'He always came across as needy. Anyway, worth going to see him if only to eliminate him. Next is Bruno.'

'He's on Facebook, I've sent a friend request but haven't heard back yet. He was gorgeous. I'd love to see what he ended up doing.'

'But connection?' asked Marcia. 'If I remember right, he was only around one summer. What made you put him on the list?'

'He was unlike any of the Manchester boys, such a great dresser, charming. We exchanged a few letters after that summer, but then it faded; we were too far away to sustain any real kind of relationship.'

'Sam Gorman. You liked him and he adored you.'

'Stoner, remember. If he got off the dope, it would be

worth seeing where he ended up. I've already messaged Kate, his sister.'

'Yeah,' said Pete. 'But we all smoked dope back then. He's probably some hotshot executive now. I remember him. He dressed like a Victorian poet.'

'That was him. Very intense too.'

'Michael O'Connor?' asked Marcia. 'Definitely a contender.'

I felt myself blush. 'Peter Pan type, and I haven't heard from him since his fleeting visit weeks ago, so maybe he hasn't changed after all and is still full of promises and plans but fails to deliver.'

Marcia was watching me closely. 'By the colour of your face, there's still clearly something there.'

'You really loved him, didn't you Bea?' Pete asked.

'Did but . . . not sure I want to go back there to all that uncertainty.'

'You mustn't let fear hold you back, Bea,' said Marcia. 'If he's The One, then of course it's going to bring up some concerns. You have to be brave to let go to love—'

'And face the possibility of loss and heartbreak,' I said.

'Better to have loved and lost than never to have loved at all,' said Marcia.

'OK. Keep him on the list. I have his mobile number now so I can chase him up.'

'OK. Next. Graham. Ah . . .' I saw Marcia put a line through his name. 'Then Richard.'

'He's not on the list,' I said. 'Nor is Joe Wilding.'

'I know, but one thing you have to consider, Bea, is that Billy and Grace never got to spend a long period of time together, from what we know; they were young lovers and never really got to do the moving in together, getting bored with each other, finding each other's faults. So who's to say that they would have stayed the course anyway? Like with Joe and Richard, you found out you weren't suited to either because you were with them for years. I think, with the right one, the years will get better, so I reckon you haven't met him yet.'

'And that brings us pretty well up to date with the list, unless there's anyone you're holding out on telling us about,' said Pete. 'Kevin, Bruno, Sam, Michael.'

I cursed that I blushed again and Eagle-eyes Marcia spotted it straight away. 'Ah. OK, I'm going to add your neighbour Jon. I know there's something going on between you two.'

'No there isn't. He fancies himself as a playboy so, no, I don't want him on the list.'

'Ah, but one night with you might change all of that. Ah . . .' Marcia studied my reddening face. 'Bea! He's already had one night with you. Really? Have you been holding out on us? You have, haven't you?'

'Oh . . . Something I'd like to put behind me, and I don't want to talk about him so don't put him on the list. If he turned out to be The One, I think I might have to jump in a river.'

Marcia didn't look convinced. 'What happened with you and Jon? When?'

'Why are we even talking about him? Jon's not a contender,' I said.

'Methinks the lady doth protest too much,' said Pete.

'Ignoring that comment. Saranya Ji said I had a pattern in my relationships but I can't see one.'

Marcia glanced over the list, 'No, nor me, not really. Richard – father figure, Michael – a Peter Pan, Joe – Flash Harry, Graham – Steady Eddie.'

'So,' said Marcia, 'to sum up, here's the final list of contenders and our course of action. One: Kevin. Bea to meet on Saturday. Two: Bruno. Waiting to hear back. Three: Sam Gorman.'

'Waiting to hear back from his sister.'

'Four: Michael O'Connor. Bea to text him. Five: Jon. We know where he is.'

'Stop it. Jon is not on the list. I mean it. And that's it.'

'Have you actually slept with him or just had a date?' asked Marcia.

'I told you, not talking about it.'

'That means yes.'

'Once, OK? Happy? Ages ago, and not something ever to be repeated. A big giant mistake which is why I have never mentioned it. OK, so moving on.'

Marcia laughed. 'OK. Moving on.'

'Five,' I said. 'No Jon.'

Marcia just smiled. 'We'll see.'

*

When I got home, the postman was standing there with a parcel for me.

I took the package inside and unwrapped it to find a beautiful red lacquered Chinese box with a dragon and snakes painted in gold and silver on top. I opened it to find it was lined with silk and stuffed with Liquorice Allsorts. Marcia. Had to be. I picked up my mobile to thank her.

'Not me,' she said. 'Heather? She knows you like liquorice. In fact, everyone knows you love those sweets; always have, ever since you were small.'

'Always will,' I said.

'Or maybe it's a mystery admirer. Maybe you won't have to go looking for Billy, it sounds as if someone is coming after you. First the flowers, now this. Could it be Richard? He was always very generous, and the Chinese box sounds like the sort of thing he would get you.'

'Doubt it. Maybe the box but not the Liquorice Allsorts. He was a control freak when it came to sugar. It was banned from the house, and if he ever bought sweet treats, they would be the type sold for diabetics.'

'Bleurgh, but maybe it's his way of saying that he's changed and wouldn't tell you what to eat or wear or think any more.'

'Or maybe it was one of my brothers and the card has gone missing.'

'Well, let us know if you find out.'

I put the phone down and took a piece of liquorice. Jon? I remembered we'd had a conversation about sweets from our childhood on one of the evenings he'd been over. He'd told me that he loved Marathon bars, now called Snickers. I'd told him that I liked liquorice. But why wouldn't he have signed it? The man had an ego, no doubt about that; I was sure if he sent a gift, he'd want to make sure the receiver knew where it came from.

Next I called Heather to ask if she'd sent the box. 'No,' she said, 'and I've been thinking about something you should do. Go back to Simon for another session and see if you can find the mosaics you saw in your second session again. See if you can explore them and find that colour match between the one that represented the present and the one that represented the past.'

'Already booked.'

'So where are you up to on the soulmate search?' she asked.

'The numbers are going down. I have to see if there's any reply from Bruno or Kate about her brother Sam, book my train to see Kevin and text Michael – oh, and drop a note to Jon.'

'Jon? Is he on the list now? I thought you couldn't stand the man.'

'I can't. It's a note to ask him to park his car somewhere else in a couple of weeks' time when the removal van comes. I want to make sure I give him plenty of notice.'

'Right, OK, do that, then get on with contacting Michael. I saw the way you lit up when he came into the shop.'

'But he hasn't been in touch and he said he would be.'

'You can't rule him out just because of a fear of rejection.'

'That's what Marcia said too.'

'She's right. Text him. You have his number.'

'And say what?'

'Was great to see you. Are you coming back this way? Bea. One kiss,' said Heather. 'Short, simple, friendly.'

'Will do, as soon as you hang up.'

'What was Bruno like?' Heather asked.

'He appeared very sophisticated to me at the time; handsome too. He was dark and olive skinned, but don't forget I haven't seen him for over thirty years. I clicked on his Facebook page but couldn't see any of his posts or photos either. I sent him a private message.'

'What did you say?'

'Am looking for a hero from World War Two. Is it you come back in a new body?'

'Yeah sure,' said Heather.

'I wrote one of your lines about looking up people from the past.'

'And what was Sam like?'

'Intense, passionate about art and literature. I think he fancied himself as one of the romantic poets. He was also a stoner who loved his dope.'

'Better than laudanum, I suppose.'

'I reckon he'd have tried that if it had been available.'

'So why's he even on the list? You had enough of addiction problems with Joe.'

I shrugged. 'Because people change and I doubt he's still smoking dope thirty years on. You never know where life has taken him since. He had potential.'

'I thought it was worth checking him out, even if it's just to eliminate him, and we did have a pact that, if we were still single at fifty, we'd hook up again.'

'You're kidding? It has to be him then.'

'I doubt if he even remembers.'

'You never know. Kevin Grisham?'

'He was a sweetie.'

'Sweetie? Sounds a bit wet to me.'

'Well, he was only fifteen when I knew him and he did sound more confident when I spoke to him.'

'Might be an axe murderer then.'

'Thanks for that. I'm meeting him on Saturday.'

'Want me to come with you?'

'I'll be fine.'

37

Bea's been in touch. I wonder if she suspects that it's me who sent her the flowers and the box. Is it time to reveal myself? Almost. In the meantime, maybe I'll woo Bea some more. Now . . . what to send her next? Balloons? No. More flowers? No. Maybe I should google romantic gifts? I got out my laptop and did just that. There were websites that had all sorts of suggestions.

A hamper. No. That's what you get an aunt for Christmas.

A crate of beer. I don't think so.

Make-up. That could be misinterpreted, like I am saying she needs some. I did learn a couple of things from being married.

A book a month to be delivered.

A keychain with co-ordinate charms that lead to my address. No.

A key to my heart. Too soppy.

A puppy, kitten, goldfish. She might not thank me for any of those, though I know she's an animal lover. There will be time for all that later; that is, if she'll have me in her life.

I'll have a think. This is important. We'll be making memories, Bea and I, and whatever I send will be part of our story.

38

It was walking past a bathroom tile shop in Muswell Hill that cemented the idea. Since my appointments with Simon, I kept thinking about the mosaics I'd seen internally in the second session. I had it in mind to create something similar as an art project – not of my own life as I'd seen it under hypnosis, but of my friends, using the colours that they'd vibrated when I'd seen them in my subconscious. I wanted to use a mixture of mediums – photographs, which would be easy enough to fragment; Perspex; the gems and bits of old jewellery that I had stored away – but I wasn't sure how to create the luminosity that I'd seen. On looking in the shop window, I'd spied a display of tiny mosaic tiles in shiny gold, silver, green, black and red. They would be perfect. They had just the right shimmer of radiance to work. They would be too expensive to buy from there, but I could find out the supplier, decide on my colours then order them at trade price. It was the first time in years that I'd been fired up about working on something new, and I wanted to start with a multifaceted portrait of Heather, in all the glorious greens that I'd seen her in on the internal mosaic of my life.

Inside, the assistant was kind enough to give me some samples. As I looked around, I saw that there were also sheets of tiny coloured-glass tiles. They would also work; they reminded me of the wonderful glass walls and mosaics I'd seen in the City Palace in Udaipur. Maybe, as Heather had said, my visit there had sparked off the idea of mosaics in my subconscious mind. Whatever the explanation, I couldn't wait to get started.

As I came out of the shop, I went over to the deli over the road to pick up some supper. Outside, I noticed Stuart and Monty on the opposite side of the road. Stuart was standing at the board where people advertised local events and tradesmen and appeared to be pinning a leaflet up on there.

'Hey you,' I said, 'what you up to?'

Stuart turned, smiled and gave me a hug. 'You first. Is the sale of your house going through OK?'

'I couldn't have asked for better buyers. I'll be moving in with Marcia and Pete soon.'

'What about the shop?'

'All good, we've managed to sell off a lot more of the stock since you came in last.'

'And any more thoughts about what you might do next?'

'Yes. I'm going to take some time off, stand and stare for a while.'

'Good for you. "What is this life if, full of care . . ."'

'. . . "We have no time to stand and stare." I love that poem. William Henry Davies.'

Stuart smiled. 'Exactly.'

I looked at the board. 'Did I see you posting something?'

Stuart nodded. 'Ad for my band. Remember I told you

I'd got together with a few musicians. We're playing in a couple of weeks' time.'

'Your band?'

'Yes. The Reckless Hearts.'

'And you're on keyboard?'

'I am; we play mainly country blues. You could come and listen if you like.'

'I would.'

Stuart handed me a leaflet. 'All the details are on there.'

'Great. I'll definitely come.'

'Good, it's a date then, I mean . . . not a date date, bring your friends if you like.'

I laughed. I'd never seen Stuart look awkward before. 'I know what you mean. Will Janet be there?'

Stuart laughed. 'Not likely. Not her kind of thing at all, and don't have too high expectations, we've only been playing a few months. But I enjoy it, it's been great; rediscovering a lost part of me and having something creative to do makes a nice change from the day job.' Monty started tugging on his lead. 'Better go. Dog duty calls, then back to work. And Bea, could you pop into the office some time? There's something I wanted to talk to you about.'

'OK, any clues?'

'Few changes coming up I'd like to fill you in on. Nothing urgent.'

*

When I got home, I saw that there had been another delivery. Inside was a black and white box that I recognized immediately. Jo Malone. I *love* her products. I opened the black and white packaging to find a Pomegranate Noir Scent Surround Diffuser. I opened the box it was in and sniffed. A gorgeous scent filled the room. I looked for a card and found one inside a tiny envelope. All it said was 'Heady stuff. x' Interesting and true: receiving gifts like this was heady stuff indeed.

39

On Saturday morning, I took the train from London Bridge to Westgate-on-Sea. As I sat on the train, I planned to catch up with admin and emails.

On Facebook, I noticed that Bruno had accepted me as his friend and that there were two private messages. One from him, one from Kate. I clicked on the one from Bruno first.

Darling Bea, how lovely to hear from you and what a surprise after all this time, though of course, I have never forgotten you and our marvellous summer. What happy days. Write and tell me all your news. I am often in London on business. Sending you kisses. Affectionately Bruno.

Hmm. A nice reply, but it doesn't sound like a message from a man who's been thinking of me of late, I thought. Now I had access to his page, I scrolled through to see if there were any pictures of him. There were. There was one of him as a young man, which of course I recognized immediately. Others I had to look at more closely. Was that him? The chubby, bald, older man? Could it be that Bruno had lost his fabulous dark hair? I clicked on the photo and enlarged it. It *was* him. He was still stylish and impeccably dressed, in that way Italian men were, but he looked so much older. *What had I been expecting?* I asked myself as I glanced out of the window. It was thirty years since I'd seen him. I clicked through the rest of the photos. Bruno in an office, in front of a sports car, on various holidays around the world. I recognized the lakes, the Amalfi coast. Could he have sent me the flowers? The box? The Jo Malone? Surely not. He'd written in his message that it was a surprise to hear from me after all this time. That didn't sound like someone who had been sending me romantic gifts. And if it was him, how had he got my address? Maybe the same way that Michael O'Connor had, through Matthew? That wouldn't have been so hard, but Matthew would have told me if that had been the case. I stared at Bruno's photo. What should I write in reply? Did I even want to respond? *Could you be The One?* I asked. I looked for the sense of recognition I'd felt when I saw Billy's photo at the house in north London, that 'Ah, there you are.' The eyes are supposed to be the window to the soul. I zoomed in on Bruno's. I didn't feel anything. So no, not Bruno. I had a gut feeling that he wasn't my mystery man and mentally crossed him off the list.

Next I clicked on the message from Kate.

Dear Bea. Hey, good to hear from you. All well here. Have moved to Alderley Edge, not far from Manchester. Am still married to Roger, three kids and even one grandchild. Can you believe it? Come and visit. Now . . . you asked about Sam. I guess you haven't heard. He's in prison. Again. He was out briefly in January but back inside again. I don't know how long for this time. Truth be told, I find it hard to hear anything about him any more. Shall I tell him you've been asking after him? Curiously, a few months ago, he did ask if I knew where you were, but I kept it vague though did tell him London. I have to warn you, he's not good news, and the family and his ex-wife have just about washed their hands of him. Sam is not the man you would remember and, unless you want to assume the role of social worker, addiction therapist and nurse, I would advise against reconnecting. I feel bad saying this about my own brother, but we tried being supportive, bailing him out so many times, but he keeps going back to his old ways and I can't see what good would come from you resuming an old friendship. Sometimes these things are best left in the past. So sorry to have to break it to you like this, and of course Roger and I would always be happy to see you if you're up this way. Much love, Kate x

I stared out of the train window. I felt sad to have read what Kate had written. Although Sam had always been a mercurial soul who could have gone in so many directions, to hear that he'd ended up in prison, and, by the sound of it, was an addict, was such a waste. Would I try and see him? Reconnect? Probably not after what Kate had written. The last thing I wanted was a repeat of my time with Joe and his drug problem.

I checked my phone to see if by chance Michael had replied to my text. Nothing. I felt disappointed and resolved to put him out of my mind. Could he have sent me the gifts? I couldn't deny that part of me had been hoping that he had but then, if it had been him, he surely would have replied to a simple text.

This list of potential past lovers is disappearing fast, I thought as the conductor arrived in the carriage to inspect all the tickets.

*

At Westgate-on-Sea, I got off the train, walked to the front of the station and looked up and down the road. It looked a charming place, with a variety of shops opposite, including a fabulous-looking greengrocer's with boxes and baskets overflowing with fruit and vegetables in the window and out onto the street. A few people were standing on the pavement outside the station waiting. *How would I recognize Kevin?* I asked myself as I stood with them. *How would he recognize me? We should have agreed to carry red carnations.* As I looked around, a white battered Skoda drove up and stopped. A chubby middle-aged man with thinning grey hair got out of the driver's seat and came striding towards me.

'Bea? Is that you?'

'Yes, I . . . Kevin?'

He looked nothing like the skinny teenager with a mop of thick hair I had known so long ago. He pulled me into a hug where I got a whiff of some strange chemical smell. 'Come on. I can't stop here long,' he said as he went back to the car and opened the passenger door for me. 'Get in.'

The car had a strong scent too, a mix of stale cigarettes and meat pies. *Oh God, this was a bad idea*, I thought but, too late, he had already started up the car and was heading off down the street.

'So good to see you, Bea. I'm so glad you got in touch,' said Kevin as he drove. 'I've rustled up some lunch at home. It's not far and you can meet my babies.'

'Babies?'

Kevin grinned. 'All will be revealed.'

He continued on and right into one of the side streets, where we stopped outside a terraced house. He got out, rushed round to the door and opened it for me. 'Allow me, madam.'

As I got out, he looked me up and down. 'Well, I have to say, you're looking good, Bea. Kept your figure.'

'And you're looking well too,' I lied. He wasn't. His complexion was pallid, like that of a man who spent a good deal of time indoors. There was zero attraction to him and I wanted to get away as soon as possible. *I'll have lunch then make my excuses*, I thought as I followed him up the pathway and into the house, where I was hit with a strong, cloying, rotten smell, mixed with some kind of chemical. It reminded me of the chemistry lab from my school days – chlorine and maybe formaldehyde – and had obviously soaked into all Kevin's clothes.

'I got us a quiche and some salad from the Co-op,' he said as he led me into a small kitchen. 'And what would you like to drink? Tea? Wine? Beer?'

'Just water, thanks. You said something about babies, so I presume there is a Mrs Grisham?'

'Was. We've been divorced over ten years. Kids stayed with her. All local so I see them regularly.'

'So whose are the babies?'

'Come with me,' he said, and gestured that I should follow him to a room at the back of the house. Heather's voice saying 'axe murderer' rang in my head and I cursed that I hadn't let her come with me.

Kevin opened a door with a flourish and I went through

to find myself in a room with four large glass tanks. This was the source of the smell and it was overpowering.

'This is my hobby,' he said, 'my passion. Come and meet Mungo.'

He led me over to a tank in the corner where I spotted a red and orange snake looking back at us.

'Christ! What is that?'

'No need to be scared. He won't bite.'

'These are your babies?' I asked incredulously, as I looked at the other tanks to check that they all had lids on them.

'Yep. Mungo's a corn snake. Want to hold him? Or feed him – do that and he'll be your friend for life.' He reached into a bin in the corner and lifted out a dead mouse.

'No thanks.'

Kevin lifted the lid of Mungo's tank and dropped in the mouse. 'Come on. Meet the others.'

I moved along to the next tank. This time, I could see a grey-green snake with a white stripe curled up in the corner.

'That's Basher. He's a garter snake, and there's Rollo,' Kevin said as he pointed at the third tank, in which there was a brown snake with beige patches.

'Yes, very handsome,' I said in an attempt to sound enthusiastic.

'Isn't he? He's a ball python. And lastly, there's Slinky.'

'Good name for a snake,' I said as I looked into the last tank, where there was a brown snake with what looked like black circles drawn on him.

'He's a rainbow boa. And I have a tarantula in the bathroom. Sidney. Want to see him?'

'Er . . . no thanks. I'm not keen on spiders. Maybe later.' *Maybe never*, I thought, and resolved not to go to the loo.

Why oh why didn't I arrange for a phone call from Heather to give me a get-out clause if I needed one? I needed an excuse – and fast – to get out of there as soon as possible.

We went back into the kitchen and had a bland-tasting quiche with a bit of tomato and lettuce, while Kevin gave me a fascinating talk about snakes and their habits.

'And for pudding,' he said as he got up and went to a drawer. 'Ta-dah.' He produced a packet of Liquorice Allsorts. 'I remembered how you loved these back in the day. We both did. Remember?'

'I do.' *Oh please, please don't let it be him who sent them to me on Valentine's Day*, I thought. *It couldn't be, surely. He doesn't have my address. Or does he?* I remembered the box the sweets had come in; it had been covered in golden snakes. *Oh nooooo. He hadn't mentioned the box. Surely he would have made a reference to the gift if he'd sent it?*

'So tell me all about you,' Kevin said. 'You're doing a book about Manchester back in the day? I suppose you've found all sorts of people doing extraordinary things, though I bet none as interesting as me.'

'You're right there.'

'Want to take some photos?'

'Good idea,' I said. I thought he meant of him, but he led me back into the snake room, where I dutifully took pictures of the snakes on my phone and one of Kevin with Slinky wrapped around his neck.

'Want a photo of him round your neck?' Kevin asked.

'I think I'm going to have to decline that very kind offer, and I really have to get back now before the rush hour hits London,' I said as I backed towards the door.

'Completely understand,' said Kevin. 'The snakes aren't

everyone's cup of tea. No worries. I'll drop you back at the station.'

He drove me back and luckily there was a train five minutes later. I got on, sank back into the seat and texted Marcia and Heather. Eliminate Kevin Grisham. Not an axe murderer but pretty weird. Has snakes. Smells strange. Not the one for me.

A moment later, a text came back. Not from Marcia or Heather. It was from Kevin.

So great to see you, Bea. Hope we can make it a regular event now that we're back in touch. I'd love to see more of you and look forward to catching up where we left off so many moons ago. Come and stay next time. Kisses from your big snake Kevin x

Oh God, I thought. He'd even put a snake emoji after the kiss.

40

'And down down, deep down,' Simon said as I sat once more in his reclining chair. As in the previous sessions, I soon found myself drifting, relaxing.

'Don't try and force it,' Simon had advised, but I couldn't stop myself, I kept thinking mosaics, *I need to see the mosaics*, but they didn't come, nothing came, nor any sense of going back to the time of Billy and Grace, nothing. In fact, I think I fell asleep, because the next thing I was aware of was Simon's voice and waking up in his office.

'Don't be disappointed,' said Simon as I put on my coat and got ready to leave. 'Maybe what came up previously has served its purpose. You have to trust that and, if there is anything else to be revealed, your subconscious mind will find a way.'

Marcia said much the same when I called her later. 'The sessions proved without a shadow of a doubt that Grace and Billy were real because they led to Eileen and the confirmation that Minty also was real, and that was what convinced you that Saranya Ji spoke the truth. So, as Simon said, purpose fulfilled, there's no need to go there again. So what next?'

'Well, it's not going well, is it?'

'What do you mean?'

'Seeking out men from the past. So far it's got me nowhere. Andrew – monk who's taken a vow of silence; Jed – gay; Sam – addict and prisoner; Bruno – just not my type; Michael – unreliable; Kevin – peculiar-smelling snake man.'

Marcia started laughing. 'Maybe it's best not to look back sometimes, but don't rule out Michael. You don't know why he hasn't been in touch. He could have lost his mobile – people do – or, as I keep saying, it may be that you still have to meet this man, so hang on in there. Who knows what we might still find, who you've yet to encounter and, in the meantime, we're narrowing down the search.'

'But we don't know who sent the flowers or the Chinese box or the Jo Malone.'

'We don't, but whoever it is will reveal themselves, so relax. You don't go to all that effort to remain anonymous.'

*

When I got home, I passed some time looking at Jed's paintings on his website. I still had it in mind to contact him and resume our friendship. I flicked on the TV and soon fell asleep. I had the most vivid dream. I was in an art gallery, similar to the one where Jed's canvases were on display but, as I looked more closely, they weren't his paintings on the wall, they were my mosaics. As I'd seen under hypnosis, there was the one depicting my present life, a massive piece filling almost the whole wall. As I studied it, I noticed once again that different people seemed to exude different colours. I looked for Graham and noted he was in browns and shades of maroon, Marcia in the colours of autumn leaves, yellow, rust, oranges, bright and glowing; Heather shimmered in greens, Joe in reds.

I remembered Heather's instruction to look at the other mosaic, the one from my past life, and see if I could make a match. I turned and there it was on the wall opposite. I went over to study it. It seemed to be shrouded in mist but, as I peered through, it began to get clearer, like a photo image emerging in developing chemicals; first a blur of grey, then I could make out figures, tiny but becoming more distinct. I knew I needed to find one that matched someone's colours in the first mosaic. I turned and looked back at the first one, then returned to the second one. *I need to find Billy*, I thought within the dream. I looked for him and there he was in blues, silvers and grey. *Not Graham then, he was brown and maroon*, I thought, *nor Joe in red. Blues and grey; I must find the man in the same shades of blues and grey in my present life.* I turned back and scanned the first mosaic, looking for the right colours. Blues . . . blues . . . There, someone was coming clearer . . . I leant closer to see whose face it was when I became aware of a shrill sound, persistent; it was annoying, distracting me. I realized that it was my phone bringing me back to my sitting room. *Nooooooo*, I thought as I awoke and reached out for the mobile.

'Miss Brooks?'

'Yes.'

'And how are you today?'

'I . . . I . . . who is this?'

'We believe that you may have been mis-sold some PPI—'

'Arghhh.' I switched the phone off and nuzzled back into the cushions on the sofa, desperate to get back to my dream and what it had been about to reveal. I'd been about to see who my mystery man was, who Billy was now. I had been so close, *so* close. But, as is the way of dreams, once you've woken from them, they disappear so fast, gone, gone, and it's impossible to recall where you'd been or who with.

*

When I saw Heather the next day in the shop, I told her what had happened.

'Interesting,' she said. 'The mosaics didn't appear in your last hypnosis session but came up in a dream. What does that tell us?'

'What we've said all along, that the subconscious often interprets whatever's been on your mind or what you've been thinking about that day. I'd been looking at Jed's paintings on his website so that probably sparked it off, but then I was back to the mosaics and, in the middle of the dream, I remembered you telling me to look for Billy. I almost had him, almost, until those blooming people called, wanting me to claim for being mis-sold PPI.'

'But you did learn something valuable. You learnt that the man we're all looking for isn't Graham or Joe?'

'Did I? It was only a dream but yes, I suppose that I did. Joe was clearly bright reds.'

'Then cross them off the list. Take note of your subconscious mind.'

'I'm not so sure. What if it told me to go out and do

something mad. I'd be classed as insane, hearing voices, listening to what dreams tell me.'

'I think you should trust what your subconscious is telling you in this case. Something deep inside of you knows that, whoever you're looking for, it's not Joe. It was giving you colour-coded clues. Trust that. If a dream tells you to go and shoot someone, don't trust it. Come on, Bea, use your brain. You haven't lost your power of knowing what's right or wrong here.'

I laughed. 'OK.'

'Another way of saying it, dreams or no dreams, is that you should trust your gut instincts. If those are telling you not Jo, then we cross him off the list. You kind of had done already.'

'Done,' I said. 'Billy was silver, grey, shades of blue.'

'Couldn't be clearer. Did you see what colour Bruno, Michael, Sam or Jon were?'

'I was about to before that PPI call.'

'And did you see what colour Graham was?'

'Browns, maroons.'

'He used to dress in those colours.'

'He did.'

'So maybe that has something to do with it,' said Heather.

'Maybe,' I said.

*

One night, soon after Graham had proposed, he had gone to give a lecture on the life of Matisse. 'Back about ten,' he said as he kissed me goodbye then headed out the door.

Ten o'clock came, then eleven, and I went up to bed.

Graham often got caught up after his talks, with eager students wanting to ask questions, and he could never resist the opportunity to adjourn to a nearby pub for further discussion.

At eleven thirty, I was awoken by loud knocking on the door. I grabbed my dressing gown, hastened down the stairs and opened the front door to find a young policeman standing there. I knew immediately that something had happened. 'Is he still alive?' I asked.

The policeman asked if he could come in. By this time, I felt as if I had left my body, but must have ushered him into our sitting room where he shook his head in answer to my question. 'I am so sorry, Ms Brooks.'

'What happened?'

'A massive heart attack.'

'Where?'

'Just outside Highgate tube station.'

'Was he taken to hospital?'

'He was, but there was nothing they could do.'

'Are you quite *quite* sure that it was Graham White?'

'We are,' said the policeman. 'Would you like to call anyone, and then I can take you to the hospital.'

I called Marcia and Pete, got dressed, then went with the police officer to the hospital. The hours after that were a blur. I walked through them as though I was barely there.

'A good death,' friends said. 'He wouldn't have known anything.' I knew they meant well. Good or bad death, the house felt empty, the bed too big, the silence unbearable, our dreams of a family and long life together gone. My world changed so fast, and the motto from my earlier life was once more reinforced: love brings pain, and those you love, leave you.

41

Wednesday evening was recycling night. I carried my various boxes to the pavement to leave them for the bin men to collect the next morning.

'We have to stop meeting like this,' said a voice behind me, and I turned to see Jon who had just come out of his house. He carried recycling boxes to the pavement. 'See, I finally got the hang of it. Plastics, glass and cardboard, all separate. Gold star for me.' He put his boxes out then looked up at the sky. 'I can think of more romantic locations.'

'Who said anything about romance?' I said as I turned to go back inside.

'Come and have a drink with me,' he said. 'I've got Chief permanently now. He'll be happy to see you.'

'I . . .'

'Are you doing something?'

'Just finishing packing.'

'God, yes, you've sold up, haven't you? Come and tell me all about it. What are your plans?'

'That's the big question. But what about you? I haven't seen you around lately.'

'Ah, so you've missed me?'

'In your dreams.'

'A man can hope, can't he? Look, Bea, I appreciate we got off to a bad start; no, actually I think we got off to a great start . . . then I messed up. I realize how things might have seemed. I'm not really that man. Let me make it up to you and let's get inside, it's freezing out here.'

He wouldn't take no for an answer, so I closed up my house and went over to his. I was curious to hear what he had to say. Inside, it looked homely and warm. He'd obviously been working on the place since I was last there and put up pictures and prints, books on the shelves, rugs on the floor.

'White or red wine?' he asked as he took my coat. 'Make yourself comfy.'

'White. Thanks,' I said as I sat on the L-shaped sofa in his sitting room. 'It's looking good in here.'

'Starting to look like someone lives here at last.'

Chief came running out of the kitchen and sprang straight onto my lap.

'Push him off,' said Jon. 'He shouldn't be on the furniture but I'm afraid he's rather spoilt.'

'Rather a dog than a snake,' I said.

'Snake?'

'Long story. I met up with an old friend. He keeps snakes.'

Jon pulled a face.

'Exactly. Not my thing either.'

Jon disappeared for a few minutes, so I took the opportunity to have a closer look at some of the prints he'd chosen. On the wall behind the sofa was a series of black-and-white photos that looked as if they'd been taken in the

1940s or 1950s. All were of scenes around North London, some I recognized. One in particular caught my eye; it was the street in Kentish Town where Marcia and I had been looking for Billy Jackson's house.

'I like your photos,' I said when Jon brought two glasses of wine in and handed one to me. 'Where did you get them?'

'I found them in a cardboard box in Camden Lock, on one of those stalls that sells old postcards of the area. These were under a table; they had all sorts in there going back years, but these drew me to them. I thought they'd look good framed and displayed like a collection.'

I pointed at the photo taken in Kentish Town. 'Do you know this street?'

Jon nodded. 'I know the pub. See it there on the left? I've been in a couple of times; in fact, I was at a gathering there last week.'

'Gathering?'

'Memorial.'

'Oh, I'm sorry.'

He shrugged. 'Not one of my inner circle, if you know what I mean, but sobering none the less. So . . . tell me everything, Bea. Why the move?'

'Time for a change.'

'I sense there's more to it than that.'

I shrugged. 'Financial reasons too. I needed to consolidate my assets, get rid of a few debts.'

'You OK with it all? The changes, I mean.'

'Sure. I wasn't at first but now it's all happening, it actually feels good, positive.'

'It's funny how your priorities change as you get older

– er, not that I'm saying you're old, but you know what I mean. You start to think about what makes you happy.'

'And what makes you happy, Jon?'

'People. Good company.'

'Hence the endless stream of beautiful blondes?'

His expression clouded. 'No, actually they didn't make me happy. I soon learnt that. Don't forget, I was married for a long while, twenty-five years. I guess I needed to run wild a bit, test the water to see if anyone would still want me. I came out of that long-term stability not sure who I was any more or what I was looking for and I needed to explore that. I realize it must have looked pretty shoddy from your point of view. A bit of insecurity in there too, I guess. I needed to prove that I was still an attractive man, but in the end, it's not about the number of conquests, it's about the quality.' He looked at me hard. 'I'll be honest. I think we had something. I don't think I realized at the time.'

'I can understand the need to run wild when something hasn't worked out. I did the same a long time ago and came to the same conclusion, quality not quantity.'

'So what are you looking for?'

'In life?'

'In a relationship.'

'Ah. I'm not sure I know any more. Loyalty, kindness, no snakes.'

'I could do loyalty and kindness and definitely no snakes.'

'What are you saying, Jon?'

'That I'd like to give it a go with you, Bea. Go on a few dates, see how we get on. What do you say? You and me.'

'Er . . . I . . . I've a lot going on at the moment.' Inwardly I was debating whether to tell him the whole truth – all about Saranya Ji; the fact that I'd been checking out a list of men – and see how he reacted. I decided not to. No man wants to be one on a list. 'I'm flattered, I really am, just—'

'You don't fancy me?'

This time, I looked at him hard. No doubt there was a spark between us. We both smiled in recognition of it.

I made a quick decision. Jon had talked about testing the water with his various women; well, I was going to test the waters with the men left on my list and see what they thought about the idea of past lives. 'OK, this might sound really mad but I'm just going to come out with it. When I was in India, I saw a fortune-teller . . .'

Jon put his hand over his heart. 'And she told you about me?'

'Stop it. No. Maybe. She said I'd known the true love of my life in a past life and I had to find him this time round.'

'Ah . . . that again. Is this your way of telling me to mind my own business again?'

'No. I'm serious. She told me that I'd known someone in a past life in the Second World War and that he'd been killed in action in the defence of Calais and that, just as I was back in this life, so is he.'

'Ah, I know all about the defence of Calais,' he said, and indicated his bookshelves. 'Look, loads of books about the Second World War. It is one of the stories that has always fascinated me; the men who fought there saved thousands at Dunkirk. So . . . your past life man, *definitely* me. And now you've found me. We've already wasted half our lives, maybe more than half. Let's go to bed.' He moved closer to me on the sofa and put his arm round me.

I laughed. 'How would I know it was you?'

'Easy. We have a connection and you can't deny we have something going on. We don't have to have sex, I didn't mean that, we could just cuddle and kiss.'

'Ah, but this connection, is it just physical? Surely there's got to be more than just good sex.'

Jon's face lit up. 'Ah, so you admit it was good. It *was* good, wasn't it?'

'Do you believe that we have all had past lives? I didn't, but—'

'Oh absolutely. Makes perfect sense, doesn't it? I've seen a dead body twice, my mother and my father, and it was so clear that, although their bodies were there, they'd gone somewhere else, as if they'd left the physical self that they'd inhabited behind like a piece of used clothing. They have to have gone on somewhere.'

I wasn't sure if Jon was just coming out with this, pretending to take it seriously just to get me in to bed. 'Yes, but where? Where had they gone? You believe the spirit lives on but that doesn't necessarily mean that it moves on to a different life.'

'That's the big question. No doubt we'll find out one day. A friend of mine had an amazing daughter; she's twenty-nine now, but she could play the piano like a concert pianist at the age of five – no kidding, complete genius. Her parents always used to joke that she was the reincarnation of Mozart.'

'He was a child genius too, wasn't he?'

'He was. Maybe that's the explanation. Be nice to think you carry some of what you've learnt over. So, OK, this fortune-teller told you that you have a soulmate somewhere?'

'Yes, but I don't know how I am supposed to recognize him.'

Jon looked thoughtful for a few moments. 'Interesting. No. I don't think you need look any further. It's me. Definitely.' He grinned, moved in again and started nuzzling my neck. I gently pushed him away.

'There has to be more to a relationship than getting physical.'

'But it's an important part, don't you think? Has to be. I mean, say it wasn't me and you found some bloke who you thought is your long-lost soulmate and the sex was crap. What then? Would you stay with him just because some fortune-teller said he might be your soulmate?'

'Good point, but there are all sorts of aspects to a relationship – companionship, kindness, shared interests, learning from each other, enjoying each other's company outside the bedroom.'

'OK. How about this then? I think we should give us a go. You and me. We get to know each other better. Think about it, take your time, but I reckon we could have a good time together. You say you have no plans for the immediate future?'

'Only that I'm going to take some time off. Stop, re-evaluate, and not rush into anything.'

'Sounds good to me. If you're taking some time off, maybe we could do that together. Maybe even go away together, a holiday, watch a few sunsets in romantic locations.'

'Sounds lovely.'

Jon smiled. 'Where do you fancy? Caribbean? Spain? Bali?'

'Italy,' I said. 'I'm not saying I'll go with you, but I do love Italy.'

'Me too. Let's go, see all of it – the lakes, the Amalfi coast, Ravello, Puglia, Sicily, Sardinia, Umbria, Tuscany. We'll be old buggers with Zimmer frames by the time we've done it all. Italy has a smell I love – not just the food, the coffee, no; it's the air there, it smells different.'

'Talking about smells. Jon, did you send me a Jo Malone diffuser?'

He raised an eyebrow as if in surprise. 'Send? A present in the post?'

If he was my mysterious admirer, he was playing it very cool. 'Yes. Gorgeous-smelling stuff.'

'And you don't know who it was from?' His eyes were twinkling. Was it from him and he was teasing me? Or letting me think it was him?

'I don't. Whoever it was, also sent a box filled with Liquorice Allsorts.'

'My favourites, and I seem to remember yours too. You had a bowl of them in your kitchen when I first came over.'

'I was also sent a bunch of gardenias.'

'A man of taste.'

'Jon, was it you?'

'What do you think?'

'I don't know, that's why I'm asking.'

'Who else would they be from?'

'No idea, but if you tell me it was or wasn't you, it gives me a better idea.'

'Of *course* they were from me. Who else?'

'I . . . So why didn't you send a card?'

'And ruin the mystery? Where would be the fun in that? So you liked what I sent?'

'I did, more than generous, thank you. I . . . I don't know

what to say.' I didn't know what to say because, as well as being surprised, some part of me doubted if he was telling the truth.

'You're very welcome,' he said.

'OK, then tell me about you? Where have you been the past weeks? I haven't seen you about in the mornings that much.'

His face clouded. 'A few personal issues to sort out.'

'You're not giving away much. You asked a moment ago what I wanted in a relationship. No secrets, that would be something pretty high up the list.'

'OK. I was clearing out my old home now the divorce is final. Hard letting go of some aspects of the past sometimes, but you have to move on, so let's drink to that, no secrets, and let's set a date. Lunch or dinner somewhere lovely. We'll make some plans. You tell me what you like to do. You tell me everything about yourself, I'll tell you everything. Deal?'

'Deal,' I said. At that moment, my phone pinged that I had a text. I was going to ignore it when Jon stood up.

'Take it,' he said as he headed for the kitchen. 'I'll get us another glass of wine.'

I took my phone from my bag and looked at the text. *Am back in London week after next week. Will call soon to arrange to meet up. OK? Love Michael X*

Men are like buses, I thought. *No dates for ages then three come at once. Jon, Stuart and now Michael.*

'Anything interesting?' asked Jon as he came back into the room.

'Old flame is back in town,' I said. It wouldn't do any harm to let Jon know that he had competition, and I wasn't going to roll over just because he'd asked me on a date.

'Old flame, huh?' he asked as he sat down beside me. 'And is the spark still there?'

'I guess I'll have to find out.'

For a brief second, Jon looked vulnerable. 'You don't think he is your soldier returned, do you?'

'Guess I'll have to find out.'

'Never go back, that's my advice,' said Jon. 'The past is done with, we have to move on.'

'You would say that, wouldn't you?'

He laughed. 'Of course.'

42

By the end of March, my house was empty and had been cleaned ready for the new owners who were keen to get in before Easter. The sale had gone through in record time with no hold-ups or complications on either side. I went from room to room reliving memories of my time there. Boris and I when I first moved there. I'd been happier then, full of hope for the shop, for a new chapter in my life. Then there were the Richard years, not my best era, with the endless boring dinner parties and lunches entertaining his dull friends. After him came freedom again, a joy at first; I could eat what I wanted again, wear what I pleased, have my own friends round, but that had soon faded and become familiar, and the nagging sense of something or someone missing had taken over.

'Time to lock up,' I told myself as I gathered my bag and coat. I thought about letting Jon know that I was going. I hadn't got back to him about his proposal and he hadn't pushed, unlike Kevin, who was beginning to be a nuisance, sending texts and phoning late at night.

As I went into the hall, the doorbell rang and, speak of the devil, there he was, standing on the step.

'Bea,' he said. He was carrying a battered bunch of flowers, the type you get from the forecourt of a garage. 'You haven't been answering my calls so I thought if Muhammad won't come to the mountain, the mountain better come to Muhammad. So here I am. Are you going somewhere?'

'I am,' I said as I stepped outside and shut the door behind me. 'Urgent appointment. I am so sorry you've come all this way but you really should have let me know.'

'I tried to but you don't reply.'

'It's been a hectic time. I'm . . .' I was about to say I was moving but didn't want him to ask where to. 'Anyway, got to dash.'

'No problem. I'll wait. There has to be a café around here somewhere. So, this is where you live?' he asked as he looked up at the house.

'Yes. How did you find out?'

'Probably the same way you found me,' he said and tapped the side of his nose. 'We have our methods.'

Fair point, I thought. 'Er . . . how long are you in London for, Kevin?'

'Just today. There's a convention on in Earl's Court which I'll be attending later today, about caring for snakes. Couldn't miss that, plus I wanted to see you. I was hoping you might like to come. Since you came down to Westgate, I can't get you out of my mind. The timing, seeing you again, it felt like destiny.'

'It did?' *Oh God, how am I going to get rid of him*, I asked myself.

'Yes. We were good together once, we could be again.'

'Oh Kevin, I am so sorry but I am in a relationship.'

'You are?'

'Yes.'

'Is it serious?'

'Very. Love of my life.'

'Can I meet him?'

Oh lord, I thought. *How was I going to conjure up a partner at a moment's notice and, not only that, one who'd play along if necessary? Of course. Heather.* 'Not a he, a she,' I said. 'We've actually been together for years.' *Not a complete lie*, I told myself, *Heather was a partner of sorts.*

Kevin looked shocked. 'So you're—?'

'Attached, yes, and I'm in a bit of a hurry here and I'm going to be busy for the rest of the day. I'm sorry I haven't returned your texts. Truth is, there's a lot going on in my life at the moment. There's no point in you hanging about here, so you might as well head off for your convention and when you go back to Westgate, I promise I'll return your calls. OK?'

He looked peeved but nodded, and handed over the flowers. 'Not much point if you're not available but you might as well have these.'

'Thank you, and you're probably right, not much point. Now, I can give you a lift to the tube if you like, it's on my way.'

He got into the car and, once again, I noticed his strange scent. I felt mean. He was probably a nice enough bloke and, like most people, just looking for love. It had been cowardly of me to ignore his texts and then lie to him. I resolved to do better and be friendly at least.

I dropped him at the tube. On my way back up to

Highgate village, I took my usual route past where Stuart lived. The road was blocked by two removal trucks. I was about to reverse when I noticed Stuart's wife, Janet, was supervising the men. She looked harassed and, as soon as she spotted me, came over to the car.

I wound down the window. 'Are you moving?' My heart sank. Stuart hadn't mentioned this, although maybe that was what he had to tell me when he'd talked about catching up on changes.

'Yes. Off we go. New start.' She indicated the trucks. 'It's manic.'

'I know. I'm in the process of moving too. But where are you going?'

'Stuart hasn't told you?'

'No.'

'Arundel. Fresh start and all that. Anyway, better go.'

'Isn't Stuart helping?'

'He's at the prison Friday mornings. Convenient, isn't it, leaving me to do all the donkey work. Typical man.'

'Prison?'

'He teaches accountancy to the inmates there once a month. Didn't you know?'

'No.'

'Has done for years. Anyway, I'd better get on.' She sighed. 'I'm exhausted and we've only just got started. I could kill Stuart disappearing at a time like this.'

'Surely he'll be back later?'

'Doubt it. Probably for the best, he'd only get in the way. That reminds me, I must make sure I haven't packed his suit. He'll need it as we've got a wedding to go to next week. Last thing I need at the moment but—'

A car behind me beeped its horn. When I turned around, a driver who was parked to my right indicated that he wanted to drive off and I was in the way. 'Looks like I'd better get going too. Best of luck with the move, Janet,' I said and reversed back up the street. I felt shocked. Stuart leaving? I couldn't imagine him not being around. *Why hadn't he told me?* I asked myself as I turned the car and drove away. Truth was, Stuart and Janet seemed an odd match. She was a neat woman, always beautifully turned out in navy or grey, but she appeared to lack humour; she was certainly not someone you could have fun with. They say opposites attract. Stuart seemed to be all the things she wasn't: slightly dishevelled in his dress, kind, thoughtful, good company and he had a quirky sense of humour on occasions. On the times I'd been to their home, I'd noticed that Janet bossed him around as if he was her personal and slightly dim slave and she was his superior. I'd told myself that every marriage has its own dynamic agreed to by both parties, but it made me feel uncomfortable to witness him being diminished by her as though she didn't really appreciate what she had. And now they were leaving. The thought made me overwhelmingly sad.

43

I've always felt that Bea is not aware of her own beauty. She's not conventionally good looking, could never appear on the catwalk or in *Vogue*, but she has a tremendous sense of style and looks interesting, the kind of person you'd want to hang out with. I would anyway. Not that she is unattractive, far from it. She has fine features, soulful eyes, and it is the spirit that shines through them that draws me in; though sometimes it is as if there is a shadow over her, a sadness or regret that I have seen from time to time. I'd like to see her come out of that shadow into the full sun where she belongs. She deserves to be loved and I hope that she will allow me to be the one who does just that. Not long now until I play my hand. Slightly scary stuff. Will she feel the same way? And what the hell will I do if she doesn't?

44

'No hurry at all,' said Marcia as I moved the last of my cases into what had been Freya's room on the top floor. It was a sweet room, painted dove grey, with a skylight window on the sloped roof, a single bed and Victorian wardrobe and chest of drawers. 'You make yourself at home and stay for as long as you like. Pete and I are totally behind the idea that you tread water for a while before making any major decisions, and we love that you're going to be with us for a while.'

I gave her a hug. 'Thanks, Marcia. I can't tell you how much I appreciate this.'

'These are for you,' she said, and gave me a set of house keys. 'I'll leave you to settle in. Will you be around for lunch? There will be plenty.'

Marcia always did a roast enough for four even though Ben and Ruby were away. Sundays always followed the same pattern at their house: a large English breakfast, reading the papers or a walk on the Heath, then a big traditional lunch around four, and a movie afterwards with a bottle of good red wine.

'Tempting but I want to get on with my new project,' I said.

'Are you going to tell me any more about it?'

I shook my head. I didn't even want to talk about the mosaic idea too much in case I jinxed it. 'Early days, but I haven't felt this inspired in a long time. When there's something to show, you'll be the first, I promise.'

'Can't wait,' she said as she went to the door.

After she'd gone, I sat on the bed and took a deep breath. It had all happened so fast. The sale, the move, my old life gone in trucks and boxes, a new life beckoning when I'd decided what, where and when. I got up and emptied the cases I'd brought with me. It didn't take long. I'd brought a few clothes, books, toiletries and essentials to see me through a few weeks. If I needed more stuff, I could always go to the lock-up.

As I was unpacking the last bag, my mobile rang and I glanced down to see that it was Michael. I clicked on answer.

'Hey Bea,' he said. 'Where are you? I called round to your house to find you'd gone.'

'I know. It was a quick sale. I've just moved in to Pete and Marcia's temporarily until I decide where I want to be. And you? Are you back in London?'

'I am, in fact, that's why I was calling. My niece's wedding is on Saturday and I wondered if you'd come along as my plus one.'

'Won't they mind? I imagine they've already done the guest list and seating plan.'

'No, it's fine. I already checked in the hope that you'd say yes.'

'Sure. OK. I'm not doing anything.'

'Fantastic. Give me Pete and Marcia's address and I'll come and get you. About eleven, that OK?'

'Perfect. Oh . . . do I need a hat?'

'No hat, but you got a party dress or something?'

I laughed. 'No. All my clothes are packed and in storage. Don't worry. I'll find something.'

After the call, I made my way to Hampstead where I could get on with my mosaic in the room over the shop. As I laid out all my materials, I thought I hadn't felt as happy or fired up about a piece of work for years. The portrait, if you could call it that, was taking shape in my mind and was to be a mix of elements – photos, glass, beads, and whatever else seemed appropriate. I had a series in mind, to portray all the people I knew, but I was going to start with one of Grace and Billy. Theirs was a love story from the war, one of the so many forgotten, unrecorded, lost in the mists of time. I wanted to honour their memory and I was going to do it through my art. I sent off for copies of their birth and death certificates. I printed copies from the censuses that showed a record of them. I scoured the Internet looking for photos and postcards from Calais in 1940. I looked for images of dressmakers and various pieces of fabric from the same time. I resolved to make a mosaic portrait of Graham, too. It would be in memory of him and a tribute to him. Apart from the evening in the lock-up, I'd barely been able to look at his photos since he'd disappeared from my life, but turning them into a work of art would be a positive thing to do and maybe help heal the wounds of loss.

When I had everything I needed, I pulled out fabrics I'd collected over the years – silks, satins and velvet in shades of pink, sepia and dove grey, as those felt like the right colours for them. As I worked, I had a flashback to when I was five, at my parents' house, collecting bits of fabric in a biscuit tin. How had I forgotten that?

I put everything out on the floor then began to place some of the items against each other to see how they looked. I cut up bits of fabric, bits of photos, switched the lights on when the light outside began to fade and, when I looked at my watch, six hours had gone by. The room looked a total mess. I quickly sent a text to Heather. *Office is banned. Please don't go up there in the morning. Am working on project and want to leave it all as it is and will continue work evenings and spare time.*

45

'You look fabulous,' said Marcia when I came down to the hall in my wedding outfit the following Saturday morning. I'd borrowed a calf-length, pale blue silk dress from Freya which she had worn to a wedding last year, and Marcia had lent me a dove-grey pashmina to wear over it. A rope of pearls and earrings to match, grey shoes and handbag and I was ready.

'Very elegant,' said Pete.

The doorbell rang a moment later and Marcia opened it to let Michael in. He looked very handsome in a navy suit and silver silk tie. As soon as he saw me, he strode towards me and lifted me into a big hug, then groaned as if he'd pulled a muscle.

Pete and Marcia cracked up laughing. 'None of us are as young as we used to be,' said Pete.

'You OK?' I asked.

He laughed. 'Absolutely, just not as fit as I was and you're not as light.'

'Cheek.'

'Oh. No. I didn't mean you've . . . oh, you know what I mean. I'm getting older, that's what. You look great by the way.'

'But are you OK? You look a little pale.'

'Virus,' he said. 'Had an absolute stinker. I was in bed for weeks, can you believe it? No wonder I left for sunnier shores. Being bedridden like that reminded me of why I left in the first place.'

'There has been a lot of it around,' said Pete and gave him a hug. 'But good to see you, man, it's been years.'

'Time for a coffee before you go?' asked Marcia.

Michael glanced at his watch. 'Maybe afterwards. I'm best man so I've got a few things to do when I get there so we'd better get going.'

Marcia opened the door for us. 'Now don't be late back,' she joked as we headed for Michael's car.

I laughed. 'You do know I'm fifty, don't you?'

We got into the car and soon we were on our way.

'I haven't even asked you where we're going. Where is the wedding?'

'Kentish Town,' said Michael as he indicated the sky, 'and look, the sky is blue, it's springtime and I have a date with a beautiful girl. What could be better?'

'You always were a smooth talker,' I said.

'Sorry I wasn't in touch earlier,' Michael continued. 'I really was laid low. Even getting up to the bathroom was a mammoth effort; the norovirus, I think it was called. It was still lingering when I got to London too, so I stayed away from people in case I passed it on.'

'Don't worry,' I said. 'I've been busy. Moving house . . .'

'. . . And your shop?'

'The landlord still hasn't got a buyer for it, but I've given my notice for a few weeks' time.'

'Great. So let's go somewhere fabulous. I was thinking about you a lot when I was ill. I thought I might take off after the wedding and see a bit of Europe before I head back to Thailand. You could come with me. France, Spain, Italy, be a lovely time to go. What do you say?'

I almost laughed. First Jon inviting me away, now Michael. 'Sounds fabulous. Tell me. . . have you been sending me gifts?'

Michael feigned surprise. 'Gifts? Why? What sort of gifts? Who? The cad. I didn't realize I had competition. I challenge him to a duel at dawn.'

I laughed. 'Seriously. Whoever it is has sent me a bunch of flowers and a Chinese box full of Liquorice Allsorts and . . .'

Michael smiled. 'Liquorice Allsorts. Did he now? They were always your favourite. You always made me laugh; so particular with eating a healthy diet, then it all went out the window when the Liquorice Allsorts were around.'

'You're evading the question. Did *you* send those things?'

'No card with them? No indication at all where they came from?'

I shook my head.

'You must have *some* idea who sent them.'

'I have my suspicions but I'm not entirely sure.'

'Well, I reckon if he didn't send a card, it's part of some master plan. Wait and see what he sends next.'

'Or you could tell me if it was you. Coincidentally, they started arriving around the time you got back to England and got in touch.'

Michael raised an eyebrow and grinned. 'Really?'

'So was it you? Tell me.'

'And spoil all the fun? I wouldn't do that.'

'You're infuriating.'

'Thank you. I try to be.'

'OK. Next question. Remember we talked about past lives last time we met?'

'I do.'

'Have you ever had a sense of déjà vu about a place or person?'

'All the time. I don't know if it means anything, though. Some people you recognize, some places feel familiar, so what? The only time that's real is the here and now. I try and live in that.'

'Very deep.'

'Do you think? That's me, deep.'

We reached the traffic lights at Kentish Town, crossed over, then Michael turned left into the street where I had been with Marcia to look for Billy Jackson's old house. 'Michael, where is this wedding?'

Michael slowed the car down and began to park. 'Just over there, that little church there on the left. The reception is in a pub, just there, so not far to go.'

I felt a shiver run through me as I looked at the small crowd gathering outside the church; to my surprise, amongst them were Stuart and his wife, Janet. *This is weird*, I thought, as Michael got out then went round to open the car door for me. *We're on the street where Billy lived, about to go into a church where maybe Billy used to go. Could this be a defining moment and Michael will experience that sense of déjà vu that we were just talking about.*

*

Fifteen minutes later, I found myself seated in the church that Marcia and I had looked at back in January. Stuart and Janet were sitting three rows in front and, so far, hadn't seen me. Michael was at the back, greeting the guests, who were still arriving. Up at the front, a nervous young groom was standing at the altar. I looked around at the stained-glass windows, the inscription on the wall where Marcia and I had found Billy's name. I wondered again if Heather was right and this was the church where Grace and Billy were due to be married. *Does it seem familiar?* I asked myself, but still nothing resonated. I thought back to Mum and Dad telling me about my imaginary friend when I was little and how I used to plan my wedding. If any of it was true, then Grace had been planning her wedding just as I had been planning mine to Graham so many moons ago. The thought made me feel overwhelmingly sad. *Stop this*, I told myself, *this is a wedding, a happy occasion*. At that moment, Stuart turned around to look at the guests and he spotted me. He looked very dashing in a grey suit; and appeared surprised to see me but smiled and waved. The bride's arrival music began to play and the congregation stood to watch as Melanie, a blonde English rose in an elegant ivory dress and veil, advanced along the aisle on Michael's arm.

It was a lovely service, and as soon as it was over and the couple had gone to sign the register, Michael went to the front and called for attention. 'The reception will be held in the Bell and Anchor next door. Not far to go, out of the church then turn right and we're in the room upstairs above the pub. Help yourselves to a drink, but please could all the immediate family stay here for a short while to get some photos while everyone can still stand up.'

The crowd laughed, stood, and some began to filter out, so I got up to join them. I hovered by the steps at the door, unsure whether to go and join Michael who was busy with the photographer, or whether to go over to the pub.

'Bea, what a treat to see you here,' said a man's voice behind me. 'Bride or groom's side?'

I turned to see Stuart. I looked around for Janet but she'd moved away and was walking towards the pub with one of the female guests.

'Neither, really. I'm a plus one for an old friend.' I pointed over at Michael. 'Michael invited me. Melanie's his niece.'

'Ah, yes, him, he's the chap from your past, isn't he? It turns out he's Rob's brother. Did you know Rob, Melanie's dad?'

I shook my head. 'No. Did you?'

'Rob was one of my oldest friends. Sadly he died before he could see his daughter married. I know how much he'd have wanted to be here today, which is why I volunteered to help organize things with Michael's help.'

'Oh, so you've met Michael?'

'Just met recently. Both of us wanted to make things easier for Jess, Rob's widow. It's a bittersweet occasion for her, I think. A happy day to see Melanie married but so sad Rob isn't here.' He offered me his arm. 'Shall we go on?'

I took his arm and looked over my shoulder to see if Michael was still busy. He was but looked over and gave me the thumbs-up.

*

Once inside the pub, Stuart was soon swept away by old friends, and I stood for a moment, uncertain who to talk to and feeling very much like the gate-crasher. Luckily Janet noticed me and came over to say hello.

'How did the move go?' I asked.

'Fine, fine – loads to do still, obviously.'

'It will be a long way for Stuart to travel though, won't it?'

'Long way? What do you mean?'

'His office in Highgate. Or will he be giving that up? I suppose accountants can work from anywhere these days.'

Janet was staring at me oddly. 'Hasn't he told you?'

'Told me what?'

'You might as well know, people soon will. Probably not the word to say at a wedding, but it begins with D.'

'D?'

'Divorce, darling,' she said.

'Oh. I am sorry.'

'Don't be. No need. Best thing for both of us. Should have done it years ago.' She saw someone she knew on the other side of the room, waved and went over to join them.

Divorced? Stuart? My mind began to reel. That meant he was free, single. I took a gulp of champagne then another one, as a tidal wave of repressed feelings threatened to break down the wall that had held them back. I'd told the world and myself that he was my friend, but I'd been secretly in love with him from the day I met him. Had he ever felt anything? Apart from the night at the lock-up, he'd never given me the slightest hint that he was attracted to me, never flirted, was always professional. The main sense I got from him was that he acted protectively, like an older brother looking out for me. I'd always felt like a silly girl with a schoolgirl crush on someone out of her reach, so had pushed the attraction I felt for him to the back of my mind and never mentioned it to anyone. It was there from that first day on the Heath – a connection, a pull, a brightness I always felt when around him. Sometimes, at our sessions in his office, he'd let his guard down and talked about his life and passions – music, animals, his love of history and art; he wanted to paint, dabbled in watercolours at the weekends. But he hadn't been available. I'd reminded myself every time I saw him until I was used to seeing him as a friend, nothing more. He was married with two grown-up children and I wasn't a home-wrecker, never had been, never would be. And I'd always thought he was happily married because I'd never heard him criticize his wife; not once. I'd told myself the attraction I felt was all in my imagination, and the feelings I had were because he was a man out of reach, which was convenient because I would never be let down by him. As long as it was only in my head, a love affair unconsummated, he couldn't disappoint me, reject me, cause me pain. My fantasy lover.

And now he was free.

I took a third gulp of champagne and looked around the wedding guests. I couldn't see anyone else I knew, so I wandered over to look at a series of old photographs on the wall opposite. As I studied them, Michael came into the room and strolled over to join me.

'It's the pub before the war,' I told him as he looked at

the frames. 'I believe the street was bombed and many of the houses on the opposite side were flattened.'

'Yes, the manager told me that too. It's amazing that the pub and church stayed standing,' said Michael, as Stuart came over to join us. I took a deep breath to steady myself. Michael, Stuart. Two men I'd loved in different ways: Michael in the past, Stuart in secret. It was overwhelming to be in such close proximity to both of them and confusing to see them both looking at me. I glanced from face to face, two sets of eyes, trying to see if I felt anything beyond just recognizing them as Stuart and Michael. Was there anything else there?

'You OK, Bea?' asked Michael. 'You're looking a bit strange.'

I coughed and looked over his shoulder. 'Oh yes. Fine thanks.'

'I hear that you and Bea already know each other,' said Stuart.

'We do,' said Michael. 'And you?'

'Old friends for years,' said Stuart. '*How* did you both know each other?'

Michael looked at me fondly and put his arm around my shoulder. 'We were much more than old friends. We used to live together in our early twenties.'

I glanced up at Stuart's face and noticed the briefest look of . . . what was it? Jealousy? Anger? His protective nature? Whichever, he pushed it away fast and smiled.

'How lovely that you've met up again,' he said. 'Lots to talk about, no doubt. *When* are you returning to Thailand?'

Subtle, I thought, and tried not to laugh.

'Oh, not for a while,' Michael replied. 'I'm trying to

persuade Bea to join me on an extended holiday, maybe in Europe.'

There was a flash of annoyance on Stuart's face again, quickly disguised. 'You *are?* Europe? And *will* you be going, Bea?'

Was I imagining that he was jealous? Or was it wishful thinking? I asked myself as I looked at him then at Michael. 'I think you know my situation better than anyone, Stuart. I have no idea what I'll be doing.'

This time, it was Michael who looked jealous. 'How exactly do *you* know Bea?' he asked.

'Oh, as well as being good friends, I've also been her accountant all that time.'

'Ah,' said Michael. 'An accountant.' He said it in a disdainful way.

Stuart ignored the insult and leant over to look at the photos on the wall behind us. 'These are fascinating, aren't they? Appears that this pub hasn't changed much, but it looks as if the rest of the street has. Good that they have these old photos as a record of how it once was.'

I pointed at one that showed the row of houses that had taken the hit from the bomb. 'Yes, especially as that side was destroyed. Can you imagine what it must have been like to live there and find that your house, your home, had gone.'

Stuart stared at the photos. 'That's if you survived the war. I'd imagine a lot of people didn't. Awful, heartbreaking.'

'Yes, I wonder what happened to the residents,' said Michael.

'And if any of them had sons who were away in the war?' I added.

'War is a filthy business,' said Stuart as he turned away from the photos. 'So many wasted lives.'

'For those left behind too,' I said. 'The families, friends, fiancées waiting for their men to return.' I glanced from Michael to Stuart to see if the place, the conversation was triggering anything, but neither looked particularly affected. Stuart knew the story about Grace and Billy and I was about to point out the photograph that showed the house where Billy lived.

'Hey, come on you two,' said Michael before I had a chance, 'we're at a wedding. Let's talk about something more cheerful, shall we?'

'Of course,' said Stuart. 'Now, Bea, can I get you another drink?'

'It's OK,' said Michael. '*I* can do that.'

Part of me wanted to laugh again. Stuart being attentive, Michael being possessive, all I needed now was for Jon to jump out of a cake and my strange love life would be complete.

46

Hmm, seems I have competition. What I need is something to demonstrate that I mean to make her life better, both our lives richer through shared experiences. Recent events have made me realize that you have to make your memories, and I want to make mine with Bea. If this works out, there are so many places I want to take her, things I want to do with her, experiences to share. That's it. An experience. Now that might be an idea instead of gifts or flowers. Something to hint at a future together. Not just idle talk, daydreaming. I'll make it real and send tickets for two to Venice or Paris. The opera in Verona. Does Bea even like opera? Or an invite to dinner somewhere fabulous? Yes, that's more like it. We could have the time of our lives. But where? And when?

47

'Three dates?' asked Heather as we sat having coffee at the counter of the shop.

'Three. I know, I'm a wanton woman.'

'Good for you. So, Jon, Michael and who's the third?'

'Stuart.'

'*Stuart* Stuart? But he's married.'

'Was. They've separated and are getting a divorce, according to his wife.'

'Wow. How do you feel about that?'

'I like him a lot but never let myself consider being with him as a possibility.'

'So you *do* like him? I'd always suspected as much. How long?'

'Ever since I met him.'

Heather rolled her eyes. 'Since you met him? That's *ages*. You are a dark horse, Bea. Why did you never say anything?'

'Because he was out of bounds, so nothing to say. Pointless. Like fancying the Pope or some movie star, just wasn't going to happen.'

'Guess we add him to the list then.'

'We do. I already have actually.'

'Any others?'

'He's the only one.'

'You failed to mention Jon in the first instance. Are you quite sure there aren't any others you've been keeping from us?'

'No one worth mentioning.'

'And are you feeling more drawn to one of them?'

I groaned. 'Depends on the phases of the moon, the weather, the menopause – oh, I don't know. I've never felt so confused in all my life. Michael, yes definitely . . . Stuart . . . yes, *yes*, though I'm still trying to get my head around the fact that he might be a serious contender, I don't even know if he thinks of me in that way and I'm so used to repressing whatever I feel for him, the wall keeping it all in is only just coming down if you know what I mean; Jon sometimes yes. Honestly, I'm not sure.'

Heather laughed. 'Don't worry. You have three dates set up then; it's a chance to spend time with each of them and I'm sure it will come clearer.'

I nodded. 'Although the evening with Stuart isn't officially a date, more the kind of invite you'd give to a pal; in fact, you could come with me, he said to bring a friend if I wanted.'

'No, you're on your own there. Think about the dates as interviews for the role,' Heather continued. 'Could be fun; in fact, make *sure* you have fun and let the best man win.'

I felt a sense of anticipation as well as so many other emotions – fear, uncertainty, self-doubt, confusion. Could I overcome my anxiety about being vulnerable, maybe hurt again, and let myself surrender to whatever or whoever revealed himself?

48

J on had told me to be ready by eleven and to bring a cardigan.

'An early lunch on the river, then a boat cruise down to Greenwich,' said Jon when he appeared at my door the next morning. 'How does that sound?'

'Like a practised routine,' I said, then added, 'only joking.'

Jon pulled a hurt face. 'I told you, I'm a changed man.'

'I'm teasing, it sounds heavenly,' I said, and looked up at the blue sky above. 'And we have the perfect day for it.'

We took a cab down to the river, which Jon insisted on paying for, then headed up to the brasserie on the eighth floor of the OXO Tower building. Inside, the décor was sophisticated and modern, with slate tables and a leather-clad bar, but it was outside that drew the eye. Through the floor-to-ceiling glass wall was a stunning view of the river and London with St Paul's Cathedral to the right,

Jon had booked us a table by the window and, once seated, he ordered two glasses of champagne. 'That OK?' he asked.

'Oh yes. I feel like I'm on holiday up here.' I did too. Since my move to Pete and Marcia's, I felt free and ready for new adventures.

Lunch was fabulous, scallops for me and cod and chorizo for Jon, and we chatted easily about the view, landmarks and places to visit.

After lunch, we walked along the riverside to Westminster and took the boat with a small crowd who were waiting there. I felt slightly giddy from the champagne and laughed at the tour guide's banter about the history of the area as the boat took off towards Greenwich.

'So much water under the bridge,' I said as we sailed under Tower Bridge.

'Funny,' said Jon.

'But true. This was one of regular trips I did with an ex many moons ago.' I told him about how Graham and I loved to be tourists in London, and he reached out and squeezed my hand when he realized that Graham had died.

When we landed in Greenwich, we passed *The Cutty Sark*, looked around the Royal Naval College then browsed bookshops, junk yards, then the market, where I bought a scarf for Heather and lavender bath lotion for Marcia. Jon was easy company, informed about the area, and I found myself looking at him a few times wondering if he was serious about us having a relationship.

'I don't know why I haven't done this for so many years,' I said as we made our way to the station to get the train back. 'I always felt like I was coming to a different country when I came to Greenwich, yet it's so near to London.'

'Maybe we could be tourists in London,' said Jon. 'I like that idea.'

*

On the train home, I found myself dozing off; before I knew it, we were back in the city and in a cab heading for Marcia and Pete's.

When we arrived back at theirs, Jon asked the cab driver to wait, then got out and came round to my side to open the door to let me out.

'It has been a perfect day,' I said. 'And please can I contribute?'

'Absolutely not. My treat. Think of it as a late birthday present.'

'You've been very generous.'

'I am hoping there will be more days like this,' he said.

As we stood on the pavement, he leant over and kissed me lightly on the forehead then got back into the cab. 'I'll be in touch,' he said, then grinned. 'I could invite you home and in for a drink but I don't want to crowd you.'

'I appreciate that and it's been wonderful. A day to remember.'

'I meant what I said about wanting us to work. I sense you're a woman who likes company but also likes her space. I will try to respect that by giving you time to come round to the idea of us as a couple. In the meantime, you can rest assured that I really have changed, my wild days are over, and I shall be waiting for you.'

And off he went. I was glad he hadn't pressed me into spending more time with him or suggesting drinks at his place and the possibility of getting physical. I needed time to think, to absorb this new turn my life had taken, and I had the dates with Stuart and Michael still to come. Seeing Michael at the wedding and spending time with him there had stirred up so many old feelings. He had been the great love of my life, a fact I'd tried to bury for so many years, not because my feelings for him had changed but because he had left and I'd had no choice but to suppress what was there. No doubt about it, he was the one who had got away, but now he was back. Perhaps it had been right man, wrong time, and now it could be the right time. He had certainly been attentive at the wedding; looks were exchanged that lingered too long and reminded me of the strong pull of attraction there had always been. I was looking forward to spending some proper time with him alone; a chance to get to know him again, find out who he really was now and what he wanted.

And then, of course, there was Stuart: suddenly single, suddenly available. How long had I wished for such a thing, never thinking for a moment that it would actually happen.

So now there were three contenders, serious contenders, for my lonely heart. Could one of them have been Billy Jackson in a previous life? Did it even matter? Surely what mattered was in the here and now, in this present life? So . . . Stuart, Jon or Michael? *You don't have to decide just yet*, I told myself as I felt my stomach knot.

49

Stuart was waiting for me outside the pub behind the square in Highgate. His face lit up when he saw me, and he strode towards me and gave me a warm hug. I felt nervous and tongue-tied, fifty going on fifteen, and out on a first date with a boy I had a crush on.

'Ready to rock and roll?' I asked in an attempt to disguise my nerves.

Stuart pulled a face. 'I hope it wasn't a mistake asking you to come. We haven't had time to practise much. Don't feel you have to stay if you hate it.'

I realized he was as tense as I was, though about doing a gig rather than seeing me. We went inside. Stuart got me a drink and a seat in the corner of the pub then went to take his place with his musician friends. There were four of them, men who, like Stuart, looked in their fifties, with grey hair and an assortment of cowboy shirts between them. Two guitarists, Stuart on keyboards and a harmonica player.

One of the guitarists introduced himself as Ed and, with a one, two, three, they went into their first number, 'Big

Boss Man'. Soon people at other tables were tapping their feet, and a couple at the back even got up to jive. I was enjoying the chance to watch Stuart without embarrassment. I resolved to tell him that he had no need for nerves, he was good and the band had a great sound. I could also see how much he was enjoying himself; there was a great camaraderie between him and the other musicians. He glanced over at one point and grinned. I gave him a thumbs-up.

In the interval, Stuart came straight over. 'How are you finding it?'

'Fanbloodytastic. The audience love you. You've been holding out on me. I've seen a whole new side to you.'

'I know. I don't know why I let it go for so many years. Actually no, I do know. I wanted to pursue my music but Janet disapproved and told me to leave it to people who could actually play.'

'About that, Stuart, we didn't really get a chance to talk at the wedding but I saw removal vans outside your house and Janet told me briefly what was happening. What's going on?'

Stuart looked embarrassed. 'Ah. Yes. I've been waiting for the right time to tell you, been planning to tell you, but the wedding didn't seem like the right occasion and before that . . . there was so much going on in your life, I . . .'

'Are you OK?'

He nodded. 'Yes, fine actually. Janet and I should have separated years ago, so in a way it's liberating.'

'But you were with Janet at the wedding?'

'Janet knew Rob and Jess, so we went along together, and I'm sure there will be many occasions when that will be appropriate, but our separation is final and mutually agreed. Neither of us was happy with each other, nor had been for a long time. I'm looking forward to a new chapter, being able to explore what I want to do, play the music I want to play, spend time with who I want to.' He gave me a meaningful look. 'But mainly there will be the freedom to be myself for the first time I can remember in I don't know how long. I feel like a young man again, released.'

'And do you have plans?'

'I do and I hope they will—'

He stopped abruptly as Ed signalled to him that the second set was about to start, and began pulling Stuart back towards the front. 'Drink later,' he called over his shoulder.

'Sure,' I called back.

The second set was even better; before long, half the pub were on their feet, dancing and singing along to old favourites – 'Sixteen Tons', 'Dust My Broom', 'I Just Want to Make Love to You'.

Who'd have thought it? I asked myself, *Stuart Armstrong, Mr Cool Dude.*

When they'd finished, the band packed up and Stuart came over. 'Next time, you must take me to hear some music you like, but for now, let's get a glass of wine. I'm ready for one.'

'Sounds good to me.'

Once we'd settled, he told me a bit more about the separation. 'We were a classic case of staying together for the sake of the children. It's not as if we were fighting,' he laughed, 'we were both very civil and good at repression, but you get to a certain age and think: is this it?'

'I know exactly what you mean.'

'Richard?'

I nodded.

'I never thought you were very happy with him and I was glad that ended. You seemed to come alive again after he'd gone.'

'I did.'

'But no partner since? Sorry, I don't mean to be too nosey.'

'Not at all. No. No one since. Truth be told, I'd given up.'

'You say that as if something has changed?'

'Possibly.'

Stuart sighed. 'The chap at the wedding.'

'No, not necessarily. He's a very old friend.'

'Seemed very fond of you.'

'He is, and I of him.'

'Ah.'

We sat in silence for a few minutes and I felt that the atmosphere between us had changed from amicable to uncomfortable.

'He lives in Thailand permanently, doesn't he?' said Stuart.

'He does.'

Stuart laughed but it was brittle. 'Good. And what about you Bea? Have you decided where you're going to live? What you're going to do?'

'No decisions. Like you, I'm going to tread water for a while. I've always rushed into things, kept myself busy, but I want some time to think about the next phase of my life and where I want to go.'

'Maybe we could tread water together sometimes, if you know what I mean.'

'I do. Truth is, what Saranya Ji told me in India – and the events that have happened since – have made me rethink a lot of things. I know it sounded outlandish, crazy, but since that day in Cherry Tree Park when I told you about it, I've begun to think that there was some truth in it all.' I told him about the hypnosis session when I remembered Minty. He listened patiently until I'd finished.

'So you think now that you were Grace Harris?' he asked.

'I do. A few months ago, I would have thought the idea was preposterous, but I've changed. I now believe it completely.'

'And this man you're looking for, the one who you say might have been Billy, have you any idea who you think he is this time?'

'Not exactly. What do you think? Could be you.'

He laughed then shook his head. 'I have no recollections about past lives, although I do believe that in the course of one life, we have many lives and different roles, are different people in the different phases we've lived through. Thing is, does it matter? Does it matter whether or not you knew someone in a past life? Surely what counts is now, what's in your heart now. Take Janet and me: we loved each other once in our way, then grew apart. I suppose you could call that a past life in this life, or maybe past chapter is more accurate. Sometimes you have to move on, think about who you are now, what you want now.'

'Are you saying you don't believe what Saranya Ji said had any validity?'

'Not exactly, but I wouldn't let it rule my heart. I hope that doesn't disappoint you.'

'Everyone's entitled to their opinion. As I said, a few

months ago I'd have agreed with you, but a lot's happened since then.'

'You sound like Alice in Wonderland talking to the caterpillar.'

I laughed. 'Exactly, and that used to be one of my favourite books, the part where she says something like, I knew who I was this morning when I got up, but I've changed a few times since then.'

'Curiouser and curiouser,' said Stuart, quoting more Lewis Carroll.

'But not just that, what's been happening has opened me up to the possibility of new experiences, like anything could happen, and rather than that being scary and to be shunned, it's rather exciting and to be embraced.'

Stuart regarded me for a few moments with an expression that was hard to read. 'That part sounds good, Bea.' He raised his glass. 'I'll drink to that.'

50

'Where have you been staying?' I asked Michael when he called to arrange a place and time to meet him.

'At Melanie's. Now she's on her honeymoon, they've let me have their flat. It's not the Ritz, but it's comfortable enough for a short stay. Would you like to come over? I'll cook us something.'

*

Melanie's flat was on the ground floor in a semi-detached Edwardian house in Muswell Hill. I rang the bell and Michael let me in. He closed the door behind me, took my jacket and hung it up, turned and pushed me up against the wall. He moved close so I could feel his body against me and looked into my eyes. The intensity of his expression and proximity sent shock waves through me. As soon as he could see the desire he awakened, he tilted my chin up and kissed me with a hunger that made me feel weak with longing. He pulled me closer to him then guided me to the sofa, where we sank into the cushions. My head was spinning. I hadn't been expecting this. It felt utterly delicious but I wasn't ready. Part of me felt locked, unable to respond.

Michael felt my resistance and pulled back. 'What's the matter? Don't you want to?'

I took a deep breath. 'I do but . . .' I sat up. 'It's too soon.'

Michael groaned. 'Too *soon*? Too soon for what?'

'This. I hardly know you any more. You can't expect me to—'

'Bea, you know me so well and I know you feel the same way. I can feel the heat between us and I know you do too.' He pulled me close and began to kiss me passionately again, and it did feel wonderful, arousing sensations I hadn't felt in years. I could just succumb, I could but . . . I gently pushed him away. 'No. I'm not that young girl any more. I . . . we . . . need to talk, get to know each other again.'

'Bea, you don't have to prove anything to me. I know that you're not a pushover. You're strong, independent and, believe me, that's so attractive.' He realized I wasn't giving in, so he got up. He looked like a small boy who'd had his favourite toy taken away. 'I suppose we could talk, but that's not what I had in mind.' He turned to face me. 'Sometimes I think you have to seize the moment, Bea. What we have doesn't come along so many times in a lifetime and I think we're both old enough to recognize that.'

'Which is why I want to take things more slowly. I don't even know how long you're going to be here for, or when you're going back to Thailand. What are your intentions?'

'You sound like my father.'

'I mean, what do you want? To reconnect or just a moment of pleasure?'

'Both.'

'Then don't rush me. I haven't seen you for thirty years then you just appear and—'

'You're worried I'd just take off again.'

'Of course I am. It's been weeks since I've even heard from you. For all I knew, you might have gone for good.'

'OK. Let's talk then. I'll finish cooking supper and we can talk. You can tell me about your life and I will tell you about mine.'

I felt bad; I'd disappointed him.

'Spag bol OK?' he asked.

'Perfect,' I said, but I sensed it was far from that. The atmosphere felt tense.

As he busied himself in the kitchen, I looked around. The place was a mess, clothes piled on chairs, wedding presents still in their boxes on the dining table. Melanie and her new husband had obviously taken off in a hurry. The thought made me smile – the build-up to the wedding, the big day, then off somewhere fabulous.

'Where have they gone?' I asked.

'Mauritius,' Michael replied. 'We could add that to our list of places to visit.'

I smiled. 'Are you going to admit to sending the gifts yet?'

'Nope. A man has to have some secrets.'

'Infuriating.'

'That makes two of us,' he said as he threw something in the pan and it began to sizzle.

'The food smells delicious,' I said as the aroma of onions and garlic filled the air. 'Your niece seemed so happy at the wedding, meeting The One, starting a new life. Do you remember how we used to talk about The One when we knew each other before – such a romantic notion. Did you ever feel you found yours?'

'I did, then let her go.'

'Celia?'

'No, you of course.'

'Ah.'

'I know you feel it too, Bea.'

'Still not going to sleep with you.'

'What? Not ever? Might as well go straight back to Thailand then.'

'What, so no Europe?'

'Maybe, but only if you come with me.'

Michael served supper and we chatted generally; it was pleasant, but the feelings that had been so charged when I'd walked in now felt stilted, and Michael became quieter and quieter as the evening went on.

'Are you sulking because I didn't succumb to your irresistible charms?' I asked in an effort to lighten the mood.

'Clearly my charms aren't irresistible,' said Michael, but he did smile. 'Sorry. Just I had such an idea of how this evening was going to go and—'

'I didn't go along with the plan.'

'Not too late,' said Michael.

'Just give me time.'

'How long? Five minutes? I'll go and strip off.'

I laughed. 'You know what I mean.'

'You've changed, Bea.'

'Good or bad?'

He looked thoughtful. 'Neither, just different.'

He didn't have to say. I knew what he meant. The Bea

he had known would have done anything for him, was there at his beck and call, lived to see him smile. And wasn't that a form of love? To give yourself completely, unconditionally? Maybe I could again, but first I needed to know that I could trust him. I heard Heather's words in my head – when you find The One, he will want you as much as you do him, so let him show it, let him come to you. Hadn't Michael just shown how much he wanted me? And I'd rejected him, despite the fire of passion between us. *Oh God*, I thought as it dawned on me, *maybe* I *was the problem?* Michael had shown his feelings and I'd backed off, pushed him away. In my mind, I blamed him for trying to rush me, but was it me? So fearful of being hurt, I was no longer able to let myself love? I'd closed off, become self-sufficient, told myself again and again that I didn't need anyone, to the point that I'd become frigid. It felt so much safer not to rely on anyone but is this what I did? Self-sabotage? Saranya Ji had hinted as much. My belief that love hurt had made me put up a wall to keep pain out but, in doing so, it also kept out love. But I also knew I wanted more now than just good sex, my priorities for a partner so different to what I wanted in my twenties or thirties. I wanted someone I felt comfortable with, a companion with shared interests and, yes, hopefully, the sex would feature, but it wasn't the be-all and end-all.

'Michael, I am sorry . . .' I started.

He held up a hand. 'No need. It was thoughtless of me to assume that you felt the same. It should be me who apologizes.'

'But I . . .'

He cleared the plates of half-eaten food away. It appeared

that neither of us had any appetite. When I rose to leave, he didn't try to stop me and, at the door, he kissed me on the cheek, not the lips.

*

I got back to Pete and Marcia's that night feeling very low and more confused than ever. I was glad that they weren't around when I let myself in. I was in no mood to talk to anyone. *Saranya Ji*, I thought as I took the stairs up to my attic room. Maybe she could help, if only we could find her.

51

I went down to the kitchen the next morning and put a wad of twenty-pound notes on the table.

'What's that for?' asked Marcia.

'Rent.'

'Don't be ridiculous, no, I couldn't take it.'

'It will make me feel better to know I am contributing.'

'So take me somewhere for lunch instead.'

'Where do you want to go?'

'Somewhere swanky – I know, how about that place Jon took you?'

'The OXO Tower?'

'Yes. I've always wanted to go there.'

'Great, done. And has Pete found Saranya Ji yet?'

'Not yet, but he's still on the case. And how about you? You've had your three dates?' Marcia asked. 'Any clearer? Who's it to be? Michael, Jon or Stuart?'

I shook my head. 'No idea, I'm more confused than ever. They're all nice and appealing in different ways. Truth is, I don't know what I want any more.'

'So give yourself a break. It's not as though there's any countdown on this.'

'Apart from Michael going back to Thailand at some point.'

Marcia laughed. 'There are planes; you could always go out there if you decide that it's him. I'd say, relax, what will be will be. You can't force love or destiny. I think all will become clear. Trust that.'

*

I booked the table at the OXO Tower for the following weekend for Marcia and me and asked Heather to join us for a chance to review what I was going to do next.

'What does your gut tell you?' asked Heather as we travelled down together on the tube.

'That I need to eat less sugar.'

'Seriously. The three contenders?'

'Seriously, I like all of them for different reasons. It's an impossible situation.'

'Surely one of them must draw you more than the others,' she said.

'I'm drawn to all of them. I feel different on different days. One day I think that it's Michael, definitely Michael, he's always been the love of my life; then I think no, best leave the past in the past. Michael was a long time ago, so start afresh, so that would be with Jon. He's the newest man in my life and he really does seem different lately, plus he's great fun to be with.'

'Fun is good. You need some of that in your life. But can you trust him?'

'I'd say yes. He says he's a changed man, and don't forget he was married for a long time.'

'Ah, but did you ever find out why he and his wife split up?'

'Actually no, he never did tell me that.'

'Could be because he was playing around then.'

'You don't like him, do you Heather?' I asked.

She shrugged a shoulder. 'Only because he seems like a player.'

'He said that was because he felt insecure, needed to prove to himself that he is still attractive. I understand that.'

Heather pulled a face. 'Sounds like a line to me.'

'And Stuart?' asked Marcia. 'I like him.'

'Me too,' said Heather.

'Me too,' I said, 'and definitely, there are days now when I think yes, it's Stuart, and now he's separated from—'

'Beware of a man who's just come out of a long-term relationship,' said Heather. 'Either they need a lot of counselling or they can be on the rebound and, a bit like Jon, need to find out that they're still attractive. Stuart probably needs some space to orientate himself as a single man and discover what he wants. I would advise against getting too involved with him too soon.'

'Yes, but don't forget, I was secretly in love with him for years but . . . we haven't even kissed but I do like being with him, always have.'

Heather sighed. 'Tough one. Maybe get drunk and sleep with all of them then we can reconvene.'

'You're both a fat lot of help. Give them space, no, no, sleep with them: your advice is completely contradictory.'

'Or we could do a sort of test for them and look at all

their skills, not just their sexual prowess,' said Marcia, 'like cooking, tidying up in the home, how are they at communication? God, the list could be endless.'

I laughed. 'A test sounds a bit harsh, they all have feelings too. In the meantime, I don't want to hurt anyone by giving them the wrong impression. I mean, three dates with different men in a week, can you imagine how they'd feel if they found out?'

'You're not in a relationship with any of them, nor have you made any commitments,' said Heather.

'All the same, I don't think any of them would be happy about it.'

*

When we reached the OXO Tower, we got the lift up to the restaurant and a waiter found us a table near the window. As he led us towards it, I did a double take. There was Jon at the corner table where I had sat with him only a week ago. He wasn't alone. He was with a very attractive blonde lady who was laughing at something he had said. I watched as he took her hand, turned it over and kissed her palm. I went straight over and the look on his face was priceless.

'Bea!'

'Jon. How fabulous to see you.' I looked at his companion and waited for him to introduce us.

'Oh yes, Bea, this is Amy; Amy, Bea.'

'Hi Amy. Lovely to meet you.' I indicated the brasserie. 'Great place this, isn't it?'

She nodded. 'Very nice.'

'Having lunch?' I asked.

They both nodded. Jon looked as if he'd like the ground to open up and swallow him.

'Me too. I'm with my friends,' I said, and pointed back to where Marcia and Heather were standing by the bar. 'So. You two? Lunch, then afterwards a boat trip down to Greenwich?'

'Yes. How did you know?' asked Amy.

'I know it's a favourite of Jon's. Anyway, better go. My friends are waiting. Have a great day.'

'You too,' said Amy.

I went back over to Marcia and Heather, who were now seated at our table.

'Unbelievable,' said Marcia.

'I know. At least it makes my dilemma a bit easier,' I said as I sat down. 'He's off the list, which leaves us with two.'

'Hold on a minute,' said Heather. 'Why's Jon off the list?'

'I think that's pretty obvious,' I said.

'Not at all,' said Heather. 'I know Jon hasn't been my favourite of the contestants, but just because he's having lunch with someone shouldn't rule him out. As we said before, it's not as if you are in a relationship, and anyway, pot? Kettle? You can't take the moral high ground here. You've just dated three men in one week. How do you think Jon would feel about that if he knew? Or Stuart or Michael feel if they knew they were names on a list?'

Marcia nodded. 'Fair point.'

'I suppose,' I said. 'Fickle, my name is Bea. I don't know what's come over me lately.' I felt disgruntled about seeing Jon with a companion, but Heather was right, I had no claim to him and we'd made no promises.

'Have you asked any of them if they sent you the gifts?' asked Heather.

'I have. Jon said it was definitely him, but then he would, wouldn't he? And I don't know why but I'm not sure I believe him.'

'Or maybe you just don't want to believe him,' said Heather. 'Secretly you know who you want the presents to be from, and I reckon that's Michael.'

'He acted all enigmatic when I asked him if he'd sent me anything, and said it would ruin the mystery if he was to say yes or no. I haven't asked Stuart yet.'

'So ask him,' said Heather. 'Text him now. Go on, get your phone out.'

I did as I was told and sent Stuart a quick message. *Hi, quick question, someone has been sending me lovely gifts, is it you? Bea.*

A message pinged back within seconds. *Am unclear. Who do you think they're from? S.*

I texted. *Not sure.*

His reply came back instantly. *Clearly you have more than one admirer if you're having to ask. S.*

'Oh dear,' I said as I read the message, then showed Heather and Marcia. 'He sounds pissed off.'

'Hmm. I wonder, is that because he sent the gifts and thought it was obvious they were from him? Or because he didn't send the gifts but now knows he has competition?' asked Marcia.

'And there's no guarantee that whoever sent them was Billy, Bea's soulmate from another life,' said Heather, 'and surely *he's* the one she wants to find. Just because someone has been sending gifts doesn't necessarily mean he's The One.'

'How do you feel about it all?' asked Heather.

'Confused,' I said. 'And, if I'm completely honest, when Jon said it was him who had sent the presents, I felt disappointed, then I felt mean because, if it was him, the gifts were generous and thoughtful.'

'You *have* to go with your gut,' said Marcia, 'and if something deep inside was disappointed that it might be Jon, that's telling you something and you have to take note of that. I would say, rule Jon out.'

'Not just yet,' said Heather. 'But I'd forget about flowers and presents. As I keep saying, OK, they show you have an admirer, but they don't mean that whoever sent them was The One, the late Billy Jackson reborn in a new body.'

'And there's still Sam Gorman hovering in the background,' said Marcia. 'They could have been from him.'

'A man who, according to his sister, is an addict who is in and out of prison – oh yes, let's hope it's him, not,' I said.

'So we're still back at square one. How do you know who Billy is now?' asked Marcia.

'By how you feel, surely?' said Heather.

When the waiter seated us, I made sure I had a seat with my back to Jon so I didn't have to witness him charming his latest conquest. I didn't want to think about why I'd found it disturbing to see him with her. I didn't really care about him, did I? When we got up to leave later, he was gone.

52

When we got back from the restaurant, there was a note from Pete on the kitchen table.

Finally tracked down Saranya Ji. Result! She can talk to you this afternoon. 009175133000.

'Timely,' said Marcia.

'Or maybe she'll confuse things even more,' I said.

I went up to my attic room so I could talk in private, dialled and got straight through.

'Bea, of course I remember you – from Udaipur, yes?' she said. 'How can I help?'

'You told me that I had to find a man I'd known in a previous life, my soulmate, known then as Billy Jackson. You said that just as I am back, so is he, and I must find him. At first I didn't believe you, but so much has happened since then and now I do believe that I have the memories of a woman who was called Grace Harris. But I am lost as to what to do about it, how to recognize the man I knew as Billy.'

'Ah. Remember I told you, first comes destiny then free will? He will come to you, then you decide what to do in response.'

'That's the problem. Three men have turned up.'

I heard Saranya Ji laugh. 'Most excellent. So you can choose.'

'That's just it. I can't. I like all of them, they like me. None of them remembers a past life.'

'And how do *you* feel about them?'

'Confused, like I'm having a nervous breakdown.'

'Sometimes that can be good, break down to break through.'

'What if I choose the wrong man?'

'Trust your heart and his heart. Remember, there are two of you in this. He will want to be with you as much as you want to be with him, this feeling will be strong in him.'

'But all three say that they do, that's what's confusing.' I thought of Michael and the heat of passion when I'd last seen him and turned him down. I thought of Stuart and the feelings I'd had for so many years. I thought of Jon and the spark between us. 'Feels like muddy water to me.'

'Then be still, Bea, only then will the water become clear.'

'You're saying do nothing?'

'Sometimes that is exactly right.'

'Saranya Ji, you're not being very helpful.'

'I cannot tell you who to choose; only you can know what is in your heart. Be still and you will find that the answer you seek is already inside of you.'

'And how do I attain this stillness?'

'Meditation, learn to be a human being instead of a human doing. We all are so busy busy, doing this, doing that, and so often don't take time just to be.'

'To stand and stare.'

'If that's how you like to say it. Go beyond the thoughts that come and go, the worries and anxieties, and find the stillness that is within you. Trust that what is deep inside of you will become clear.'

When we'd finished our call, I sat quietly and just breathed. I thought of Stuart. I thought of Michael. I thought of Jon. Stuart. Michael. Jon. Stuart. Michael. Jon. I breathed again. I imagined myself with one and then the other and then the other: on the Heath, on holiday, in bed, in the supermarket, with one, then the other then the other. Stuart Michael Jon, Stuart Michael Jon. I could make their names into a mantra in the way I'd been taught in meditation classes, where you say a word over and over until it becomes a vibration of sound, usually Om, which becomes ommmmmmmmm. Stuart Michael Jon, Stuartmichaeljon, stmjnnnnnnnnn.

53

I think I might have blown it with Bea. What do I have to do to make her realize that I am serious and sincere about her? Have I scared her off? It's hard to tell. She's unreadable: one minute she's warm and responsive and I know that she feels the same way as I do; another she's closed down and I have no idea what she's thinking or even if she's already involved with someone else. And even if she wasn't, would she be prepared to take on someone like me?

Nothing lost, nothing gained. Sometimes in life, you have to take a risk, in this case my heart. It's time to make a grand gesture, show Bea my hand and send her something that will reveal not only who I am without any shadow of a doubt, but also the kind of life we could have together.

54

Over the next few weeks, I decided to put men, soul-mates and matters of the heart to one side and do what I'd learnt to do so well, and that is immerse myself in my work.

Every day, I took Saranya Ji's advice and would start with a short meditation to try and find the stillness that she had spoken of. Afterwards, I looked on my phone to see if there were any messages from Michael, but nothing appeared from him, nor from Jon, nor Stuart. All had gone quiet, apart from a short message from Kate saying that Sam was due out of prison should I want to contact him. No signs, no more declarations or promises from any of them, and no gifts or envelopes in the post. I missed them and the intrigue and excitement. *I have to let it all go*, I told myself, *and trust that all will be revealed in time*. I let Heather take care of the shop while I spent every spare hour immersed in my mosaic for Grace and Billy, working some days into the late evening, and God, I loved it. Time flew by and I realized I was never more content than when being creative, dabbing paint, choosing bits of fabric, adding texture. I felt whole and inspired. My old survival mantra that I didn't need anyone became a reality, not a fabrication invented to placate myself. I *was* happy. I *didn't* need anyone.

Every night, when I'd finished, I covered the work with a large sheet so that no one could see it, but at last, in mid-May, it was finished and ready to show. After much trial and error, I'd kept the colours simple. I knew that, as with creating a garden, if I used too many elements it would look fussy and overdone, but using a few well-chosen images, repeated here and there, and the effect would be more pleasing. As part of the backdrop, I'd made small patchwork pieces from grey and faded pink vintage fabrics, some of which were found on one of my many trips to the markets in Notting Hill. The tiny glass tiles in sepia and pink gave luminosity, and they were complemented by small mirror squares in grey and dark brown, placed to give some depth. The main focus, though, was on the jigsaw pieces I'd made from photos showing scenes from the defence of Calais; images of men at war, marching, on the field, but also streets back in the UK that had been bombed; others showing workers amongst the debris, two young women in aprons, standing near a pile of bricks, having a break and sipping mugs of tea. At intervals, I glued strips that I'd cut from the copies of the birth and death certificates and census records that showed Grace and Billy's names and dates. I added words here and there in different fonts: soldier, dressmaker, Kentish Town, Fortis Green, Minty. When I'd finished, it was exactly as I had imagined it, the whole effect an abstract mosaic depiction of a scene from a time in history.

One morning, I invited Heather up to the office. 'Ta-dah,' I said as I whipped away the cloth.

'Oh!' she gasped then was silent as she studied it.

'What do you think?'

She turned to me. 'Bea, this is fabulous. Amazing. For Grace and Billy?'

'It is. They really captured my imagination, and I wanted to make something in remembrance of them so that their story lives on. I'm going to make some more, though my next work will be from this century. I've already done rough sketches. I can't stop thinking about what I want to do and seeing people in colour. I'm going to do Graham next, then you and Marcia and Pete.'

'I think that's a brilliant idea. Will you sell them?'

'I hadn't thought about that. Maybe. I thought I'd just make them for friends to start with.'

'Oh Bea, you must make more. People would pay thousands to own one of these.' She turned back to the mosaic. 'I've never seen anything like it.'

After she'd gone and I'd locked up the shop, I headed back to Marcia and Pete's to find the house empty and a note telling me they'd gone out to the theatre. I went into the kitchen, poured a glass of wine and sat at the table. It struck me that for all that had happened since India, and the excitement of a possible mystery man, I was still alone. Something had changed, though. I felt liberated and open to new possibilities, and that feeling that I had to control my life and my work by keeping endlessly busy had been replaced with a sense of what would be would be, and whatever that was would be revealed in time.

Next to the note that Marcia had left, I spied an envelope. It was addressed to me. A silver envelope. I felt a shiver of anticipation as I ripped it open and read the card inside.

To Bea Brooks,
I am inviting you to join for me for cocktails at 6.30 p.m. at the Bar Terrazza Darsena at The Grand Hotel Villa Serbelloni in Lake Como in Italy, followed by dinner on the terrace in the Mistral restaurant on June 14th. Plane tickets in accompanying envelope. Make sure your passport is up to date as I hope this will be the first of many. X

Wow. The Italian lakes? That's some invitation, I thought as I turned the card over to see if it was signed. Needless to say, it was blank. *Who sent this?* I asked myself as I put the card aside. I got out my laptop and tapped in Grand Hotel Villa Serbelloni. It took me to an elegant-looking, five-star hotel on the shores of Lake Como. I clicked through the pictures. The Mistral restaurant showed a terrace with tables that looked out over the water. Another shot showed the view at sunset. The Bar Terrazza showed another terrace looking out over the lake. *You couldn't find a more romantic location*, I thought as I clicked through. Whoever had sent the invite was clearly making a big effort. Join me for cocktails, he had written on the invite. So either he planned to reveal himself, or else I was going to be sitting on that terrace on my own. I opened the accompanying envelope and found that it contained details for a flight from Heathrow to Milan, a plane ticket, and a message saying that a car would pick me up at the airport so to look out for a driver who would be holding a card with my name on it when I arrived in Italy. Hah, so someone *was* still thinking of me. Who? It appeared that I would find out soon.

55

My flight left at midday and would take around two hours, then the drive up to the lakes would be about an hour and a half. By my calculations, and the fact that clocks were one hour ahead in Milan, I reckoned that I'd get to the hotel between four and five. Time for a bath and to get ready, then down to meet my mystery man. I couldn't wait.

My taxi arrived on time in the morning and soon we were speeding through the rain towards Heathrow. When we reached the motorway, we found that the traffic had slowed down to a standstill and for the next twenty minutes, we crawled along.

'Must have been an accident,' said the cab driver as we heard an ambulance's siren behind us, then saw it overtake and weave its way forward as cars swerved aside to let it through. 'Want me to try and find another route as soon as we can get off this road?'

'Whatever gets me there in time,' I said, as my vision of a leisurely hour cruising and trying on all the perfumes in duty-free went out the window.

The driver pulled off at the next junction but it appeared

that a lot of other cars had had the same idea and we hit another traffic jam.

'Looks like we'll just have to sit it out,' said the driver. 'We'll get you there but I can't guarantee when. Where you off to?'

'Italy.'

'Lovely. With friends?'

'On my own.'

'Oh. Meeting friends out there?'

'One friend.'

'Ah. A romantic holiday.'

'I hope so.' *If I make it*, I thought. I felt a knot in my stomach as the minutes went by and we were still hardly moving, then half an hour . . . an hour . . . as we crawled forward. I started to panic when I glanced at my watch and realized that I was going to miss the flight. I got out my envelope with the travel schedule to look for any clue of a contact number, but there was nothing. I sighed with relief as cars started moving, nudging forward, then we were on our way again. I glanced at my watch again and felt my heart sink. The flight would be being called. No way was I going to get there on time.

At the airport, the driver drove as close as he could to the departure area before dropping me off. I paid him and raced into the airport then looked at the board. Flight 6224. Milan. I fully expected to see it say 'boarding now', but no, my heart lifted when I saw the word 'delayed'. I might make it after all, depending on the delay. I found the right queue for check-in and joined the line of people who had probably all been stuck in the same traffic as I had been. As the line nudged forward, I kept glancing at the board then, oh *no*,

I saw that the word 'delayed' had changed to 'cancelled'. *Cancelled?* All around me, other passengers had noticed the board and were muttering to each other, all anxious to find out what was going on.

'I am so sorry. We can get you on a later flight,' the lady at the desk informed me when I finally reached her. 'It leaves at six p.m.'

My mind went into overdrive. Six o'clock, two hours' flight time, add another hour for the time difference then the drive from the airport. It would be late in the evening when I got to Milan, and there was no way to let whoever was supposed to meet me know that I was on a later flight. The invite had said to meet in the bar at the hotel at six thirty. I called Heather.

'I don't know what to do,' I said after I'd filled her in.

'Take the later flight. And if there was to be a car waiting, they'll know that the flight is cancelled. They will check, they always do. They might even work out that you'll be on the next flight in. Have you got Stuart's number?'

'Yes.'

'And Jon's and Michael's?'

'Yes.'

'Text all of them. Just say, flight cancelled, coming in later. Whoever it is will understand. Whoever it isn't will probably text back asking what you mean and you'll know it's not him.'

'And what if it's not one of them?'

'There are taxis, buses, just get yourself there. Look on it as an adventure. In the meantime, get a trashy magazine, go and get a glass of overpriced champagne and do your best to enjoy the trip.'

'Will do.' I clicked the phone shut, then made my way over to the bar where I intended to send out texts. It was then that I saw that there was going to be no need, because sitting at the bar was a familiar figure. He was turned away but I knew immediately who it was from the shape of his back, his head. I stood for a moment as I took in the implication. Mystery over. It was Michael. Beautiful Michael, dressed in a navy linen suit and looking cool and unruffled. At that moment, my mobile rang and I moved over behind a display to take the call.

'Bea,' said Marcia's voice, 'I'm so glad I caught you.'

'Oh. Why? Has something happened?'

'Yes and no. Sam called about an hour after you'd gone. He said he found us through Harvest Moon. He wanted your mobile number.'

'Sam Gorman?'

'Yes. I didn't give it to him because I remembered what you told us about his sister saying he was trouble. I said I'd have to ask you first, so he's waiting for me to call him back. Maybe he's The One?'

'Oh! No. Definitely no. I know who is. I'm standing looking at him now.'

'What? Who?'

'Michael. Long story short, I was late getting to the airport, but I'm here now and the flight's been cancelled—'

'Oh no—'

'It's OK. I'm getting a later one . . .'

'I don't understand. So how do you know it's Michael?'

'He's here, at the bar, six feet away. He hasn't seen me yet.'

'Ah. So he was booked on the same flight.'

'Looks like it.'

'And planned to surprise you on board? So romantic.'

'Yes but . . . Marcia, strange thing is, I'm not sure how I feel about it.'

'What do you mean?'

'About it being him. You know more than anyone how I felt about him back in the day – thought he was the one who got away – but now he's here, I feel . . . I feel . . . I think I feel disappointed.'

'Disappointed?'

'Well, not the elation I thought I would feel if it was him. I didn't realize this until now, standing here, faced with the possibility of being with him, only now I realize I *don't* want it to be him. We're over. We were over a long time ago.' At that moment, Michael turned around and spotted me. 'Oh God, he's seen me. I have to go.'

'Call me,' said Marcia, as I clicked my phone shut and went to greet Michael, who had got off his stool and was coming over with a huge grin on his face.

'Bea,' he said. 'What are you doing here?'

I laughed. 'No need to keep up the pretence any longer.' I indicated the departure board. 'Best-laid plans and all that.'

Michael looked up at the board. He looked confused.

'Nice try, Michael. I never knew you were such a good actor.'

'I . . . I'm afraid I don't know what you mean.'

'Flight? Cancelled? The lady at check-in offered me a seat on the six o'clock flight. I presume she made you the same offer so we can travel together after all.'

'You're coming to Paris?'

'Paris? No. Italy.'

'Italy?'

'Of course. You can drop the game now.'

Michael looked utterly confused.

'You sent me a ticket and an invite to Lake Como?'

His expression cleared and changed to embarrassment.
'Of course, of course. Your mystery lover and his parcels.
You're travelling today?'

Now it was my turn to look confused.

'Bea, it's not me,' said Michael. 'I'm going to Paris. I . . .
I told you I was going to see a bit of Europe before I went
back to Thailand. I did ask if you'd come with me—'

'You mean it wasn't you who sent the invite? The tickets
to the Italian lakes? Or the gifts?'

'Not guilty,' he said, then cocked an ear as an announcement came over the intercom. 'Last passengers for flight
3312 to Paris please go to Gate Seven immediately as the
flight is boarding.'

'That's me. I'm so sorry, I have to go. Better dash.' He
hugged me close to him.

'So it wasn't you who sent the gifts either?'

Michael looked sheepish. 'Afraid not.'

'So why did you insinuate that it might have been you?'

He grinned. 'Hey, I wasn't going to give in without a
fight.'

'But you lied.'

'All is fair in love and war but . . . it appears someone
else will be waiting for you in Italy, lucky man. I'm sorry
to leave you like this but,' he glanced up at the departure
board, 'good luck, hope he's everything you want and more.'

And he was gone.

I called Marcia and told her what had happened.

'Meant to be, meant to be,' she said after she'd stopped laughing. 'Can't you see, Bea, it was good that he was there, otherwise you might not ever have realized how you really felt about him.'

'I guess.'

'Closure. So what do you want me to do about Sam?' she asked. 'How would you feel if it was him? He might already be over there and have heard about the flight delay and be trying to contact you.'

As she talked, I noticed a couple of the people who had been in the queue for the Milan flight were waving at me. 'Hold on a mo, Marcia.'

I went over to them to see what they wanted.

'Come on,' said the lady, 'the flight's going after all. They're boarding now. Gate Thirty-Two.'

'Marcia, I have to go, flight's leaving,' I said into the phone.

'Oh. OK, but what about giving your number to Sam?'

'Don't, please don't,' I said as I ran after the couple. 'It's not him, I just know it.'

*

As we rose above the clouds, I sat back in my seat and thought back over the last months. So much had happened. My shop gone, my house sold, my future still uncertain, and now I was on my way to meet a mystery man on the shores of Lake Como. Would it be a surprise? Or a disappointment? I needed to mentally prepare myself for whatever the outcome. I knew now that it wasn't Michael, so I could strike him off the list. He was on some other plane heading to a different location. I'd been so convinced it would be him, especially so when I saw him at the airport, but I was glad that it wasn't. A life with him would have been fraught with uncertainty and I would always have had to dance to his tune. That was how it was with Michael. He was a restless soul, always moving on. I wanted someone I could trust, someone who really wanted to be with me. Marcia had said Sam had called. I hadn't seen him for thirty years, but we had made that pact about getting together if we were still both single when we were fifty. Had he remembered? It would be so like him to make a grand romantic gesture and choose such a poetic location. I took a few deep breaths and asked myself how I would feel if it was him who had somehow managed to organise such a trip. Disappointed, that's how I'd feel. It would be an awful anti-climax. He wasn't someone who featured in my life any more and I couldn't imagine him ever doing so. Maybe one day I'd agree to meet up, grab a quick coffee for old times' sake but nothing more.

Or would it be Jon? Who knew what really went on in his head? All I knew was that he was full of surprises. Although there was a physical attraction, I wanted more than to be charmed and enjoy good sex. Four days away with him could be fun but, if I listened to my heart, I hoped it wouldn't be him either. If it was, we could have that holiday he'd talked about, enjoy being in Italy as companions, but I couldn't really imagine a future with a man who I didn't feel I could ever completely trust.

Which brought me to Stuart. I felt a flutter of hope,

anticipation. *But I can't go there*, I told myself. *It might not be him.* I still didn't know if he even liked me in a romantic way but if, for a moment, he did . . . I let myself imagine it was him waiting for me and felt a smile deep inside. I could see his face light up when I arrived, his eyes, his expression, his smile. I imagined him reaching out for me. *No. Stop this*, I told myself. *Why would it be him? Out of the blue? Just decides to pursue me? Why would he do that? Wishful thinking on my part, but something worth exploring when I get back to the UK if it is Jon or Sam waiting for me in Italy.*

And what if one of these men had been Billy Jackson in a past life? Did it really matter? I didn't care any more. Back in the days when Grace Harris was alive, it was so different. Women didn't have many relationships. That generation usually married one man and stuck with him; never got the chance to play the field and discover what or who they really wanted. Grace hadn't had time to do that. She'd died so young, as had Billy. Who knows how they would have got on had they lived, married, got older and more familiar, after the first flush of love had faded. My generation had more choice when it came to love. I certainly had. I'd had various love affairs in my life, made some good choices, made some bad, but I'd learnt from them all. Never mind past lives, as Stuart had said, in this life I already feel I've had different lives, even been different people: the schoolgirl, the student, the photographer's assistant, barmaid, jewellery designer, shop owner, lover, partner, singleton, but those labels weren't who I was, they were just parts that I'd played as my life evolved.

I gazed out of the window at the clouds and the planet

far beneath and, for the last time, did a mental scan of the men who might be waiting for me. It was so clear. I knew exactly who I wanted to be there and, if it was him, hoped that despite the travel delays, he would still be waiting.

56

Once I got to Milan and through customs, I noticed a handsome, olive-skinned man holding up a board with the name 'Bea Brooks' written on it. He was dressed in a smart black suit and was wearing shades.

'You speak English?' I asked.

He nodded. 'Yes. Speak good English. I Fabio.'

'I'm so sorry I'm late, Fabio. I didn't even know if the flight was going to go.'

'Is no problem,' he said as he took my bag, then indicated that I should follow him out to the car park. 'Flights always late, early, cancelled. I have phone app that tells me what's happening.'

He led me to a black Mercedes and soon we were on our way, speeding past Milan and up to the lake area.

'Drive take hour and a half, maybe longer, maybe not so long, you relax,' he said.

After the commotion of the day so far, I felt exhausted, and put my head back on the leather seat. My phone pinged a message. I glanced at the screen expecting to see a text from Marcia or Heather wishing me well but no, it was from Kevin. I groaned.

If you ever change your mind and allegiance, it said. With love and hope to see you soon, your snake charmer man, Kevin.

Oh no, I thought, *please, please don't let it be you*. I dismissed the image of him being there waiting for me. In my gut, I knew it wouldn't be. From our brief encounters, I knew enough about him to know a hotel in the Italian lakes was not his style at all. *Please, please let it be the one I hope for*, I thought as our journey continued and I fell into a light doze.

When I awoke and looked out of the window, the scenery had changed from urban to scenic, with mountains to the left, glimpses of a lake behind shuttered villas and cypress trees to our right. I glanced at my watch. It was early evening and I was late. My stomach knotted in anticipation when I saw a sign for Bellagio and I tried to focus on the stunning scenery and put all thoughts and questions out of my mind.

'Almost there, signora,' said Fabio as he reduced his speed and we drove into a picturesque village with cobbled lanes, lined with centuries-old honey-coloured buildings with balconies displaying red geraniums. Nearer the water were cafés, restaurants and shops, and we moved on through a square, past a church with a bell tower. 'This is Bellagio, known as the pearl of the lake. Is first time here?'

'It is. It looks very charming and elegant.'

'I think you will like and there is Grand Hotel Villa Serbelloni.' Ahead of us, on a slope on the edge of the promontory, was a palatial-looking building with a red tiled roof. Fabio turned into a lane lined with cypress trees and stopped outside the hotel. After he had got out my bags, I tried to give him some money as a tip, but he refused to take it. 'No money. Is taken care of. *Ciao*.'

He got back into the car and, with a wave, started up the engine and drove away. I put my bags down and walked round the side of the hotel to look around. Below, to my right, I could see a large swimming pool with sun loungers that looked straight out over the lake. I took a deep breath of the clean air and marvelled at the shades of blue, the turquoise water of the pool, the deeper blue of the lake and the sky blue above me. Around were terraced formal gardens and, further up and behind, I could see woodland.

I went back to collect my bags and went inside. The interior was that of an old palazzo decorated in an ornate traditional style, with wooden floors, old rugs and domed painted ceilings and pillared archways. At the reception desk, a dark-haired Italian girl had all my details on the computer.

'Has anyone left a message?' I asked.

The receptionist nodded and handed me an envelope. Inside was a note saying, *See you on the terrace bar at 7.30 p.m. X*

I glanced at my watch: 7.35 p.m.

Inside my bag, my phone pinged that I had another message. I got it out and glanced at the screen. It was from Heather. *It's not Jon*, said the text. *I'm on my way home and saw him drive past, literally five seconds ago.*

I felt a sense of relief and a surge of hope. Two down. Not Jon, not Michael.

The receptionist handed me a room key. 'Would you like to go up now?' she asked.

I was about to say yes. I'd had it in mind to go and change, do my hair, fix my make-up, but another part of me was impatient; there was an urgency now to find out who was there in the bar that would not be ignored. *I cannot wait another minute*, I thought. 'Later, thank you, though if you could have the bags sent up, that would be great. First, I'd like to go to the bar.'

She indicated that I should go down a corridor that led to the back of the hotel.

'Thank you,' I said again, then took a deep breath. *Right, this is it*, I thought as I set off towards the bar. A sense of calm came over me as I walked towards the terrace, a feeling that every moment leads to the next to the next and all those moments in my life had been leading up to this one. I soon found the terrace that looked out over the lake. It was a beautiful evening; there were hues of rose and gold in the sky from the fading sun reflecting on the water. At first, I couldn't see anyone there, then I spotted a tall figure. He was standing, facing away, looking out over the view. Stuart. He turned, saw me, his expression pleased to see me but also uncertain, his eyes searching my face to gauge how I was. From some deep, buried place inside me came a rush of joy and, with it, tears.

'It *is* you!' I said as I went over to join him.

'Bea, you're crying. Oh. Was your journey so bad? Or . . . is it so disappointing that it's me?'

'No, not at *all*. It's wonderful here and I'm *so* glad it's you. I was hoping it would be.'

The relief showed on his face and he held out his arms. I moved into them and, as he embraced me, it felt so completely perfect that more tears came.

'What is it?' he asked. 'Why the tears?'

I half sobbed, half laughed. 'Because this feels so . . . so right that it's almost painful and, despite appearances, I can honestly say I have never *ever* felt happier.'

He held me close again and, with the warmth and proximity of him, I felt a sensation of belonging that I'd been missing all my life, as if I had come home. I pulled back a fraction and looked into those kind eyes I knew so well and there was that 'Ah, there you are,' sensation. I'd felt it before in my hypnosis session when I'd first glimpsed Billy. This time, however, the man in front of me was real, alive, in the present, not a man from another century, no more than a shadow of a memory in my mind who could disappear at any moment.

He laughed. 'This is you when you're happy?'

I nodded. 'You're here, we're both here.' I gestured towards our surroundings and the lake.

'I wanted to take you somewhere fabulous. See, I reckon we could have the time of our lives together, you and me, Bea Brooks. More blues concerts, experiences to share, places to visit, and not to forget walks with Monty on the Heath. I have a long list of places to show you.'

'And me you.'

He sighed. 'I did wonder back there at that wedding if you were going to go off with that other chap; that's why I didn't come forward sooner. I wanted to give you space to explore that.'

'No, he was not the one for me. So what made you change your mind, send the invite to come here?'

He laughed. 'No way would I have ever given up. I wanted to send you something to show how things could be.'

'I'm so glad.'

'And your Billy? Are you still looking for him? Looking for an experience of déjà vu? Does that still matter?'

'Not now that I'm here with you.'

'Good,' he said, and held me close, 'because surely that's what counts. Here and now. Us together. Whether time after time or just this time.' He let me go and held me at arm's length. 'I don't want to think about the past. It's gone, over. I want to focus on the present and our future together. What is a feeling of déjà vu anyway? It's a recognition and, for me, it's not about a place, it's about a person and that person is you. I felt it every time I saw you, since that moment we first met.'

I nodded. 'A feeling of coming back to someone I know. Déjà you.'

'Déjà you.'

Epilogue

Eileen Jeffrey had decided it was time to update some of the upstairs rooms at the old family house. The builders had been in working for over a month, stripping out old carpets, replacing floors. One morning, the young, skinny one with ginger hair called Adam came downstairs with an old tin box. 'Found this under the floorboards in the back bedroom,' he said.

Eileen took the box and opened it. Inside were a few trinkets, a lock of blonde hair, a medal, a sprig of dried lavender, a photo which she recognized was of Minty smiling out from her pram, a vintage postcard depicting a dusty pink rose amidst grey and sepia foliage. She turned it over and read:

Grace, my darling girl,
In these dark and uncertain times who knows if I'll make it home but the thought of you keeps me going. Presently we are lost to each other, distance and this war separate us, but be assured, what is lost

can be found, and I will find you wherever you are. Don't be downhearted. I will carry you in my heart always. It may be goodbye for now, but I will return to you, somehow, sometime and we will be together again. God be with you and keep you safe, forever yours Billy. X

ACKNOWLEDGEMENTS

With thanks:

To my fab editor Kate Bradley for getting behind this book, her incisive comments as always and for coming to Bath for such enjoyable meetings when we discuss everything from books, writing, life, art, relationships to the best place to buy knickers.

To Claire Ward for coming up with another great cover.

To all the team at HarperCollins for their support, enthusiasm and hard work getting my books out there.

To Penny Isaac for her eagle eye when going through final drafts. Much appreciated.

To my agents, Christopher Little and Emma Schlesinger for their constant encouragement and enthusiasm.

I feel very lucky to have two such great teams behind me.

And lastly, to my husband Steve for the endless cups of tea, willingness to listen to me talk over plot points and for being my greatest supporter.

Discover more warm,
funny and uplifting fiction
from Cathy Hopkins

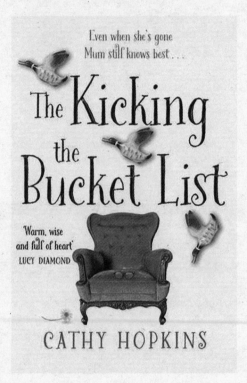

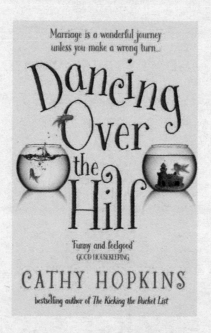

Marriage is a wonderful journey
unless you make a wrong turn...

Dancing Over the Hill

'Funny and feelgood'
GOOD HOUSEKEEPING

CATHY HOPKINS

bestselling author of *The Kicking the Bucket List*

Praise for Cathy Hopkins:

'Funny and feelgood'
Good Housekeeping

'Warm, funny and uplifting'
Reader's Digest